EDEN'S DELIVERANCE

RHENNA MORGAN

Copyright © 2016 by Rhenna Morgan

All rights reserved.

No part of this book may be reproduced in any form or by any electronic or mechanical means, including information storage and retrieval systems, without written permission from the author, except for the use of brief quotations in a book review.

This book is a work of fiction. Names, characters, places, and incidents are the product of the author's imagination or are used fictitiously. Any resemblance to actual events, locales, or persons, living or dead, is coincidental.

Ebook ISBN: 978-1-945361-02-9

Print ISBN: 978-1-945361-03-6

ACKNOWLEDGMENTS

I remember the first day I sat down to type the first words of *Unexpected Eden* as clearly as I do the day I typed *The End* on *Eden's Deliverance*. Between those two monumental days are four books, a whole lot of memories, and a huge number of people who helped make every story happen.

Penny Barber, you will forever be the editor who first gave me a chance. I doubt I'll ever be able to thank you enough for your patience along the way or your encouraging words through each revision, but the lessons you've taught me won't ever be forgotten. (And if they are, I'm claiming old age.)

I've got an amazing team that always keeps me moving forward and tirelessly answers my endless questions. Cori Deyoe, Juliette Cross, Veronica Forand, Dena Garson, Audrey Carlan, Jaci Burton, Kyra Jacobs, and Lauren Smith—thank you for always being there. (Even when I don't always make sense.)

To my daughters, Abegayle and Addison, and my partner, Joe Crivelli, goes a never-ending thank you. The three of you are my core. The ones who not only see and deal with my personal brand of crazy every day, but love me despite it.

And of course, a huge THANK YOU to the readers who've journeyed through the series and experienced the highs and lows of every hero and heroine. Without you this gig wouldn't be nearly as much fun.

For my fellow dreamers. Never give up, but remember—getting there is half the fun.

CHAPTER 1

A human will stand as judge, one versed in both races and injured in similar kind to the one wronged this day.

Brenna Haven staggered down the castle's darkened hallway toward the servants' staircase, echoes of the Great One's booming proclamation dogging every unsteady step. Streaming tears and the vision she'd unintentionally shared with Ramsay blinded her to the thick maroon rugs in front of her. Even now, awake and alert, the flashback burned as bold as real life in her mind's eye. The gold and silver flecks amid a rainbow-laden sky. The standing stones. The ancient Myren warrior who'd brought the prophecy to pass—and his dead human mate splayed across his lap.

She couldn't be the judge the Creator had referred to. Surely God wouldn't put the weight of all races on her shoulders. Not after all she'd been through. Not now that she finally had a chance at peace.

The vicious knot at the base of her throat blossomed thicker and larger, the specters of her past clawing their way free and unleashing her buried terror until she could barely breathe. She shook her head and hurried forward. The dead woman she'd seen wasn't her. The vision was of the past, and she was alive. Safe. Free from the bruises and shameful way she'd been used. Maxis was dead and couldn't hurt her anymore.

Her footsteps quickened, and her blood raced. The room spun around her, hazy and out of focus, but the cool stone walls were steady beneath her palms, guiding her to the soft glow ahead. Air. She needed air. And space.

Freedom.

Grasping the wrought-iron stair rail, she padded down the gray stone steps, careful to silence her sandaled steps. Freshly baked bread and cinnamon weighted the air, and muted feminine chatter drifted from the kitchen. Most likely Orla and the other morning castle workers, maybe even Lexi and Galena, preparing for another day full of hungry warriors and family members. Compassionate people who'd saved and sheltered her, but came with keen eyes and probing questions.

Skirting the voices, she cut through the formal dining room and angled to the main foyer and the massive gardens beyond. Midmorning sunshine slanted through the open two-story arched windows, and the salt-tinged ocean breeze swept her tear-streaked cheeks. Her heart kicked at the scent, calling her as it had all those years ago with her parents. The day before Maxis kidnapped her and destroyed everything.

She shoved one of the two thick mahogany doors wide, gasped, and staggered backward.

A warrior, backlit by the rising sun, towered in her path. A big one, dressed in full warrior garb of black leather pants, boots, and silver drast. He caught the door before it could shut in a quick, easy grip, and stepped out of the sun's glare.

Her lungs seized. Not just any warrior. This was Ludan Forte, right hand and somo to the malran. Six-foot-six of pure intimidation with twice the muscle mass of his peers.

Framed by the brilliant light behind him, he loomed like an avenging legend come to life.

He cocked his head and assessed her head to toe, a wayward strand of wavy, blue-black hair falling across his forehead. His mouth tightened. Framed by his closely cropped beard, his frown reeked of menace.

"You're crying." An accusation and a demand for information all rolled up into one, as crisp and gruff as everything else he did.

"I…" Her thoughts fizzled, any hope for words drying up on her tongue. She ducked her head and swiped her cheek with the back of her hand. Her feet refused to move, frozen beneath his searing ice-blue gaze. "I'm fine, I just—"

"Ludan, you going to let the poor girl by, or glare at her until she keels over?" Ian Smith's raspy voice drifted from behind her, his heavy tread sounding on the main foyer staircase. A perfect distraction.

"Excuse me." Her breathy words barely registered as she ducked beneath Ludan's arm and stumble-scurried across the castle's veranda. Her sandals slapped against the stone. Her lungs burned with the need for a full, unimpeded breath, and her heart slammed against her sternum in time with each footfall. Just a little farther. Around the castle's edge to the cove and the ocean's peaceful rhythm. Then she could stop. Reevaluate. Smother the past so it couldn't touch her. Couldn't blemish the tiny scrap of good she'd finally found.

Rounding the final corner, the wind whipped her loose, dark hair and tangled her simple sapphire gown around her ankles. The bluff's waist-high wall stretched along the cove's crescent edge, gray and taupe stone blending with the perfect azure and rainbow-laced Myren sky. Chocolate wood gates marked each quarter mile interval, the closest one unlatched and open, welcoming her escape.

She trudged across the vibrant green grass, the color

3

similar to what she remembered from her home in Evad, but tinged with silver that glinted off the red-rimmed Myren sun. Memories from before her capture barely registered anymore, only foggy snippets remaining where there were once finite details. So much lost. Her family. Her future and any hope for tenderness or love. No man could ever want her, not with her tainted past. And now this? Thrust into the middle of a prophecy hinged on the very cruelness that had shaped her life? It wasn't fair. At the very least she deserved a fresh start. Peace and contentment, if not solace.

Below, the turquoise waves crashed against the powder-white sand and black stone walls. As deep as the soaring three-story castle was tall, the turbulent waters seemed forever away. She inched closer to the edge, the toes of her sandals lining the bluff's rocky edge.

The dead human from the vision wavered in the forefront of her mind, her twin not just in appearance, but in the fate they'd suffered. Except that Brenna had lived.

That's not the only difference.

The snide, biting thought razored across her heart and left a frozen wake in its path. That woman had been loved. Her mate had mourned her death. Avenged the damage brought upon her and offered his gifts to protect those like her. She had no one.

A pebble slipped from beneath her feet and bounced off the black stone walls once, twice, then plummeted to the water below. All this time she'd believed. Clung to the hope of going home and finding her family. Kept the faith that she'd someday set her misfortune behind and build something new and fresh. For what? To have the weight of all races thrust on her unwilling shoulders?

The wind whipped faster, and reality blurred, only the back and forth of the waves below in focus. In the distance, a larken trilled a string of singsong notes. Fifteen years she'd suffered, no choices left to her but life and death.

No more.

She was done with accepting what others thrust on her. If she didn't want this role in the prophecy, she didn't have to take it. Didn't have to play the parts deemed appropriate by others. This was her life. To build however she saw fit. Myren laws and prophecies be damned. No one could force her life or her choices.

Lifting her head, she focused on the horizon and sucked in a deep breath. She could do this. For once, she'd stand up for what she wanted and make this life her own. Voice her demands. Her needs.

She shifted to look back at the castle.

The rocks beneath her crumbled, and her body pitched to one side. Her feet slipped past the bluff's edge, and she flailed her arms, barely catching the ledge. Wind whipped her gown and tugged her dangling legs. Her heart galloped and lurched, fueled by panic. She couldn't die. Not now. She'd barely had a chance to live.

Straining to pull herself up and over the ledge, she dug her work-roughened fingers into the damp earth and pushed with everything she had.

The clay fragmented, slipped between her fingers, and surrendered her to the water below.

～

SHE'S NOT YOUR CONCERN.

Ludan tightened his grip on the castle's thick mahogany door until he thought the wood would snap. He'd fed himself the same damned mantra since the first time he'd seen Brenna, over and over in an endless loop.

Along with all the other voices.

Ian ambled up beside him and stared down the veranda in time to see Brenna disappear around the far side of the castle. "What the hell did you say to her?"

"I didn't say anything." Forcing his fingers free, Ludan let the door slip shut. The land on the far end of the castle was quiet. No other energy patterns registered near the ocean where Brenna had headed, nor in the forest beyond. Only blinding midmorning sun and the bold blue Myren sky filled the quiet landscape in between.

He still didn't like it. Too much weirdness had gone down in the last few months. Serena and Angus's page, Sully, disappearing. The Spiritu. The prophecy. He glanced at Ian beside him. "Go find Lexi. Have her take you to Evad today. I'll find Brenna and bring her back."

"You sure that's a good idea?"

The bite in Ian's tone cut through Ludan's focus. "Why wouldn't it be?"

"Because you looked like you were an inch away from ripping her head off."

Hardly. A hopeless junkie would surrender his fix before he'd hurt Brenna. Not that Ian would know that. None of them would. Ever. "I had things on my mind." Like how anytime she got within fifteen feet of him the nonstop racket in his head downgraded to a more tolerable decibel.

Ian cocked his head and anchored his hands in the pockets of his jacket, studying Ludan with a level of scrutiny that probably came in slow-mo precision. The son of a bitch was too damned perceptive. Cops—or former-cops turned PI in Ian's case—usually were.

"Track down Lexi," Ludan grumbled before Ian could latch on to any ideas. "The sooner I find Brenna and you're in Evad running reconnaissance, the sooner I can get back to guarding Eryx."

He strode away and shook the weight of Ian's stare off his

back. This whole damned place was one giant microscope lately. Suspicious stares. People digging into his personal life and asking questions they had no right to ask. Ian could think whatever the fuck he wanted. Tracking Brenna and making sure no other shit storms were on the horizon was just common sense, nothing more.

Justify it however you want, but you'd follow her with or without a prophecy.

His conscience's uppercut nailed him square in the gut and yanked him to a halt at the castle's edge.

Beyond the stone safety wall, Brenna stood staring down at the cove. Her dark hair whipped in the heavy ocean winds while the rest of her stood still as a statue. In the past few months, he'd watched from the sidelines as she'd fought her way back from near death. Seen her creep from the timid shell she'd survived behind after fifteen long years with Maxis. Studied how every day her posture got a little taller, her shoulders squared, and her chin had raised a fraction higher.

Today was different. Something in her near-black eyes seemed fractured. Broken. Off in a way that tripped all kinds of warning bells.

Pushing his Myren senses out along the cove, he gauged for any disturbance he might have missed. A larken swooped and sang high overhead, his deep blue body a near perfect match to Brenna's gown. Except for the bird and Brenna, no other forms of energy stirred. No visible threats, which meant whatever plagued her had already happened, or originated in her head.

He should leave her be and get Lexi. Combat and stealth were all he had to offer. If either were worth a damn when it came to emotions, he'd have slain his own demons years ago. Histus, even Ian would be better at this than him. At least Ian shared something in common with her. Two humans whose lives had been turned upside down by Maxis Steysis.

A memory surged to the forefront of his mind, and his knees nearly buckled. His mother, bloody and battered. Defiled and broken in a way no woman should ever know. Her screams roared above all the other memories battling for space in his head, sending painful shards between his temples.

He shook his head and focused on the grass beneath his boots. How the silver on the bold green blades sparked on the morning sun. How the rich, dark soil beneath it was still damp from storms the night before. It was just a memory. The worst of all the ones he had to relive, for sure, but in the past. This was now.

Brenna still hadn't moved. She probably just needed time alone, a concept he of all people understood, but he could check on her without making her uncomfortable. Pulling his mask into place, he blended with the elements, hiding his presence as he took to the sky and circled up and over the cove. A desperate, almost palpable propulsion urged him faster, directing him no more than twenty feet in front of her.

She stared out at the sea, her gaze empty and unfocused. He knew that look. Resignation and defeat. Had staggered beneath the weight of both for too damned many years. Her hands were fisted tight at her sides, and her toes touched the bluff's edge. Surely she wouldn't try to take her life. Not now. Not after all she'd survived.

As if in answer to his thoughts, Brenna's head snapped up, and her focus sharpened on the horizon.

The muscles along his shoulders uncoiled, and he huffed out a relieved exhale. Whatever had gripped her was gone now. Even her energy sparked brighter than moments before, as if the ocean's breeze had slipped beyond the confines of her skin and swept the sleeping monsters from her soul. Still, he'd be smart to keep an eye on her.

The dark, untamed presence inside him lifted its head, ears perked. The clawing hunger and compulsion he kept hidden and buried from everyone else rippled to the surface. Too close. An animal scenting the most succulent prey.

He forced himself an extra twenty feet away. Being closer to Brenna was a bad idea. Blissful in the way she dampened the backlash of his gift, but far too risky with the beast. That ugly, unpredictable part of him was only fit for battle. He'd mention his concerns for Brenna to Lexi or Galena. Brenna would be more comfortable with them anyway.

He turned for the castle, the memory of her soulful, near-black eyes and the way they'd focused on his lips this morning superimposing on the brilliant sunrise in front of him. For the sweetest, most torturous moment, he could have sworn she wanted him. Craved him the way he wanted her. But that couldn't be right. She was afraid of men. All of them.

Beneath him, the tossing seas transitioned to the plush green grass surrounding the castle. He had a job to do. The job he was born to do. The sooner he got back to it, the sooner that taut, insistent tug that stretched between him and Brenna would go away. At least he hoped it would. Either that, or he'd have to spar and drink himself into a stupor like he had the last few weeks.

A shriek rang out behind him, the sheer terror of it searing white-hot shrapnel inside his chest.

Before his mind had fully registered Brenna as its source, his body acted on instinct. The distance he'd created between them swept by in a blur. The only object in perfect focus was Brenna, her fingers digging into the loose clay and her slender arms pushing with all she had.

The slick, moss-covered edges crumbled.

Brenna's fingers slipped through the clay, and she dropped out of sight.

The beast roared and lashed him from the inside out. Fear supercharged his powers and shot him through the air so fast the wind burned his face. The powdered sand and black boulders rushed closer, Brenna only two arm spans away.

Three feet from the ground, he swooped beneath her and angled up at a sharp pitch. His heart slammed an angry protest, and his lungs burned for air, but Brenna was flush against him. Shaking violently in his arms with a brutal grip on his shoulders, but safe.

He held them there, high above the ocean, and cradled her closer.

Her breath chuffed against his skin, and something wet trailed down the side of his neck. Tears. A river of them mixed with gentle sobs.

And he could hear them. Each raspy inhalation as clear as a whisper in the dead of night. The ocean and the larken, too. No voices clouding the sounds around him. No memories trampling each other for headspace. They weren't just dimmed the way they normally were around her, they were gone. Absolute silence. His first reprieve in over a hundred years.

His arms tightened on instinct, as though she might somehow fly away or dissipate into nothingness. Rubbing his cheek against the top of her head, he savored the silk texture against his skin and lowered his voice to a near whisper. "You're safe."

She huddled closer, drawing her knees to her chest as her whimpers continued. The ocean tossed bold and loud beneath them. Probably not the most reassuring view from a non-flying human's point of view.

Fuck, like she'd have any other response. She'd nearly

died. He couldn't exactly expect her to lift her head and beam sunshine and roses.

He drifted to a flat-topped boulder at the cove's base and settled with the bluff wall behind him. Leaning back, he gave the wall his weight and pulled his knees in to angle Brenna closer.

Damn, but she felt good. So tiny and soft. Her hand opened and closed against his chest, dragging the slick-rough fabric of his drast against his adrenaline-soaked skin in a way he probably shouldn't enjoy, but abso-fucking-lutely did. Considering Brenna couldn't get a solid breath in, it was also entirely the wrong thing to think about. There had to be something he could do. Something to help her find her balance.

For once, a decent memory came to mind. The day he'd tried to imitate his father by jumping off their cottage roof in an attempt to fly. He'd been too little to comprehend that flight required an awakening, something that didn't happen to eight-year-old boys. His mother had healed his wounds and held him in her lap while he cried, rocking slowly side to side.

He'd liked that. A lot. So much so, he'd pretended to cry longer so he could stay.

Gently, he imitated the movement, albeit more clunky than his mother. He stroked a hand from the top of her head to the small of her back, her glossy hair slick against his callused palm. Since the first time he'd seen her, he'd been fascinated by it. The darkest chocolate to match her eyes.

Wind whispered through the cove, wrapping a faint vanilla scent around them. He dipped his head, his nose only inches from her temple, and inhaled deep. It was Brenna, either her hair or her skin, but whatever it was, was perfect. Comforting and soft.

The darkness inside him settled. Stilled in a way he hadn't

felt since before his awakening. Countless battles he'd fought, and bone-chilling memories he'd absorbed in the name of protecting his malran and his race, but no act felt as important as this moment. This was what armies fought to provide. What men died to protect.

Brenna let loose a long, body-shuddering sigh. Uncoiling her arms from around his neck, she smoothed her hands across his shoulders and down to his biceps.

His muscles tightened, every inch of him poised for her touch. Her presence.

Her fingers tightened, a tentative combination of exploration and reflex, before she pushed upright. Her nearly black eyes were glassy with the last of her tears, and her cheeks were a mottled red. It shouldn't have impacted him the way it did, but damned if he didn't want to pull her back against him and demand she stay put.

She didn't meet his gaze, but neither did she avert her face. Definitely a step up from the first day he'd met her.

"Thank you," she muttered.

Her voice. Praise the Great One, it was beautiful. He'd heard it plenty of times before, always shy with a breathiness born of well-earned caution, but now it was clear. Unhindered by the noise in his head.

He dipped his chin in acknowledgment. There wasn't much he could say she'd appreciate at this point, and all he really wanted was to hear her say something else. Anything. Histus, she could recite the damned alphabet and he'd be happy.

Instead, her focus drifted to where her hands rested on his biceps. A curious light flickered for a second, maybe two, before she blinked, shook her head, and tried to wiggle off his lap.

Ludan tightened his hold. "I'm not gentle." The words came out rougher than he'd intended, driven solely by compulsion and a need he couldn't quite define. "My words aren't as pretty as Eryx's, but I can listen."

For the longest time she stayed locked in place, studying him with a deep scrutiny he felt clear to his soul. As though she gauged the meaning of his entire existence from her gaze alone. A fresh tear slipped down her cheek.

He traced its path, captivated by the contrasts between them. Her smooth, creamy skin, to his dark, roughened fingers. His brutish-sized paw against her pixie face.

"I don't want to talk about where I've been." Her voice ripped him from his thoughts, the angst behind it prodding the beast out from his brief respite. "I don't want him to have any more of me than he already got."

And by *him* she meant Maxis. That bastard.

Ludan exhaled slowly, but held Brenna's gaze. In that moment, he'd give a lot to resurrect the son of a bitch and kill him all over again with nothing more than his fists. "Then tell me what made you run."

"Only my memories." She looked away, scanning the cove with the pretense of gaining her bearings, but he recognized it for what it was. Diversion. The same tactic he'd used for years to throw people off track.

She smoothed her gown along her thigh, all business but for the sniffles that came between her still uneven breaths. Whatever it was that had chased her from the castle this morning was tucked neatly back in its place. For now. "I need to get back. Ramsay's awake, but Trinity's in a bad place. I told them I'd tell Eryx and Galena he was okay, and give them some time alone."

The casually dropped information punched through Ludan's languid state as little else could in that moment. Ever since Ramsay and Trinity had come back from Winrun, Ramsay out cold and Trinity a mess of nerves, Eryx's temper had run sharper than any blade Ludan had fought against. He nodded and set her on her feet, clinging to her hips until she was steady.

The second he lost contact, the voices rose. Nowhere near their normal levels, but the quiet vanished, the chatter of memories he'd consumed the last hundred plus years kicking back into full gear.

So, it wasn't a fluke. Brenna really was the key. The calming presence he'd sensed from the beginning.

He stood and shook the thoughts off. Eryx needed him. Ramsay needed him. The tiny break was more than he deserved anyway. He'd already learned in the worst possible way what happened when responsibilities went ignored. "I asked Ian to find Lexi before I came after you. Eryx is at the training center, but I'll contact him and have him meet us at the castle."

He stepped forward to pick her up, but she staggered back a step and raised her hands to hold him away. "What are you doing?"

"Getting you back to the castle." Ludan glanced up and over his shoulder at the towering bluff behind them. "Unless you'd rather climb."

This time she ducked her chin, but it was sweet and paired with a pretty flush on her cheeks. "All right."

He scooped her up, and the voices disappeared. Amazing. A damned miracle in sweet, innocent form. He stepped forward, ready to launch to the skies.

"Ludan."

He stopped and nearly choked at the depth in her dark eyes. Large and full of emotion, full of knowledge no woman her age should know. "You're wrong."

Like before, the pleasant brush of her voice sent him sideways, enough so it took at least a seven-second delay before the meaning of her words registered. He lifted an eyebrow, wanting more of her beautiful voice no matter what she had to say.

Her gaze slid sideways, and her arms tightened around his neck. "You might not use pretty words, but you were gentle with me."

CHAPTER 2

*S*erena was screwed. Well and truly backed into a corner she'd never anticipated. Tugging the tattered gray blanket tighter around her shoulders, she huddled deeper into the corner of Uther's dank cellar. Only a single candle burned on the small scarred table beside blank parchments and the translation tome they'd stolen. A blessing, really. Any more light than that and she'd be privy to whatever scampered along the floor and the filth covering her cot. With its bare clay walls and the moldy stench, she felt barely a step up from a rodent burrowed into the earth. The only plus was the thin stretch of zeolite above her. Without the gift-stripping crystal fully surrounding her, it had little impact on her powers, but it might do a decent job of muddling her location. Odds were good it was the only thing keeping her alive.

She reached for the sun's position with her Myren senses. Its energy sparked in an erratic pattern, definitely above the horizon, but beyond that she couldn't be sure what time it was. Uther had to be back soon with news. And food. Hopefully even clean clothes. For the umpteenth time since Uther had hustled her into the shelter beneath his home in the Underlands, she rehashed her hasty grasp for the upper hand with Eryx. Rushing home before the guards could find her missing would have been the safe play. Definitely the more comfortable play. But then she wouldn't have the journal.

Reaching beneath the cot's crude mattress, Serena slid the chocolate leather book from its hiding spot. The pages were ancient and yellowed with heavily slanted, masculine bold script in the old language. Tucked in the center was the pendant, a black filigree ironwork that fit the palm of her hand on a simple black chain. It was too ugly to be fashionable, but it matched Lexi's prophetic mark perfectly.

The mark of your family will be the key, the tool that will feed its bearer the powers you give freely this day, or that will keep the wall in place forever more.

She traced her fingertips atop the ivory-twined sword. If this was the key, no man would ever lord over her again. Not her father. Not Eryx, or any mate. *She* would wield the power and take the throne for her own.

The heavy clunk of Uther's front door and purposeful footsteps pounded on the wood floors above.

Her heart lurched and she scrambled off the cot, praying it was Uther. If Eryx and his warriors had managed to track her, everything she'd learned about the prophecy would be for nothing. The malran would happily carry through on her sentence, stripping her powers and banishing her to Evad. If he even deigned to let her live.

Looping the chain around her neck, she tucked the pendant under the neckline of her tunic and stashed the journal back beneath the mattress. She settled in the old ladder-back chair behind the rickety table as the door swung open.

Her breath whooshed out in one giant exhale. "Uther."

Her dead mate's strategos ducked through the tiny opening. A self-made warrior who'd murdered his way up the rebellion ranks, he seldom showed signs of fatigue, but today his power was muted. Dark smudges arced below his deadened sage eyes, and his usually prideful shoulders hung heavy.

She fisted the blanket wrapped around her shoulders tighter. "What happened?"

Pacing toward her, he scanned the tiny ten-by-ten hovel, then raked her with a passive, almost disdainful assessment. The harsh lines of his square jaw and sharp cheekbones were even more pronounced in the dim candlelight. With his cropped black hair, his appearance was twice as sinister as in daylight. He tossed a semi-folded bundle of drab, brown fabric on the table and then ambled to the cot. "You're officially a fugitive. I trailed the guards. From what I gathered, your family's agreed to cooperate with the malran."

"That's it? You've been gone for hours, and that's all the news you've got?"

He sat on the cot and crossed his ankle atop his knee, exhaustion whispering through his heavy exhale as he reclined against the rough wall. "Eight hours, to be precise. Eight hours masking and risking my life around elite Myren warriors on your behalf." He motioned toward the bundle of fabric with a lift of his chin. "And getting you fresh clothes. I thought you'd be thankful."

Those were clothes? She clasped the top item and unfolded it, pinching it between her fingers and holding it high to cover her grimace. Granted the loose tunic was functional and decently made, but it had the style of a burlap sack. "Where did you get them?"

"The market. You know, where the average people go."

The bastard. He knew damned well she'd never bought a thing from Cush's market. Still, she needed something clean to wear, and he was the only provider she had. She schooled her face into a serene mask and smiled, folding the garment in her lap. "Thank you."

He smirked, an insolent quirk to his lips that made all too clear how much he enjoyed her discomfort.

"How exactly does my family plan to cooperate?" she said.

"They've already undergone questioning. None of them were able to report your location via link. Your mother put on quite a show, claiming you were dead, but your father screwed you and said the link wasn't completely mute. Only indistinguishable. They've all agreed to share their memories so long as a solicitor is present."

Of course, her father would put a caveat on his support. Only solicitors were capable of blocking irrelevant memories in a scan, and Reginald Doroz had more than enough dirt on people to want to keep it contained. *Knowledge begets leverage.* The damned phrase should have been blazoned beneath her family mark. "So, now what do we do?"

"We?" Uther sat up and rested his elbows on his knees. "How is it you think there's a *we* in any equation pertaining to your future?"

"Because I need out of this hole, and the only way to do that is to either sever my family links, or take my family out of the equation another way. Maxis never figured out how Eryx broke his link to Reese, so that's not an option. That leaves dealing with my family."

"Thanks to your impetuous decision, we've got the malran's translation tables, which means he'll be doing no more work on the prophecy. I've already got my family's journal. As far as I'm concerned, the best place for you is right here, finishing your work. Getting you free from this predicament isn't in my best interest."

And there it was. The unexpected ramification she'd ruminated about since Uther had hustled her into this dreary burrow. "Actually, I *had* your family's journal."

Uther punched upright, his hands fisted at his sides. "What's that supposed to mean?"

"I mean, before we left for the castle, I stored it, the work I'd already done, and the other translation table in my father's office."

"I thought it was in your solicitor's safe?"

"I only worked in Thyrus's office for a change of scenery and his texts. I never kept things there." Not entirely true. There was a third translation table in Thyrus's safe, one that had proven far more accurate than the one she'd shown Uther, but Uther didn't need to know that.

"Fuck!" He paced the tiny space, three angry strides consuming the distance before he spun and headed the other direction. "Where are they?"

"Hidden in my father's office."

"Where?"

"Behind some books in my satchel. There's no way they'll find them unless they know where to look."

Uther halted and hung his head, hands braced on his hips.

As advantages went, the hidden information wasn't much, but it was all she had. "We need my satchel if we're going to get you what you want. The last thing we need is Eryx getting his hands on the translations I've already completed."

Rubbing the back of his neck, he stared down at the dirt floor. "There's no way I'm getting in right now. Not until some of the guards clear off." He pinned her with a glare. "Who else knows where they are?"

"Aside from you, no one."

"I want details. Enough I can walk right in and find what I need."

She scooted to the edge of her chair and folded her hands on the table. "They're in the bookshelf. The section closest to the door, the shelf at shoulder height." She noted Uther's towering stature and corrected, "*My* shoulder height."

"And the books they're behind?"

"*The Myren Compendium*. There are four of them. Or maybe five."

The muscle at the back of his jaw twitched. His gaze slid to the stack of papers on the table's edge. "Write it down."

"What?"

"Write it down. Exactly as it shows on the book."

The quiet amplified, and her instincts prickled. The request was a bit overkill for someone as mercenary as Uther. Still, she wasn't in a position to push him further than she already had. She dragged the papers in front of her and wrote the name clearly at the top.

As soon as she set her pencil down, he snatched it off the pile and studied it. "What color are the books?"

"Blue leather with gold leaf."

His eyes narrowed intently on the paper as though trying to memorize it.

It was just three words and not altogether difficult ones at that. Why in the world would he make such a big deal about her writing them down?

Unless he couldn't read.

That had to be it. Or maybe he could, but not very well. He'd once shared he'd been raised without station in Myren society, which usually meant no education. It also explained why he'd agreed to work with her in the first place.

For the first time since she'd gone into hiding, the muscles at her core unwound and she sucked in a slow, grateful breath. This was the hook she needed. The one saving grace that might get her out of here.

He folded the note, stuffed it in his pocket, and turned for the door. "I'll sleep today and try tonight."

"Wait."

He stopped, propping the door open with one hand.

An idea flickered, soft as the candlelight beside her, but

glaring as risks went. Still, if her hunch was right and he couldn't read, she'd buy some solidarity. "There's something I want to show you."

Rising from the table, she lifted the mattress and slid the journal from its hiding place. She fingered the aged, quality leather, and then held it out where he could see. "While we were at the castle, I found something else."

He crept toward her. Suspicion colored his gaze as it dropped to her outstretched hand. "What is it?"

"I think it's a journal like yours. While you were gone, I studied it a little. The markings look similar, except this one has more. New markings I didn't recognize plus a lot more content."

He opened it, scanning the pages without lingering long enough to really take anything in.

Her hunch was right. It had to be. If he could read, he'd at least hesitate over a few of the pages.

"You kept it to yourself." He handed the journal back to her. "You never planned to tell me."

"I really didn't know what it was at the time, but since they looked similar, I took it. Then I was distraught about my situation and forgot about it."

"But you hid it."

"Because I didn't know if it was you." The lies rolled easy off her tongue, certainty growing with every one. "Your link wouldn't register through the zeolite. If it was Eryx, I didn't want him to find it on me."

Uther's scowl deepened.

"I want to help you. If I didn't, why would I share it now?"

"You never do anything without a reason, Serena." His mouth quirked in a wry smirk, and he turned for the door. "Then again, neither do I. You'd be smart to earn your keep translating those journals while I'm gone."

CHAPTER 3

*S*o, this was what flying was like. Wrapped in Ludan's strong arms, Brenna surrendered her fears for the future to the cool wind stinging her cheeks and inhaled the ocean's salty breeze. Soft, buttery sunshine from the red-rimmed sun bathed the landscape. Moss-green grass with flecks of silver and random patches of closely cropped white flowers undulated over soft-sloping plains. In the distance, a forest with lavender leaves and rich chocolate-colored trunks lined the ridge beneath a mesmerizing pearlescent mountain range. "It's beautiful."

Ludan's gaze snapped to hers, roving her features in sharp assessment. "You've never seen it like this?"

She shook her head and stared behind them at the turquoise ocean with its rainbow-kissed sky. Better that than to let him see too deep. "I've only flown twice. Once the day Maxis captured me, and again the day Eryx brought me here." Explaining beyond that wouldn't be necessary. Ludan had been there the day she'd stepped in front of a bullet for Lexi. Eryx had healed her and brought her unconscious body home, not knowing the effects of his healing on her human body.

They knew the consequences now. Or at least some of them. Mirroring the gifts of the Myrens around her was likely the only reason she'd been able to see Ramsay's dream of the prophecy.

Ludan's thumb swept a disconcerting path along her shoulder, leaving warm tingles in its wake. "I can take you again."

Shock more than wisdom forced her gaze to his. "You would?"

He nodded, the motion slow and solemn as though offering an oath. His wavy black hair tossed in the wind and tickled her arm where it wrapped around his neck. It was shorter than Eryx's, only a little past his shoulders, but it was every bit as thick and kissed with hints of blue.

She'd give a lot to touch it. To see if it felt as soft as it looked and comb the gentle waves through her fingertips. She fisted her hand instead. A man like him would never stand for such a thing. It was too girly. Too soft. "I'd like that."

His eerie blue eyes stayed trained on her face, pinched with an awkward uncertainty. He swallowed and jerked his attention to the ground below. "Eryx is on his way, and Lexi's in the office waiting for you." Fast as a snap, the glimpse of vulnerability vanished, replaced with the bulldozer persona he kept cinched around him night and day.

The castle's stone veranda with its shimmering gray stone and ivy-covered balustrades drifted closer and closer. A handful of seconds at most and she'd be back on her feet and faced with reality. She ducked her face in the crook of his neck and held her breath.

Ludan touched down with a soft thud. The scruff of his beard whispered against her jaw, and his deep, mesmerizing voice rumbled near her ear. "You're safe."

Twice now he'd uttered that phrase, both times unfurling unfamiliar sensations that neither her mind nor body could process. Lifting her head, she pulled in a fortifying breath. His scent permeated her lungs, a mix of leather and earth that brought to mind forests and steadied her nerves better than any of Galena's tonics. "Sorry. I shouldn't let my fears get to me."

"We'll work on it."

They would?

The confusion must have shown on her face because his mouth quirked in an almost grin. He urged her forward with a hand at the small of her back, the span from his pinkie to his thumb nearly covering her hip to hip. His touch burned through her simple velvet gown, the contact so distracting that the walk from the veranda to the royal couple's office didn't register.

Lexi stood alone at the far end of the room, staring out the soaring arched window. Lexi, but no Eryx.

Brenna stopped so suddenly that Ludan barely checked his steps before crashing into her. "Why is Eryx at the training center? He was waiting for Ramsay to wake up when I saw him last."

Lexi faced them at the sound of Brenna's voice and pushed away from the window. As usual, she'd forgone the more traditional gowns favored by Myren high society and wore a simple scarlet tunic and leggings. The malran's mark covered her right arm, a black winged horse reared back on its hind legs, wings spread high and ready for flight. Her attire might have been casual, but the tension in her face screamed of warfare. "They're tracking Serena and Sully."

"What?" Brenna swiveled and gauged Ludan's face for some trace of information.

Unfortunately, his mask was firmly back in place. Bored and teetering on insolent.

25

"I thought she was under house arrest," Brenna said. "And who's Sully?"

"She was." Lexi paced toward her, popping her knuckles along the way. "Sometime yesterday afternoon she disappeared. Sully is Angus's page, and he's the one person who can help us hang Serena and Angus once and for all, but he's missing, too. Warriors have been searching for them since last night."

"That's what Eryx was so upset about," she said mostly to herself. Multiple times, Eryx and Lexi had checked in on Ramsay when he'd been unconscious, anxious to see if he'd woken. Every visit, Eryx's agitation had grown a notch higher.

An eerie cold whispered across her skin. "She's free."

Ludan moved in close behind her, his presence as tangible as heated armor. "No one will get to you." It was a promise, spoken low and for her only.

"Maxis is dead." Lexi stopped right in front of her. For a second, her gaze slipped to Ludan behind her, but shifted back to Brenna's and softened. "Most of the Rebellion men turned themselves in for a chance at leniency, and Serena's not capable of doing her own dirty work. She's not a threat to you."

Maybe not physically. But Brenna had seen firsthand Serena's disgust for humans. And God help her if Ramsay's vision proved true and Serena ever learned of Brenna's role in the prophecy.

Eryx and Reese strode through the arched entrance, each of them dressed the same as Ludan in standard silver drast and black leather pants and boots. Like most mated Myren men, their hair was bound, Reese with his tawny blond hair pulled in a knot at his crown, and Eryx with his commitment braids bound by platinum beads and nearly reaching his waist.

Eryx halted only two steps in and scanned the room, ending on Ludan. "What's the news?"

"Ramsay's awake," Brenna said. "He woke a little over an hour ago."

He spun and headed for the main staircase. "And I'm just now hearing about it?"

Reese stayed close beside him. "I'll get Galena."

"Wait!" Brenna hurried after them. She'd barely managed a few strides before Eryx turned back. Raw, crackling energy slammed against her, and she staggered backward.

Ludan stepped between them, and a low, menacing growl rumbled through the room.

The hairs at the back of Brenna's neck lifted. Without thinking, she laid a comforting hand on Ludan's shoulder and crept beside him. "Ramsay's fine. Better than fine, actually, but he asked for time alone with Trinity. She's hurting."

Eryx noted Ludan's stance, then Brenna's hand on his shoulder.

She snatched it away and edged closer to Lexi, who'd paused beside her.

Still keeping his gaze locked on Ludan, Eryx asked, "What do you mean, better than fine?"

Brenna swallowed and gripped her hands tightly in front of her. No way was she sharing the details with Eryx, not while he was in such a foul mood. Or ever, if she had a say.

"Don't let him get to you." Lexi wrapped her arm around Brenna's shoulders. "He's just in a snit because of Serena, not because of anything you've done. Tell him about Ramsay."

Beside her, Ludan fumed lasers at his malran. His shoulders were thrown back and his towering body angled forward and ready for action. Despite their questions about Ramsay and his awakening, every other gaze was aimed on him as well, particularly Eryx and Lexi. Surely, Ludan wouldn't lash out at his king on her behalf. They were best friends, nothing short of brothers even if they didn't share blood.

"Trinity's dad didn't hurt Ramsay." Everyone's focus darted to Brenna, Ludan's included. "Kazan gave him knowledge. That's why he came back unconscious. He was reliving the prophecy in his head."

Eryx stepped toward her, but Ludan blocked his path just as fast.

Lexi held up a hand and scowled at them both. "You boys think you can nip the testosterone long enough for us to learn something before you scare Brenna half to death?" Planting her hands on her hips, she gave both men her back and went one-on-one with Brenna. "Okay, let's try this again, with a few more details this time."

"Kazan gave Ramsay all the details on the prophecy," Brenna said. "What caused it in the first place, who was involved, and how it works. For him to get those details, he sort of relived it. That's why he was unconscious." Who resolved it could wait for later, like when Eryx was in another region.

Eryx's voice cut from behind Lexi, more calm and slightly baffled. "Everything?"

Brenna kept her gaze on Lexi and tried to ignore the clammy moisture dotting her forehead and neck. She was just sharing information. Not agreeing to participate, or even hinting at her involvement. "Everything. But he needs time alone with Trinity. She wasn't in the best shape after he woke up. I don't think she told any of you, but the information Kazan gave Ramsay came with a price."

"Trinity had to pay?" Lexi said.

"Not Trinity." Brenna wiped one sweaty palm on her hip. "Her dad forfeited his life."

Eryx twisted and stared in the direction of Ramsay's room in the far wing. His eyes grew distant for a handful of seconds, then snapped to Brenna. He nodded. "He wants to get Trinity settled. He'll share what he knows at dinner. Reese and I will head back to the training center and make sure the search keeps going until then." He eyeballed Ludan. "You coming?"

Before Ludan could answer, Reese held up a hand. His gaze stayed rooted to the floor for another beat before he focused on Eryx. "The quaran at Serena's house says the family's solicitor just arrived. They'll be ready to testify within the hour."

"I thought Reginald had Serena's back these days," Ludan said.

Eryx rubbed the back of his neck and glared out the windows along the far wall. "Reginald supports his bottom line, first and foremost. That's probably where Serena gets it." He narrowed his gaze on Ludan. "They're offering their memories, albeit through the solicitor's protection. You up for it?"

Ludan crossed his powerful arms across his chest and frowned. "Aren't I always?"

Eryx volleyed a look between Ludan and Brenna and opened his mouth.

"Enough," Lexi said before he could speak. "If you two want to beat on your chests, you can do it without us. Though you might not want to get blood on the carpet. If you do, Orla will string you both up by your nuts." Waving Brenna forward, she stole a peek back at Ludan. "Unless I'm reading things wrong, you in particular might need those later."

~

NONSTOP CHATTER, music, and noise jangled through Ludan's head, punctuated now and then by a random scream. The capital region of Cush zipped by below him, and the cool air whistled in his ears. Usually flying helped, the peacefulness of the act and the focus it required offsetting the noise, but not today. Not after being so close to Brenna.

Eryx flew beside him, Reese flanking Eryx's other side. For all the flack he'd given Ludan in his office, his best friend hadn't uttered a word since they left.

Ludan clenched his jaw and tried to focus through the ruckus in his head. He had five minutes tops to get his shit under control. If he didn't, he'd never make it through the Doroz family scans, and that would be a topic Eryx wouldn't be so willing to couch for later.

Eryx's cool voice slid through Ludan's head, the lack of echo telling him the conversation was solely between the two of them. *"You want to explain what your posturing in my study was about?"*

So much for couching topics. *"Depends. Be more specific."*

Eryx's mental scoff rang loud and clear. *"We practically shared a cradle. What just happened in my office hasn't ever happened before. I doubt I need to be more specific than that."*

"I've gotten in your face plenty."

"That wasn't getting in my face. That was a threat."

True. And if he'd have been less off balance by his response to Brenna, he'd have checked it a helluva lot better. *"I never said a word."*

"You didn't have to." Eryx shifted so his feet aimed toward the ground and dropped to the earth. As soon as Reese and Ludan touched down beside him, he fixed Reese with a pointed look. "Let the Doroz counsel know we're here. Ludan and I will be a minute."

Reese gauged the two of them as though he wasn't entirely sure the lack of supervision was wise, then shook his head and strolled away.

Eryx stared after him, waiting until he was well out of earshot. "You've been acting strange for weeks now."

No denying that. Everyone had commented on it, and he wished like histus they'd all butt out. He glared back at Eryx, keeping his expression void.

Cocking his head, Eryx scratched the stubble he hadn't bothered to shave this morning. "The more I think about it, things went a little off the day we brought Brenna home."

It was all he could do not to look away. To pace, or just slug his friend for a diversion. The last thing he needed right now was Eryx connecting dots. Not yet anyway. Not until Ludan understood what was going on better himself. "You're imagining things."

"I didn't imagine you getting between me and Brenna."

"You scared her, and it pissed me off."

"I've scared a lot of people in my years, and not once have you stopped me. What makes her different?"

He swallowed big before he could catch it, and Eryx's gaze dropped enough to note it.

Fuck, he didn't need this. The voices rose another notch, and his temples throbbed with ice pick precision. He was sick of the lies. The secrets. For once, he considered letting it out. All of it. Every sordid detail he'd stuffed since he'd found his mother dead, then sentenced and killed his uncle for the crime.

But Eryx didn't deserve that. He'd heap all kinds of guilt on himself for asking Ludan to consume memories in the first place. He had a whole damned race to look out for. It was Ludan's job to look out for Eryx.

"When I figure it out, I'll let you know." It was the closest he could get to the truth, and hopefully enough to buy him some time.

Eryx studied him, his shrewd eyes working overtime.

Ludan clenched his fists.

Letting out a resigned breath, Eryx shook his head. "Sometimes the best way to figure things out is to not try to unravel it alone. Hopefully, you'll figure that out sooner rather than later." He spun for Serena's front door. "Let's get this done. I want to see my brother and hear what he learned on his little adventure."

Three tense minutes, and boom, it was over. Before Ludan even had a chance to unwind his defenses, the creepy Doroz butler ushered them through the stark, black and white foyer and into the formal receiving room situated off the main entrance. Every time Ludan came here, an eerie vibe settled on him. Between the pale purples and pinks decorating the room and the museum stuffiness, the place was more like an Evad mortuary than a home.

"My malran." The family's solicitor hustled forward and dropped to one knee, lowering his head in the most formal of greetings. Unlike the more vaunted attorneys in Cush, he wore a simple ivory overrobe and an unadorned maroon stole. "My name is Yaron Dost, counsel for the Doroz family."

Under normal circumstances, Eryx barely tolerated ceremonial protocol, but this time he left the middle-aged man on his knee and glowered at Reginald and his family still seated behind them. Three picture-perfect citizens dressed up in their Sanctuary best. "You've served them how long?"

To his credit, Yaron kept his head down. "Over fifty years, sir."

"More than enough to build loyalty."

"My loyalty is to the throne and the ellan first, my clients second."

A smart answer, considering the circumstance. Not that Eryx wouldn't have seen through a lie. Being a Shantos male, he carried the sum of all Myren gifts, including Lexi's scary emotional radar. Thank the Great One, Eryx wasn't as in tune with the gift as his mate, or he'd have called Ludan on his secrets years ago.

"I'm surprised you didn't send for your daughter's lawyer," Eryx said to Reginald. "They say Thyrus hides memories better than most."

Reginald cocked his head arrogantly, crossed one leg over the other, and circled his foot. His fitted black pants, tall leather boots, and tailored gray duster were the standard for wealthy merchants, but Ludan doubted any of Reginald's peers used such quality fabrics. "If I were a part of her schemes, that would have been a reasonable response. However, given my family's desire to cooperate, that would be counterintuitive."

Eryx huffed a disbelieving chuckle and studied Yaron, still kneeling at his feet. "Rise." Not waiting for the man to reach full height, Eryx circled the solicitor and paused before Serena's mother. "Any hints as to your daughter's whereabouts, Fatima?"

"Not a word, Your Highness." She bowed her head and clasped her tiny hands in her lap. Her pink velvet gown covered her neck to toes, and it matched the wingback she sat in so well it was a wonder anyone noticed her at all. Rumor had it she'd been as lovely as her daughter in her youth, long hair the color of the moon, a classic face, and unnaturally beautiful blue eyes. Now it was hard to imagine beyond the wrinkles lining her face and the veins running beneath her pale skin.

For Serena's brother, Eryx only raised an eyebrow in silent question.

Callen scoffed and rolled his eyes, a brave move considering Eryx's waning patience. "Believe me, if I locate her, I'll be the first to share. She's a spoiled brat and always has been." He mimicked the raised eyebrow back at Eryx. "I'd think you of all people would know that."

Fatima gasped.

Reginald surged to his feet with a sharp reprimand. "Callen." He smoothed his duster over his stomach and affected a stiff bow for Eryx. "I hope you'll forgive him, my malran. My son is young. The events of late have left him short-tempered and thoughtless."

"The boy doesn't know what short-tempered is." Ludan prowled forward, giving his beast a little extra rope. Adrenaline surged and partially dulled the ruckus in his head. "I can show him, though."

Yaron glided between Reginald and Eryx and urged his client back to his chair. "Perhaps we'd do best to proceed with the scans and let everyone get back to their business. While the Doroz family is most disappointed in Serena's violation of her sentence, they hold the safety of our race as the highest priority. So..." He folded his hands in front of him and tilted his head. "What are the time barriers needed for today's work?"

"Two months, at least," Eryx said.

Yaron smiled and dipped his chin, but not fast enough to hide the patronizing glint in his eyes. "I can understand Your Highness's need for the most information necessary. However, Serena already provided her memories following the trial as a part of her sentence. Two months is an excessive time span considering she's only been under house arrest for four weeks. Perhaps we could agree to the beginning of her sentence?"

Ludan crossed his arms. "Or I could just take what I want without your interference."

"No way." Callen perked up and twisted toward his father. "He's doing it?"

Fatima covered her mouth with a dainty hand, but Reginald just resumed his bored pose from before. He waved a dismissive hand toward his solicitor. "Two months...one month...just give him what they want. I want my family free of this mess."

Ludan advanced.

Yaron held up a hand. "One other thing, if I may. Memories will be limited to those with Serena present. Others are invalid for the purpose of this interview." He focused on Eryx. "Agreed?"

"For now." Eryx motioned Ludan forward. "Let's get this done."

Heading for the mouthy youth first, Ludan crowded close and snatched his hand. The solicitor's memory-filtering gift slid into place a half a second before Ludan could get an unfettered peek. Not that there was much to look at. In seconds, he was in and out. Callen didn't just dislike Serena. He'd had nearly zero interaction with her in the last few months.

Fatima held out her hand, palm up, before he even looked at her. Her fingertips were ice cube cold and trembling against his palm.

"It won't hurt." At least he wouldn't make it hurt for her. Like Eryx, he could take memories with as little or as much pain as he wished. He could also take them fast. A whole lifetime in the space of seconds without a solicitor's intervention. Without the blocking influence, Ludan was pretty damned sure he'd find evidence Reginald was more the source of her tremors than Ludan.

Weeks from Fatima's memories zipped past, only random blips coming into focus where Serena was present thanks to Yaron's intervention. Aside from dinners and a trip to Sanctuary, there was very little. Nothing of substance.

He loosened his grip, and she snatched her hand away.

"Thank you," she whispered.

Yeah, there were secrets there. Dark, ugly secrets. He shifted his focus to Reginald.

He smiled back at Ludan, confidence bordering on defiance, and offered his hand. "You see? As I stated, my family is innocent of my daughter's schemes."

A weird, offsetting pulse rippled through Ludan a split second before he gripped Reginald's hand. His thoughts scattered, and the room went hazy. There was a purpose to his visit. A mission. He shook his head and took a deep breath. Memories. Reginald's memories. Closing his eyes, he tunneled through Reginald's mind.

Praise the Great One, no wonder Serena was screwed up. The man looked at her with nothing but distaste and disgust. How could anyone ever come out of this household unscathed?

A scene flew by so fast and muddled he nearly missed it. Serena stood in a darkened kitchen, her hand on the door to the outside. Reginald spoke to her, but the words were muffled. An urge to bypass the whole scene burned hot as a torch aimed at his skin. Damn it, why couldn't he focus?

"Sir?" Yaron's voice sounded like he stood at the end of a long tunnel. "Sir, is your scan complete?"

Ludan released Reginald's hand and nodded, turning away until he could catch his breath. Serena hadn't left, of that he'd been certain, but the words spoken between her and Reginald were too broken and muffled to understand.

All the other memories he'd consumed in the past surged in one deafening wave. His eyelids twitched and a piercing stab burned at each temple.

"Anything?" How Eryx's simple question made it through the chaos was a miracle.

Ludan shook his head but didn't dare make eye contact. One thing about Eryx, not much escaped his notice. One look at Ludan's face and he'd start digging. *"Nothing."*

Behind him Eryx and Yaron exchanged commentary. Reginald and his family wisely held their tongues.

God what he'd give for the silence Brenna offered right now.

Eryx's voice cut through his thoughts. "This isn't a political opportunity for leverage, Reginald. The council has ruled her a fugitive and a risk to our race."

"My son might be careless in his mannerisms, Your Highness, but I assure you, we all want Serena dealt with. The moment any of us sense her via link, your guards will be alerted immediately."

"Good." Shooting one last intimidating glare at Callen, Eryx shifted for the door. "Because if I find her alive or outside of zeolite without your assistance, I'll consider all three of you accomplices in her escape."

CHAPTER 4

*B*renna trailed two steps behind Lexi and Galena on the way to the kitchen. They'd met up with Eryx's sister, the healer, on their way to find Orla, and neither had stopped their rapid-fire chatter since. Understandable given the information Galena had missed out on while checking on patients, and more than a welcome respite for Brenna. An idle time to unwind her thoughts.

Tall windows lined the castle's back hallway and cast narrow beams of light on the gray stonework and handmade tapestries. So bright and beautiful. Still, if she could've found a way to politely extricate herself from the two women and ruminate in private, she'd have leveraged it in a second, but there was no escaping Lexi once she got her mind wrapped around a task. Right now it seemed her task was keeping the women busy until the big reveal tonight.

Gliding through the kitchen's arched entry, Lexi's gaze locked on to Orla—or more like the lower half of Orla— hovering inside the pantry. Without the gift of flight, Brenna had given up trying to access the two-story storeroom, but for Myrens, the awkward space was a breeze.

Lexi tugged on the hem of Orla's cornflower gown. "Knock, knock."

"Oh! Lexi!" Orla lowered to the ground. Her silver hair hung loose to her waist and her cheeks were a tad pink, but her cornflower-blue eyes sparked with a mix of happiness and mirth. "My goodness, you scared me.

"Sorry." Lexi hefted the sack of flour from Orla's arms and peeked at the higher shelves. "What are you doing, anyway?"

"It's nearly harvest. I'm inventorying for winter before I place my orders with the market. I got a little overexuberant with the briash last year, and I'd like to avoid another miscalculation." She wiped her hands on a faded ivory hand towel, then tossed it to the cobalt tile countertop. "What's got all my girls gathered in the kitchen when they should be out in the sunshine before it turns cold?"

"Dinner." Lexi peeked under a towel covering a large ceramic bowl. "As in a big one. Ramsay's awake and has news about the prophecy. He's sharing over food."

"Oh, thank goodness." Orla bustled back into the pantry and started pulling out supplies, handing them over her shoulder to Lexi and Galena. She might have been nearing her five hundredth birthday, but the energy pouring off Orla seemed on par with a teenager. With the simple yet fitted cut of her gown and the intricate silver chain sloped around her waist, she looked more like a socialite than the castle's chatelaine. "Shouldn't we send him something up beforehand? He was out for a long time, and those boys never go long without food."

"He'll live." Galena pulled a barstool from underneath the oversized square island and perched on the edge. "Besides, Brenna said Trinity's in a rough spot. Kazan got us the information for the prophecy, but it cost him his life."

Orla spun, her eyes wide and her mouth agape. "Mercy."

She scanned the kitchen, then swung back to the stores behind her. "Well then. We need comfort food. Lots of it."

"That's why we're here." Lexi checked the ingredients already laid out on the counter. "So, what's on the menu?"

Orla stared up at the shelves and tapped her lips with one hand, the other anchored at her hip.

"The amber wine roast," Brenna blurted.

Everyone swiveled toward her.

Where the idea had come from, Brenna didn't have a clue, but she was certain it was the right suggestion. "You made it for Trinity right after she came here. She loved it."

Galena propped an elbow on the countertop and nibbled on a skinny breadstick. "You're right. And you don't get much heartier than roasted aron. I swear I put on five pounds just smelling that dish."

"Will Graylin be coming, too?" Orla twisted for a confirmation from Lexi, but spun back around before she got an answer, piling items in her arms. "Viccus goes well with the roast, and he's partial to it."

Lexi smirked and unloaded Orla's newest haul. "I'd say he's partial to anything that comes out of your kitchen, but I'll eat whatever so long as we get dessert."

"Lastas," everyone said at once.

Lexi beamed. "Exactly."

Shifting into action, Brenna hustled to the vegetable bin, while Orla set Lexi and Galena to work crushing home-grown herbs. That was Orla's real specialty. The woman could coax a plant bound for the compost pile back from the dead with little more than a brush of her finger.

Moment by moment, the chatter and the simple task of peeling the fuzzy sage husk from the viccus soothed Brenna's jangled nerves. The process was familiar. Simple. Although, having warm and welcoming women around her was far more enjoyable than the isolated years she'd slaved at Maxis's estate.

Heavy footsteps sounded behind her, and a second later Jagger, Lexi's somo, sauntered into the room.

"Hey, Jag." Lexi motioned to the honey-stained trestle table centered in the cozy nook nearby. "Have a seat and we'll get you something to tide you over until dinner."

"No need." He helped himself to a cup of coffee, then moseyed to the table a stone's throw away. How anyone could stomach the stout brew without a nearly one-to-one ratio of sweet cream Brenna couldn't comprehend.

She finished off the last of the viccus and plodded to the sink, brushing close enough to Lexi that she could mutter, "What's he doing here?"

"He's my somo," Lexi answered just as quietly. "He goes almost everywhere I go."

Sprawled in one of the hand-carved chairs near the corner, Jagger stared out at the private garden that lined the back of the castle. He might stay beside Lexi whenever they left home, but inside these walls, Jagger gave her free rein.

"He's only with you outside the castle."

Lexi hesitated long enough that all the women stopped what they were doing and gave her their full attention. "To be honest, I don't know. Before he left, Eryx insisted Jagger stay and keep an eye on us while they were gone. Something about Ramsay making him promise to keep you safe."

More like make sure she didn't escape. The mere thought grated her patience and goaded her to take a long, unsupervised hike on principle. She might not be running around in a gown that could pass for a burlap sack anymore, or suffering Maxis's cruelty, but apparently she was still a prisoner.

"Is everything okay?" Lexi abandoned her herbs and urged Brenna away from the sink. "The last few weeks you've seemed pretty happy, but you're jumpy today. And don't think I missed your red, puffy eyes when you walked in the library."

Brenna shook her head and went back to washing the viccus.

"Okay, then tell me this much. Ludan didn't have anything to do with the tears, did he?"

"No." The denial came out way too fast, right on par with how her blood flow shot from normal to light speed. She braced her fists on the countertop and took a slow breath. No matter what she'd seen in Ramsay's vision, or what her future held, Ludan didn't deserve suspicion. Not from people he considered family. She twisted so all three women were clearly in sight. "If it wasn't for Ludan, I wouldn't be here right now."

All three spoke at once.

"What?"

"What happened?"

"Ludan?"

Brenna couldn't help but smile at Lexi's shocked expression. "Yes, Ludan." She dried her hands and carried the cleaned vegetables to the island, snatching some flour along the way. "You know how I like the bluff. I was there, thinking. I got a little too close to the edge, and…" She shrugged a shoulder and sprinkled some of the fresh herbs into the flour.

"And?" Orla said.

"And I fell."

Galena laid her knife down on the counter. "Fell as in tripped? Or fell as in off?"

God, this was awkward. "Off."

The tension in the room thickened, and the silence was so stark the room may as well have been empty.

Brenna huffed out a tired sigh and looked up. "It wasn't

what you think. Something reminded me of Maxis and my past and I got distracted. I guess Ludan followed me, saw me fall, and caught me."

Quiet.

"It's okay." Brenna met each woman's gaze individually, then waved them back to work. "I'm fine. Crisis averted. Now can we get back to work?"

They did, but not before they did the scary eyeball communication thing that always went with their telepathy. Unlike Ian, she hadn't really seemed to latch on to the whole Myren hearing thing yet, but she sure needed to spend some time learning. If nothing else, they'd be forced to wait until she wasn't in eavesdropping range before they shared their private thoughts.

"So." Lexi cleared her voice and scooted the small glass bowl full of ground herbs closer to Orla. "I guess Ludan gets our 'hero of the day' award."

Galena's husky laugh came out more relieved than humorous. "Sounds like it."

"You girls don't give him enough credit." Orla rubbed a mix of herbs and oil along the oversized roast. "He might be gruff, but no one's heart is kinder. Not for those he cares about."

"Well, he definitely cares about Brenna." Lexi pulled the cork out of a gallon-sized ceramic jug and tipped it toward the roasting pan. The rich crimson wine trickled into the basin, filling the room with a sweet cider scent.

"Well, of course he does," Orla said. "We all do."

"No, I mean he *cares* about Brenna." Lexi glanced away from her task long enough to make sure Jagger wasn't paying too much attention and lowered her voice. "As in I was picking up some seriously discombobulated mojo while we were in the library."

"Ludan?" Galena's gaze shot to Brenna's. "I mean, you're

totally worth his notice, but Ludan's never so much as blinked at a woman. Not like Eryx and Ramsay used to."

"You've got it all wrong." A man like Ludan wouldn't give a woman like her the time of day. Especially one who knew her history like Ludan did. "He was just being protective."

"You sure about that?" Lexi asked.

Brenna laid the flour-coated vegetables out on the roasting pan and shook Lexi's question off. She couldn't believe anything else. Letting her thoughts wander that direction would only twist her head up in knots and make her want something unrealistic. Though the memory of her time with him wasn't one she'd soon forget, if ever. Where most men made her scramble for distance, Ludan's closeness had calmed her. Even when his arms had tightened around her to keep her on his lap, she hadn't registered the slightest alarm.

Quiet settled over the room.

Brenna looked up and found all three women studying her with curious expressions.

"It's nothing. You're overreacting." Brenna scooped up the pan and headed for the oven. "Orla, can you light the fire? I could use the matches, but you're faster."

Almost on autopilot, Orla spun, opened her palm to the arched stone oven, and cast a thin stream of fire to the waiting coals.

"Thank you." Brenna propped the wide pan on the ledge and scooted it toward the back with the long-handled wooden peel.

Orla took the hint on the need for a topic change and hustled to the sink to wash her hands. "Galena, you haven't said much about you and Reese. How's the new cottage?"

"It's perfect." No one could have missed the dreamy wisp in her voice. "I think we spend as much time by the falls as we do inside. I couldn't have asked for a better home."

Brenna turned in time to catch Lexi waggling her eyebrows. "Yeah? How about the love life? Is that perfect, too?"

Galena dusted the cinnamon off her fingers, and her cheeks tinted a pretty pink. "Well, you won't hear me complain, that's for sure." She peeked at Jagger, leaned into the island, and whispered, "Are all men that creative? I mean, it's like he's constantly coming up with..." She did the universal sign for *and-so-on* and straightened. "Well, surprising ideas."

Lexi flat-out laughed, but it was Orla who answered around a polite snicker. "Only if they care, dear. Only if they care."

Shifting into clean-up mode, the women tidied up their work space, but Brenna couldn't quite shake their easy banter. How they were so comfortable talking about something that had caused her only pain.

"What's it like?" Brenna froze the second the question slipped out. She hadn't meant to say it. Had more thought it, only to have it rip past her lips with far too much volume.

Everyone paused, their confused gazes locked on hers.

"What's what like?" Lexi asked.

Brenna swallowed, her mouth too dry to do the task much justice. She shook her head. "It's nothing."

"No, no, no." Lexi hurried around to Brenna's side of the island and cupped Brenna's upper arm. "Tell us what you want to know."

Brenna rubbed her thumbs and fingertips together, and the clumped flour spilled onto the bright tile countertop. God, what she'd give to have smooth hands and pretty nails like Lexi's. Not the jagged tips and callused palms she'd earned slaving for Maxis. "I've always wondered what it's like to be kissed. To be touched and not be afraid."

For long seconds, no one moved. The silence pressed

heavy around her, and if the weight on her neck was any indication, even Jagger stared from his corner perch.

Lexi moved first, pulling her into a tight, almost fierce hug, but not before Brenna spied the tear on her cheek. "If that bastard wasn't already dead, I'd rip his guts out with my bare hands." She held her long enough that Brenna's arms wrapped around Lexi's waist of their own accord.

Giving in to the embrace, Brenna closed her eyes and soaked up the moment. A second later, a soft, steady hand stroked the back of her head. Galena, given the light herbal scent that drifted in along with it.

It wasn't until Lexi finally released her and stepped away that Orla moved in and gripped her with firm hands at each shoulder. "You listen to me, Brenna, and mark my words. These girls don't need to tell you anything. Do you know why?"

Brenna shook her head, feeling more like a lost, innocent child than she'd felt in years.

Orla gripped her chin with delicate fingers and smiled. "Because you'll have it for yourself someday. And when you do, it will be perfect. Enough to erase the harm of your past. It'll be beautiful. Just like you."

CHAPTER 5

A perfect princess room in a real-life castle. Brenna braced her elbows on the stone window ledge and leaned forward, sucking in a deep, soothing breath. At seven years old, this kind of view and the luxurious room behind her had been all she'd wanted. Her mother had done her best, draping pale pink tulle over her twin-size bed and painting the walls a pale lavender. Now she had the real thing. Rich tapestries depicting Eden's fantastical landscapes, a luxurious bed with an elaborate headboard and thick posts carved out of ivory, and pale gray stone walls that glowed luminescent white.

Only she wasn't a princess, and the price she'd paid to get here wasn't nearly worth the outcome.

Outside her second-story window, stars twinkled against a deep blue backdrop, and silver swirls of surplus Eden energy sparked like the one falling star she'd seen back home. All that showed of the ocean were reflections of the crescent moon on the tossing waves below, but she could hear it. The swooshing push and pull, and the crash of waves on the sand and rock.

The Shantos clan would be gathering for dinner now. Gathering and learning what she'd already seen. And then what?

All the certainty and determination she'd muscled up beside the ocean this morning had vanished. Gobbled up and crushed between her plummet off the bluff and Eryx putting a guard on her. She couldn't escape now even if she wanted to.

The Shantos family and their mates had been nothing but kind to her, and she'd wanted for nothing since the day she'd awakened here, but the idea that she was the one who'd determine the fate of all races? She didn't want that responsibility. She wanted the small things that had been taken from her. Her parents. A chance to make her own way. To learn what she liked and disliked. To build a new dream. A new life.

Three sharp raps sounded on her door.

Not Lexi. Her knock was softer, and she seldom waited for Brenna to answer. This was a man's knock, confident and strong enough to reverberate through the thick wood.

It came again.

"Brenna?"

Eryx. Or Ramsay. She'd learned to tell them apart on sight, but their voices were too similar to discern without a visual.

She hung her head, resting her forehead in her hands. Wishing him away wouldn't do any good. After all, if wishes held any power, she'd have been home years ago, this whole realm less than a flash in her memory.

"Brenna?" Trinity's voice sounded this time, just a second before the iron latch thunked and she peeked around the door's edge. Her blonde hair glimmered in the candlelight, and the dark circles that had marked her eyes this morning were gone. Like the rest of her, her haircut was spunky and stylish—a long pixie cut Lexi had called it.

That was another thing she'd do if she ever made it home. Try out a new hairstyle, or maybe go shopping and see what fashion appealed to her.

Trinity pushed the door a little wider, revealing Ramsay behind her, backlit in the hallway torchlight. "You okay?"

"I'm fine." Her stomach lurched on the empty answer. God, she was tired of that expression. She wasn't fine. So why the heck did she keep saying it? She smiled as best she could at Trinity. "You look like you finally got some sleep."

"I did." A blush stole across her cheeks, and a big grin spread ear to ear.

Guess she'd gotten more than sleep while they were holed away in Ramsay's room. Though how the women found sex enjoyable was beyond her.

Ramsay pulled Trinity against his chest, his large hands cupping her shoulders. "We thought we'd swing by and walk to dinner with you."

"I'm not going." She turned back to the window and inhaled deeply on a strong gust of air. A hint of woodsmoke from Orla's oven blended with the ocean's brine.

Ramsay's booted footsteps sounded behind her. "Why not?"

"Because all they'll do is look at me funny and ask a bunch of questions I can't answer."

"You're not giving them enough credit. They'll be curious, yeah. But no one would try to talk you into something you're uncomfortable with."

"You think Eryx wouldn't if it meant protecting his race?"

"Not if it meant forcing someone against their will, no."

Trinity sidled closer and rested her hand on Brenna's shoulder, turning her from the window. "I think if you gave them a chance, you'd see we're in this together. They'll support you, whatever that looks like. If it gets to be too much, we can leave. You and me together. But you being there, sharing your perspective, will be so much better than just relying on what Ramsay remembers."

Like she'd want to remember it. Every time her mind flashed back to the human's battered face and contorted body, Brenna's stomach heaved. Experiencing the shame she'd felt at Maxis's hands the first time was bad, but rehashing the gruesome image she'd seen was a hot poker to an already festering wound.

"Please," Trinity whispered. "Give them a chance."

They'd helped her. Healed her when she would have welcomed death. "Who'll be there?"

"Eryx and Lexi," Ramsay said. "Galena and Reese, Trinity and I. I'd like to include Graylin and Ian. They're both smart and bring good perspectives to the table, but we don't have to if it makes you uncomfortable."

A subtle tug registered beneath her sternum, an impulse she couldn't quite identify. "What about Ludan?"

Ramsay shrugged. "He's always with us for dinner, but he'd understand if we asked him not to. With what's happened to you, he'd more than understand."

"What's that supposed to mean?"

Ramsay glanced at Trinity and then back to Brenna and scratched his chin. Rather than speak right away, he eased into one of two Byzantine chairs covered in smooth lavender velvet near the window. He splayed his legs wide and rested his elbows on his knees. "No one talks about it much. The woman you saw in the vision? His mother died much the same way. Only it wasn't six strangers, it was his uncle. Ludan found him still covering her dead body. No one knows much of what happened, but I think it's safe to say his uncle didn't live longer than a few seconds after Ludan found them."

The room dimmed, and her vision went hazy. Her knees buckled so fast she staggered two steps before she found her balance. When her eyes came back into focus, Trinity stood to one side and Ramsay on the other. Each had a steadying hand on her arms and studied her with a mix of confusion and concern.

Trinity smoothed Brenna's hair away from her face. Her cool fingers were a blessed relief to her clammy skin. "You okay?"

No. Not even close. No wonder Ludan had been so kind to her. So gentle and understanding. She could all too easily imagine what he'd endured finding his mother and the grief he would have carried after. Maybe it was their common past that guided her instincts. The unspoken bond that allowed her to trust him when most other men caused only terror.

"He should be there," Brenna said. "They all should. Your family's been good to me, and I want what's best for you." She fisted one hand, willing even a fraction of the bravery she'd felt by the bluff to wind its way to her lips. "I just don't know if being a part of all this is what's best for me."

Ramsay nodded. "That's fair enough. We'll share what we know together tonight. After that, I'll make sure everyone gives you space to figure out what you need."

~

EVEN BEFORE BRENNA started down the main castle staircase, the sweet cider scent of amber wine and herbs wrapped around her. Chatter, laughter, and the clink of plates and cutlery made the night sound like every other, but her heart hadn't pounded this hard since the day she'd first awakened here.

As if sensing her need to flee, Trinity let her mate prowl ahead and laced her fingers with Brenna's. They rounded the corner into the massive dining room a few steps later. Lexi, Galena, and Orla carried in platters laden with food, while the men milled in a loose circle to one side. Eryx's voice wasn't loud enough to piece together the conversation, but Graylin, Ian, and Reese all listened with relaxed intent.

Ludan was more like his father, Graylin, she'd realized. Same build. Same eyes. Same powerful presence. But unlike Ludan's preference for warrior attire or jeans, Graylin always wore the loose pants, tank, and overrobe favored by the older, more traditional generations. Today was no different, the charcoal color of the silk he'd chosen accenting his shoulder length silver hair.

Ludan stood slightly behind Eryx. Dressed in leather and drast like Eryx, Reese, and Ramsay, his arms were crossed and his shoulders pushed back so his muscled torso was even more imposing.

Funny how his size hadn't registered this morning. Only that he was warm and seemed content to let her rest against him as long as she needed.

Trinity tugged her hand enough to gain her attention. "Brenna?"

Brenna shook off her thoughts and hurried toward the table.

Across the table, Ludan's dreamy blue gaze bored into hers, shrewd and focused with such intensity it burned clear to her toes. Her heart kicked in a painful rhythm, and her mouth ran too dry to swallow. The battered survivor inside her urged her to look away. To curl up into a ball so tight no one would notice her presence. But a new and curious, almost defiant, part of herself held his stare. How had she failed to really look at this man before? How unique and compelling his eyes were. And while his posture might have telegraphed a warning to those around them, she would swear his gaze sparked with concern. Or maybe it was camaraderie. Two souls wounded by the same tragedy, albeit in different ways.

"Okay, everyone. Grab a seat." Lexi's commandment snapped the rest of the room into focus. Eryx and Lexi took their place at either end of the table, while Galena, Ramsay, and their mates paired off on either side.

Orla gently guided Brenna to the chair beside hers. "Call me sentimental, but it's been too long since I've had all my chicks around one table. It seems to me we'd do better to make this the norm instead of an exception."

With Trinity comfortably situated, Ramsay eased into his seat. "You just had us all together at Lexi's awakening party a few months ago."

"And it's even better now with their mates beside them." Orla handed a heaping bowl of salad mixed with an oddly colored blue fruit Brenna had never seen before in the opposite direction. "All the more reason to make it a practice. Children should know a solid family unit."

Ramsay winked at Trinity beside him. "Gee, no pressure there."

"I don't know." Reese wrapped his arm around Galena's shoulders and pulled her in for a kiss. "I think the idea of kids running all over the castle is a pretty good one."

"You would." Lexi scowled at Reese and snagged a fresh roll. "You're not the one who has to waddle around with a baby growing inside you for nine months."

"Twelve," Galena blurted.

Lexi froze mid breaking her roll in half. "Twelve what?"

"Twelve months. Human fetuses develop more rapidly than Myrens do. Probably has something to do with the longevity of our race."

Lexi's gaze drifted down the table to Eryx. "Greeeat."

The whole table chuckled, but it was Orla who offered comfort. "It's not that bad. On the bright side, there's very little chance of morning sickness, and we're not too prone to stretch marks."

Galena dipped her head in agreement right before she sampled the breaded viccus. "There is that."

So easy and light. Their banter bounced between them as though the night's agenda didn't have the slightest chance of upending their very existence. By the time they'd worked their way through most of the meal, the tension in Brenna's shoulders unwound enough she actually enjoyed the sumptuous food. She'd even dared a few glances down the table and caught Ludan's gaze pinned on her. Its impact scrambled much of her worries, knocking what lay ahead aside in favor of the palpable buzz he set blazing beneath her skin.

Eryx edged his plate away and crossed his arms on the table. "All right, let's get this done. Beyond what Brenna shared this morning, the only thing we know about Ramsay's trip to Winrun is that Brenna needs our protection and support." He nailed Brenna with an unflinching stare. "Usually, the best way forward is quick and factual, but seeing as you're somehow tied in to what's going on, I'm open to what works best for you."

Just that fast, her anxiousness bubbled to full boil. Across the table, Ramsay studied her, eyes soft with compassion.

Eryx was right. Quick and factual was probably best, but there was no way she'd recount it without getting emotional. "It was Ramsay who experienced it. He should be the one to share."

Ramsay held her stare and nodded. "All right." He switched his focus to Eryx. "Though in fairness, you should know Brenna saw the whole thing, too. Probably through the mirroring she's experienced."

Eryx appraised Brenna for long, awkward seconds. If she gauged the furrow cutting across his brow correctly, he wasn't too thrilled Brenna had kept information from him. "Go on."

Ramsay exhaled and reclined against his seat back. "We were in Winrun, and Trinity was about to accept her gifts. Kazan was there, too, and wasn't any more thrilled than I was about Trinity accepting her gifts to learn about the prophecy." He paused long enough to cover her hand in her lap with his own and squeezed. "He made a deal with the White Queen. He pushed the memories into me and offered his life as forfeit."

Ian cleared his throat and set his fork aside. "That's a generous gift."

"I shouldn't have gone." Trinity hung her head. "He was forced into it because of me."

"Nonsense," Graylin said. "He had choices, just as you do. And a good parent isn't afraid to make the difficult ones when their child's happiness is at stake." His gaze slid to Ludan for the barest of seconds, then rested back on Ramsay.

As if sensing the sudden tension, Lexi straightened taller in her chair and fiddled with the stem of her wine glass. "So, the information just popped in your head?"

Ramsay shook his head and huffed out a broken laugh. "Hardly. It was more like being awake one second, then free-falling, but without landing. The next thing I knew, I was seeing… or more like reliving another life. Our first ancestor, Kentar Shantos, was there with me. Only I wasn't me. I was someone named Hagan Xenese."

Graylin's attention snapped to Eryx.

"Something significant in that piece of information?" Eryx said.

"I haven't heard that name since my history lessons before my awakening." Graylin's gaze drifted to the tabletop, and he tapped the surface in a random rhythm. "There aren't many accounts of him, but legend has it his line was as powerful as the Shantos family. The two were best friends, both carrying the sum of all gifts. No one gave much credence to the stories, though, given no such line exists today."

"Actually, it does," Ramsay said. "If I'm interpreting things correctly, Hagan Xenese was Lexi and Trinity's grandfather."

"But Kentar and Hagan would have existed more than six thousand years ago. Myrens live a long time, but not long enough to be so close to their generation."

"Those six thousand years were his penance." The words shot out of Brenna's mouth.

Everyone shifted their attention to her, but her gaze was rooted to Ludan. Something in his expression gave her strength, knocking the weight of those watching off her shoulders. "Six thousand years was his sentence for killing the Myren men who raped and killed his human mate."

"What?" Lexi's outraged question barely registered over the grumbles and disheartened sighs.

Brenna couldn't bear to look away from Ludan, not even when Ramsay continued the story.

"In that time, humans and Myrens were both here," Ramsay said. "When Hagan found his mate had been killed by Myren men, he cut them down. Used his powers to torture and kill them unmercifully for the pain they'd caused her. When it was done, the Great One appeared and told him he had to pay."

"Sounds to me like the bastards got what they deserved," Reese said.

Ramsay leaned in, resting his muscled forearm beside his empty plate. "Yeah, but Hagan didn't argue. He agreed to whatever punishment the Great One deemed fitting, but asked that the other humans be protected. He said he didn't trust that other Myrens wouldn't do the same. The Great One agreed. Said he'd build a wall between the two races, so long as Hagan agreed to surrender his powers to fuel it. In exchange, Hagan would have to live among the humans he'd sacrificed for, loving and watching those close to him die, even as he propagated his Myren race among them."

Ian whistled.

Lexi flopped against her seat back, clearly flabbergasted. "Damn."

"Exactly," Trinity said.

Quiet settled around the table. The only sounds came from the rustle of clothes as everyone shifted and studied each other.

It was Reese who spoke first. "So the prophecy is about the wall coming down?"

Ramsay nodded. "The Great One said a reckoning would come, marked by the joining of one who leads and one who bears Lexi and Trinity's mark."

"Hagan's heirs," Ian said.

Ramsay wrapped on arm around Trinity and urged her closer. "Yep."

"And the reckoning?" Eryx said.

Ramsay paused and looked at Brenna.

She managed a terse shake of her head and clenched her hands tight in her lap. This was it. The minute everything would change.

Ramsay cleared his throat, low and awkward. "He said a human will stand as judge, one who knows both of our races and has been injured the same as Hagan's mate. He said Hagan's mark would be the key, the tool that will feed its bearer the powers he surrendered that day, or that would keep the wall in place. The choice is up to the judge."

Silence.

A slow, deafening buzz whirred in Brenna's ears, and her nape grew clammy and damp. The partially eaten food on her plate blurred, and a tear slipped down her cheek.

57

Galena's soft, honeyed voice reached from the far end of the table. "You think you're the judge, don't you?"

Brenna jerked a nod and held her breath.

Beside her Orla shifted, making her wooden chair creak. Her aged yet still elegant hand covered Brenna's on her lap. "I can see how you and Hagan's mate have history in common, but that doesn't necessarily mean—"

"It was me." Brenna lifted her head, and her eyes sought Ludan on instinct.

His face was an angry red, and a muscle ticked at the back of his jaw in a frantic rhythm. Was he upset on her behalf? Or mad she hadn't told him?

"What do you mean it was you?" Orla said.

"Hagan's mate looked just like me, only she was dead."

"And you saw the whole thing." Ian tossed his napkin to the side of his plate and exhaled so loud it sounded closer to a hiss. "Jesus, no wonder you didn't want to share."

She hiccupped and pushed away from the table. Standing, she glared at Eryx. "Do you have what you need now?"

Eryx nodded.

She threw her napkin to the table and strode toward the exit.

"Brenna."

She froze at Eryx's sharp command, closed her eyes for a second, and pulled in a steady breath before turning.

He stood, slow and purposeful, and met her stare head-on. "You are your own person. Your choices and your decisions are yours. There's not a person at this table who would ask you to do anything you don't want to."

The confidence and determination she'd so fleetingly stoked this morning resurrected itself, surging bold and furious. "My life hasn't been my own since I was eight. I don't even know what kind of clothes I like or what color I'd paint my room if given an option. What makes you think I'm suited or ready to make a decision that could impact your throne and the fate of two races?"

She'd expected him to scowl. Maybe throw one of those scary death glares around like he did with his men, or command her obedience. Instead, he smiled, the look on his face more understanding than she'd ever seen. "You're suited to that kind of a decision because you're you."

CHAPTER 6

Serena shivered beneath the tattered, musty quilts and tucked her knees tighter to her chest. Praise the Great One, it was cold. With no outlet to the outdoors save the entrance, warmth in the way of a fire wasn't an option, but Uther could have at least brought her a warming brick or two. Then again, the bastard was probably dead to the world, sleeping near his roaring hearth. She'd scented the soft woodsmoke shortly after nightfall and had cursed him nonstop ever since.

You'd be smart to earn your keep translating those journals.

Definitely a bastard. One she'd string up by his nuts when she found a way out of here. There had to be a way to bring him in line. His illiteracy gave her some leverage, but offered little in the way of meaningful threats.

A fresh shiver racked her, and the pendant shifted between her breasts. That was another thing she needed to figure out. Risking the journal was one thing, but her instincts insisted Lexi's family mark was important. Having it anywhere Uther could find it was dangerous.

Footsteps sounded on the wooden steps beyond, slow and

heavy. The door groaned open a second later, and Uther ducked inside the opening. "I'm heading out."

Serena forced herself upright and clenched the blanket around her torso. She'd snuffed out all but one candle, now burning low on the table. "What time is it?"

"A little before two in the morning. I'll try to slip in when they change the guard." His gaze slid to the journal on the desk. "You learn anything?"

"Enough to know it's about the prophecy. I found an almost identical section to your family records, but there's more before it. A story from our first generation. It got too cold in here to go much farther." A fresh quaver rattled her torso, and her teeth clattered so hard it hurt. "I need out of here."

"No one's stopping you."

"You know I can't leave." She pulled her knees in tight and huddled against the bare earth wall. "The minute I do they'll track me."

"And you want me to what? Kill your family? They're innocent."

"Ha!" The harsh bark scraped her achy throat. "My mother, maybe. But my father's far from innocent. My brother's growing up just like him."

"So you want me to do your dirty work."

Beneath the blanket, Serena fisted her hand and winced at the stabbing pain it sent jolting up her arm. "Believe me, if I had the strength or the opportunity, I'd handle it myself. I've suffered plenty at my father's hand, as has my mother."

It was more than she wanted to admit to herself, let alone Uther, but a flash of compassion slid across his face. He wrapped his fingers around the doorknob. "We'll talk after I get my family's journal, if I can even get past the guards. If I'm not back before sunrise, odds are I'm not coming back."

The door thunked shut behind him.

Damn him. Damn her father and the rest of her unfaithful family. Damn Eryx Shantos and her hasty decisions. She tucked her nose beneath the blanket's edge and exhaled through her mouth. The warmth ricocheted off her knees and wafted across her cheeks. She'd figure something out. She always did.

Pulling the pendant free, she curled her fingers around it. The iron filigree scraped her fingertips, twice as harsh as the smooth backing that had lain against her skin. The first thing she needed to do was find a safe place for it.

Black clay covered the floors and walls. The only furniture was the three-by-three table, a simple wood chair, and her cot, nestled in the corner. The only place to hide anything was beneath the ratty mattress, and Uther wouldn't fail checking there going forward.

Too frustrated to stay locked in one spot, she shoved from the cot. Pain stabbed through her heels and the balls of her feet, the cold leaving her toes almost numb. Maybe she should consider hiding the pendant outside Uther's cottage. If she picked someplace close, she could access it easier without Uther knowing. Plus, she could pick up a warming brick on the way back inside.

She spun for a fresh lap of her cramped cell and shrieked, freezing so quickly she nearly overturned the table beside her. The candlelight flickered and nearly went out, but there was no mistaking the presence in front of her.

A woman she'd never seen before stood in front of the doorway with her arms crossed. Her black gown was loose and made of a shiny material with a low V at the neck, and a looped silver chain circled her waist. She'd have been elegant had it not been for her coarse, salt-and-pepper hair that hung loose and uncombed to her shoulders.

"Who are you?" No way had Serena missed the door opening. It groaned as loudly as her stomach had the last five hours every time it opened, but it was shut tight behind the woman. "How did you get in here?"

Her visitor pursed her lips and glared with enough hatred the room's temperature felt warmer by five degrees. "How I got here doesn't matter. My name is Patrice. I'm a widow. By your hand."

Prickles scampered down Serena's neck, and her heart kicked harder than it had when she'd found Patrice rooted near the doorway. "I don't know what you mean."

"I think you do." Patrice dropped her hands and straightened to an imposing height. It had to be a trick of the light. No one could actually grow an extra four inches in a single heartbeat. "You've only slaughtered one man in your life and made us both widows in the process."

"Maxis." The word left her on a breathy hiss, and a fresh wave of cold slithered down her spine.

"Your mate and mine, all at once. Quite efficient of you." Patrice drifted forward, her feet unmoving while the rest of her moved like a cloud. She surveyed the tiny space and wrinkled her nose as though offended by a foul stench. "For a woman who had so much going for her, you've certainly found yourself at a dead end."

Serena couldn't move, couldn't muster one decent thought.

Patrice scowled. "My mate was a visionary. Hungry enough to free all the Dark Spiritu, but short-sighted in his manner of getting there. If he hadn't acted rashly with Maxis, he'd still be alive and the passions closer to being out of balance."

"The Spiritu?"

"Guides of inspiration." Patrice trailed her fingers along the table's edge, her head cocked to one side, thoughtful. "We have two contingents—the light and the dark. One feeds the more compassionate side of nature, while the other speaks to the headier passions." She smirked. "The more enjoyable passions."

Stepping back from the table, Patrice crossed her arms and lifted her chin. "My mate chose yours to bring the two sides out of balance. To unhinge the Dark Spiritu from their balance with the Light and let the dark desires run free. But Maxis buckled. Failed my Falon and put the two sides back in balance. Now I'm alone. Ostracized from my kind with no human or Myren interaction to feed my soul."

"Then why are you here?" The question came out with far more defiance than Serena felt, adrenaline spiking her tone with a powerful mix of anger and fear.

Patrice's dark eyes glinted in the candlelight. "Maybe I thought to aid you."

Silence burned long and loud between them. "Why?"

For the first time since Serena saw her, Patrice's bravado wavered, sadness glossing her face and painting deep creases across her brow. "Because I want to join my mate. The one sure way to do that is to help you."

"How?"

The candle's flame grew bigger, and the room blossomed with a rich, spicy scent. "You're in a bit of a bind, aren't you? Worrying on how to leave this hovel without your family tracing your link? Wondering how to use that pretty pendant hidden beneath your gown? How to leverage the prophecy you've deciphered? Surely answers to those questions would be valuable to you."

"How could you know those things? Know what's going on in my head?"

"Because that's what Spiritu do. We listen to those we guide and offer encouragement. It just so happens your needs will get me what I want. Assuming you want my help?"

Yes. A million times over, yes. Her blood surged so fast the cold vanished, and a fuzzy warmth surrounded her.

Patrice lifted a finger and shook her head. "Ah, ah, ah. Not so fast." She pursed her lips and glided toward the door, her head down as though deep in thought. "If I give you what you need, I'll pay with my death, a price I'm happy to remit, but that doesn't mean I'll willingly leave this realm without a parting shot. I want to fulfill my husband's mission. To free the Dark contingent from the Light and create a world laden with debauchery and free of remorse."

Debauchery and no remorse. Two components that fell perfectly in line with the reign she envisioned.

"Exactly that," Patrice said. "I see you were as in sync with your mate as I was with mine. A shame it's the two of us who have to see their goals through in the end."

In sync was pushing it. True, she'd mourned Maxis's passing, or at least the upheaval his death had heaped upon her. But the chance to live without dependence on any man burned brighter now than any dream she'd had before.

Patrice's low, raspy chuckle filled the room, so sinister and heavy Serena wondered if she was truly safe in the woman's presence. "I've met many people in my time, Serena, and yet I've found few as narcissistic as you." She grinned, the expression one of a self-satisfied woman only moments from gaining her most prized accomplishment. "If you want my help, it comes with a price, one sealed with a blood vow."

"What kind of price? And what's a blood vow?"

"Actions you vow to complete prior to a predetermined time. Failure to abide by your oath means your life is forfeit. And before you harbor thoughts otherwise, there is no escaping a blood vow. Ever."

Pressure squeezed Serena's heart, so painful she wondered if perhaps Patrice hadn't thrust her hand into Serena's chest and fisted it in her palm. Everything Serena needed was here. All the answers in exchange for a chore.

"Well?" Patrice glided forward. "Just how dedicated to your purpose are you?"

Surely the vow would be worth it. Especially if it meant shaking the chains she'd worn her whole life. Her pulse thrummed frantic and heavy at her neck and wrists, and a fevered buzz bellowed loud and demanding in her head. This was right. A gift preordained by the Great One himself if she only dared to accept it. She sucked in a bracing breath. "Tell me what I have to do."

CHAPTER 7

*P*raise the Great One, Ludan needed a fight. A good, drawn-out, bloody one with enough sweat and fatigued muscles he couldn't walk when it was over. He tossed his light blanket aside and glared at the sun barely lifting over the horizon. The ocean's breeze drifted through the open window and slicked across his naked body.

It still didn't help. Nothing did. The only time he found deep sleep was at the bottom of a strasse bottle or after a fight. Or a long, dirty fuck, and he couldn't remember the last time he'd indulged in one of those.

Maybe Reese would be up for a spar this morning. Surely Galena's new mate would take it at face value. A warrior in need of some old-fashioned stress relief.

Without conscious direction, his senses stretched down one floor toward Brenna's room. It'd been all he could do not to go after her when she'd stormed from the dining hall. Histus, leaving the castle to join the search for Serena and Sully had been nothing short of a miracle. The need to be near her was three times more powerful since he'd touched her. Since he'd witnessed her pain laid bare for his friends and family. Whether it raised eyebrows or not, he'd make damned sure no one pushed her into anything she wasn't comfortable with from here out. And he'd kill any stranger who got too close to her.

The animal in him stalked the perimeter of its cage, snarling with pent-up frustration. Maybe he should sweep the castle perimeter. The Great One knew he wasn't getting any more sleep.

You mean make another pass by Brenna's room.

He grumbled at the dig from his conscience and knifed out of bed. So what if he'd patrolled her hallway more than once. It wasn't like he'd stopped and enjoyed what little dampening her presence on the other side of the door made. He'd wanted to, yeah, but the key was making sure she was safe inside. No warrior ignored his instincts, and since the day he'd laid eyes on her, his beast had gone on high alert. More so now that he'd touched her.

He tugged on his leather pants and shoved on his boots. Something was up. His brain hadn't put it all together yet, but he knew it was important. Whether her impact on him was part of it, he couldn't tell. It would be nice if he had someone to bounce his thoughts off, but he didn't dare mention anything to Eryx. Or Ramsay. Both of them were so lovesick they'd chalk it up to Brenna being his mate.

No way was that the case. He didn't deserve the love they had. Even if he did, he wouldn't know how to honor a woman like Brenna. She needed someone tender and thoughtful. Not some ham-fisted brute.

Drast in place, he pulled his warrior's torque and cuffs from their onyx chest. His mother's favorite pendant, an opal with vibrant colors shaped in the form of a dove, winked in the candle's glow from the rich black velvet inside. If she were still alive, he could've talked to her. Lexi, Trinity, or Galena would all yap to their mates or jump straight into matchmaker mode, but his mother would have listened. She'd been good that way. Patient despite the hotheaded warriors in her life.

You could talk to your dad.

The thought jolted through him, carried on his mother's warm molasses voice. Goose bumps lifted up and down his arms, and the hair on the back of his neck stood on end. Could he? Since his mother died, they hadn't had many deep conversations, but before that they'd been inseparable. They'd grieved together, but afterward his father had never looked at him the same way. Not with blame, though the Great One knew Graylin should have, but with pity. If the roles were reversed, Ludan wasn't sure he'd have been able to abide his son's presence, let alone keep from killing him.

He picked up the pendant. The stone lay cool against his callused palm, as bright and beautiful as her smile. Before he could second-guess himself, he traced his link to his father. The ice-blue thread so like his own pinged from the castle instead of his father's isolated cottage. Odd. His dad usually preferred isolation to the castle's noise.

Ludan squeezed the pendant tight. *"You up?"*

His father's link jangled as though startled. *"I am indeed. Though I'm surprised you are. You had a late night."*

Later than his father could possibly imagine, not that Ludan had any plans on cluing him in. Not at that level of detail anyway. *"You spend the night here, too?"*

"No, I got here about an hour ago. Eryx approached me before he and Lexi retired. He's concerned about the men being preoccupied with the search and wanted me to oversee the castle guards."

That made sense. Maxis had infiltrated once and swiped Lexi. As somo to Eryx's father, Graylin had an elite background few could compete with, and the last thing they needed was for someone to make inroads to the castle and snatch Brenna.

Over my dead body.

He peeled his fingers away from the pendant before he could crack it in half and tucked it back against the velvet.

"Something wrong, son?"

His father's voice shook him back on track. He'd never told a soul of his gift's impact, but if there was one person he could trust to keep it quiet, his dad was the guy. No one had more honor than Graylin Forte. And if his prickling instincts or Brenna's impact on him had anything to do with the prophecy and keeping her safe, he'd be a fool not to share. No matter how awkward it felt. *"You got time to talk before Eryx is up and ready to go?"*

Stunned silence ricocheted through their connection. *"I always have time for you. I'm in the kitchen when you're ready."*

Disconnecting the communication, Ludan headed down the hallway and jogged down the steps to the second-story landing. He hesitated before heading down to the first floor and rerouted down Brenna's hallway.

You were gentle with me.

Damn it all, he couldn't get Brenna's words out of his head. Not her words or the feel of her curled against him. As tiny as she was, he'd felt even more like a giant than usual. Like he could conquer the world if she so much as whispered the request.

He shook his head and realized he stood rooted outside her doorway. What the hell was wrong with him? He shouldn't feel like this. Shouldn't feel the kind of responses thoughts of her generated. He was her protector, nothing more.

No, not Brenna's protector. *Eryx's* protector. Brenna was just an extension of that security. He strode down the remaining hallway to the workers' stairway and stomped to the first floor. The rich, nutty scent of Orla's coffee drifted to him before he reached the kitchen. The first hints of baking bread followed right behind it. He rounded the corner and halted.

Beside the kitchen island, Graylin stood in front of Orla, one hand cupping her face. Their close bodies conveyed a comfortable intimacy, and Orla practically glowed. Was that a smile on his father's face? Not the polite and gracious one he used with Eryx and everyone else, but that of a man excited about life. A young man.

His father glanced up, spied Ludan standing at the entrance, and slowly lowered his hand. If he was upset at having been caught in such a situation, he didn't show it. Quite the contrary, he placed a familiar hand at the small of Orla's back and turned her to face Ludan. "Orla made breakfast if you're hungry."

How in histus was he supposed to process this? His whole life, the only woman he'd ever pictured next to his father was his mother. Sure Orla was a fantastic woman, but she wasn't his mother.

Orla and his father stared at him, both with eyebrows raised.

Fuck, his dad had asked a question, hadn't he? What was it? Ah, right, breakfast. He shook his head and took two smaller steps into the room. "No, thank you."

Orla glanced back at Graylin, smiled shyly at him, and wiped her hands on her apron. "Well, if either of you change your mind, I've left it warming on the counter. I'll leave you two alone to talk."

Desperate for something to take his mind off the thoughts sprinting circles in his head, Ludan paced to the coffeepot. Behind him, wooden chair legs scraped against the stone floor.

"Does it bother you?" Graylin said. "Seeing me with Orla?"

Bother him? Not really. If anyone deserved happiness it

was his dad. Not once since his mother's death had he seen his dad with another woman. "It just surprised me."

"I imagine it did. I probably should have said something."

Ludan set the coffeepot aside and turned. "I'm a grown man, and you've been alone a long time." He took a drink.

Graylin stared back at him with his all-too-knowing gaze.

Eryx would know what to say. Something supportive and wise. "Orla's a good woman," he finally managed. "You deserve that. You both do."

The second the words left his mouth their weight hit him square in the gut. His dad was happy. Truly happy and experiencing something good on a personal level for the first time in more than a hundred years. He couldn't share what was going on with the voices and Brenna now. Nothing got by Graylin. The minute he learned what happened after Ludan consumed someone's memories he'd put two and two together and realize how often Ludan relived his mother's death. No way could he burden his dad with that kind of knowledge.

Graylin leaned back in his chair. "What did you want to talk about?"

Ludan sipped his coffee and blanked his expression. Graylin could scent bullshit thirty leagues away, especially when it came to Ludan. Unless he stuck close to the truth. "This thing with Brenna, do you think it's too much? More than she can take with everything she's been through?"

Graylin studied him. "I think the Great One never gives a person more than they can handle. Sometimes we heap more on ourselves than we should, but seldom will our Creator place a burden on our shoulders we can't bear." He paused and tapped his thumb on the tabletop. "What are your thoughts?"

That was easy. If it were up to him, he'd cart Brenna out of here, let her go home like she wanted, and stay as close as he could without getting locked up for stalking. He shrugged instead. "Just seems unfair. She's had enough forced on her. She should get a fresh start."

The intensity behind his father's eyes deepened, pain and remorse eking past his usual somber demeanor. "Life is often unfair."

A scratchy burn clawed inside Ludan's throat, and the air around him grew dense, wrapping him in an unforgiving grip. They might have started the conversation with Brenna, but he was pretty damned sure she wasn't the topic now. Sharing his gift and the penalty that went with it was one thing. Digging up the ghost between them wasn't happening. Not today.

Ludan pushed away from the countertop and took a last swig of his coffee. "It was just a random thought, and I wanted your opinion." He laid the empty mug in the sink and headed for the entrance. "I gotta check in with Eryx. Let us know if you need anything."

"Ludan."

Ludan stopped, schooled his expression, and turned. "Yeah."

Over a hundred and fifty years Ludan had watched his father move through all kinds of situations. Happy ones. Dangerous ones. Even those where he was bored to tears. But not once had he seen Graylin so uncertain. So hesitant to speak.

As if finally grasping his courage, Graylin gripped the top of the chair back and squared his shoulders. "Listen to your instincts, son. I know you blame yourself for your mother's death, but you're a good man. A smart one. Listen to your spirit. Your Spiritu, or whatever that quiet voice inside belongs to. To deny it is to deny your soul."

Ludan couldn't move. Couldn't have budged so much as an inch if the diabhal himself had come barreling through the kitchen. Graylin couldn't possibly know what he'd really wanted to talk about, but his comment addressed it head-on. Maybe he was wrong not to share. Histus, he could at least say thank you.

He opened his mouth, uncertain what would come out.

Eryx's voice blasted through his head, the echo behind it and the way his father flinched telling Ludan it was a mass broadcast. *Lock the castle down. We've had a breach.*

CHAPTER 8

*I*n only a second, Ludan marked Eryx's position in the castle via link. He lurched forward and froze, years of loyalty and preprogrammed response knocked sideways by an equally brutal pull in Brenna's direction.

The beast rattled its cage, and an unholy roar reverberated in his head. Over his shoulder, the kitchen exit and the back staircase stood empty. The side trip to check on her would cost him time. Time that could cost his malran. His race.

His father's low but urgent voice breached his hesitation. "I've got her. Go."

It was all Ludan needed. The castle rooms blurred past him, workers filing in for the day and warriors' voices shouting around the perimeter. His link to Eryx pulsed strong and healthy, a bold and glowing silver in his mind's eye, guiding him to the royal office. Brenna would be fine. His father might be old, but he could still kick half the elites' asses on experience alone.

The royal library doors stood open, Eryx and Reese safe and sound inside and scanning every detail. No, not scanning. Tracking. Very few tracked as well as Reese, which was why they'd put him in charge of the search for Serena and Sully. For all the good it had done them.

Two guards stood at the castle entrance, their backs propping the mammoth doors open and flooding the foyer with early-morning sunlight. On the far edge of the veranda, Ramsay barked orders to the guards.

Lexi paced the soft yellow rug covering the stone foyer and scowled, her arms crossed tight as though she feared giving them free rein. Trinity held her place to one side, watching her sister and nibbling on a fingernail. That meant all were present and accounted for, save Galena.

Ludan stalked into Lexi's path. "Who's missing?"

She barely looked up and turned for a fresh loop. "It's not who, it's what. The journal and the translation table from the archives."

"And my pendant," Trinity added.

Better the artifacts than a person. Though with three times their normal guards even that should have been impossible. Granted, the artifacts weren't the kind of information they'd want in the wrong hands, but at least they weren't the sole source of information anymore. "How long have they been missing?"

Lexi stopped and planted her hands on her hips. Unlike the usual Myren attire, she'd thrown on a pair of Levi's and a girly purple tank top. "Day before yesterday. Around six, I think. Maybe a little earlier. I put the pendant in right before Ramsay headed to Winrun. I swear the journal was there then." She huffed a frustrated breath. "I should have locked it up."

"Stop it." Trinity bustled from her ringside spot and grabbed Lexi's arm. Her bold red tunic and leggings were as vibrant as the rest of her, a bullfighter ready to engage the bull. "No one could have anticipated this."

EDEN'S DELIVERANCE

"Um, yeah," Lexi said. "I could have, seeing as how I was the last thing Maxis swiped."

The comment jogged Ludan's focus. "Where the hell is Jagger?"

Lexi waved Ludan off and plodded to the bench situated on one side of the huge hall. "They had a lead come in on Sully right when we figured out the journal was gone. Reese is the better tracker in this kind of situation, so Jagger went to check it out."

A sensible decision, especially with all the guards around, but Ludan still didn't like it. "I'm checking in with Ramsay. You two stay in my line of sight."

Lexi dropped her head back against the stone wall and screwed her mouth up in a semi-playful/ironic twist. "I see you're in your usual glorious mood."

He grunted in lieu of an answer and strode toward the veranda. He should have paid more attention. Should have listened to his instincts. He reached for his father through their link. *"She safe?"*

"Safe and getting dressed. I caught her coming out of her bedroom after hearing shouts on the castle perimeter. I told her it was just a precaution and that I'd walk her down when she's ready." Graylin paused and the link buzzed with something odd. Uncertainty maybe. *"I like her."*

Nope, not uncertainty. More like hope. *"You're reading too much into it."*

"Probably. But old men are allowed their wishful thinking. I'll bring her to you...err...Eryx when she's ready."

Ludan dropped the link. Better to say nothing than dig a deeper hole at this point. He halted beside Ramsay, who was finishing up with orders.

"Wes, you scan the warriors stationed here for the last forty-eight hours. Troy, I want all castle workers rounded up and questioned. Any missing people, or suspicious memories, warrant them being taken into custody. That room was off limits to non-family. If anyone so much as stepped a toe in there in the last month, I want to know."

The two men nodded and launched skyward.

"Another inside job?" Ludan said.

Distraction and a whole lot of pissed off colored Ramsay's answer. "If it is, it's fresh. Everyone who's been on duty here the last month has volunteered for unfiltered, regular scans. Warriors and workers."

"Any chance someone could've gotten past the guards?"

Ramsay shook his head and watched two guards patrolling the massive garden fronting the castle. "Not likely. It's been too calm. Unless there's some kind of chaos, energy patterns are easy to detect, especially with my elites." He hesitated, spun, and studied the open entrance. "The day I went to Winrun."

"What about it?"

Ramsay snapped to attention and hit Ludan's gaze head-on. "Shit got crazy right before I left for Winrun. Men were all over the place looking for Trinity. That would have been a perfect time for someone to slip in if they were skilled enough."

Ludan scoffed and crossed his arms. "Serena's not that skilled."

"Doesn't mean she hasn't found a new lackey."

True. Though how people, particularly men, always fell for the sweet-talking blonde never ceased to amaze him. Even Eryx had fallen for her shit for a short time. Right up until he'd had his first dream of Lexi.

Eryx's voice cut through his head, disgust mingling with the echo that went with his multiperson message. *"The place is clean."*

Ludan and Ramsay took the message as the summons it was and headed to the library. By the time they got there,

Lexi and Trinity were already inside, Trinity at Eryx's desk and Lexi at her own, rifling through the drawers like they weren't yet convinced the whole thing wasn't a misunderstanding.

Eryx glared out the towering window at the end of the room. Ludan knew that posture. Aggression and raw power barely leashed. He'd bet his Evad bank accounts the whites of Eryx's eyes glowed brighter than the sun outside, a warning sign that his malran was a breath away from all histus breaking lose.

Reese strode toward them, more contained than Eryx but still sporting a wicked scowl.

"A big goose egg, huh?" Ludan said.

Reese glanced over his shoulder at Eryx. "Not a trace. Definitely a feminine residue around Lexi's desk, but I'd expect that since it's hers. Nothing stands out that shouldn't already be there."

Cocking his head to one side as though listening, Ramsay paced a few steps away. He braced one hand on his hip and fisted the hair on the top of his head a second later. "Damn."

Everyone's attention shot to Ramsay, though Ramsay kept his focus on the thick maroon rug. Two heartbeats later, he snapped his head up. "They found Sully. He's dead."

Reese grumbled low beside Ludan. "Fuck."

"Figures," Trinity said.

"Damn it all to hell." Lexi reined in her tirade as fast as she'd let the curse fly, took stock of her silent mate, and beat feet to ground him with a comforting hand on his chest.

His eyes dimmed a fraction, but the nearly palpable and deadly energy emanating off him burned as powerful as a nuclear reactor gone rogue.

Ramsay kept going. "Jagger says they double-backed with Angus for details on Sully's last assignment. They followed the most likely path to complete the errand and found the poor guy just outside Cush's outskirts in an unharvested wheat field. From the looks of his body angle, Jag says something probably took him out of commission midflight and he crashed."

"They move the body?" Eryx said.

"Not yet."

"Don't. Galena will want to look at him first." Eryx pinned Reese with a glare so potent it had to hit the guy like a fist. "You got this?"

Reese nodded and quick-stepped it to find his mate.

"All right. So what have we got?" Ramsay paced toward Trinity. "We think Angus is the one who stole the translation tables, and Angus visited Serena just before they went missing. If you put the two together, then why would Serena want them to begin with?"

"Are you sure the prophecy isn't documented somewhere else? Maybe Maxis had one," Lexi said.

"Maybe. His library is huge." Eryx grumbled and anchored Lexi to his side with one arm.

"I still don't think it was her," Ludan said. "She can barely mask against a human."

Ramsay perched on the edge of Lexi's desk, crossing his arms over his chest and one boot over the other. "Okay, so maybe she's got help."

Lexi whipped her attention to Trinity. "The rogues. They were willing to help Maxis. What if they're the ones helping her now?"

"I thought every time someone hit for the bad guys, the good guys got a turn at bat," Ramsay said.

"The law of reciprocity." Trinity chewed on her lip. "Dad mentioned that a time or two, but I don't know much in the way of details."

For the first time since Ludan had walked in the room,

Eryx's tension ebbed. "Any chance you can use your pretty rock and make a visit to Winrun? See what's going on?"

Ramsay shoved upright and squared his shoulders. "Not without me she's not."

"I can try." Trinity laid a placating hand on Ramsay's shoulder and tugged him out from in between her and Eryx. "I can't say the king or queen will tell us anything, but it's worth a shot." She frowned up at Ramsay. "I'm not stupid. I'm not out to do anything that might compromise my existence."

Curling his hand around the back of her neck, Ramsay eliminated the space between them and pulled her against his chest. "You I trust. The Black King seemed pretty eager to add you to his ranks."

"It still doesn't make sense." Eryx eased into the chair behind his massive desk and propped his elbows on his knees, his hands clasped tightly between them. "If I'm a rogue Spiritu, why point Serena to anything written? Why not just give her the info the way Kazan gave it to Ramsay?"

Everyone traded stumped expressions, the same clueless faces most prevalent in a teenage classroom when no smart-asses were available to bail them out.

"She's got to be somewhere." Eryx sat back in his seat and lasered onto his twin. "What's the latest with her family? Have they picked up anything with the links?"

"Not since I checked in with them last night. I'll have the men check again. Wherever she's hiding, she can't stay there long. Serena's not known for keeping her head down."

"What about Angus?" The idea pinged out of nowhere, but the minute the question slipped past Ludan's lips, he knew it was a solid target. If they'd learned anything in the last few months it was not to underestimate the cagey bastard.

"We've got nothing on him right now," Eryx said. "He's

fully cooperating, and his memories at the time in question are clear as can be, though he's still not divulging his conversation with Serena. I think it's time I petition the council and force the issue."

"Or you bluff a little and make Angus think Sully's alive." A job Ludan would get a kick out of considering how Angus treated those he considered inferior. "Angus might get nervous enough he'll spill about his visit with Serena. He might even know where she is or how she might have known to steal the journal."

"What do you mean the journal's gone?"

Everyone spun to face Brenna in the entrance beside Graylin.

Praise the Great One, she was pretty. Gone were the gaunt angles that had plagued her face when she'd first arrived, and her gown clung to curves a man couldn't help but appreciate.

But she wasn't for him. Couldn't be, no matter how much he might like to imagine otherwise.

Lexi's voice cut from behind him. "Trinity and I were hoping we could spend some time looking through the journal and figure out if it was Hagan who wrote it. Maybe see if he's really our grandfather. But it's gone. The pendant and the translation table too."

"It's more of a sentimental loss at this point than a tactical one," Trinity added. "Nothing to worry about."

Brenna's stare cut to Eryx. "Unless Serena's the one who got it and that's why she's missing. That's what you think happened, isn't it?" Her gaze trailed the room, stopping on each person long enough to get a firm read. She ended on Ludan. "Isn't it?"

He slowly dipped his chin, unable and unwilling to give her anything but the truth, even though it probably terrified her.

Her spine stiffened, and her fingers fluttered at her sides. She focused on Lexi. "You said there was mention of a fight in the beginning. A part you didn't fully translate."

"Probably the part you saw where Hagan killed the guys who hurt his mate."

"Then odds are good the whole thing is in there. Everything I saw with Ramsay."

"That doesn't give her much advantage." Eryx stood and prowled beside Lexi. "She'll have to translate it first, and you know how slowly that goes."

"But she can."

Eryx nodded. "Yes, she can."

Brenna held so still Ludan couldn't even gauge her breathing, but her eyes burned with vulnerability. He'd bet anything that what her body lacked in movement her mind more than made up for with churning thoughts. She glanced at Graylin beside her and turned. "If you don't mind, I'll go back to my room."

Casting a quick check at Ludan, Graylin waved his arm toward the hallway. "I'll escort you back."

"No need." She pierced Eryx with an empty glare over one shoulder, one most warriors would think twice about using on their malran. "I'm perfectly safe here, right?"

In three quick strides she was out of sight.

The room dimmed. Whether the sun slipped behind a cloud or she took the brightness with her he wasn't sure, but the shadows left him hollow. Empty.

His thighs bunched and his feet itched to move. To follow and comfort her like he had on the beach.

"She'll be fine." Lexi smoothed her hand over Eryx's shoulder and glided toward the door. "I'll talk with her while you guys run down what to do next."

Ludan's temples pulsed from the strain of his clenched teeth, and his breath huffed hard and labored. *He* wanted to go to her. Not Lexi. Not Eryx or anyone else. His gaze snagged on Graylin still at the entrance.

Graylin dipped his chin, a slight, barely perceptible motion loaded with encouragement.

"No." The simple command rumbled up his throat and resounded through the room. He strode past Lexi, locked in place by the door with eyebrows high and jaw dropped low. Along the way, Graylin nodded his approval.

Ludan glanced back at the rest of his stunned audience before he stomped out of sight. "The only one talking to Brenna is me."

CHAPTER 9

*B*renna calmly closed her bedroom door and leaned against it. Her heart ka-thumped in a deep, steady rhythm and a weird, otherworldly calm grounded her. Odd considering the thoughts racing through her head. One blink. One tiny second and a flash of realization, and her whole life had changed. Ever since the day Maxis had taken her, she'd prayed that someday, somehow, things would change. Well, it was going to change. Today. No more waiting for someone else to fix it for her.

She pushed away from the door and padded through her tidy room. The ivory and plum comforter was made from the finest fabrics in Eden. The tapestries depicted lavish gardens and spectacular landscapes, and the accents gave the sizable suite a homey feel.

But none of it was hers. Not really.

She opened the closet and assessed her wardrobe. Gowns. Casual tunics and leggings. More than she'd owned even before she'd been kidnapped and all in rich, jewel-toned colors that accented her olive skin, or so Jillian had claimed. Ian's long-lost daughter had been more than generous upon

Brenna's arrival, offering a good chunk of her overflowing closet to make Brenna feel welcome. But what would she choose for herself? Did she like gowns and leggings? What other options could she try? And what would they be wearing now in Evad?

It was time to find out.

She pulled a few of the darker tunic and legging sets made of sturdier cloth from their hangers and tossed them on the bed. She was done waiting around for her happily ever after. Done with drifting along the passive path those around her created. Done with letting other people dictate her life, however innocently. And she sure wasn't sitting around waiting for Serena to put any more pieces together.

The sapphire dress she'd worn the day before hung toward the end. She stroked the soft velvet and closed her eyes, remembering the safety she'd felt in Ludan's arms. For that brief stretch of time, she hadn't worried. Had just let herself go and trusted him to keep her safe.

Pulling in a deep breath, she opened her eyes. A dress wouldn't do her much good on foot, especially this one. She started to step away and stopped. She wanted it with her. It might be foolish, but if she wanted it and was willing to haul it around, then why not? Wasn't this about her following her own desires for once?

She pulled it from its hanger and set about folding her selections.

A sharp, heavy knock sounded on her door, and Brenna flinched. The peace that had grounded her scampered into hiding and left her alone with her racing heart. It couldn't be any of the women, not with such a firm knock. She scooped up her belongings and strode to the dresser.

"Brenna?" Ludan. He'd never come to her room before. Not once. "Let me in." His deep, rumbling voice rang firm as though the door didn't stand between them. No sweet talk.

No placating. Just a simple, straightforward request laced with something close to a plea.

Setting the clothes on the top of the dresser, she opened the door a crack.

His hands were anchored on either side of the doorjamb, as though braced to wait forever. His head snapped up, and the pinched, almost painful expression on his face cleared. He straightened and swallowed. "I was worried about you."

Warmth skated across her skin, and a delicate flutter issued behind her sternum. Such a simple statement. Common courtesy on the surface, but the emotion that went with it sounded as though it had been ripped from his soul. All warrior, and yet gentle. Another perfect memory to take with her. "I'll be fine. I'm going to make it fine."

Fast as a warrior braced for attack, his gaze sharpened and he tensed. "Make it fine how?"

Oh no. No more backing down. Not from him, or anyone else. She mirrored his defensive stance and tightened her grip on the door.

His focus shifted to her hands, the door, and how she'd limited what was exposed of her room. He planted his massive hand on the thick wood and pushed it the rest of the way open, careful and cautious of hurting her, but relentless all the same.

Brenna stepped in his path and splayed one hand in the center of his chest. "I didn't say you could come in."

He paused long enough to study her hand, an odd, almost shaken expression scuttling across his face.

He wasn't the only one. Beneath her palm, his heart beat strong and steady, and his body heat radiated up her arm. She lifted her other hand, wanting, almost needing more contact.

His gaze drifted over her shoulder, and his face hardened. "You going somewhere?"

"Just putting up some clean clothes."

Ludan edged around her and lifted one garment after another. "All pants, one gown." He twisted and scowled over his shoulder. "Try again."

"No." Fire burned through her bloodstream, and her lungs stung with a need to yell, even shout if that's what it took to make a stand for herself. She lifted her chin instead and steadied her voice. "I don't have to explain anything. To anyone."

His head snapped back as though she'd physically slapped him. With a tight grimace, he spun, paced toward the window, and planted his hands on his hips. For the longest time he stared out the window, his loose, dark hair ruffling in the steady breeze. "You're right. You don't owe me. You don't owe them. If anything, we owe *you*."

He turned and dropped his hands to his sides. His beautiful blue eyes were pinched and hazed with pain. "I wasn't asking if you were okay for Eryx. Or for the prophecy. I asked because I was worried about you. You're not safe on your own."

"And you think I'm safe here? Maxis got Lexi. Serena waltzed in with a ton of guards and stole right out from under Eryx's nose."

"I doubt it was Serena."

"Well, someone did. Can you honestly tell me you think I'm safe here?"

For the first time since he'd pushed his way into her room, his face sparked with determination. "We'll guard you."

"I've been a prisoner for fifteen years. I'd rather not add to it." She strode to the stack of clothes on the dresser, grabbed one of the two outfits she hadn't yet folded, and set back to her task. "I want to leave. I want to go home. If I can't do that, then I'll make my own way. I lived through Maxis. I'll live through this, too."

Ludan shifted so fast his movement barely registered. His mammoth hand clamped around her wrist and stilled her folding before she could squeak. "You won't be a prisoner. You can do whatever you want. Go wherever you want."

Despite his control, his touch was gentle. A delicate brand against her skin, warm and powerful. His thumb skated along her pulse. God, what she wouldn't give to curl up against him again. To pretend, even for a minute, someone would protect her.

But she was done with that. Her future was up to her and no one else. She tugged her wrist free and piled the clothes into one stack. "I want to go home."

She turned for the closet and pilfered the simple leather tote Jillian had used to cart up a load of clothes. Stuffing her neat selections into the bag, she tried to ignore Ludan's towering presence where she'd left him by the dresser. No small feat with the tension radiating off him, a manifest presence that clawed her skin.

"Okay."

She startled at his grated voice.

He swallowed so hard his Adam's apple lurched and his fists were knotted tightly at his sides. "Pack what you need and I'll take you."

"What?"

"Pack what you want," he said, "but most everything from Eden stands out there."

"What do you mean you'll take me?"

"I mean I'll port you over and stay with you."

"But you live here. I want to make a life for myself. I want to find my mother, and—"

"You have no money. No knowledge of life in Evad. No

identification, and no passport. You can't make a living without one. I do." He stalked closer, stopping with only inches between them. His body heat slicked across her exposed skin. "Humans are stirred up over people being brought here and our altercation with Maxis in Texas. If they found out you'd been here, you'd end up the star of a three-ring circus. And even in Evad, Serena could find you. I won't leave you alone."

"But Eryx—"

"Don't worry about Eryx. I'll talk to him. Give me thirty minutes and you'll leave with his blessing."

The clothes she'd been clutching slipped from her fingers, and her body seemed as if it might break the field of gravity at any moment. Dreaming about going home was one thing, but actually realizing it might happen jetted her adrenaline to dizzying levels. Surely he wasn't serious. But if he was...

Her parents. She'd be able to see them. Talk with them. Pick up her life and start over. "What if he says no? What if you can't talk him into it? Then I'll never get away."

He stilled and for a handful of seconds let a glimpse of raw defenselessness show through his mystic eyes. As fast as the vulnerability had come, his face hardened and he squared his shoulders. He held out his hand palm up. "Take my hand."

A shiver skated down her spine, the timbre of his voice on par with approaching thunder. She should've been afraid. Should have shied away like she did with every other man who offered contact, but with him it was different. The mere idea leaving her centered and her muscles loose and languid.

She placed her hand in his, the calluses on his palm scraping against hers in a not unpleasant way. Warm and solid. The same protective sensation she'd felt in his arms.

"I give you my vow." His voice coiled around her, a snug cocoon that tingled and soothed. "Whether Eryx gives us his blessing or not, I'll take you to Evad."

~

VOICES FILTERED through the library's open doorway as Ludan reached the foyer landing. The quick, staccato rhythm of whatever those inside debated tapped on his frayed nerves, another layer on top of the noise that had come roaring back the second he'd left Brenna.

He rounded the corner and paused in the entrance.

The chatter halted, and all heads turned to him.

His pulse thrummed wild and angry at his neck, and his lungs felt as though they'd been weighted down with wet cement. He was out of his mind. No somo had ever broken his vow. Not in the history of their race. And yet, he'd just superseded it with a vow to a woman he'd known all of a few months.

Listen to your spirit. Your Spiritu, or whatever that quiet voice inside belongs to. To deny it is to deny your soul.

His father's words flared bright and powerful in his head, overriding all the superfluous noise. This was his chance to make up for failing his mother. A window of peace, however long it lasted.

The stinging silence and the weight of everyone's stares pressed through his thoughts. He locked his gaze on Eryx, reclined in his chair with one elbow propped on the arm. "We need to talk."

Eryx lifted his eyebrows as if to say, *"And?"*

No way. No way was he airing his plans with an audience. He'd cast enough shame on his family when word got out. "Alone."

With no more than a subtle chin lift from Eryx, everyone headed for the door. On her way past, Lexi squeezed Eryx's arm and cast Ludan a soft, almost sympathetic smile.

Graylin stood from the wingback in front of Eryx's desk, his shoulders squared and a confident, proud look on his face. Halfway between Ludan and Eryx, he paused, looked back at Eryx, and opened his mouth as if to speak, but then closed it. Instead he clasped Ludan's shoulder on the way out and dipped his head. *"I'm proud of you, son. Whatever you're up to, I trust you. You'll always have my support."*

Ludan's knees nearly buckled, stubbornness and shock the only things keeping his legs locked. Yeah, his dad had always been supportive, but he was a warrior, too. A man's man. He'd just as soon spar and work his emotions out physically than try to put words around an issue. Direct praise and spoken confidence was nothing short of a blessing from the Creator.

But then his dad didn't know the whole of what he was about to do. Praise the Great One, could he even do this?

The double doors thudded shut behind him. The quiet pressed thick and heavy around him.

Eryx leaned back farther in his chair, kicked his feet up on his desk, and folded his hands across his chest. "All right. You've got my attention, along with about four other people pacing outside those doors."

A slow, painful squeeze surrounded his heart, and a chilled sweat set up shop between his shoulder blades. He wanted to breathe, to steady himself and balance his voice, but damned if he could get enough air. "I want to take Brenna to Evad."

To his credit, Eryx didn't move. Didn't even flinch. "I've got to admit. I didn't see that one coming."

Yeah, he hadn't either, and he still couldn't believe it. "It's what she wants. I think we owe it to her."

"Yeah, well, she made an oath to me and the council otherwise."

"She was afraid when she made the oath. Alone in a world where she's an outsider. What else could she do with no way home? And now she's a target for Serena. We owe her."

"No, Maxis owes her."

"Bullshit." The need to pace or punch pummeled him from the inside out. "Someone from our race hurt her. That means *we* failed. She's had zero choices since she was eight. She deserves to call her own shots for a while. And it's safer there. Harder for Serena to find her."

"I could reason it's more dangerous. Only one of you to watch over her versus a whole guard."

"Which makes her feel like a prisoner. You think she wants more of that? After the life she's led?"

Eryx sighed, sat forward, and hung his head.

He'd seen too much of that fatigue on his friend lately. For as far back as Ludan could remember, Eryx had always been the reasonable one. Grounded and optimistic. Now here Ludan was adding more to Eryx's plate.

But he still had to do it. With every word he'd spoken on Brenna's behalf, the firmer his resolve had become. As if his life were picking up steam and clicking on all the right gears after years of operating on idle.

He stalked closer. "You want her help with the prophecy. I know that's not your end goal, and I know you'd never push her, but think about the big picture. She's known no freedom. No choice. Give it to her. Let her explore. Give her reality instead of dreams. In the end, when you need her, her head will be in a better place. More open and willing."

Eryx huffed out a laugh and scratched the back of his head. "I think that's the most I've heard you talk since that night we tried to outdrink each other on strasse." He cocked his head to one side. "Not a bad argument either, but it still doesn't get me out of hot water with the ellan."

"You're the malran. Your command trumps the ellan, and there's no one on the council who can challenge you."

Eryx just stared at him. Whether he was bored, mulling it over, or just not buying it, Ludan couldn't tell.

Fine. He'd pull a full-court press. "If Lexi wanted something, you'd break every damned one of their rules."

Fire sparked in Eryx's eyes, and a cunning, almost pleased expression flashed across his face. "True." He rubbed his chin and studied his boots. A second later, a low chuckle shook his chest. "I have to tell you, I'd enjoy this a whole lot more if it didn't come at such a shit time."

"Enjoy what?"

Eryx grinned. One of those triumphant, know-it-all smirks that rubbed Ludan ten different ways of wrong. "Watching you fall."

Ludan might have masked his flinch outwardly, but his insides were a whole different story. "That's not what this is."

The bastard's smile grew bigger, and for the first time in months Eryx looked like the easygoing, fair man he'd grown up with. "If you say so."

"It's a simple case of doing what's right and what's safest."

Eryx leaned forward and planted his elbows on the desk. "My somo is breaking his vow for a human."

"I'm doing what's right for the prophecy. And it's not forever. She'll get settled, this will pass, and I'll be back."

Eryx lifted an eyebrow.

"You're blowing this out of proportion." Praise the Great One, didn't he get it? "And I'd die for you whether I was your somo or not."

"But if you had to save me or Brenna, who would you choose?"

An unguarded slug to his jaw couldn't have thwacked him harder than that question. Fuck. Surely Eryx knew he could count on him. He'd always put him before anyone else.

But would you?

Eryx's voice cut through his thoughts, lower now and loaded with wisdom. "There's not a wrong answer to that question. More something for you to think on." Pushing away from his desk, he stood and lumbered toward Ludan. "And if you're wondering, I love you as much as I do my own brother, but I'd save Lexi before either of you."

Holy histus, Eryx really thought he'd save Brenna over him. Though after that hiccup in his head, he couldn't really blame him.

Holding out his hand for a warrior's clasp, Eryx paused in front of Ludan. "Go with my blessing. Use Ian to track down what you can on her family. Keep her safe and stay in contact."

For longer than he should have, Ludan stared at Eryx's outstretched hand. Hell, staring was all he could do because his whole damned body felt as if it had been disconnected from reality. He'd actually done it. Upended his whole life on nothing more than instinct.

For a woman.

He grasped Eryx's hand. Over a hundred years he'd stood by Eryx, and now his whole life was different.

"Now who's the one who's over thinking it?" Eryx clapped Ludan on the shoulder and released his hand. "You went with your gut. Don't second-guess it now."

That was the weird part. He wasn't second-guessing it at all. More like anticipating the things he could show Brenna. The things he could teach her.

He felt more than heard Eryx stride toward the door, but he paused before he opened it. "And Ludan?"

Ludan turned and blinked his eyes into focus.

Calm contentment filled Eryx's expression. "While you're there, what's mine is yours. Make sure her time there is a good one."

CHAPTER 10

*B*renna hustled toward the far side of the castle gardens as fast as her legs would allow without breaking into a jog. If Ludan had any notion how difficult it was keeping up with his long strides, he didn't show it. In fact, the only thing showing on his face was resolute determination. As if he had to complete the task in front of him before anyone could stop him, or worse, he changed his mind.

Her heart punched the same insane rhythm that had started the second he'd stomped into her room without knocking and announced it was time to go.

She was going home. And Ludan was the one taking her there.

He paused just beyond the farthest manicured flowerbed and peered over his shoulder to the castle's front tower. The wind tossed his hair around his face, the dark strands accenting his pale blue eyes. The emotion emanating from behind them was one she'd never seen in him before. Not sadness, exactly. More like acceptance. If it weren't for the T-shirt and jeans he'd changed into, she could have easily painted him as a knight from one of her bedtime stories.

Following his gaze, Brenna twisted.

A lone figure stood behind the waist-high wall.

Eryx.

A cold, foreboding shiver snaked down her spine. "Are you sure he's okay with this?"

"The decision was mine. But yes, he supported it." Ludan's gaze slid to hers. "Are you ready?"

Goose bumps rippled up her arms, and her breath hitched in her throat. Ready was the understatement of the century. She nodded in lieu of an answer and wiped her palms on her hips.

He noted the awkward gesture, and his tension ebbed, leaving behind a crooked, barely there smile. "It's just a portal. Nothing to be afraid of."

Easy for him to say. He'd been through them countless times. Even preferred Evad where others favored Eden, if the stories she'd heard at the castle were true. She, on the other hand, had only been through once as a hysterical girl. Not exactly something on her list of positive experiences.

He lifted his hand, palm facing out. His fingers were loose, but spread as though ready to catch a ball, and his eyes narrowed.

The breeze stilled and the sounds of nature silenced. Several feet in front of them, the air shifted, swirling to a pearlescent gray mist. Bigger and bigger it grew, continuing until a cave-like circle stabilized with a tunnel formed inside. Foggy tendrils wavered from the edges, and beautiful sparkles glimmered in the setting Myren sun.

Ludan lowered his hand. "Time to go."

Fifteen years she'd waited for this moment, and yet she was so pumped with adrenaline that moving seemed coun-terintuitive. Forcing herself forward, she placed her hand in his outstretched one. The second she made contact, her tension eased and his warmth rippled through her.

Guiding her forward, he stepped over the misty edge.

Brenna followed. Two steps in, the ground beneath her shifted like sand on an outgoing wave and she stumbled.

Ludan caught her around the waist. "Sorry. I forgot the feel of things takes getting used to." He swept her into his arms, and her startled squeak echoed down the dark corridor. "We'll do it this way your first time around."

Her arm around his neck tightened, but her muscles didn't seem interested in her mind's command to relax. The portal wasn't anything like she remembered. Even though the walls were a smoky gray, a soft, welcoming light pervaded the space, and the glittery sparkles she'd seen at the entrance winked as they walked past. "Where are we going?"

"Dallas. You said you were born in Allen. Dallas isn't far from there, and Eryx has a place downtown we can use."

Memories from her youth flickered. Big buildings and highways packed with so many cars it took forever to get home. "I think I remember it. Mom and Dad took me to a huge mall around Christmastime. We went ice skating and then shopping."

"Sounds nice."

It had been, even when her parents had argued on the way home. Something about backseat driving. She hadn't paid much attention to their light bickering. Her feet had hurt too bad from all the walking, and the darkness that had enveloped her had been a welcome respite from the mall's chaotic sounds. The whir of tires against the pavement and the soft motion of the car had lulled her to sleep in almost no time. The next thing she knew her dad was tucking her into her bed.

She gave in to the memory and rested her temple on Ludan's chest, letting loose an easy sigh. "I like that memory.

There was a Christmas tree. A big one in the middle of the ice rink."

Quiet settled around them, even Ludan's footsteps swallowed by the peaceful mist. The farther they walked, the more the air changed. "Why does it feel different?"

Ludan glanced at her. "Different how?"

"The air. It seems…" Nothing in her vocabulary felt right. "I don't know, maybe damp? Empty?"

Surprised flickered across his features. "It's the energy. There's less of it in Evad. I guess you can sense it now because of Eryx's healing. Most humans can't."

Low rumbles sounded all around them, a cross between thunder and what she'd imagine an earthquake sounded like. A flickering light appeared in the distance. "Are we there?"

"Almost."

Beneath her shoulder, Ludan's heartbeat thumped steady and powerful, far more stable than the erratic lurch of her own. Seconds passed. Or maybe it was minutes. All she could focus on was the growing light. The closer they drew, the more the rumble increased.

"What's that noise?"

"The highway. I set the portal exit to a park near downtown, but there's a major highway right beside it. The portal masks most of the sound, but once you're outside of it, you'll get the full force."

This was the muffled version? The end of the tunnel lay only twenty or thirty feet ahead, and the droning noise was already enough to make her jumpy. "Wait. There's a park near a highway? That doesn't make sense."

Ludan chuckled. "Yeah, you'll see a lot of things that don't make sense. Entertaining for sure."

A haze covered the portal's edge, but she could still make out a deepening blue sky, twinkling lights, and tall, box-like structures.

Pausing at the exit, Ludan closed his eyes.

"What are you doing?"

He kept his eyes closed, but one corner of his mouth twitched in an almost-smile. "Checking the surroundings. I need to gauge who's close by and keep us and the portal masked. Don't want to step out in the middle of something awkward."

Well, that made sense. It also proved how she'd have bungled this in a jillion different ways if she'd somehow managed to build a portal of her own.

Pulling in a deep breath, he opened his eyes and stepped over the portal's edge.

The rumble burst to a roar, and a high-pitched hum buzzed all around her. It wasn't until she felt Ludan's big hand stroking her spine that she realized she'd buried her face in the crook of his neck.

His deep, comforting voice sounded at her ear. "It's just the highway. Look around. You're safe."

She peeked over his shoulder, and her breath left her on a shaky exhale. The sun had just set, leaving the skies a rich blue. Trees formed a perfect line through the simple green grass, and a wide sidewalk stretched behind them. Or maybe it wasn't a sidewalk. More like a patio for the large covered structure with the all-weather picnic tables beneath it.

Ludan's chest shook on a nearly silent chuckle, not that she could have heard him laugh with the noise behind them. "Want to try it on your feet now?"

God, how stupid could she be? He'd been carrying her for at least twenty minutes. "I'm sorry. Put me down. You must be tired."

Even though she loosened her grip, ready to stand on her own two feet, he held her right where she was and locked his gaze with hers. "You're not a burden to me, Brenna. Not in weight or in time."

"Oh." Her heart did a weird twisty-twirl, and for a good second or two, the chaotic din around her dropped to background clutter. His hair ruffled against her knuckles where she cupped the back of his neck, and her fingers lifted to comb through the wavy strands on instinct. "Thank you."

His eyes darkened, more like a morning sunrise than their normal high-noon blue, and his gaze dropped to her lips. Before she could make any more of his reaction, he eased her to her feet, steadying her with a hand on her arm.

"I'm okay." Actually, *okay* was pushing it. Standing with all the adrenaline coursing through her limbs was more of a challenge than she cared to admit.

His hand slid down and clasped hers, never losing contact. "All the same, I'm here if you need me, but keep your hand in mine until I drop the mask."

The mask. She spun to where they'd stepped out of the portal and nearly fumbled their point of contact when she found it gone. In its place were towering buildings, one with an exterior that looked like row after row of mirrors, and sparkling lights as far as her eyes could see. "Where's the portal?"

"I let it close." He tugged her hand. "Let's move out of sight. After I drop the mask you can take your time looking around."

Fifteen minutes and a casual stroll later, she paused beside a tall wrought-iron lamppost. Dozens like it lined the walkways. She stared up at the glowing light. "That's the buzz."

Ludan nodded. "Electricity. Do you remember it?"

She should have. When Maxis had first taken her to Eden, doing without lights had been the hardest hurdle to overcome. Yet somewhere along the way, the concept had evaporated from her memories. "I do now. It's loud." Unnatural, like all the other greenery around her. The park was beautiful, but it was so sculpted and rigid that it felt more like a picture than part of nature.

Ludan's gaze locked on a small cluster of people gathered nearby. "You okay if we hold off on the rest of the tour until we get you some clothes to help you blend in?"

She flinched and glanced down at her deep-blue tunic and leggings. Compared to the rest of the people, it was a bit out of place. "I guess that would be smart." She considered the buildings around them. "Where does Eryx live?"

"Not far from here. We can walk if you want, but flying would be faster."

And more inconspicuous. He might not have verbalized it, but the agitation in his posture and the way he constantly surveyed their surroundings broadcasted it quite clearly.

"Flying is fine." More than fine really. She could use a minute to center herself without the highway's drone. Not to mention the added benefit of being in his arms again.

She gave herself an internal shake as he guided her into a hidden spot, and tried to ignore the feel of his arms around her when he picked her up. Letting any wishful, intimate thoughts of Ludan burrow into her imagination was a dangerous game. Hoping for a nice, normal relationship someday was one thing. Fantasizing about Ludan was something else altogether.

Around them, the skies had darkened to full night, though the color here leaned more toward drudge-gray than the rich, velvet black of Eden. The August air was thick and sultry. Cars zipped beneath them, and buildings of different heights and blacktop streets covered every square inch. It looked odd. Void and empty. Soulless.

They'd barely been in the air five minutes when Ludan touched down on a tall rooftop. Outdoor furniture circled a stone fire pit, and off to one side was a brick arrangement that made her think of Orla's wood stove back home.

No, not home. *This* was home.

Ludan cupped her shoulder. "Hey."

Brenna snapped from her thoughts. "Sorry. I was thinking."

"About?"

She shook her head and surveyed the rest of the concrete-covered space. "It's just..." Not at all what she remembered. "Different."

He splayed his hand low on her back and guided her to a plain black door near the corner. "It is, and it isn't. The environment and the culture are different, but the people are basically the same."

They took the barren, concrete stairwell down one flight and came out in a posh elevator landing decorated in deep grays and black. Only a few pearl and silver accents broke the dramatic décor. One entrance sat directly opposite the elevator, a double door made of ebony wood with intricate details carved in the smooth surface.

Ludan stopped in front of it, focused on the door handle for all of two seconds, and then twisted it.

"Don't you need a key?" She was sure she remembered her parents using them when she was little.

"If I know where the lock is, I don't need a key." He tapped his temple and grinned. "A Myren perk."

That *was* a perk. One she'd be smart to learn if she ever got a chance. Then again, Ludan wouldn't be here forever, and she wouldn't have any other Myrens to mirror from, so maybe learning was a waste of time.

Behind her, the door clicked shut. It should have been still and quiet, but the rush of traffic and city noise still droned beyond the windows. And there were a lot of them, an entire wall of nothing but glass that ran the length of the apartment. Outside, downtown's yellow and blue-tinted lights dotted an otherwise sea of black.

"The apartment's not huge, but it's got everything we'll need." Ludan stalked to a row of switches just inside the entrance and flipped them all with the flat of his hand. "Kitchen's to the left. Bedrooms are to the right. You can take the master at the end of the hall. I usually sleep in the one next to it."

The words registered, but she couldn't quite get past the fact that he thought it wasn't big. Sure it wasn't the castle, but she was pretty sure the house she'd been born in wasn't this large. In keeping with the colors in the elevator landing, the space was decorated in dove gray, black, and soft white, but unlike the outside, it was cozy and welcoming. Thick black beams ran floor-to-ceiling in fifteen or twenty-foot segments, and warm lighting shone on them to create elegant warmth.

She paced toward the center of the room. Leather and lavender scented the air, fueled by a showroom-new, over-sized couch centered in front of the windows and the bowl of potpourri on the glass and wrought-iron coffee table. "I would never have imagined a place like this for Eryx." She dragged her fingers along the back of a white and gray club chair. "It suits him, but at the same time it doesn't."

"You've only seen one side of him. He's been alive a long time. Seen more than most."

Because they lived longer than humans. As in a lot longer. Lexi had mentioned some Myrens lived into their mid-six-hundreds. A huge difference to her expected lifespan.

Ludan prowled toward the kitchen. "I'll need to run out and get some food and cash." He flipped another set of switches and glanced over his shoulder. "You think you'll be okay for about an hour?"

Trailing behind him, she soaked in her surroundings, fully aware her that mouth hung open, but she was too far gone to care. She smoothed her fingertips against the silver refrigerator. She'd forgotten about those. And ovens. Though her parents never had one as huge as the one in this kitchen. God, what she would have done for either of those in the last fifteen years.

On the stone countertop sat a large leather-covered box with five slim rectangle boxes with shiny glass fronts. Ludan plucked one from its stand and swiped the front with his thumb. Colorful lights blazed to life with more appearing the more he touched the glass.

He nodded and handed her the one he'd picked up. "If you need me, just call."

The device was cold in her hand and so skinny she was afraid she'd drop it. Bright squares with bold designs sat lined up in tiny rows. "What do I do with it?"

For a second, Ludan's jaw slackened. He closed it and scratched the back of his head. "Shit, I forgot. They didn't have mobile phones like this when you were little." He sidled up behind her and pointed to a green square with a telephone on it at the bottom. "Push this."

She did and a white screen popped up.

"Now push the star."

Every instruction she followed to the letter, only vaguely registering what she was doing. Nothing could register beyond the tingles scampering along her skin and the wishful thoughts that fired when he was this close.

"You think you've got it?"

Not even close. She nodded anyway and set the phone on the counter, hoping he wouldn't ask her to prove it.

The frown he aimed at her said he knew better than to believe her, but instead of pushing it, he strode to the refrigerator and yanked it open. He scanned the inside and shook his head. "Nothing in here worth keeping except the beer." He shut the door and opened an onyx cabinet above a built-in desk at the back of the kitchen. Rows of keys jingled on hooks inside, and Ludan snatched a set in the middle. "Anything in particular you want from the store?"

She blinked, mentally scrambling for anything she'd liked when she was little. "All I remember are Lucky Charms. And peanut butter. And marshmallows, but I only got those in the winter when we went camping."

He smiled so big Brenna staggered back a step. It was beautiful. Easygoing and open, it transformed his entire presence. Prowling closer, he cupped the side of her face and traced her cheekbone with his thumb. "Lucky Charms, peanut butter, and marshmallows it is."

CHAPTER 11

*L*udan stepped from the portal into Ian's backyard and bright morning sunshine. As power drains went, portals were the end all be all, but flying to Tulsa from Dallas would have taken twice the time. At a four-hour one-way trip, driving was out of the question. Brenna might have been happy to be home, but she was damned jumpy. She'd tried like histus to hide her less-than-magical reintroduction to human society, but the constant flinches and frowns spotlighted her disappointment.

Striding across the manicured lawn with the ridiculously high privacy fence they'd had installed for convenience, Ludan cracked his neck for the fifth time in less than an hour. Sleeping in a chair was for shit no matter the circumstance, but the second Brenna had padded from the master bedroom with a troubled pout and a claim she couldn't sleep, he'd clicked off the TV without a word and offered to sit with her.

She'd looked at him like he was a god in that moment, and damned if he didn't feel a good ten feet taller stalking behind her to the bedroom. Though, if she knew how selfish his reasons for jumping at the chance, she'd probably be terrified.

He slid open the sliding glass door to Ian's kitchen and poked his head inside. "Ian?"

Jillian's voice drifted from the adjacent living room. "He's in his office."

Shutting the door behind him, Ludan headed to the half-empty coffeepot. Compared to what he normally pilfered from Orla's kitchen, Ian's java was closer to flavored hot water, but at least he'd get a little caffeine. Then again, if he'd spent more time sleeping instead of staring at Brenna while she did, he wouldn't need it in the first place.

He snatched half a bagel out of an Einstein bag and strolled into the living room.

Jillian sat stretched with her feet and legs up lengthwise on the old orange and chocolate woven couch. Like everything else in Ian's house, it matched the late-seventies wood paneling and thick rock fireplace. The only thing new was the huge flat panel mounted in the big wall unit. Oddly, it was set to one of those old-school comedies TV Land always played. The one with the hot sixties witch.

Jillian glanced up from her laptop. "Hey, Ludan."

"Hey, Squeak. Your dad busy?"

The question was no sooner out of his mouth than Ian ambled down the hallway on the opposite side of the room. "I thought I heard your grumpy rumble." He jerked his thumb over one shoulder toward the spare bedroom turned makeshift office. "Eryx said you'd be coming by. Come on back and tell me what you've got."

The hallway was all of ten strides long. Built like every other home from the late seventies, it was compact with a ceiling height that made him claustrophobic. Still, between their all-too-public altercation with Maxis in Texas and the mystery person stirring up panic by taking humans on guided tours through Eden, it had made for a handy and private PI Central.

Ludan glanced down the hallway at Jillian. Her knees were drawn up so the laptop screen rested against them, and her eyes were narrowed as though she were tracking down life's lost secrets. "You got her working, too?"

The smile that split Ian's face was pure fatherly pride. For more than sixteen years, he'd tried to find his missing wife and unborn child with no luck. Thanks to fate and Ian's friendship with Lexi, he'd found Jillian in Eden, safe and very Myren. Granted, it had taken Ian being captured and near fatally tortured to bring all the pieces together, but Ian sure looked like he'd pay that price a few times over to stay with his kid.

"For a girl who'd never touched a computer before two months ago, her aptitude is off the charts. She picked it up a hell of a lot faster than I did. She's got great instincts, too." Ian slid around his desk and dropped into his worn leather banker's chair. "You see the latest news?"

Ludan sat in one of the two uncomfortable chairs opposite the desk and braced his elbows on his knees. "The bit about the military upping their interest? Yeah, I saw it." Actually, Brenna had been the one to see it after she'd figured out where the TV was while he was out running errands. It'd taken him an hour to peel her away from all the news channels. "Any word on how they plan to do that?"

Ian clicked his email program. "Word is they've corralled all of the people who claimed they'd been taken to Eden and are comparing stories."

"Not going to win a PR contest with that approach."

"Nope. And let's hope they don't dig up anything new. It's already going to take a long time for this ruckus to die down." Turning from the computer, Ian picked up a plain manila file and tossed it across the desk. "Eryx said you needed some background on Brenna. I haven't been able to do much since Lexi brought me over this morning, but that's a start."

Ludan thumbed through the printed versions of newspaper stories and police reports. On the left-hand side of the file were Ian's scrawled notes in thick black ink.

Brenna Haven
Disney World disappearance.
Suspected kidnapping.
Cold case.
Hometown: Allen, Texas
Mother: Abigail (Abby) Haven
Father: David Haven (deceased)

Ludan snapped his head up. "Deceased?"

"Yeah." Ian frowned and tapped his thumb on the desk. "Two years to the day Brenna disappeared. From what I can tell, the couple burned every dime they had traveling back and forth from Texas to Florida trying to find her. Looks like the mom moved to Orlando shortly after his death. I'll need a little more time to validate that and find an address. Assuming she's still there."

Unable to sit with that kind of news rattling around in his thoughts, Ludan pushed upright and paced to the window. Brenna would be devastated. Her magical fairytale ending was already a disappointment. How in histus was he supposed to tell her she was minus one parent on top of losing a good chunk of the life she should have had? As news went, it was a shit sandwich. "How much longer do you need?"

"Give me a few days. If the goal is to keep her safe, the last thing you two need is to go hunting on your own. I'll narrow down a good address and place of business. Probably wouldn't hurt to see if Mom's holding things together better than Dad."

"You got Brenna's old address? The one she lived at before? She said she wanted to see it."

Ian spun the folder around, rifled through the papers, and handed one over. "Right here. No clue yet what condition it's in or who owns it yet."

Ludan snatched the info and studied it. "You got my number?"

"Got 'em all."

"Good. You get the information, give me a call." Grabbing his coffee off the edge of the desk, he headed out the door. "I appreciate the effort."

"Ludan."

Ludan paused and looked back.

Ian leaned his elbows on the desk and clasped his hands in the middle. "I think it's good what you're doing. What you're giving her."

All Ludan could do was blink and mentally stutter. He'd been in countless dangerous and difficult situations, but this one was on par with a woman handing him a squalling newborn baby. The irony was off the charts. Ian thought he was doing something noble when, in truth, he was the biggest beneficiary. "I'm not doing anything special."

Ian smiled and nodded, but damned if he didn't have the same smug look as Eryx. "If you say so."

CHAPTER 12

*I*f Brenna thought the highway noise from the park was loud, actually being on the highway, surrounded by tons of other cars zipping in and out of the lanes around her, was worse. Way worse. She checked the seat belt strapped across her chest. "Is it always like this?"

Ludan glanced at her face, scanned her body, and semi-scowled as he stared back out the windshield. He'd been grumpy ever since he'd come back from visiting Ian, but the sour grapes had gotten worse after she'd tried on a T-shirt and jeans she'd found in Lexi's closet. The T-shirt wasn't too bad, but the jeans felt weird. Not uncomfortable, but awkward.

"Ludan?"

"Sorry." He pulled in a deep breath and let it out. "This actually isn't bad. It's lunchtime right now. Nothing like rush hour."

"What's rush hour?"

His head snapped toward hers, and his eyes softened. "Today is Monday. That's the first day of the work week for most humans. Rush hour is in the morning or afternoon when they're driving back and forth to work."

Another detail she didn't know. She huffed and scowled out the window. Colorful signs and businesses flew past, most of which she could only guess their purpose. The ones that were easy to pick out were the restaurants, and after the food Ludan had brought back last night, she wasn't in a hurry to visit one. She'd remembered the word *hamburger* from when she was little, but the taste was way too fatty for her to eat.

The Hummer's tires droned and vibrated against the highway, lulling her thoughts deeper and deeper. She really didn't have a clue about this world. Even the things she'd remembered were so different in today's world that they might as well be foreign. Like those phones. Granted they were pretty and it was nice to walk around without a cord, but they were confusing. Life in Eden was so much simpler. Cleaner.

She sat up straighter and glared out the windshield. This was home. Not Eden. So what if she needed to catch up a little? She'd figure things out eventually. The same way she'd done in Eden.

The engine's growl dropped a notch, and Ludan exited the highway, veering onto a side road. Beside it was a single-story building that seemed to go on for two or more blocks with cars packed in the parking lot. "What's that?"

"They call it an outlet mall. Lots of popular stores all clumped into one place like the one where you went ice skating, only outside."

Huh. There sure were a lot of places like that. She didn't remember her mom shopping very much, but maybe that's what people did now. She craned her neck as they drove, looking for anything she'd recognize. A carved wooden sign on the side of the road said, *Welcome to Allen!*

She plastered one hand on the glass. "This is my town." She spun back to Ludan. "This is the place I lived."

Ludan smiled, but there was a sadness to it. Or maybe regret. "Yeah, this is your town."

"Are you taking me…" She couldn't say it. Didn't dare for fear she'd jinx it.

"To see your home?"

The stoplight turned green.

Ludan turned the corner and glanced her direction. "Yes. That's where we're headed. Just to see the house though, nothing more."

All the melancholy she'd nursed throughout the thirty-minute drive evaporated, replaced with an almost unbearable antsy crawl beneath her skin. She scanned every block, desperate for something to remember. Something to anchor her and bolster her hopes.

A few miles down the road, Ludan pulled into a neighborhood. The homes were small and all had the same look and feel. Different paint colors, different brick, or wood trim, but siblings all the same. Tall, mature trees dotted the front yards, and sidewalks cracked by time lined either side of the street. Off the driver's side, a small pond stretched behind the span of three or four houses. Covered picnic tables and playgrounds lined the perimeter.

A memory flashed in her mind. Her on a swing and giggling while her father pushed her higher. "This is my neighborhood."

Ludan kept his silence, winding through the streets with intermittent glances at the tiny map built into the Hummer's dashboard.

She scanned the row of houses on her right. "It doesn't look as familiar as I thought it would."

"This neighborhood's over twenty years old. Time changes things. Plus, new owners like to add their own mark." He turned a corner and parked at the entrance to a cul-de-sac.

Four houses rounded the circular plot, but it was the one closest to them that snagged her attention. A one-story surrounded in carnelian red brick. The roof's pitch was shallow like those around it and was covered in dove-gray shingles. Neatly trimmed hedges lined the front, and a stonework path ran from the front door to the sidewalk.

"That's it." She fumbled with the door handle, missing the first two attempts for failing to take her eyes off her child-hood home. The air-conditioned cold metal barely regis-tered against her palm as she pushed the door open and slid to the asphalt. One majestic oak tree towered near the center of the front lawn with rich black mulch surrounding its base.

She traipsed closer.

Behind her, Ludan's car door thumped shut and his clipped, booted footsteps rounded the front of the truck.

She pointed at the neatly stained wood slats surrounding the backyard and the greenbelt behind it. "They replaced the fence. When I was little, it was chain-link. I'd climb over it and almost always scraped my legs." She glanced back at Ludan.

Despite her story and the location she'd pointed at, his focus was solely on her, his eyes hooded with an unsettling weight.

She shrugged and turned her attention back to the house. "I was little for my age. Dad said he liked me being little because I wouldn't always be that way."

"He was right." Ludan's hand settled between her neck and shoulder, warm and comforting. A steadying presence while her insides churned and relived memories long forgot-ten. "But you're still tiny to me."

She snorted and giggled before her pride could prevent

otherwise, and glanced over her shoulder. "Everyone's tiny compared to you."

She froze. Heat—or maybe need—radiated from his cool blue gaze, plucking her from her thoughts and plunging her headlong into the present.

His thumb skated along her spine near her nape.

The noonday summer sun beat harsh against her skin and wavered off the blacktop street, but she shivered as though it were twenty degrees. Under his heated stare she could forget anything, or anyone, and never regret it.

He relinquished his hold and stuffed his hand in his front pocket. "I'd take you in if I could, but there are people inside."

The comment shook her from her haze as little else could have. She spun back to the house, her heart lodged high in her throat. "My family?"

"No. Not anymore."

Beside her home stood another made of ivory brick and chocolate trim. Her best friend, Renee, had lived there. Opposite the cul-de-sac lived another little girl who'd been five. She'd tagged along behind Brenna and Renee when they'd play and drove them both crazy. What was her name? Samantha? Savannah? "Do you know where they live now?"

Ludan crammed both of his hands deep in his front pockets and hung his head. "Your mom moved to Florida a few years after you disappeared. Ian thinks it was so she could have a better chance of finding you."

"You mean Mom and Dad."

Closing his eyes, Ludan's shoulders sagged on a long sigh. He opened them a second later and met her gaze head-on. "No, I mean your mother."

She looked back at the house. "Dad stayed here? Why would he do that?" When Ludan didn't answer, she turned back to him.

Anguish pinched the corners of his eyes, and his lips were mashed in an angry line.

Dread slithered down her spine, frigid and unforgiving as fractured ice. "Something happened to him."

"In a manner of speaking." He swallowed and scanned the horizon as though it might hold answers he didn't have. He studied his boots a second, then looked up and cleared his throat. "You have to understand, losing a child, especially a young one, can be hard on a parent. Sometimes too hard."

Too hard? What could possibly be harder than what she'd endured? What she'd lived and suffered through? "Tell me."

He jerked one hand free of his pocket and cupped the back of her neck. His thumb traced the line of her jaw. "He's gone, Brenna. He died two years after you disappeared."

"What? How?"

He cupped her face with his other hand and pulled her closer. "It doesn't matter."

"It does matter. I deserve to know."

He studied her face, eyes roving her features. He frowned before he spoke. "He killed himself."

"Suicide? How?"

"Please don't ask me that."

"How?"

Ludan growled low in his throat, and his jaw looked like it would snap at any moment. "The death certificate said asphyxia. Ian couldn't pull up much beyond one news story that confirmed it was a self-inflicted death."

Asphyxia. Another word she didn't recognize. Judging from the look on Ludan's face, it was one he wouldn't be willing to describe either.

The neighborhood faded to nothing but white noise and haze. There wasn't anything about this world she knew. Not really. She could barely read beyond that of a fifth or sixth grader. Her father was dead, and God only knew where her mother was. "It's my fault."

Ludan tightened his grip on her neck. "What?"

Her vision cleared enough to train her gaze on his. "It's my fault. They told me to stay close to them. Both of them did, over and over again. But then I saw a pretty princess tiara in a store window, and I wanted to get a better look." She studied the house. "I should have listened. If I'd listened, he'd still be here. I wouldn't have lost them."

Ludan cupped the side of her face and urged her focus back on him. His fingers pressed firm against her skin, refusing any give. He dipped his head so close his warm breath fanned her cheeks. "This isn't your fault. Maxis is the one who set things in motion, and adults are responsible for their own actions. You've taken enough since you've been gone. Don't take this, too."

Tears welled in her eyes and blurred his perfect face. She wanted to say something, anything that wouldn't make her appear as lost and worthless as she felt, but nothing came. Not so much as a thought beyond the craving to curl up in his arms and let her tears have free rein.

Sliding his hand to her back, he pulled her against him.

Her tears spilled down her cheeks, leaving cold tracks despite the Texas heat. His earth and leather scent surrounded her, and his heart pulsed strong and steady beneath her ear. Twice now he'd been the one to comfort her. To hold her steady while her past and the lack of a future tore through her soul.

She surrendered to it. To his strength. To the unpracticed, but oh-so-genuine stroke of his massive hand up and down her spine. His lips brushed her temple, and his breath tickled her skin.

God, he made it easy to let go. Lifting her head, she

dashed her tears with the back of her hand and sniffled. "Sorry."

With his callused thumb, he swept aside a tear she'd missed and softly smiled. His deep voice drifted smooth and tranquil across her senses. "Nothing to be sorry for."

Easy for him to say. He wasn't the one who'd broken down twice in less than a week. Forcing herself from his embrace, she stepped back and straightened her stance. "Can I see my mother?"

"Ian's looking for her. He said he needs a few days to track her down, but after that, yes."

Across the street, a little girl with a bright pink helmet and a blue romper peddled on a tiny bicycle down the sidewalk. Her mother jogged beside her, one hand poised near the back of the bike to catch her if she wobbled.

She'd been that little girl once. Mindless of problems or the cruel world.

Only days to wait. In the scheme of what she'd been through, the timespan was nothing. She could use the time to her advantage. To adjust and learn about the life she'd missed. "Okay. A few days it is."

CHAPTER 13

*L*udan stuffed his change in the front of his jeans pocket and took the second of two glutton-sized chocolate frozen custards from the cashier. Texas might be a bitch in the summer, but everyone who lived here knew how to take the edge off an August evening.

He ambled back to Brenna who was perched on the edge of a picnic bench and facing away from the built-in table. The custard place they'd stopped at on the outskirts of lower Greenville was packed with single nine-to-fivers and families in sore need of a midweek retreat. He was pretty sure the only reason he and Brenna hadn't had to share their little all-in-one, table-and-bench combo was sheer intimidation on his part. Not that he cared. More time alone with Brenna was worth it.

Handing off her waffle cone, he sat and stretched one arm behind her so it rested on the table.

Her eyes lit with delight, and her pretty pink tongue licked the frozen curlicue at the top. Her eyes dropped, and a slow, decadent *Mmmm* hummed past her lips.

Fuck, he needed to get a grip. The last two days had been

some of the best of his life. Peaceful and mostly quiet while they'd driven all over the huge-ass state so she could soak up everything from downtown to ranches. Even his beast had taken a breather, content to laze in Brenna's presence.

Still, every time he so much as glanced at her, a weird tug pulled him, like they were connected somehow. Damned if it didn't freak him the hell out.

He took a big enough bite to obliterate half of his custard.

Brenna's playful taunt cut through his thoughts. "You're supposed to enjoy it."

"I'm a guy. Savoring's for when we're already full."

"We just ate a few hours ago."

Ludan shrugged and devoured another bite. He'd have to start getting creative with ways to occupy her if Ian didn't call soon.

Well, ways that didn't entail some of the lecherous thoughts scooting around in his head. Those he had in high supply, and every one of them made him feel like a Class-A dick.

He'd thought their shopping trip to the Galleria would've taken up a whole day, but it'd turned up surprisingly short-lived. Instead of dragging him from store to store for hours like he'd expected, Brenna had drawn into herself and eyeballed the people as though she expected them to sprout three heads. After an hour, he'd nixed the outing and taken them to a park.

Brenna watched a teen jump into a midsized truck across the parking lot, fire up the engine, and whip out of his parking place. Ever since he'd pulled over on the outskirts of town the day before and told her to slide in the driver's seat, she'd paid twice as much attention to how people navigated their cars. As spontaneous ideas went, teaching her to drive had been one of his better inspirations.

"You sure I won't get in trouble driving?" she said.

"Not unless you do something stupid."

Actually, she could do 120 down Highway 75 with no clothes on and no one would fuck with her. He'd kill them first.

The phone in his back pocket vibrated. He pulled it out to find Ian's name and number on the home screen. He punched the answer button and stood, pacing out of Brenna's hearing. "Yeah."

Ian's chuckle rumbled through the connection before his voice did. "Well, aren't you a chipper fella."

"More like a man who's short on patience."

"With Brenna? She's one of the most easygoing people I've met, and I've met more than my share."

"Not her. Just trying to keep her occupied while she waits. My ideas aren't always the best."

"What?" Ian said. "Cage matches and warfare aren't her cup of tea?"

Praise the Great One, that shit got old. If they knew why he fought and sparred as much as he did they wouldn't give him such a hard time. "You gonna talk my ear off or tell me what you know?"

Ian paused at that. He might be a slash or two past middle age, but he didn't intimidate easily. No, that pause said his cop instincts had whirred into gear, and he was gearing up for an armchair psych evaluation. "I found her mom."

Thank the Creator. "Tell me what you've got."

Less than five minutes later, he tossed the remnants of his custard and stalked back to Brenna, still taking her sweet time licking toward the cone and looking damned good doing it. He sat beside her and planted his elbows on his knees, his head cocked sideways so he could catch her expressions. "Ian found your mom."

A firecracker couldn't have gained her attention faster.

She shot to her feet and nearly fumbled the keys to the Hummer. "Where? Can we go now?"

He coiled his fingers around her wrist, took the keys, and stuffed them in his pocket. With a gentle tug, he pulled her back down beside him. "Here's the deal. Your mom's definitely in Orlando. She's got a minimum wage job at a hobby store but spends most of her time volunteering. The real problem for us is getting there."

"Is it far?"

Damn it all, he'd stepped right into that one. The last two days, he'd tried to couch things in a way she could slowly build her confidence. Now here he was lobbing a curveball at her. "About sixteen hours by car."

"Oh." She said it matter of factly, but the disappointment came through loud and clear.

"You've got no identity," he said. "Not without you coming out of the woodwork after a long disappearance, and I don't think you want, or need, that kind of attention. Ian's getting you a bogus ID, but until then, you can't fly commercial. Me flying you there isn't an option." Not if he wanted to have any energy left. Even rationing his powers the way he'd been since they got here, he'd be lucky if they lasted three weeks.

"So what other options do we have?"

"It's either a trip via portal," which was another power suck he didn't want to give up, "or we road trip."

"Road trip?"

He jerked his head toward the Hummer in the parking lot. "The scenic route. Sixteen hours of sightseeing. That work for you?"

For a moment, sadness overtook her features. Then her gaze slid to his pocket, and a shy grin slipped into place. "Can I drive some of the way?"

Man, she was amazing. Kicked and punched over and

over by life, but she still found goodness where she could. "Absolutely."

He stood and offered his hand.

With not an ounce of the trepidation she'd shown that day by the ocean, she laid her palm against his and strolled beside him to the Hummer. Her gaze slipped across the crowd. From the time he'd spent with her, there wasn't a doubt in his mind she'd catalogued twice the details most people would see. Nuances too many people took for granted.

Her attention snagged on something to his right, and she trailed to a stop.

Ludan twisted for a better look.

A young couple stood beside the custard stand, the woman with her back to the brick wall and the man in front of her, leaning in close. He'd propped one hand against the wall beside her, but between the way he'd angled his torso and the girl's answering shy smile, it didn't take a genius to know a clinch was imminent.

The thought had no sooner drifted through Ludan's head than the man cupped the back of his girl's neck and lowered his head, sealing his lips against hers.

Brenna held stock-still, her lips slightly parted and her eyes rounded in a rapt wonder. If she had any inkling as to the rest of the world's existence, she didn't show it. In that moment, she seemed lost in the couple's affection, as though their emotion had swept out, yanked her into its orbit, and cemented her in place.

Praise the Great One, he wanted to touch her. To feel her soft skin beneath his palms and fit his lips against hers. To see if she kissed with the same abandonment she offered every other task.

One of the toddlers behind them shrieked.

Brenna jolted from her trance and scanned the patio as

though gauging where she was.

He gently squeezed her hand. "You okay?"

"Yeah, sorry." Smoothing her hand across her heart, she hustled toward the truck. She didn't even try to talk him into letting her drive. Just climbed up into the passenger seat and clicked her seatbelt into place.

The trip to Eryx's apartment took all of fifteen minutes. Brenna stared out the passenger window the whole time, one elbow anchored on the door ledge with her fingers curled loosely in front of her mouth. Every now and then, she'd drag a fingertip back and forth across her lower lip.

He pulled the Hummer into its reserved spot in the underground garage and shifted into park.

The second the locks disengaged, Brenna popped back to reality, opened her door, and jumped to the ground. The whole damned thing was weird. He'd seen her draw into herself like this a ton of times since she'd first awakened at the castle, but never since they'd arrived in Evad. At least not to the point where she excluded him.

They rode the elevator in silence, and a cold, painful discomfort thrust behind his sternum. More than anything, he wanted to pull her against him. At least hold her hand or hear her voice. He flipped the apartment lock with his mind and opened the door with a mental push. Before Brenna could cross the threshold, he caught her by the wrist and held her in place. "What's wrong?"

She blinked over and over as though waking from a dream. "Nothing's wrong." Her gaze drifted to where his fingers coiled around her wrist. "I was just thinking." She gently tugged against his hold.

Heeding his barely audible voice of reason, he let her go.

The beast rattled its cage and stomped an angry tirade, not at all tolerant with watching her walk away.

Ludan shut the door behind him and tossed his keys to

the entry table. There had to be something he could say, something he could do to get her to talk. How could he fix what was wrong if she wouldn't share what she was thinking?

She padded to the walled window overlooking downtown and stared out at the bright lights. The early evening glow radiated soft against her pretty face and accented her sad smile.

Maybe he should reach out to Lexi and ask her what to do. Then again, knowing Lexi, she'd show up at the front door inside of five minutes. The last thing he wanted was anyone between him and Brenna.

He ambled to the light switches.

Brenna's quiet voice drifted across the room before he could flip the first one. "What's it like?"

He bypassed the lights and prowled closer. "What's what like?"

Even when he stood right beside her, she wouldn't look up, but her eyes were clear in the window's reflection, bright and burning with something that flipped all kinds of dangerous triggers. Her voice came out scratchy. Little more than a whisper. "To be kissed."

Three little words, but they almost flattened him. If his heart didn't calm the hell down he wouldn't live long enough to think of an answer, let alone speak it. His lungs, on the other hand, had stopped functioning. He rubbed his jaw and waited for his mind to give him something, anything to work with.

Give her the truth.

The thought punched through his stymied state, as clear as someone standing beside him.

He knocked the idea aside as fast as it had come to him. She'd think he was an idiot if he told her the truth. Still, she'd bared her demons with him. Was he such a coward he couldn't do the same?

He inched closer so they were side by side. "I don't know if I'm the best judge."

Her gaze shifted, watching him in the reflection. "You don't like it?"

He huffed out a half laugh and shook his head. "I like it. I just haven't done much of it."

She gave up the view entirely and faced him. "Why not?"

Now there was a topic he wasn't broaching. "I just haven't."

She pulled her lower lip between her teeth and waited.

God, he wished she wouldn't do that. Granted he hadn't done much kissing, but that didn't mean he didn't think about it. A lot. Most of it in the last few months with her in a starring role. He stuffed his hands in his pocket and pretended indifference.

"Would you..." She clasped her hands in front of her, digging the thumb of one hand into the palm of the other. "Would you consider kissing me?"

Fuck.

His whole damned world pulled a Tilt-a-Whirl, and every muscle went I-beam rigid. He couldn't have heard her right. It had to be his head playing tricks with him. Too much time out of Eden or something.

She ducked her head. "I'm sorry. I shouldn't have said that." Tucking her hair behind one ear, she shook her head and turned toward the bedrooms. "It was a silly idea. I just wondered—"

His hand whipped out and stopped her with a clench on her shoulder before his conscience could get a word in edgewise.

"It wasn't stupid." He moved in close, needing the proximity more than he needed air. Maybe giving her the truth wasn't such a bad idea. At least then she wouldn't think it had anything negative to do with her. He cupped the back of her neck, and her silky hair brushed his knuckles. "Kissing is hard for me."

She cocked her head, fully engaged and eager for his answer.

He swallowed around the monster lump in his throat and wished like histus he had a fresh beer handy. Or a shot of strasse. "It's intimate, and I don't do that well. Not with the noise."

"What noise?"

With her closeness and the physical contact, the chatter wasn't there, but an entirely different buzz blazed between his ears. "You know all Myrens have unique gifts?"

Curling one hand around his wrist at her neck, she nodded.

"Do you know mine?"

"You read memories."

"No, I consume them. Rapidly."

Her eyebrows lifted. "And?"

He was out of his mind sharing this. If she ever let it slip to Eryx, or anyone else, they'd never reach out when they needed him again. "Once I have them, I hear them. All the time. Good memories, bad memories, it doesn't matter. They're always there. And they're loud."

She frowned, and her grip on his wrist tightened.

"Kissing is intimate," he said. "It's hard to be in the moment with all the voices in my head. So I haven't done much. I'm not sure I'd be any good at it."

"The voices never stop?"

The thumb he hadn't even been aware he'd been stroking along her hairline stopped. For all the battles he'd been in, never once had his hands shook the way they did now.

Truth. She deserved it, especially with the gift her presence brought him. But what if she took it the wrong way? He tightened his hold and pulled her closer. "Not until a few days ago."

Her muscles tightened beneath his hand, and she braced both palms on his chest.

"I knew you were different the first day I saw you," he said. "You were unconscious, and Ramsay had you in his arms. We were about to fly back to the castle. When I got close to you the noise got quieter. Not completely gone, but bearable."

"That's why you acted funny around me."

He dipped his head. "I wasn't sure what to do about it. What it meant. And then the other day by the ocean, when I caught you, they stopped."

"They're gone for good?"

"No." The Great One be praised, he couldn't read her. Couldn't gauge if she was pissed, happy, or disaffected. "They're only completely gone when I touch you."

Her fingertips pressed deeper against his chest, and her voice rasped low in her throat. "Like now."

"Yeah, like now."

Quiet snapped between them, the energy more charged than the Eden skies at night.

The reflection of lights from downtown shimmered in her dark eyes, and her pretty pink lips parted. "Is that why you came here with me? For the quiet?"

"No." He might not have been willing to admit it before, but the second the answer came out, he knew it was true. "I came because it was you. Because something told me to."

Her breath came faster, warm and buffeting softly against his T-shirt. She dipped her head just a fraction, still holding his stare, and licked her lower lip. "So we could both have a first."

His conscience urged him to step away. The beast fisted

the bars on its cage and strained for release. Her scent wrapped around him. That sweet, innocent hint of vanilla that made him think of home and simple, peaceful days, soothing him the way it always did.

"You deserve someone better for your first." He'd probably kill anyone who tried, but it was his last-ditch effort at giving her an out.

She lifted one hand and smoothed her fingertips across his lips. Soft. A butterfly touch that fired lightning bolts straight to his dick.

His lips parted on instinct, tasting her skin with a quick flick of his tongue.

Brenna gasped and jerked her hand away, but only by a few inches. As fast as she flinched, her pupils dilated, leaving almost nothing but black. Her eyelids grew heavy, and her demeanor shifted, the shy, tentative girl shrinking beneath a curious, hungry woman. It was beautiful. The most perfect thing he'd ever seen in his life.

Her gaze roamed his face, and she trailed her closely-trimmed nails through the scruff along his jaw. "I don't want anyone else for my first." Her gaze locked on to his, and her hand curled around the side of his neck. "I want you."

Reality and common sense clicked off. With three simple words she'd shorted out all thoughts save those necessary to please her. All that was left was touch, sensation, and an all-consuming need to taste her.

He exhaled slow and shaky, fear and desire spiking his adrenaline higher than any battle. It was just a kiss. Something people did all the time. Surely he could do her first one justice.

He cupped the sides of her face and inwardly cursed the subtle shake of his big paws. Lowering his head, he focused on her perfect pink lips, pale with a subtle shimmer where she'd licked the bottom one. He wanted his tongue there, to savor the plump surface and feel her lips part.

"The truth?" He closed his eyes and slid his nose against hers, only a fine blade of air and crackling tension separating their mouths. "I want you, too."

He sealed his lips against hers before she could respond, capturing her sweet, broken sigh in a light, teasing contact. He licked the seam, urging her to open, and groaned at her perfect taste. Remnants of ice cream and an essence uniquely hers.

Hesitantly, she opened for him, her tentative tongue meeting his and growing bolder with each decadent stroke. The world dropped farther and farther away. Nothing mattered beyond them. Beyond her and the silky, passionate glide of her lips against his. Too many nights he'd imagined a moment like this, but not one fantasy matched reality.

As if she sensed his thoughts, a tiny whimper slipped past her lips, and she urged him closer. Her soft whisper brushed across his kiss-slackened lips and kicked his pulse to a whole new level. "Ludan."

A growl slipped free, and he held her steady as he deepened his kiss. He needed more. To feel her skin beneath his palm. To watch her respond to his touch. He pinned her hip with his other hand instead. Better that than to risk too much and jar her from the moment.

He surrendered her lips and sampled the smooth stretch along her jaw. She angled her head so the vulnerable line of her neck was exposed.

He took full advantage, teasing the sweet spot behind her ear and nipping the tip of her earlobe.

A sensual moan rumbled free, and she arched against him, gripping his shoulders and pressing her full breasts against his chest.

He snapped, pulling her to him with a firm hand at her

ass and pressing his hips into hers. His aching cock pressed against her soft, welcoming belly, and the animal in him roared.

Brenna locked up, her body going ruler straight.

Loosening his hold, he eased away. The frigid terror stamped across her features nearly cut him in half. "I'm sorry."

Bit by bit, her tension eased, but she took two steps back, breaking contact. "No, it's okay. I…" She looked away, one hand pressed above her heart. "I'm fine. I just…" She met his eyes and blushed a deep red. "I should go."

She spun and was halfway down the hall before his mind pried itself from its kiss-stung stupor. How could he be so stupid? He, of all people, should have understood what she'd been through. Should have been gentler. Instead he'd mauled her like the fucking brute he was.

Her bedroom door clicked shut. Such a small sound, but it rang more ominous than any sound from the castle dungeons.

Beyond the glass wall, the downtown skyline shimmered with its pretty lights and deep night skies. One chance. He'd had one chance to give her something good. To give them both something good, and he'd screwed it up.

A mournful, devastating wail rang out from somewhere deep and dark. A memory. The beast. A shout from the world outside, or his soul. He couldn't tell which one it was. Only knew that watching her walk away shredded him from the inside out. Whatever he'd done wrong, he'd fix. The bond they'd built was too good to let it be ruined by greed on his part.

Yeah, he'd fix it. Then he'd make sure he never crossed that line again.

CHAPTER 14

*D*ressed and out of excuses to face the morning, Brenna sucked in a deep breath and opened the master bedroom door. She padded down the hallway, her loose cotton skirt and matching tank top ten times more comfortable than Lexi's jeans and a whole lot more attractive. She'd need it today. That and anything else to help her face Ludan given the humiliating way she'd bailed on him.

Early morning sun slanted through the living room windows, buffered only by thin ivory shades lowered nearly to the floor. The apartment was silent, but Ludan was definitely up. He might not make a peep when he moved, but the scent of freshly brewed coffee wasn't something he could hide.

Sure enough, she found him perched on a kitchen stool with his back to the entrance, his elbow propped on the gray granite countertop and his forehead resting on his hand.

The heel of her sandal barely clipped the hand-carved ebony floors before he snapped upright and faced her. "Hey."

Like always, his deep voice sent delicious tremors through her, but there was an edge to it today. She'd have labeled it fear, but that couldn't be right. She'd never seen Ludan afraid of anything in the months she'd known him.

She tucked her hair behind her ear and tried to smile. "Morning." She puttered to the coffeepot and tried to still the three-ring circus flipping through her stomach. "Can I fix you something to eat?"

"I thought we'd grab something on the way out of town. No point in you cooking before a road trip."

She reached for a coffee mug.

"We might want to get you decent coffee somewhere else, too."

Pausing with the mug halfway from the shelf, she peered at him over one shoulder.

Ludan shrugged and nudged his cup an inch away from him. "I screwed it up pretty bad. I thought if I added more coffee than normal it might get closer to Orla's. It didn't work."

She put the mug back in its place, shut the cabinet door, and sidled to the counter.

Crescent shadows marred the space beneath his eyes, and while he always scowled a little, today he seemed a little sad. "Didn't you sleep?"

He studied the countertop, then perked up and slid off the stool, heading for the built-in escritoire at the back of the kitchen. "I gassed up the Hummer already. I grabbed you these while I was out." He snatched a small brown bag and handed it over, still not quite meeting her eyes.

She uncoiled the wrinkled top and couldn't help but giggle. "It's gum." She scooped out a handful, everything from individual Double Bubble to packaged Bubbalicious filling her palm.

For the first time since she'd entered the kitchen, he really looked at her, and a shy smile crooked one corner of his mouth. "You said you wanted some."

"I did?"

"Yesterday. Right after we left the mall you said you remembered always having a stash when you were little." He stuffed his hands in his pockets. "So I got you some."

Of course he had. It was his way, quietly catching even her tiniest interests and handling them with infinite care. The same way he had last night before she'd gone and blown it. She dropped the handful of gum into the bag and folded the top shut. "Thank you."

He did one of those manly chin lifts and pulled one hand free of his pocket. The Hummer's keychain dangled from his fingers. "The Hummer's all packed up with snacks and stuff for the trip. I got a little suitcase for you, too. I'll get it so you can pack up your stuff." He spun for the living room.

"Ludan, wait."

He stopped and faced her, but his posture said he'd rather do anything except stand still.

She shuffled closer and swiped one sweaty palm against her hip. "I need to apologize."

"No." He shook his head and braced. "You don't. I shouldn't have let things go so far. That was on me, not you. But you don't have to worry. It won't happen again. I promise."

A painful jolt lanced through her, nearly knocking her back a step. She wasn't sure what was worse, him thinking he'd done something wrong, or his vow to never repeat it. She gripped his forearm. "I didn't run because of anything you did."

He glanced at her hand on his arm, then slid his gaze to her.

Heat spread up her neck and across her cheeks. Despite what she needed to admit, her tongue seemed frozen. She dropped her hand and took a step back. "I didn't know what to do."

For the longest time, he just stared at her, motionless without so much as a hint as to what was going on behind his blue eyes. It was probably for the better. She already felt like a complete moron for the way she'd acted. Him laughing at her would only make it worse.

His rough fingers captured her chin. "There's no reaction you could ever give me that's wrong. If it's the truth, then it's all I need." He pulled her against him, wrapping her tight in his strong arms and pressing the side of her face against his chest.

God, she loved the feel of him. The strength and care he gave with every touch. Even his scent wielded a certain power, buffeting her emotions until she felt she could endure anything or anyone.

"I thought I'd made you relive the past." He smoothed his hand along her back. "I don't want to make you remember what you've been through. Ever."

She lifted her head enough to make eye contact. "You don't make me think about the past. You make me believe I can have a future."

CHAPTER 15

*B*renna fiddled with the Hummer's air-conditioning vent, sighed, and plunked back against her seat. The way Ludan had described a road trip it had sounded fun, but reality was another matter entirely. Eight hours they'd been on the road, and all she could claim from the experience was a stiff back and a queasy stomach. She leaned her head against the headrest and stared out the passenger window.

Knee-high grass bobbed in the wind alongside the highway. Not the bold, beautiful colors from Eden, but a pale sage color that looked sick in comparison. Even the sky seemed a little off, closer to gray instead of blue. Smog, Ludan had called it, which probably explained the smell.

In the distance, a cityscape peeked across the horizon. The buildings rose and fell at different heights, but with their deep gray color, they barely stood out against the skyline.

"It's not as pretty as I remembered it." The confession burned a little as it came out, but she was tired of keeping it in. "Eden's colors are prettier. And it's quieter. It feels funny here. Even when we drove through the countryside, the earth felt antsy or something."

Ludan scanned the open field beyond her. "Sometimes the things you don't want are the things you end up missing." His gaze slid to her, and he assessed her features. "Or wanting."

A pleasant tremor rippled low in her belly, and all thoughts of scenery and distant realms fizzled.

As if uncomfortable with what he'd said, he shook his head, reached toward the radio, and punched the buttons. "We're coming up on Mobile. We'll stop there for today and make the rest of the trip tomorrow."

Thank the Great One. She'd give a lot to stretch her legs. "What state are we in again?"

"Alabama." He paused on a news channel and upped the volume. "I'll see if we can get a hotel somewhere close to the bay so you can get a change in scenery."

He'd barely lowered his hand from the controls before the announcer shifted to a new story.

"New developments have surfaced in the ongoing reports of people around the world being taken to a mysterious place referred to as Eden."

Ludan shifted in his seat, planted his elbow on the center console, and clenched his fist.

"Three new individuals have come forward stating they, too, were spirited to this magical place, but also proclaimed their source promised upcoming developments that will greatly impact the human race. Government officials, already sorting through reports with past visitors, have begun interviews with the newest travelers, and report they've as yet been unable to prove their claims a hoax. Special task forces have been engaged to ascertain the powers behind those from this mysterious land and to gauge what, if any, risk they might pose."

Brenna clicked it off before the man could say any more. "Is it Serena?"

"Has to be."

The engine's steady growl filled the quiet, and Ludan scowled out the windshield. She knew Eryx checked in with Ludan daily, but he'd never passed the details on to her. She'd thought that was a good thing, but maybe that was the coward's way out.

"Eryx still doesn't have any leads on where she is?" she said. "I thought she couldn't move around without her family knowing."

"The link is dead. The family claims Serena's link went from barely discernible to completely gone right about the time we left."

"Maxis told me links were unbreakable."

"Eryx and I broke Reese's link to Maxis, but no one else knows how. At least not that we know of."

That explained why he never let her leave the apartment without him. Even when she'd wanted to run to the little bakery across from Eryx's apartment the second day they were in Dallas, he'd insisted on going with her. "You think she's free."

The frown on Ludan's face lifted, and his expression softened. "I won't let anyone hurt you."

He wouldn't, at least not if it was within his power to stop. But as powerful and strong as he was, he was still human. Okay, maybe not human, but fallible.

She covered his fist with her hand and squeezed. "You can't be everywhere all the time, but I'm glad you're here with me. That's enough."

Half an hour later, Ludan parked the Hummer outside a hotel that looked like it belonged in the mountains. Huge trees with low, gnarled branches spanned heavily manicured grass on either side of the entrance. Down the road, a quaint marina stretched along the bay with smaller sailboats and powered vessels bobbing in a long line of slips. The water was flat as glass, and the setting sun rippled burnt-orange on the reflection. Not as pretty as Eden's, but nicer than anything she'd seen so far.

They strolled inside, Ludan's hand a comforting presence low on her back. Funny how she'd grown so accustomed to his touch, craving it when it wasn't there.

The clerk looked up from her computer and smiled at them both. "Welcome to the Grand Resort and Spa. How can I help you?"

Brenna ambled through the lobby while Ludan checked them in. The large octagonal space strengthened the lodge décor with rough, honey-stained wood and cozy sitting areas upholstered in gold and evergreen. At its center, a huge fireplace finished in dark chocolate rocks reached to the high vaulted ceiling.

She'd barely made one circuit when Ludan turned, picked up their bags, and strode toward her. He scanned their surroundings with shrewd eyes. Pointing to the elevators at the back of the room, he guided her forward with a protective grip on her arm. "We're on the top floor. I had two choices, a king-size bed with a view of the bay, or two doubles overlooking the parking lot." He punched the up button.

One of the three elevators dinged and whisked open.

To heck with a view. The thought of sleeping with Ludan, even if he got nowhere near her, fired the equivalent of ten oven fires in her stomach. "Which one did you choose?"

The doors slid closed, leaving their reflection in the chrome finish.

His thumb shuttled against her bare skin, and in that second she made a silent vow to always wear tank tops so she wouldn't ever miss such perfect contact. "You need to see something pretty. I don't sleep that much anyway. If I get tired, I can crash on the floor."

They reached their floor before she could argue. He hustled them down the hallway, his booted footsteps muted by the thick hunter-green carpet. Taking what looked like one of his credit cards out of his back pocket, he swiped it through a little slot on the door.

"What's that?"

He pushed the door and held it open. "A key card. It's based on electronics more than a key mechanism. I could monkey with it mentally, but the old-fashioned way is faster."

The carpets inside were nicer than the hallways, a pretty pattern of forest green and russet with ivy woven into the design. The room was bright and light, and sage walls and ivory curtains opened to a pretty view of the bay beyond. A big bed graced the center with an ivory headboard, crisp white sheets, and a pretty teal accent throw near the foot.

Ludan stalked to the window and slid it open. A black rocking chair with homey cushions was angled into one corner of the balcony, and a small iron loveseat anchored the other. He ignored those and gripped the wrought-iron railing, gauging the grounds below.

She waited until he finished his walk-through, then dug in with her questions. "When you say you don't sleep much, is that because of the voices?"

He paused mid digging through his duffle, then shrugged and started up again. "Yeah."

No wonder he was moody. Given the same circumstances, she wasn't sure if she'd have stayed sane. She bypassed the suitcase he'd left for her on the foot of the bed and stilled his rummaging with a grip on his forearm. "Then doesn't it make sense for you to sleep in the bed?"

His muscles beneath her palm went rigid, and the twitch at the back of his jaw kicked into high gear.

God, had she screwed things up between them so badly? "I'm not asking you for anything. I'm offering you a little peace. You said it's better when I'm close. You don't have to touch me if you don't want to, just let me give you this. Something valuable after everything you've given me."

Before she could blink, he'd freed his arm and gripped her by both shoulders. "Everything about you is valuable. Don't underestimate what being with you has meant for me." He dropped his hold on her. If she read the surprise on his face right, his little outburst wasn't something he'd planned on confessing.

"I wasn't devaluing myself. I was offering someone I care about something they need." She unzipped her bag. "It's just sleeping. You're the one making more out of it than it needs to be."

The next ten minutes passed in silence, Brenna unpacking what little they'd bought for her so far and Ludan scowling out the window with one hand braced on the wall. He shoved away from his brooding so fast she nearly jumped. "I'm going to check out the restaurants. Maybe see if I can find some food you can tolerate."

So, he'd noticed that. She really shouldn't be surprised. He noticed everything. Taking her brush and pajamas with her, she headed to the bathroom. "Don't worry about it. I've got to get used to it eventually, right? Besides, after all that time in the truck, all I want is a bath and to stretch out in bed."

Shutting the door behind her, she rested her forehead against it and let out a shaky breath. What a crock of crap. Brenna had heard that expression a hundred times from Lexi since she'd arrived at the castle, and now she really understood what it meant. A bath and a bed to stretch out in indeed. What she really wanted was to curl up next to Ludan and forget about everything for a good long while. No

Serena. No rebellion. None of her past and no disappointing future. Just Ludan, his strong arms around her, and a quiet night with a pretty view.

Only when she heard the hotel door open and click shut did she jump in the bath, zipping through her routine faster than she'd intimated. In no time, she'd donned the pink cotton nightshirt she'd pilfered from Lexi's stash and slipped beneath the covers. She plucked the TV remote from the bedside counter.

She still couldn't get over all the channels there were to choose from. Foreign languages, stations just for men, and others just for women. Channels with nothing but reality shows or music, and broadcasts about nothing but food. The Food Network had captivated her for hours her first night. She'd walked by the skinny black panel mounted on Eryx's wall a dozen times thinking it was horrible art. Eventually, she'd spied the little button on the bottom corner, pushed it, and nearly leapt out of her skin when it flickered to life.

She punched the up button on the remote, and a news channel popped up, one with an anchor positioned on the right of the screen and a smaller box showing video on the left. At the bottom was the graphic, *Is It Real? Or a Hoax?*

Excellent. More Eden. She'd kept the volume low, worried that the people in the other rooms might be disturbed by the sound, but it was still high enough to hear the cheering from the spectators in the top left box. They danced around with signs that said, *Take me!* and, *I'm ready to go home!*

Every damned one of them were certified idiots. If they had any inkling just how powerful Myrens were and how they could completely upend their powerless lives, they'd run and hide. Maybe that was why she was the judge. Maybe her whole purpose was to keep the wall up and protect her race.

Too angry to tolerate any more of their nonsense, she clicked to the next channel.

Slow, sultry music pulsed through the speakers, and a shadowed image filled the screen. A woman and a man, both naked, but beautifully so. The camera switched to a shot of their hands, the man's fingers intertwined with the woman's and squeezing tight. A low, broken moan blended with the music, one filled with passion and pain.

She clicked another channel and tossed the remote to the bed. Her heart galloped as though she'd sprinted a mile from a dead standstill, and she couldn't convince her lungs to function properly. She swallowed and tried to process what she'd seen. It wasn't cheap or gaudy. Quite the contrary. It was beautiful. Intimate.

The remote sat where she'd tossed it, stark black against the vivid white sheets.

She could turn it back. Hadn't she wanted to know what something decent looked like? To know what normal looked like? No one would know but her.

She snatched the remote and leaned back against the headboard. Her fingers shook as she pushed the up arrow.

Music filled the room as it had before, this time stronger and more potent in its rhythm. The man trailed his lips along the woman's neck and she arched for him, giving him better access. Lower and lower he kissed, licking the space below her belly button before the camera shifted to show the woman's response.

She knew that look. It was exactly how she'd felt when Ludan had kissed her, needing so much more but not having a clue how to get it. Brenna's fingers tightened on the remote, so much so the plastic groaned beneath her grip. She soaked it all in, letting the actors' passion ratchet hers along with theirs. So what if it wasn't real. It was twenty times better than what she'd experienced by Maxis's hands and gave her hope for what could be.

A click sounded from the entrance, and the doorknob turned.

Brenna pried her tight fingers from the remote and almost fumbled it trying to change the channel.

Ludan ambled in carrying a huge tray loaded down with plates and bags. He paused at the foot of the bed. "You okay?"

Her cheeks burned. "I'm fine." At least it hadn't been a whisper. A little on the husky side, but she could chalk it up to being tired.

Ludan glanced at the TV, then stalked to the table in the corner of the room. "You sure you're okay?"

Slowly, she peeled the covers back and glided to the table. The space between her legs felt funny. Wet and achy, but also very nice. "I promise. I'm better than I've been in a long time."

CHAPTER 16

*W*armth and a soft tickle skated along Brenna's jawline. Lips, the same full, delicious ones she'd craved since Ludan had kissed her, the scruff of his beard leaving the same unforgettable impact as his mouth. His wavy hair slid through her fingers, a weighted silk that teased her forearms. He slanted his mouth across hers and licked inside.

Perfect. The slide of his tongue, his taste, the way he groaned into the kiss and sent perfect trills coursing down her spine. Nothing on earth was better.

He lifted his head. His ice-blue eyes glowed with need and so much passion it resonated in her soul. "This is what you want."

Odd. It was Ludan's voice, but her own was superimposed with it. And it wasn't a question, but a statement.

Candles surrounded them, and a scarlet satin comforter stretched beneath them.

Not real.

"This is what you want," Ludan said again, ghosting his

knuckles along her collarbone and slipping his fingers beneath the neckline of her nightshirt.

Her heart leapt at the touch, his caress only hinting in the direction of her breast, but drawing her nipples to hard points. "Yes."

He smiled and lowered his gaze, a long lock of hair falling over his forehead. "So beautiful."

Cool air assaulted her flesh, sending goose bumps along her torso. Her nightshirt was gone, whisked away by her dreams.

Inch by inch, he trailed his fingertips down her sternum, his expression so reverent and caring she was afraid to move.

He cupped one breast, and she arched into the contact, too overwhelmed with the sensation to do anything but close her eyes and surrender to its magic. She tightened her grip on the back of his head, urging him closer. "Ludan, please." She didn't know what it was she needed, only that she did, and badly.

"Shhh." He dipped his head and smoothed his lips along the path his fingers had taken.

More.

Over and over, the word echoed through her head. Nothing else mattered except the feel of him against her. His weight, the warmth of his skin, and the safety of his arms. She closed her eyes and splayed her hands across his wide shoulders. So much strength. Power as rigidly contained as the man. "Ludan."

One of his big hands cupped her shoulders, and his lips disappeared.

She squeezed her eyes and willed them back. "Ludan, please."

He spoke again, but this time it was different. Farther away and muffled. "Brenna."

No.

She rolled her head back and forth on the pillow. No, no, no. She couldn't lose him. Not again. She hadn't done anything wrong this time. Had she?

The hand at her shoulder tightened. "Brenna, wake up."

Heat registered beside her. Not the kind from her dream, but real. Tangible, deliciously masculine heat and muscle.

Her eyes snapped open.

Ludan lay propped on one elbow beside her, the other hand holding her shoulder as she'd felt in her dream. In the daylight, his form was intimidating, but in the night's shadows, he was downright scary. "You okay?"

Not really. Sweat misted her skin, and her heart jackrabbited in an out-of-control rhythm. The covers were too heavy, pressing against her tight breasts. She shifted her legs and nearly moaned at the throbbing pulse between them. "I'm fine."

The comment earned her a sharp frown. He relinquished his hold and leaned back far enough that the bay's moonlight brought him out of shadow. At some point after she'd fallen asleep, he'd removed his T-shirt, leaving his perfect body on prime display. "You didn't sound fine."

She pushed upright and leaned against the headboard, careful to hide her aching nipples with the sheet. Looking at him only made the ache worse. In that moment, she'd give a lot to let her fingers have free rein. "It was just a dream," she whispered.

He stared at her, then lowered his gaze to her clenched fists in the sheets. "You're afraid."

"No." It came out too fast, and his eyes snapped to hers. "I mean, it was an intense dream, but not something I'm afraid of."

An odd look flittered across his face, caution or suspicion. "Tell me."

This is what you want.

Clearly, her subconscious wasn't in the mood to mess around. And while she'd happily go there in dreams every night, she wasn't so sure Ludan would appreciate the concept of them together as much as she did. Especially after what had happened last time.

"I..." What could she say? "I'm not sure it's something you'd want to hear. It was personal."

His eyes narrowed. "Personal, as in..."

"Personal." She pulled her knees up and wrapped her arms around them. "It was about the two of us."

His head snapped back, and his breathing accelerated. He clenched the sheet at his waist, and his nostrils flared. "What about us?"

A strange yet not unpleasant sensation swirled low in her belly, and the pulse between her legs ramped to blistering demand. She could keep the dream to herself. Never say a thing and let it slide.

Or she could take a chance.

She licked her lower lip. "We were intimate."

His gaze dropped to her mouth, and a low, animalistic growl rumbled from his chest.

It should have terrified her. Made her scramble far away or run for the door. She reached for him instead.

He knifed out of bed and snatched his jeans off the floor. "It's my fault. I should have given you distance. I gave you my word."

She needed to stop him. To say something, anything, to keep him from storming away, but her tongue wouldn't work. Couldn't, considering the sight in front of her. Muscles, head to toe. Not the overdone weightlifter kind she'd seen on convenience store magazine covers her first day in Evad, but solid, strapping bulk.

And not one stitch of clothing to block his glorious form.

"I liked it." The confession slipped out as breathy as the moans from her dreams.

He hiked the denim over his perfect ass and twisted enough that the dim lights accented the cut V at his hips. "Come again?"

Her eyes took their sweet time trailing up his torso, committing every inch to memory before she locked onto his stare. "I said, I liked it."

The twitch at the back of his jaw kicked fast and furious. He finished buttoning up his jeans. "You can't."

"Why can't I?"

He spun so fast she gasped and whacked her head on the headboard. He held his hands out to his sides as though begging for a punch. "For fuck's sake, Brenna, look at me. Take a good hard look at me."

Oh, she was looking. And while seeing the back of him completely bare had loosened her jaw, the front scrambled her wits. Especially the fierce erection straining behind his faded denim. He might say he didn't want her, but his body said otherwise.

"Maxis hurt you," he said. "Did things no person, Myren or human, should ever inflict on another. I could snap him like a damned twig. Make anyone bleed and scream for hours if I needed to and wouldn't lose a minute's sleep."

"You wouldn't hurt me."

"You can't know that." He planted a hand at one hip and fisted his hair at the top of his head with the other, his eyes trained on the floor. "I tried, remember? I barely let go, just for a second, and you ran. You think I want that? To see someone as sweet and good as you running from me?"

"I told you, I was flustered. It had nothing to do with you."

"And I'm telling you I can't see that again. You've already hurt too much. I don't want to be the one who hurts you

150

more." He frowned, turned on his heel, and stomped into the bathroom, slamming it shut behind him.

He thought she was sweet. And good. Not dirty and ruined.

Letting out a slow, cautious breath, she let her eyes slip closed. He wanted her. Ludan Forte wanted *her*. His body wouldn't lie, not in this. And if he thought she'd ever run again, he was very, very wrong. She'd just have to find a chance to prove it.

~

FISTS BRACED against the bathroom door, Ludan hung his head and clenched his jaw, fighting back the frustrated roar clawing up his throat. It was his fault. He'd known better than to sleep beside her. Should never have given in to the lure of real sleep.

And look what it had gotten him. As if he didn't have enough dirty images on his own, now he got to imagine hers, too.

We were intimate.

How in histus could a woman who knew nothing of healthy sex take three simple words and turn them into a plea? His dick had gone from dead to concrete in seconds, more than ready to take her up on the offer.

He pushed away from the door and winced at the unforgivable press of denim against his raging cock. "Fuck." He ripped the button fly open, and his length sprang free, the air-conditioned temperature doing nothing to cool his thoughts. Leaning back against the door, he tried to slow his breath and erase what he'd witnessed while she'd dreamt. Her eyes might have been closed, but her lips had parted, ready for contact. The way her back had arched and pressed those sweet, hard nipples against her nightshirt.

He fisted his shaft, thrusting his hips against his brutal grip. His conscience lashed him for the weakness. The last thing he deserved was release, but damn it, he hurt. No torture could be worse than glimpsing what she'd be like, seeing how responsive she was, and knowing he'd never experience it in reality.

I liked it.

Her words rattled through him, and fantasy took over. Her lips against his skin and across his chest. Down his abdomen and farther until his shaft brushed her mouth.

Faster he stroked, the memory of how she'd savored her ice cream superimposed on his depraved imagination, her delicate pink tongue licking his glans as she lifted heavy eyelids to meet his stare.

A growl slipped free and release ripped through him, his cock jerking and jetting his seed against his sweat-slick skin. He rode the waves, feeling her with him. The soft give of her breasts against his chest, her warm breath against his neck, the slick clasp of her sex around his dick.

He'd never deserve that. Even if he did, he wouldn't trust the beast not to hurt her. She was sweet. Giving and gentle, where all he had to offer were rough edges and dirty thoughts.

He opened his eyes, and the bathroom's cold white tiles shattered what was left of his dim and sultry dream. He was weak, at least where Brenna was concerned. The evidence coated his fist and belly.

Snatching a towel from the rack, he started the shower with a mental push and set the temperature to full cold. No doubt about it. He was the last thing Brenna needed.

CHAPTER 17

*B*renna shifted out of the morning sun and into the shadow cast by Ludan's body. August in Florida didn't seem to faze him in the least, but paired with the humidity, it'd sapped what energy she had the minute she'd slid out of the Hummer to the asphalt parking lot. "You sure we can't watch from in the car?"

Ludan shook his head enough to let her know he'd heard her, but he kept his gaze trained on the second-story apartment. "Not if we want to be able to get a closer look and not tip her off. I can mask us, but not two car doors opening."

Another polite yet distant response. The same type she'd garnered for two days straight. She'd tried everything short of prancing around naked, but nothing broke through.

She shook the frustration off and focused on the door marked with a black fifty-three. According to Ian's latest update, her mother lived behind it. The complex looked more like a hotel than other apartment buildings she'd seen. They'd yet to catch anyone coming or going, and Ludan insisted they get visual confirmation before Brenna approached. "What makes you think she'll show this early on a Sunday?"

"Ian gave me the name of the missing children's group she volunteers for. They've got a booth at the farmers' market this morning."

Over a week she'd been home, one disappointment after another dousing the hopeful embers she'd nursed in her years away. This time things would be different. She felt it to her bones, warm and bright as the sun lifting in the sky. The world around her buzzed a little brighter, and her vision went a little glitchy. She clenched Ludan's bicep to steady herself.

Beneath her palm, his muscles tensed, then slowly released.

Funny, her mother had always scolded her father for being too stubborn. Now here she was poking and prodding a giant who made a brick wall look flexible.

He wanted her. She was certain of it. If the erection she'd glimpsed before he'd stomped into the bathroom didn't prove it, then the low, broken moan she'd heard behind the bathroom door did. Like a junkie, she'd followed him after his tirade and stood on the opposite side of the door with her forehead pressed against it. With every ragged breath and quick movement that reverberated through the thin partition, she'd built her own fantasy. Imagined his corded neck strained and his eyes shut in bliss while his big hand worked his shaft. She'd nearly collapsed when he found his release, the rumble vibrating down her arms and spearing straight between her thighs.

A thunk in the distance ripped her from her thoughts.

Before she could focus, Ludan shifted behind her and cupped her shoulders. His warm breath whispered against her ear. "Quiet. You can see her, but she can't see us."

A woman with dull brown hair cut in a chin-length bob shuffled toward the metal staircase.

Ludan guided them forward, his steps slow and panther silent. They reached the front row of cars as the woman rounded the bottom stair. Glancing down the parking lot, she hefted her big purse higher on her shoulder, and her keys jangled against the quiet. This close, the gray that lined her hair was more prevalent, and deep wrinkles etched her brow and the corners of her eyes, but it was her. Abby Haven.

Brenna jerked forward, ready to rush the rest of the way there. "M—"

Ludan's hand covered her mouth, and he pulled her back against him, holding them both still while her mother stopped and tried to pinpoint where the sound had come from. Only when she'd given up and hustled to a little gray car in one of the reserved spots did he lower his mouth to her ear and loosen his grip. "Not yet. You pop out of thin air and you'll scare her to death. I know where she's going. We'll find her there."

She jerked her head in agreement and tried to calm her adrenaline-overloaded lungs. It didn't work. Watching her mother back out of the parking spot and drive away made it worse. With every second, a suffocating noose wrenched tighter. "You're sure you know where she's going?"

For the first time since he'd woken her from her dreams, he touched her with something more than detached civility. Wrapping a possessive yet comforting hand around the base of her neck, he aimed his confident, beautiful gaze on her. "I'm sure. And even if we can't find her, we know it's her now."

Her mom. Finally, after all this time, she'd have family. Her own flesh and blood. "She looked tired."

"Ian said she's never given up looking." He trailed his

hand down her arm and laced his fingers with hers. "Let's go fix that."

Something light glimmered inside her, a sensation she hadn't felt in so long she'd forgotten it existed.

Joy. Pure, unfiltered delight so light and airy it was a wonder she didn't float off the ground. And Ludan had helped her find it. Had guided and protected her through every moment. "Okay."

What she lacked in words she made up for in quick footsteps, almost running to the truck.

As if sensing her mood, Ludan kept his silence through the twenty-minute drive.

Would her mother cry? Laugh? Maybe get lightheaded? Since the day Maxis had taken her, Brenna had imaged every scenario possible, but now that real life was close to actually happening, her mind was locked in a state of paralysis.

The traffic drew to a near standstill at a big intersection. On the opposite side was a small lake with families crowded along the shoreline tossing food to a swarm of ducks. White, square-top tents dotted a stretch of land, and black mangrove trees filled the space between them.

"Do you think she'll recognize me?" Brenna said.

He covered her fisted hand on the center console and squeezed. "I can't imagine any parent not recognizing their child. Especially one like you."

Just that quick, her worry disengaged, replaced with the steady hum of anticipation. "Thank you."

Ludan didn't answer, but he kept his hand where it was, steering them closer to the market and the ambling crowd ahead.

The second he parked, Brenna yanked the door latch.

Ludan snatched her forearm before she could jump down. "We need to talk first."

Something in his tone put her on alert. Or maybe it was the worry clouding his eyes.

"No matter what you do, you can't share where you've been," he said. "Not who I am, or what you've seen."

"I wouldn't—"

"I know you wouldn't on purpose, but things can slip. Details that might seem normal to you aren't normal here. There's too much focus on Eden and what our race can do. I don't want you on anyone's radar."

Warmth blossomed behind her sternum, and a languid contentment as cozy and soft as a down blanket coiled around her. He cared. More than just as a physical desire, he was looking out for her like he always did. Protecting her the same way he protected the people he loved. "I promise. I won't say a word."

He jerked a tight nod and released her hand. Meeting her in front of the Hummer, he ambled beside her through the slowly moving crowd toward the tents beyond. Couples and families meandered from booth to booth, everything from purple and white orchids, to beer, and fresh produce offered for sale. The soft pecan mulch that lined the shaded space gave a muted crunch with each step.

Ludan paused and gripped her upper arm. "You ready?"

Why? Was she here? Brenna twisted and scanned the packed tables around her.

"Easy." He steadied her with another hand at her shoulder. "Just breathe and focus on me."

Without conscious direction from her brain, her hands found their way to his chest. She splayed her fingers across his tight pectorals and let his heat seep beneath her anxiety.

He pulled her closer, and his strength wrapped around her like a physical shield. "You'll be fine. She'll see you and everything else will just happen." Tucking her hair behind one ear, he crooked a cockeyed smile. "So, let's try again. You ready?"

Absolutely. More than ready. "Yeah."

Stepping to one side, he urged her to the booth behind him. "Then go say hello to your mom."

The woman they'd seen at the apartment stood no more than fifteen feet away. She leaned over a folding table, smiled at a little redheaded girl, and handed a card to the parents who flanked her on either side.

Brenna crept forward.

Abby's light soprano voice tripped across Brenna's senses and sent goose bumps up and down her arms. "We recommend every family have identification cards for their children. It gives first responders all the information they need to get word out on missing children quickly." She pointed to a spot at the bottom of the card. "If you go to our website, we've got an e-identification program, too."

The little girl's father picked up two more of the cards, shook Abby's hand, and waved good-bye.

Brenna's heart lurched, and for a second her brain offered nothing but white noise. "Abigail Haven?"

Her mother twisted, eyebrows high and lips poised for a warm, welcome greeting—and froze.

Stepping closer, Brenna fisted her hands. "You're Abigail Haven, right?"

Her mother's mouth opened, then closed. Then did it again, her lower lip trembling in the process. "Brenna." It came out like a whisper, but Brenna felt it in every inch of her body. "Brenna, baby, is that you?"

The chatter and laughter of people around them faded into nothing, and her cheeks trembled on a smile she felt all the way to her toes. "Yeah, Mom. It's me."

CHAPTER 18

So many voices. Men, women, children, it didn't matter. They all overlapped each other. Some talking, some shouting, but every one of them competing for attention.

Ludan shifted his legs beneath the sheets. His quads and hamstrings protested, a relaxed languor permeating the muscles with a sedated weight he hadn't felt in years. Histus, more like in centuries.

Images flickered in his thoughts, flashes of the dream he'd had fading in an out like a weak radio signal.

But there'd been no noise.

The thought whipped him upright and punched his heart into top gear. He'd actually dreamt. Easy, peaceful dreams with him and Brenna at his father's lake in Eden. One of those sunset perfect, intimate picnic encounters human marketers used to sell everything from teeth whiteners to ED medication.

He dropped back to the down pillow and stared up at the white ceiling. It shouldn't be possible. The only time he remembered such deep sleep and vivid dreams was before he'd learned about his gift.

And the one night he'd dared to sleep beside Brenna.

Vanilla. Just a hint of it scented the air, but it was there. As sweet and innocent as the woman who wore it. He rolled his head and pushed up to an elbow. The pillow beside him had a slight indention. The covers weren't as messy as his side of the bed, but they weren't tidy either.

She'd slept with him.

He pushed his senses through the small but tricked-out apartment he'd rented, stretching his power like a translucent bubble and analyzing every energy source.

Brenna's unique pattern pinged from the kitchen, the same pearl-like ivory most common with humans, but now with shafts of Myren silver and gold woven through it. Remnants of Eryx's healing influence on her life essence.

Pans clattered from the far end of the apartment, followed by the swoosh of running water. He checked the sun's position with his mind. Early, not even six o'clock yet, but she was up, dressed, and based on the scent of bacon and coffee, tackling breakfast.

Not once had he seen her sleep in. Not in all the time she'd been at the castle. Granted, the day she'd planned with her mother gave her an extra incentive to get up and around today, but just once he'd like to see her relax and not feel the need to cook or clean.

He tossed the sheet aside and padded to the adjoining bath. As relaxed as he was, he couldn't decide whether to hug her for the good night's sleep or throttle her for getting so close. She'd been pushing his boundaries a lot lately. As in constantly. No matter how much distance he put between them, she'd close it and find an excuse to touch him. To tempt him. It was like somewhere between leaving Eden and her dream of them together, she'd shifted from castle mouse to honey badger. If shit didn't even out soon, he'd lose his damned mind.

Showered and halfway out of his sleep hangover, he stepped into a fresh set of jeans and snatched a light-blue T-shirt. He had to give her credit. She'd handled the meeting with her mom like a champ, standing strong and holding her mother while Abby sobbed like a teenage girl mid-breakup with her first love. Not once had Brenna slipped and spilled details of Eden. Instead, she'd told her mom her disappearance was in the past and something she'd rather not revisit.

He pulled on his last boot and glared out the window overlooking downtown Orlando. Details or not, Abby knew what her daughter had been through was bad. He'd taken them both to a little downtown diner and kept quiet while the two chattered back and forth. The questions had stayed light, but the second Abby spied Brenna's short, split nails, she'd caught her daughter's hand, ran her fingertips along Brenna's work-roughened palm, and then lifted it to her mouth for a reverent kiss.

Stalking down the hallway, he shook the gut-wrenching scene from his thoughts. It was either that or bloody some innocent bystander to take the edge off. He beelined for the coffeemaker. "You know you don't have to get up and do all this anymore."

Brenna pushed a bacon strip to one side of the skillet, her gaze distant and her smile soft and dreamy.

At least she was happy. She deserved that and so much more. Not many people thought of other people first, but Brenna did, always factoring in the consequences of her actions.

Well, not all consequences. "You slept with me last night."

While she kept her eyes cast downward, her hand froze above the skillet and her fingers tightened on the tongs.

He poured a cup of coffee and waited for an answer.

When she flipped the burner off and scooped the slices onto a plate instead of answering, he pressed further. "You can't do that. I told you I don't want to hurt you. When I'm asleep—"

"Stop it." The simple command barely carried over his deep voice but was strong enough to halt his tongue. Calmly, she lined up the plate of bacon, a bowlful of scrambled eggs, and a side plate of toast in the center on the black granite countertop. She turned and crossed her arms. "Did anyone make you come here?"

The determined glint in her eye nearly made him take a step back. He sipped his coffee instead. "No."

"Did anyone make you follow me the day I fell off the bluff?"

"No."

"Did you sleep?"

He blew across the top of the mug and sent the steam dancing. "That's not the point."

"Actually, it is. Did you?"

He took a sip, then set the mug aside. "Yes."

Brenna straightened, tore two squares from the paper towel spindle, and gathered up the utensils and plates she'd set aside with her breakfast prep. "Well, me giving you that gift was my choice. You can't take that from me. Not you or anyone else." She rounded the counter to take her seat. "And you're welcome."

His cock stirred, and a slow, but vicious burn fired in his gut. Damn, but an attitude looked good on her. Her near-black eyes sparked bright like he'd never seen before. Tempting and unbreakable. As if he needed any more damned fuel for the fire she'd lit. He prowled forward, the beast in him taking control before common sense could debate otherwise.

A heavy knock rapped against the front door.

Brenna jolted on her barstool, checked the digital clock on the microwave, and hopped down, headed for the entrance. "Wow, Mom's early. She said she wouldn't get here until eight."

Ludan caught her by the arm and hauled her back. Brenna might be surprised her mom was early, but he wasn't. He'd practically had to pry the two of them apart the night before, and he'd been the killjoy who wouldn't let her spend the night at her mom's place. No way was he letting her stay anywhere he couldn't easily defend. And until he trusted Abby to keep Brenna's reappearance quiet, her mom wasn't staying here either. "No answering doors. Not for anyone."

"But it's just—"

"No one." He stalked around her, sweeping the landing outside their apartment with his senses.

Two Myrens, both with energy patterns he knew all too well.

He yanked the door open and scowled at Lexi and Eryx. "Kind of early for a visit."

Not waiting for an invitation, Eryx cocked an eyebrow and urged Lexi through what little space Ludan allowed. "Well, I kept thinking my somo would pull his head out of his ass and figure out he needed to recharge if he wanted to keep his woman safe, but it seems you left all your common sense at home."

"Cool it with the 'my woman' shit," Ludan said before the couple could get any deeper in the room.

"Still in denial, huh?"

Wandering into the living room, Brenna eyeballed their unexpected guests. "What does he mean, recharge?"

Ludan opened his mouth to divert the topic.

"He needs to recharge his powers." Lexi strolled through the living room, surveying the place like her color commentary wasn't a huge info bomb. "Myrens can't maintain them longer than a few weeks in Evad. Not enough energy here. It's been ten days."

Brenna pegged him with an accusing glower. "You never told me that."

"I would have handled it." He refocused on Eryx. "It doesn't take a personal visit to harass me. What gives?"

"Just a few updates." Eryx glanced at Lexi. "And to ask for a favor."

"Updates?" Brenna said.

Done with her casual perusal, Lexi eased onto the pretty orange couch that reminded Ludan of Eden sunsets in summer. She folded one leg under the other and propped her heel on the cushion's edge. "Trinity finally got news from the Black King. It took her nine trips to Winrun before he'd even see her. When she got an audience, all he said was we were on our own."

"You're leaving off the suspicious part." Eryx perched on the sofa arm beside Lexi. "He also said no actions had been taken without a balancing sacrifice and that we should heed our individual Spiritu until something changes."

"What the fuck is that supposed to mean?" Ludan said.

Eryx huffed out an ironic laugh. "Exact same thing I said. Given all our other little chats with them, I'm suspicious."

Beside him, Brenna crossed her arms and ran her palms up and down the backs of her arms.

Instinctively, he pulled her in front of him and ran his hands along the same path, pulling her back against his chest. "As allies go, they're pretty useless."

"I don't know. They helped me find Lexi." Eryx's gaze dropped to Ludan's hands anchored on Brenna's shoulders. "Matter of fact, they seem to be working miracles all over the place."

Lexi ducked her head and covered her mouth, but not before Ludan caught her grin.

Eryx didn't bother to hide his, and it was way too smug.

Damn it all. Ludan dropped his hands and stalked to the oversized chair opposite Lexi, sinking onto the thick cushion and fisting his hands on the armrest. "So, what's the favor?"

"We got a ruling from the council," Eryx said. "Full dispensation on Angus's memories. As soon as the verdict came down, Angus got real mouthy, sharing details on Serena and her dearly departed, but I'm not buying it. I want his memories. They've assigned an ellan for the job, but I want you. I need someone I can trust. Someone who'll know what to look for."

"No." Brenna glared at Ludan. "You can't. You know what it does to you."

Shit.

He shook his head only enough to send her the message she was stepping into territory she shouldn't.

"No," she said anyway. "You can't do it. It hurts you."

The room got scary quiet, every gaze rooted on Ludan.

Eryx's was the heaviest. "You want to tell me what she's talking about?"

"It's not important."

"The heck if it isn't." The same confidence Brenna had shown in the kitchen minutes before revved back into top gear, and damn it was hot. If it weren't for the mountainous pile of worms he had to wrestle back in their can, he'd prod her a little more just for the chance to feel her fire.

Lexi cut into their heated starefest. "Actually, you going with Eryx could be a good thing. You can go to Eden for a recharge, and Brenna and I can do some girl time. Shopping, nails, movies. You know, spend money and chitchat."

"No," Ludan said. "She needs protection."

"Of course she does." Lexi waved his concern off like it was no big deal. "Jagger will be with us, and—"

"Jagger's *your* somo. He'll protect you first, not Brenna."

Lexi rolled her eyes and smirked at Eryx. "Which is why I was about to say we brought Wes and Troy, too. Seriously, Ludan. You need the time in Eden. One night. That's all. We'll stay with her the whole time. And no offense, but shopping with me will be a whole lot more fun than it ever could be with you."

Brenna padded up beside him, her voice low. Though in the tiny room, Eryx and Lexi couldn't miss it. "You should go. If you need the boost, then you should do it." She glanced at Eryx. "But I still think you should talk to him about the other."

Eryx narrowed his eyes, way too many questions piling up behind his scowl.

Opting for diversion, Ludan focused on Lexi. "She's supposed to spend the day with her mom. The three of us were going out to dinner. How are you going to explain three warriors?"

Lexi grinned, not the least bit daunted. "I'll come up with something. Besides, compared to you, Wes, Troy, and Jag look like choirboys."

Ludan shoved to his feet and paced a handful of steps away, staring out the window overlooking downtown Orlando. It didn't make sense. His whole life he'd gone wherever and whenever Eryx wanted and never gave it a second thought. But now it felt like someone had poured concrete in his boots and snatched away his favorite toy. He twisted enough to meet Brenna's gaze. "You'll stay with Wes and Troy?"

Brenna nodded, though she didn't look like she enjoyed the idea any more than he did.

"Geez, Ludan." Lexi stood and wiggled her fingers toward the door. "Relax. Go recharge and work your mojo with Eryx. We've got this."

Easy for her to say. Within five minutes the voices would

be full throttle, and that darker, angry part of himself would be a raging animal bent on self-destruction. Fuck, just the idea of being away from her made him jumpy.

But Eryx was right. If he didn't recharge, he couldn't protect her. "Get Wes and Troy up here. I want their vow before I go."

~

LUDAN STEPPED out of the portal back to Eden, expecting to find the training center where Angus was detained, but finding the castle gardens instead. "I thought we were going to scan Angus."

"Tomorrow." Eryx strode toward the main path that wound through the flowers and the wrought-iron gazebo covered in ivy. "Today you rest and give me answers."

"I thought—"

"You thought you'd scan Angus and hightail it back without juicing up first. So, you juice first, then you scan Angus." He spared Ludan an angry glance. "I've been where you're at, or have you forgotten?"

"You didn't walk away."

"No. I brought Lexi with me and put my throne at risk. Believe me, brother. I get it."

Ludan clamped his mouth shut. Much as it pained him to admit it, Eryx was right. He needed energy, and Brenna would be fine with Wes and Troy. They were elites. Smart and deadly.

He glanced at Eryx. "You hear about more humans getting surprise tours of Eden?"

All he got in answer was a quick nod.

Weird. Eryx might get pissed, but he seldom got tight-lipped. Not when it concerned his race. "Any updates on Serena's link?"

"Not a thing."

"If she's the one taking people to Eden, she can't be in zeolite."

Eryx took the stairs up to the veranda two at a time, still not weighing in.

"Ian tell you about the new promises their guide is making on the tours?"

That one at least struck a nerve, drawing a grumble before Eryx answered. "Yeah, I heard about the pending revelation. Can't wait."

"You think there's any chance she's dead?"

Eryx waved a hand toward his and Lexi's private office. The double doors flew wide with far more force than necessary. "We couldn't get that lucky. And I'd still want to see a dead body before I believed it." He spun in front of his desk and crossed his arms. "You seem eager to talk, so let's talk. Tell me what Brenna meant about your gift."

Fuck.

Ludan halted a good twenty feet away and, for the first time in his life, gave serious thought to going AWOL. "That's between me and Brenna."

"Like histus it is. If something I've asked you to do for years endangers you, it's very much between you and me. Now talk."

He stared back at Eryx, scrambling for something, anything he could say that wouldn't leave his skeleton jangling in broad daylight. Nothing came. Just white noise and a barely couched need to fidget. "The memories don't leave me."

Eryx stayed locked in place, waiting.

Praise the Great One, how was he supposed to explain this and not sound like a pussy? "I hear them all the time. They're always on. Loud. Like one of those stereo stores in Evad with every radio and TV turned to a different station."

Eryx uncoiled his arms and leaned back on the desk's edge, his hands fisting the edge. "And you never thought it important I should know this?"

"What would you have done?"

He huffed out an ironic laugh. "I'd have quit asking you to do it."

"Exactly." Out of nowhere, Brenna's bravado this morning blazed through his thoughts. How proud and uncompromising she'd been about offering her gift. Funny how he'd been guilty of the same thing, only for about a hundred and thirty years longer. "I do it because it helps you. I vowed my life to protect yours. A little noise in my head is nothing in comparison."

"You don't face down the grim reaper every day." Eryx frowned and hung his head. "No wonder you never sleep. Or talk." His head snapped up. "That's it, isn't it? You can't because you can't get a word or dream in edgewise."

Ludan shrugged and stuffed his hands in his pockets. "Something like that."

Eryx glared and drummed his thumb against the desktop. After thirty or more seconds that felt like a year, he pushed upright and stalked around his desk. "You're not scanning Angus. I'll have the ellan go first, then I'll follow up."

"Bullshit."

Dropping to his chair, Eryx picked a big leather book up from the center and plunked it off to one side. "Bullshit is what's stored in that head of yours. Give me one good reason why I should let you at Angus. Or at anyone after what you've withheld?"

"Brenna." The second it came out, the shield he'd kept around himself and his emotions wavered, and he wished like histus he could take it back.

Eryx raised that imperial fucking eyebrow and stared him down. "What about Brenna?" The way he said it, Ludan

169

wasn't sure if Eryx was prepped to rip Ludan's head off or ready to take her out.

"I don't hear them when I'm with her. They're silent."

One second and Eryx's whole demeanor shifted, the tension and anger morphing into shocked, almost pitiful understanding.

Ludan ambled to the window behind Eryx's desk, the dregs of all he'd kept from his friend eking out with every step. "I told you there wasn't anything between us." Nothing more than his overactive imagination and wishful thinking.

The worn leather covering Eryx's chair groaned as he shifted. "It might have been how things started between the two of you, but that's not what it is anymore. Lexi and I were in the room with you for less than an hour and I could see it. Sense it. A stranger could have done the same. Is it so damned hard for you to comprehend there might be something more for you with her than just quiet?"

He wished that were the case. Maybe if he hadn't seen the things he'd seen, or done the things he'd done, it would be different. "I don't even deserve the quiet she gives me. I sure don't deserve more."

"Ludan." Not a request for attention, but a command.

Ludan sucked in a lungful of air and faced his malran.

"I've never met a man more deserving. But if you keep hiding behind excuses, you'll never know for sure."

CHAPTER 19

*B*renna ambled beside her mother through another huge department store surrounded by endless racks of colorful outfits while Lexi scouted other sections still in earshot. Like yesterday, Abby kept a tight grip on Brenna's hand and cast frequent glances as if checking to see if the contact was real.

Brenna didn't mind. If anything, the connection grounded her. Anchored her amidst the mall's noise and chaos and reminded her the past was truly behind her. "I remember us shopping."

Her mother halted and caught her breath.

"I hated the clothes," Brenna said, "and my feet were always tired by the time we left, but I loved hiding in the clothes racks to see if you could find me."

Tears welled in Abby's eyes, and a shaky smile stretched into place. "You remember that?"

Nodding, Brenna scoured her memories for more details, tiny nuggets she'd tucked safely out of Maxis's reach. "I remember you called them our special days. We got cinnamon rolls from some diner near our house, and you'd let me pick music from the jukebox."

Abby laughed, her gaze trained on the shiny industrial tile even though her thoughts seemed years away. "You always picked the same one. Some boy band that drove the waitresses crazy, especially so early in the morning."

She remembered that, too. The name and the band were just fuzzy scraps now, but the way she'd danced beside the table had made everyone around them laugh.

"You were so bright," Abby said. "So full of life and happy."

Where she wasn't now. Brenna understood the unspoken ending her mother held back. More than Abby knew. But she was working her way back, one minute at a time.

Shaking off the weighty mood, she refocused on the bold colors and dizzying noise around her. A headless white mannequin stood perched on a display, its arms positioned in a way that said, "Look at me!" The teal shirt it featured had a peasant design with pretty crocheted edges, a relaxed almost wistful feel that fit her mood. The jeans, however, had rhinestones on the pockets and ratty tears above one knee.

"I don't get it." Brenna fingered the strings draped across the gaped opening and glanced up at her mom. "They put holes in them on purpose?"

Surprise flashed across Abby's face a second before she frowned. "How can you not know that? They've been that way for years."

Lexi bustled up behind them with an armful of clothes, deftly cutting off any chance for Brenna to answer. "People don't like to wait for a good thing anymore. When I first started wearing jeans, we had to work 'em in the hard way." She held up her selections by their hangers. "Any of these work for you?"

Abby's gaze snagged on something behind Brenna. Her

expression hardened, and she lowered her voice. "Tell me again why they have to be here? Are you in some kind of trouble?"

"No, Mom." Every time her mom laid eyes on Wes, Troy, and Jagger, her demeanor vacillated between terror and cautious curiosity. "Just trust me when I tell you they're good people. If it weren't for them and Lexi, I wouldn't be here."

Abby scowled like she wanted to argue, or at least press for more. Instead, she clamped her mouth and nodded. "Lexi's right. The real faded look is much better." One corner of her mouth quirked in an almost grin. "I've still got a pair from college in the back of my closet. I probably couldn't get one thigh in them anymore." She cocked her head slightly. "If you want, you could try them on. I was about your size at your age."

"Awesome." Lexi elbowed Brenna's arm and winked. "I'd pay good money to see the look on Ludan's face when he sees you in Levi's the first time."

Brenna sighed and turned away, searching for more of the comfortable cotton skirts she liked. Maxi skirts, Lexi had called them. "He already did. I borrowed some of yours when we got to Dallas. I don't think he was all that impressed."

Abby hurried to Brenna's side. "You and Ludan are together?"

Now there was a tricky question to answer. Half the time she thought there was something between them, and the other half it felt like his attention was based on pity.

"They will be." Lexi paused to pick up a flirty blue tank top with spaghetti straps.

Brenna and her mother both stopped dead in their tracks.

Lexi lowered the top and cocked her head. "What? They'll totally end up together. Everyone with eyeballs knows it."

"But he's so..." Abby opened and closed her mouth twice and still couldn't find a word to finish her sentence.

Lexi chuckled. "Huge? Daft? Stubborn?" She checked to make sure the men trailing them were far enough out of earshot. "Aren't they all?"

Brenna shook her head, snatched the clothes from Lexi's arms, and headed for the fitting room. "You're wrong. He doesn't want anything to do with me. Trust me. I know."

She must have made her point because Lexi dropped the subject and focused on helping Brenna find her own style. Her mom seemed happy with the change in topic, too. It was hard to tell whether her mom was relieved that she and Ludan weren't an item, or if she was simply uncomfortable with discussing her daughter and relationships. All Brenna knew was the whole tone of their outing shifted, one focused solely on enjoying the moment. Three women, laughing and indulging in mindless chatter.

Until they stopped at the food court.

Abby excused herself to go to the restroom.

She'd barely made it two tables away before Lexi chimed in. "I'm not wrong."

Brenna broke a bite off her chicken strip and tried to peel off some of the overcooked batter. "About what?"

"You know damned well what I'm talking about."

Sure she did. She just didn't want to go there. "I told you. Jeans are uncomfortable. I like the skirts better."

"I'm talking about Ludan. Talk to me, Brenna. Let me help."

Sighing, Brenna pushed her plastic tray far enough away that she could fold her arms on the table, an act that her mother would have scolded her for when she was little.

"Come on. It's obvious there's chemistry between the two of you," Lexi said. "Ludan's a good guy, and he's been chummy with me since we got past the awkward how-are-ya's, but I've never seen him this protective of anyone save Eryx. He broke his vow for you, for Christ's sake."

"He what?"

Lexi gaped and tossed the fries she was about to eat back to the tray. "Holy shit. He didn't tell you."

"Tell me what?"

Glancing over her shoulder at Wes, Troy, and Jagger, Lexi leaned in and lowered her voice. "A somo takes a vow for life. They protect the person they're sworn to until they're too old or unable to do so. No warrior, not once in Myren history, has left his post before his time. Except Ludan. He did that for you."

The drone of voices around them wavered, drowned by the increasing thrum of her pulse.

Lexi kept going. "You can't tell me he did that if there wasn't something between you. Maybe he doesn't know it yet, but I felt it in him. A blowtorch couldn't be hotter than his emotions when he's around you."

He wanted her. Enough to forgo his future and give her hers. So why wouldn't he give in?

"We kissed," she whispered. She lifted her gaze from the white tabletop to Lexi's. "I saw a couple kissing, and I asked him what it was like. If he would give me one."

"And?"

"It was perfect." All the sensations she'd tucked away from that first night rushed through her, shame and shock close on their heels. "Until I messed it up."

"Messed it up how?"

Her cheeks burned and tears welled in her eyes. "He was…" She bit her lip, searching for the right words. "When he pulled me against him, I felt him. I freaked out and ran."

Lexi grinned, one of those juicy, lascivious smiles that said she was seriously enjoying herself. She anchored her elbow on the table and propped her chin on her hand. "You mean he was hard."

Their very public environment crashed in on her. The

food court was packed with bodies, none of them looking directly her way, but it still felt like they could hear every word. She nodded anyway.

"So? He knows what you've been through, Brenna. I'm sure he understands."

"You don't get it. Now he won't have anything to do with me. He says he'll hurt me. That he doesn't ever want to see me run from him again."

Lexi dropped the hand beneath her chin to the table and glowered. "You're kidding me."

"No. There are times I think he wants me. Times I've seen him..." She swallowed and forced herself to be as outspoken as Lexi. "Hard."

Lexi grinned.

"I heard him in the bathroom, too."

"Heard him what?"

Brenna semi-ducked her chin and motioned toward Wes, Troy, and Jagger at the table beside them. "You know. What guys do."

Lexi's voice dropped to a sexy, husky rasp, not unlike the way her own had sounded after she'd listened to Ludan climax. "He got off."

Brenna nodded.

Pursing her lips, Lexi leaned back in her chair. She draped one elbow over the back, crossed her legs, and tapped her fingers on the table. "So, basically, he wants you, but he's got it in his head he'll hurt you."

"Basically." She dragged her finger along the condensation on her drink, exhausted, but glad she'd finally shared with someone. "I thought I could change his mind. I've tried to get close to him, but the only time he lets me is when I'm sad or scared. Like you said, he's stubborn. I'm not sure I've got enough in me to get past it."

"But getting past it is what you want?"

Brenna folded her hands in her lap and picked one jagged nail. "I think if anyone could replace my past with something worth remembering, it would be him."

"You feel safe with him."

More than safe. She felt special. Even cherished. A tear slipped free and splattered on top of her hand. "Yeah."

Lexi's chair legs scraped against the industrial tile, and her hand covered Brenna's. "Then no more tears." She lifted Brenna's chin and pinned her with such a confident stare it resonated clear to Brenna's toes. "Remember what you want and throw his stubbornness right back at him. He can't fight you forever."

"I wish you were right."

Lexi settled back in her chair and winked. "Oh, I'm right. I felt what he felt, remember? And sister, let me tell you. I can't wait to watch him fall."

CHAPTER 20

*L*udan owed Brenna an apology. A big one wrapped up in groveling and ass kissing. Outside the library window, the ocean's waves rolled to the shoreline. The breeze was warm and devoid of the taint so common in Evad, not that he was in a frame of mind to enjoy it. He hadn't even been gone twenty-four hours, but the voices were driving him nuts. Less than two weeks he'd been with Brenna, almost always close enough to dampen the hubbub in his head. Apparently, that was enough to soften years' worth of the mental calluses she'd built.

He shouldn't have jumped her shit for sleeping with him. What kind of jerk read someone the riot act when all they'd done was show kindness?

Yeah, huge ass kissing was in order. Histus, if she asked him to, he'd grovel naked in Times Square and give her a month to sell tickets.

"Once upon a time, I would have thought you being here waiting on me meant you were eager to get in Angus's head," Eryx said.

Ludan flinched. The fact that his friend had gotten so

close without Ludan hearing him only proved how scattered his sabbatical with Brenna had left him.

Eryx sauntered the rest of the way into the room and braced his hands on the open windowsill. "Now I know it's more you slept for shit." He pegged Ludan with a glare. "Last night any different?"

No point in dodging it now. While he hated the remorse he might have caused Eryx, it felt damned nice not to have the secret between them. "Not really."

"That why you're always ready for a fight?"

"It helps." He twisted the empty tumbler of strasse he'd left on the ledge a quarter turn, wishing he could take another belt before they headed for Angus. "Booze helps, too."

Letting out a tired sigh, Eryx hung his head. The metal beads that held his commitment braids clicked against the quiet. "I can't ask you to do this. Not now. Not ever."

"Don't." Ludan pushed away from the ledge and stalked to the liquor cabinet. Fuck being levelheaded when he scoured Angus's head. Crazy thoughts and inane chatter he could tolerate, but pity would kill him. "You don't ask me to pull my punches when we spar. Don't ask me to roll over when it matters."

"Roll over? You think me looking out for my best friend's sanity is some jacked-up form of sympathy? Damn it, Ludan. I can't remember the last time I saw you really sleep. Or smile."

The night before last, thanks to the pretty little black-eyed nymph he'd left in Evad. He sure as hell wasn't sharing that with Eryx, though. He threw back another slug and thunked the glass on the sideboard. "Let's go. I want to get back to Brenna."

"The Great One take it, you're a stubborn ass. I can scan

Angus just as good as you and not add more to what you're already wrestling."

"You can do it, but you're not as good as me. I'm faster and far more thorough. You know that." Ludan stalked to the library doors. "It's one voice on top of hundreds. You can come with me, or I can do it on my own."

Eryx's hand clamped down on Ludan's shoulder and yanked him around with enough force that Ludan's neck cracked. "No."

"You can't stop me."

"Like histus I can't. I've got a whole row of zeolite cells downstairs that would suck the fire right out of you."

"Then you might as well cut my nuts off while you're at it. Maybe you could hang 'em in the hallway so everyone can get a visual to go with the gossip."

"Fuck!" Eryx spun so fast the beads at the end of his braids whistled a quarter inch from Ludan's nose. He planted his hands on his hips and scowled at the ceiling. "This is insane."

"This is important. I'm not scooting around in someone's head to see what they had for breakfast. I'm trying to cut Serena off at the pass and make sure Brenna stays safe."

Eryx turned, a shell-shocked expression on his face.

Damn it.

Ludan looked away and swallowed, the weight of what he'd just admitted smacking him square in the jaw.

"You want it for her," Eryx said.

"I want it for all of us." Not a complete lie. A giant, bull-shit foul, maybe, but not a lie.

Eryx half scoffed, half laughed and shook his head. "Yeah. You keep telling yourself that." He jerked his head as he sauntered past. "Let's get this done and get you home."

The trip to the training center elapsed in silence, the riot between Ludan's ears notwithstanding. By the time they crossed the wide open arena and wound through the under-ground tunnels to the detention cells, the lower-ranking warriors already had Angus bound to a chair in the main interrogation room.

Eryx motioned one guard stationed behind Angus toward the door. "Bring the ellan in."

The warrior dipped his chin and strode away.

Angus watched the man leave with a healthy dose of dread radiating from his eyes. "I already told you, I'll tell you what you want."

Ludan held his place by the door and crossed his arms, waiting for Eryx's cue.

Eryx paced the room, cataloging Angus's disheveled appearance. Where the uppity old man usually sported white council robes so crisp they could stand on their own, today's looked as though it hadn't seen a wash in weeks. His thin white hair always looked a little on the manic side, but Ludan would bet the wild edge to it now came from a long night of tossing and turning.

"That chance came and went weeks ago." Eryx paused behind him. "You claimed council protection. Now I've got dispensation, so I'll just take what I want."

Angus tried to crane his neck and keep Eryx in his sights, but the bonds around his ankles and chest held firm. His breath kicked in stronger, coming out as a strangled chuff. "Please. No."

The ellan padded through the doorway, an unimposing young man in an ivory robe that marked him as a newer council member. His brown hair was bound in a low pony-tail. Surprising. He barely looked old enough to be awak-ened, let alone mated. He dropped to one knee and bowed his head. "My malran. I'm at your service."

"No need for ceremony, Theodore." Eryx clapped Angus on the shoulder. "You know Theodore, don't you, Angus?

Your esteemed colleagues sent him here to retrieve what you claimed as protected information." He grabbed one of the ladder back chairs lined up along the bare gray wall, spun it around, and straddled it, crossing his arms casually along the back. "Given your hesitancy to share, I'm guessing what's between those ears of yours isn't exactly pretty."

Angus swallowed, genuine fear racking his body so strongly his aged jowls trembled. He lowered his voice. "I'm begging you. He's just a boy. No one should see my past. Least of all him."

Eryx cocked his head. "I never took you for the compassionate type."

"He's innocent."

"So was your page, Sully, but he's dead. He's the one who took the translations from Maron's home while you distracted him, isn't he?"

Angus hung his head.

"You killed him to keep him quiet, am I right?"

Shoulders sagging, a ragged sob shook Angus's chest. "Yes."

"How?"

"Poison." Angus's gaze dropped to the floor. "He had an allergy to coconuts. It wasn't a problem since they're rare here, but any contact to him was lethal. I laced the package I gave him to deliver that day with it."

Eryx glanced back at Ludan. "Serena asked you for the translations?"

Angus's answer came out devoid of emotion, dead and broken. "Yes."

"Tell me who she's working with."

He lifted his head. "I was contacted by her solicitor, Thyrus Monrolla. He never confessed to knowing what she was up to, but I know he supported the Rebellion."

"Who else?"

Silence.

Eryx leaned in. "Who else, Angus?"

Angus shook his head. "Maxis is dead. She knew Reese, but no other warriors…" His focus sharpened. "Maxis's strategos. The one who replaced Reese. She mentioned him the day she asked for the texts. Said there would be a new ruler. When I asked if it was him, she didn't deny it."

"What's his name?"

"I only met him once. He found me and took me to the Rebellion camp." Angus's gaze drifted back and forth as though scouring his memories for any crumb. He jerked his head up. "Uther. Uther Rontal."

"Who is he?"

"I don't know. He barely said a word to me."

Eryx's voice slid through Ludan's head. *"Ever hear of him?"*

"Nope."

Surging upright, Eryx spun the chair with his mind and slid it to the back of the room. "Why did she want the texts?"

The sudden movement must have fired Angus's adrenaline to a fresh high, because his answer came out close to a shout. "You know why. She wants you off the throne. She said she had something that might make that happen. Something to do with the prophecy."

"And that was?"

"I don't know!" Angus's eyes filled with tears, and they spilled down his weathered face. "Yes, I got the texts for her because I wanted vengeance. I wanted you off the throne as bad as she does, but I swear to you, after I handed them over, I never saw her again. Not once." Angus glanced at Theodore, motionless near the far wall. "Please. I've told you all I know. Don't ask the boy to do this."

Eryx looked away so Ludan couldn't see his face. *"I don't like this."*

"You don't have to like it," Ludan said. *"One way or another, I'll have his memories, even if I have to go through you to do it."*

Their open link pulsed with tension, a palpable energy that crackled and snapped.

Ludan glared at the back of Eryx's head, willing him to understand. *"I told you why I need this. Put yourself in my place. What would you do?"*

Eryx twisted and met Ludan's stare. His jaw looked tight enough to snap, and the whites of his eyes glowed with thinly leashed fury. *"Swear to me you'll make it fast. In and out. Only what we need."*

Ludan dipped his head, never breaking Eryx's gaze.

It took three more agonizing seconds before Eryx spoke. "Theodore, your role here has changed."

The ellan took an eager step forward. "However I can be of assistance, my malran."

Eryx stalked behind Angus. "You'll serve as witness. Given the severity of the crimes committed, I'm exercising royal command and accessing his memories otherwise." He pinned Angus's shoulders and leaned in close to one ear. "You should brace."

Ludan prowled forward, the protector in him salivating at the chance to bring Serena to an end, even as his beleaguered mind demanded he abort. He shook the latter off and gritted his teeth. Any crumb of information was worth it for Eryx. For his race.

For Brenna.

"No." Angus joggled his head and tried to push away, but the rope at his ankles only made the chair legs bob against the stone floor. "Please. Not him."

"It won't hurt." Ludan clamped his palm over Angus's head, his thumb anchored at one temple and his pinky at the other. "Much."

Before he could overanalyze the action, he yanked the barrier on his gift and seized Angus's mind.

Fire blazed through the connection and seared all the way down his spine, the pain so agonizing he nearly dropped the link. The memories were all there, imprinting themselves in his head in crystal detail. Serena asking for the translations. Angus's conversations with the solicitor. The strategos, Uther. Maxis and his cronies. The Rebellion camp and the warriors they'd recruited. It whizzed by in what was likely only a handful of seconds, but tick-tocked at the span of eons.

More images swarmed, time so regressed it went beyond Ludan's birth. To Angus's childhood and the source of the pain. Lashes stung his back.

No, not his back. Angus's, the welts so deep blood blossomed and seeped down his young skin. Tortured screams filled his head. Screams and the merciless shouts of Angus's father as he struck again.

He couldn't let go. He was stuck there, feeling what Angus felt, living the torture that had lasted for years.

"Get out."

He knew that voice. Needed to listen to it, but it was so far away.

"Ludan, let go and get the fuck out."

Angus's bellows deepened, mingling with Ludan's mother's cries. The way she'd begged and pleaded for mercy. He'd failed her. Failed both his parents, putting his friends and personal pleasure first instead of being where he should've been.

Brenna's voice breezed through the hell that gripped him, her voice quiet and gentle as a cool breeze in the midst of a heat wave. *You were gentle with me.*

His fingers unclenched, and he stumbled back. The world righted itself and drifted into hazy focus. He blinked over and over, but all he saw were generic outlines surrounded by the light piped in from above ground.

"Now you know." Angus's voice trembled, so much fear and shame in the sound Ludan tasted its bitterness on his tongue.

"What's he talking about?" Eryx's fuzzy image shifted.

Ludan staggered to the side, trying to keep upright. A steady throb pounded at the back of his head. With every heartbeat it grew, each pulse stronger and more grueling than the last.

"He told the truth." The words came out even more jumbled than his vision, his tongue refusing to work right. He turned and stomped on shaky legs out the door. The rough stone walls scraped his palms as he staggered down the hallway. Surely he could make it outside. He knew this place by heart. All he needed was a portal and Brenna. She'd help him. The same way she'd pulled him from Angus's memories.

Heavy footsteps sounded behind him. "Ludan!"

Eryx's roar ricocheted down the corridor and nearly knocked Ludan to his knees. He didn't dare stop. If he did, he wouldn't get up again. His muscles groaned with every step, and his back shrieked as if he'd taken all of Angus's pain in one strike.

Sunshine blazed up ahead. The exit. Almost there.

He turned and a big hand gripped his upper arm, yanking him to a stop. "What in histus is wrong with you?"

"Brenna." The world spun and darkness pushed the edges of what little light was left in his sight. "Need…" He pulled in a strangled breath. His head sagged with too much weight and one leg gave way. He listed to one side.

Two arms caught him a second before the world went black.

CHAPTER 21

*1*0:18 a.m.

The clock glowed a soft neon blue at the top of the microwave like the gold stars Brenna's parents used to make such a big deal out of in kindergarten. It *should* be a gold star. She couldn't remember the last time she'd gotten out of bed later than sunrise, but today she'd indulged, intimate daydreams of her and Ludan playing through her head.

She fingered the scoop neckline of her pink nightshirt. It hadn't looked like much when Lexi had recommended it the day before. Just a clingy tank design with two pearl buttons in the center and a length that hit her mid-thigh, but it felt amazing. The second she'd touched it, she'd snatched the shirt from Lexi's hand and riffled through the racks until she'd found two more in other colors.

"I told you it would look good." Lexi shuffled into the kitchen, one side of her blue-black hair more mussed than the other. Somehow she still looked sexy. "You wear those babies around here and I'll give it twenty-four hours before Ludan caves."

Heavier footsteps sounded in the living room.

Brenna peeked behind Lexi in time to spy Jagger settling in one of the oversized chairs in the living room. "Maybe now's not the best time to wear it though."

"Oh no. It's the perfect time. If Ludan learns you paraded around like that in front of Jagger, I'll cut my prediction to twelve hours." Lexi slid onto a barstool and reached for a large white box Brenna hadn't noticed. It had green and red lettering and lots of green polka dots on it.

"What's that?"

Lexi reverently opened the lid. "I really need to talk Eryx into giving Wes and Troy a promotion." She spun the box so Brenna could see inside. "Behold the mother of all breakfast delights."

Evenly placed along the bottom of the box were three rows of little round pastries with different colored tops. A memory from her childhood flared from out of nowhere. Her mom and dad stopping at a bakery before church. "Doughnuts."

"Damn right." Lexi snatched one of the chocolate ones. Her hand had barely cleared the lid before she bit into the fluffy dough. Her eyes slid shut and she moaned. "I love Orla, and I don't think I'll ever get enough lastas, but holy schamoly, Krispy Kremes kick ass."

Brenna padded closer to the counter, silently playing eeny-meeny-miny-moe in her head. Her gaze locked on the one with red, white, and blue sprinkles, and her mouth watered. Then again, the chocolate ones like Lexi's looked pretty good too.

"Oh, for Pete's sake," Lexi said. "Just pick one. If we run out, we'll send the boys out for more."

Right. Gluttony and sloth, the two primary goals Lexi had set for the day. She couldn't wait until Ludan got home so she could share her big accomplishments.

"So." Lexi licked her fingers and hopped off her seat,

headed toward the coffeepot. "What time is your mom supposed to get off work?"

Brenna bit into her doughnut and moaned the same way Lexi had. There had to be a pound of sugar in one bite. Her taste buds weren't complaining one little bit, but she'd bet her bloodstream rioted in another five minutes. "Five o'clock," she managed around a mouthful. "She's got an outing with the missing children's group tonight, though. She tried to back out of it, but I told her she should go. I think she's afraid I'll disappear again."

"You don't think she'll say anything to anyone, do you? About you showing up out of nowhere?"

"I don't think so." Brenna snagged one of the napkins stacked near the box. "The day we found her, I told her I didn't want to talk about it. Not with her or anyone else. I just want to be home and start over without questions."

In a single blink, Lexi's expression shifted. One second attentive and thoughtful, and the next hyper alert and focused inward.

"Lexi? You okay?"

Jagger shot to his feet and stormed toward the front door, tossing the remote to the coffee table as he went. It clattered across the glass surface and tumbled to the floor.

Lexi's gaze cut to hers, eyes wide and uncertain. "Brenna, there's a problem."

Yanking the front door wide, Jagger disappeared down the hallway.

"What? What problem?" Brenna started after Jagger, but Lexi gripped her arm and held her back.

"It's Ludan. Something happened when he scanned Angus's memories. Eryx is on his way here with him now. Galena and Reese are on their way, too."

The sugary residue in Brenna's mouth turned to acid, and

the few airy bites she'd swallowed plummeted like lead weights in her stomach. "Galena's a healer."

Lexi nodded, the intensity in her blue-gray gaze the only thing that kept Brenna on her feet. "He's unconscious. Eryx doesn't know what caused it, only that he wanted you, so he's bringing him here. Jagger's the only person outside family who knows. He's running interference with Wes and Troy so we can keep this private."

He couldn't be hurt. He'd said he'd be back. She had things to tell him. Things to show him. "Where are they?"

The words had no sooner left her lips than a gust swept through the opening, slamming the door hard in its wake. Eryx shimmered into view, Ludan a complete deadweight across his shoulders in a fireman's carry. Sweat painted a path down Ludan's spine, and his wavy black hair hung loose so it hid his face.

Her warrior. Her gentle giant, wounded. She hurried toward the bedrooms, pure instinct and possession shoving every other thought from her head. "Bring him in here. How far out is Galena?"

Eryx followed, his breaths heavy as he spoke. "Five minutes. Maybe less."

She sped to her room and tossed the unmade covers aside. She'd barely cleared the way when Eryx levitated Ludan off his shoulders and eased him to the mattress. Kneeling beside him, she peeled the damp T-shirt up and over his head. His breath came in short, uneven pants as though he'd been running or fighting through a terrible dream.

"Jesus." Lexi crawled to the other side to help, glancing at Eryx behind Brenna. "What the hell happened?"

"I have no idea."

Galena powered into the room, Reese tight on her heels. "How long has he been out?"

"Since a few minutes after the scan," Eryx said, prowling closer to the bed. "One minute he clamped on Angus's head, and the next he was stumbling out of the place. He said he'd only take what he needed, but the look on his face..." An angry wind that shouldn't have been possible in the enclosed space snapped through the room. "He saw something. Something nasty. He wouldn't let go."

Lexi scrambled out of the way to make room for Galena.

"That doesn't make any sense. He takes memories all the time." She lifted each of Ludan's eyelids and studied his pupils.

"Yeah, but you haven't heard what it costs him," Lexi grumbled.

Galena hesitated. "What does that mean?"

"It means the memories hurt him," Brenna snapped. She had no place in this conversation. No reason to be outspoken between people who'd known each other their whole lives, but she couldn't have contained her anger if she tried. She glared at Eryx. "Did he tell you how every single memory he's stored in his life plays nonstop in his head? How they never let him alone? Never let him sleep?"

Eryx swallowed, guilt etching every line on his face. "He did."

"And you let him do it anyway?"

His gaze cut to Ludan, then back to Brenna. "Some things one man can't stop another from doing. I don't expect you to understand. Not yet. But you will."

Galena straddled Ludan's hips and gripped either side of his neck. "Whatever he saw must have pushed him over the limit." She closed her eyes and let out a slow breath.

The room around them stilled, only Ludan's jagged breaths upsetting the quiet.

Brenna smoothed Ludan's sweat-dampened hair off his

forehead. His cool, clammy skin felt all wrong, not at all the comforting warmth she'd grown accustomed to.

With a gasp, Galena released her grip and nearly toppled sideways. "Praise the Great One." Her focus shuttled around the room as though trying to ground herself.

Reese steadied her with a hand at her shoulder. "What was it?"

"Angus." Galena covered her mate's hand with her own and clenched it tight. "No wonder he's the way he is. He's cruel because that's all he knows." A shudder racked her torso, and she squeezed her eyes shut. "No one should be treated that way. Least of all a child."

"I don't give a shit about Angus." Eryx pulled Lexi against him and gripped her shoulder. "How do we help Ludan?"

"I don't know." Galena shook her head and braced her hands on her thighs, scanning Ludan's unconscious body. "He's got a diffuse neural contusion like what I'd see with traumatic injury, but I can't heal it. I can access his memories, but when I try to heal him, the energy refracts back at me. It's like his mind has locked up as a self-defense mechanism."

A shield. It made sense if his body wanted to protect itself from further harm.

But she was different. "Let me try."

Every gaze shot her direction.

"When I touch him, the voices stop." She tightened her grip on Ludan's hand, the clasp so strong her fingertips pulsed in time with her frantic heart. It might be insane, but there was no way she'd sit here and watch him like this a second longer than necessary if she could help. "I mirrored Galena before. Maybe if you show me—"

"She's right." Eryx rounded the bed, headed toward Brenna with a fierce scowl in place. "Galena, scoot over. Brenna, climb up and hold on to him like Galena did."

Brenna scrambled into place and wiped her hands on the

tail of her nightshirt. When Eryx planted one knee on the bed beside her and splayed his big hand between her shoulder blades, she flinched. "What are you doing?"

"You mirror our gifts, right?"

She nodded, suddenly more self-conscious and way too uncomfortable with everyone's focus squarely on her.

"Then you're about to get a big boost." Eryx jerked his head toward Ludan. "Show her what to do, Lena."

Galena moved in beside her. "Just relax and press your hands against him."

Relax. Right. Like such a thing was possible under the circumstances. She splayed her hands across his chest.

Up and down he heaved short, jagged rasps. Even his heartbeat felt labored and off.

"Close your eyes." Galena lowered her voice and placed one hand over Brenna's. "Remember, you did this before."

"I healed a torn cuticle."

"That counts. Now close your eyes."

Brenna let her eyes drift shut.

"Take a deep breath," Galena said. "Think about how you felt that day and exhale. Focus on my touch and my energy."

How she'd felt? She scrambled for the memory and tried to tamp down the swirling panic in her stomach.

Think, Brenna. Relax and focus.

She'd been with Galena in her garden, planting little seedlings. The sun was warm against her shoulders. The freshly tilled soil soft beneath her knees and the rich, moist scent of earth all around her. She'd been peaceful.

No, not peaceful. Curious. Light and free of everything except the moment. Something had stirred behind her sternum, warm with soft tingles like what she'd felt when her mother had tickled her back to help her fall asleep.

"That's it." Galena squeezed her hand. "Feel your spirit and channel it through your palms."

Her spirit. That's exactly what she'd felt. The same thing she'd wrapped around her at the worst of times with Maxis. What kept her safe and lulled her to sleep at night. She inhaled deeply, building the sensation until it glowed bright inside her mind's eye, then visualized it flowing down her arms and through her hands.

"Almost," Galena whispered. "One more time."

Willing the muscles in her neck and shoulders to relax, she built the energy again, bolder and more powerful than before. It coursed through her veins, lifting the fine hairs along her arms and firing from her palms.

The world fell away, and black surrounded her. Her body no longer existed, only darkness with a shimmering, pearlescent glow that undulated in front of her.

Galena's voice sounded nearby, the tenor of it filled with awe and resonating through Brenna's incorporeal presence. "Oh, Brenna."

Wait. Was she still awake? Or was she in a dream? "Where am I?"

"You're with Ludan. You made it." An emerald ribbon wound its way beside the ivory one, its motions lazy and elegant the way smoke coiled from a slow burning fire. "Do you see the pretty glow?"

She imagined herself nodding, and the glow wiggled in response.

Galena's light laughter echoed all around her. "That's you. Your energy. I've never seen one so beautiful." The green light circled the ivory one again, and Brenna felt it like a physical tug on her heart. "Come on. Let's go let you work your magic."

The darkness lightened, a radiant silver blossoming like a mystic flashlight from somewhere behind her. Her spirit resonated with a blast of power, and the pearl glow became a

EDEN'S DELIVERANCE

shimmering beacon, as striking in its depth as Galena's. She tried to turn toward the silver presence.

It nudged her forward, as tangible as the hand still pressed against her back. "Follow Brenna."

Eryx. No wonder he was the malran. Compared to hers and Galena's, his energy burned in a sun-to-stars ratio.

With his essence fueling hers, she slipped and glided beside Galena's. White flashed like lightning followed by a labored *ka-chunck*. Over and over the awkward rhythm continued. "What's that?"

"Ludan's heart," Eryx answered from behind her.

Galena's spirit powered forward, pulling Brenna's alongside it. "The white is the electrical charge that fires his pulse. His heart and his other vitals are strong. It's his mind I'm worried about."

Together they shot upward, but the space around them changed. Where she'd felt warm and somewhat safe before, now the air prickled with an uneasy dread. "It feels strange. Like an old haunted house."

Eryx's silver aura inched closer behind her, bolstering her with quiet strength. "It's just the wound. Your spirit knows there's something wrong and gives you the impression to draw you to it."

Haunted. How long had Ludan lived this way? Isolated and alone with no one to breathe light into his world. She drifted closer, moving ahead of Galena's stream and delicately brushing her light against the murky gray.

A spark lit beneath her touch, and the ashy coating flittered away like dust mites on a spring breeze. The space beneath it glowed a healthy pink.

Galena's voice whispered behind her. "He let you in."

"Again," Eryx said almost as quiet. "Use my power. Funnel it through yours."

195

So much gray. Years and years of memories dimmed the beauty beneath. A slow, burgeoning heat built in her gut. No more. No one deserved this, least of all Ludan. She reached for Eryx's strength. Threading her mental fingers through his presence, she streamed it through her own and spread her glow as wide as she could reach. It shimmered and sparkled, hints of pink, teal, and yellow dancing across Ludan's mind and scattering the ugly ash. Over and over, she repeated the process. With each sweep, tiny sparks ignited beneath the healthy pink.

"Brenna," Galena said. "It's okay. He's fine."

The words registered, but the meaning didn't penetrate. The space around her was nice now. Peaceful and warm. Content.

Eryx's voice rumbled with a sharp edge. "She's crashing. Wrap her up, Lena. I'm getting her out." A second later, his glittering silver stream cinched around her.

Gravity hit and her arms collapsed, her torso flush against Ludan's and her face nestled close to his sweat-slick neck. She was back. Exhausted and so damned tired she couldn't open her eyes if God himself walked through the door.

A hand caressed the top of her head, and Lexi's voice whispered beside her. "You did it."

She had. Her ears rang and every muscle ached, but Ludan's heart thudded strong and steady. His body heat radiated through her thin nightshirt, healthy and comforting like the night she'd slept beside him. His chest rose and fell in easy sleep.

Hushed murmurs floated around her.

The bed dipped beside her, Eryx's presence registering even with her eyes closed. The sheer brilliance of his spirit still echoed through her own. "Rest and hold your mate. We're right outside if you need us." He moved away, and his slow footsteps sounded on the carpets.

The door snicked shut.

Her mate. She giggled and snuggled closer, drawing Ludan's earthy scent into her lungs until they sang with it. She'd never be so lucky. And besides, she was human. But for the moment, he was safe and breathing easy next to her. She'd take what she could get.

CHAPTER 22

$\mathcal{B}$it by bit, Brenna roused from sleep, her thoughts drifting from soft-spun dreams and bone-deep relaxation. She yawned and flexed her fingers. Taut, warm skin and unyielding muscles cushioned her cheek, and delicious heat blanketed her torso and the tops of her thighs.

Ludan.

Her eyes snapped open and she sucked in a happy gasp. He hadn't woken. Though sometime as they'd slept, he'd shifted, rolling to his side and wrapping her tight against him so his big hands anchored at her nape and the small of her back.

So this was what it felt like to cuddle. She wiggled her toes and nestled closer. Their legs were tangled, and his jeans rasped against her bare legs, drawing all kinds of wishful thoughts. Too bad she hadn't had the presence of mind to peel his pants free before she'd passed out. Then she'd really have fuel for her eager mind.

The room was nearly dark, offset only by soft glowing light beyond the open bathroom door, but enough to high-light his handsome face. His chest rose and fell in an easy rhythm. With his eyes closed, he was model perfect. An aquiline nose, sharp jaw, and a tightly trimmed beard accenting slightly parted lips no sane woman would willingly walk away from. But his eyes...open, they changed everything. Fearsome and powerful. Enough so even the strongest men stopped in their tracks and rethought getting within arm's reach.

She'd never walk away from him. The Great One only knew how long he'd be in her life, but it would be him who walked away, not her. She gently cupped his jaw, reveling in the tickle of his beard against her palm. She traced his full lower lip and replayed the way he'd moved his mouth against hers. Soft and yet firm and confident.

Slowly, she lifted her head, nothing more important than reliving his kiss, even if only for a stolen second. She leaned in, lips tingling in anticipation. Breathing in his soft exhalations, she skimmed her mouth against his, a barely there touch that sparked to her toes.

At her nape, his hand tightened, a tiny shift of his fingers in her hair that sent goose bumps down her spine.

She smoothed a hand up his sternum and palmed his neck. Beneath her thumb, his pulse increased, still steady and strong, but more urgent than before.

He wanted her. She'd felt and seen his response more than once, and she'd move a whole darned mountain range if it meant exploring what she craved.

Remember what you want and throw his stubbornness right back at him. He can't fight you forever.

Lexi was right. Ludan was a warrior through and through, but so was she. Her battles might have been different, but they were no less fierce. And warriors fought for what they wanted.

Adrenaline and fear clambered inside her chest, excitement and inexperience wrestling for supremacy. She licked her lip. She could do this. After all, she'd kissed him once. Granted, she'd been more the recipient than the giver, but it couldn't be all that different.

Slowly, she pressed her lips against his and let her eyes slip shut. The dream she'd had came back in perfect clarity. The way they'd fed from each other's mouths, and his taste on her tongue. She flicked her tongue along his lower lip and he groaned, opening to the intimate touch. She took what he offered and deepened the kiss, licking inside and coaxing him to join her.

He shifted his head, stroking his mouth against hers, once, twice. His arms tightened, and he slanted his lips against hers, rolling her to her back and taking over in one, all-consuming assault. His hands framed her face, fingertips pressed hard against her skull as if he feared she'd slip away. His thigh lay heavy between her legs, a perfect weight against the growing ache at her core.

She sighed into his mouth, reveling in his weight and the unguarded moment. No hesitation. No worry. Just perfect, raw emotion.

He undulated his hips, and his hard cock pressed firm against her thigh.

Oh yes. He wanted her as much as she needed him. She splayed her hands at the small of his back and lifted her hips, grinding her core against his leg. "Ludan."

He froze. Her voice had been little more than a whisper, but his eyes snapped open. His gaze locked onto hers and he shot backward, flying so fast through the air he nearly slammed against the door. He ran one hand through his hair and paced to the far side of the room. "Fuck!"

Brenna threw the covers back and scrambled out of bed.

He spun and planted his hands on his hips, chest heaving. His eyes shuttled back and forth as though searching his thoughts. "I'm sorry. I don't…I don't know what happened."

"You were kissing me." She risked another few steps closer. "And I was enjoying it."

He still wouldn't look up, just scowled at the floor and shook his head. "How am I here? The last thing I remember I was in Eden."

"You passed out." She fiddled with the hem of her night-shirt, the throb between her legs insistent on skipping the conversation and getting back to business. "Eryx brought you here, and we healed you."

His head snapped up, and his eyes sharpened. "We?"

"Galena couldn't do it. Your mind wouldn't accept her healing." She lifted her chin an extra inch, pride and fear scampering through her belly. "So I did it."

His crazy-intense blue eyes bore into her. He stood so still, she wasn't even sure he was still breathing. "How?"

"Eryx and Galena helped me."

His hands fisted at his sides. "You touched me."

Heck yes, she'd touched him. In more ways than one. And she wouldn't apologize for a second of it. "It was beautiful."

"You could have hurt yourself."

"Well, I didn't." She crept forward. This was her chance to be brave. To reach for what she wanted. Ludan wouldn't hurt her, though if he didn't give her what she needed, she might hurt him. "And afterward, we slept. You never once pulled away. You held me." She stopped just an arm's length away. "When I woke up, I kissed you."

"You shouldn't have done that."

"Why? I want you. You want me. The only thing stopping us is you and your stupid idea you'll hurt me."

Be brave. Fight for what you want. Over and over, she chanted it in her head. "I'm not weak. I'm strong." She held his stare and lifted the tail of her nightshirt. "Strong enough to make my own choices." Sucking in a bolstering breath, she whipped it over her head and let it fall to the floor. Cool air assaulted her breasts, tightening them and lifting her nipples to hard peaks. She pushed her shoulders back, channeling all her pent-up defiance into her words. "I choose you."

His jaw slackened, and his gaze locked on her bared breasts.

The need to fidget, or at least cover herself, prodded from all quarters, but she beat the reflex back. She might be out of her mind doing this, but she was tired of hinting. Tired of following him around like a lost puppy and hoping for change. This was right. *They* were right. Or they could be if he'd stop his stubborn nonsense and embrace what she offered.

She closed what remained of the distance between them, only inches separating their bare torsos. Fear and passion vibrated through her. "Tell me the truth."

His gaze snapped to hers, and his shoulders bunched as though bracing for a punch.

"Do you want me?" she whispered.

He shook his head, his excuses piling up so fast she could almost see them dashing to his tongue. "It's not that simple."

"Yes it is. Just tell me the truth. Yes or no. Do you want me?"

He clenched his jaw, looked away for a handful of seconds, and hung his head. "Yes." He frowned and met her stare. "Damn it, yes. But don't you see how dangerous being with me is?"

Yes.

The sweetest word she'd ever heard, intoxicating and flooding her with courage. She touched him, smoothing her hand down his forearm until her fingers circled his wrist, then lifted his palm to her waist. "Do you think I'm weak?"

His gaze slid to the point of contact, desperation pooling in his beautiful eyes. The muscles in his forearm strained even though his touch shook with heartbreaking caution. "You're anything but weak."

She guided his hand higher, the warmth of his touch setting every nerve alight. "Then trust me to know what I need. What I want."

He cupped her breast, and her knees nearly buckled. Her lungs refused to work, but her heart thrummed in triple overtime.

His free hand clamped onto her hip, whether to push her away or pull her closer she couldn't tell. He grumbled low and shaky, a man at war with temptation. "You don't know what you're offering." He swept his thumb against the inner swell of her breast, then rasped it across her nipple.

She arched into the touch, reveling in the scrape of his work-roughened fingers. "I know exactly what I'm offering. And there's no one I'd trust more than you." She trailed her fingertips down his stomach, toying with the faint trail of hair that disappeared beneath the low waist of his jeans. "Stop fighting. If you truly want me, stop fighting. Give us both what we need."

Sucking in a breath, she pressed lower, dragging the heel of her palm over the denim covering his powerful erection.

His strangled growl coiled around her a second before he yanked her flush against him and slammed his mouth against hers.

This was what she needed. Wild and unrestrained desire. Bruising, almost feral kisses fueled by primal instinct. She buried her fingers in his hair and surrendered to the moment. To the press of her breasts against his chest and the urgent thrust of his hard length against her belly.

He cupped her butt with both hands and lifted her, barely easing his mouth from hers. "Wrap your legs around me."

She did as he asked, twining her arms around his neck and locking her ankles at the small of his back.

Holding her close, he ambled to the bed, the corded muscles in his shoulders bunching with delicious power. It was as if she weighed nothing. A feather to be stroked and petted. Even when he crawled across the bed, one arm braced against the mattress and the other slanted across her back, gravity held no bearing against his strength.

Easing her down, he trailed slow, languorous kisses along her jaw, licking and sucking a devious path down her neck. His fingertips traced soft, enticing circles from the outside of her knee toward her hip.

Angling her head, she savored his warm breath against her skin and the tickle of his beard. She sifted her fingers through the silky scruff. "I've imagined this," she whispered. "How your skin would feel against mine."

He lifted his head. His lips were full and swollen, his pupils so wide they nearly gobbled up the blue. The hand he'd slowly worked toward her waist teased up her ribcage. "So have I." He placed a reverent kiss above her heart and lifted his eyes to her. "More than you know."

He cupped her breast in his big palm, and her breath caught in her throat, her body sparking as though every cell danced with electricity. Before, his touch had been passive. Leashed and careful. This was different. More demanding and possessive, plumping her needy flesh and building the steady ache to insistent demand.

She fisted her hands in his hair, urging his wicked mouth and tongue closer to her nipple. "Ludan."

Ignoring her efforts, he teased a lazy path around her areola, whispering his tongue oh so close. His warm exhalation drifted across the tight peak, and his voice whispered against her skin. "Hold on."

Wet, scorching heat surrounded her nipple, and her back bowed off the bed, pleasure spearing between her legs and stealing her breath. She couldn't breathe. Couldn't comprehend anything beyond the carnal connection he'd created and the unbridled sensations spurred with each pull of his mouth.

He palmed her other breast, rolling and gently tugging the nipple between his finger and thumb while his tongue provoked its mate. Slowly, he lifted his head, studying the outcome of his work. He toyed with the rosy, swollen tip. "You like that?"

A shiver coursed through her, his deep voice resonating like a million teasing fingers across her skin. "Yes."

His gaze slid to the neglected breast cupped in his palm, and he licked his lower lip. "Me too." He laved a decadent path toward it. "I can hear everything. Feel everything. Your little whimpers. Your hands in my hair." He teased the sensitive underside of her breast with his beard, then swirled his tongue around the tip, his eyes locked on hers. "Nothing better."

He closed his lips around her and suckled deep.

She bucked her hips and held on tight, the ever-growing ache he'd built low in her belly rocketing to a whole new level.

His shoulders snapped back, and he groaned around her flesh.

She uncoiled her fingers, relieving the place she'd dug her nails deep and stroking the indentions she'd left behind. "Sorry."

He released her nipple with a slick pop and growled against the reddened peak. "Don't apologize for marking me. I want it." Easing back to his knees, he skimmed his rough palms down her sides and over her hips. His gaze locked on the little white hipster panties she'd bought the day before. "I want to know you're with me. Hear you pant and beg." He fingered the little pink bows just below her hipbones, then dragged his thumbs across her mound. "I want your taste."

One thumb dipped down, gently rasping against the cotton and the growing dampness beneath.

She ground into the touch and covered his hand with her own. "More." Her eyes slid shut, every molecule focused solely on the delicious friction. With each pass, the fabric slicked against her swollen folds and ratcheted her need another notch. "Please, Ludan."

"You're soaked." The tenor of the simple statement wafted through her, a mix of triumph and disbelief. He pressed against her center, the panties blocking the deeper contact she craved. "So wet. For me."

"For you." She pried her heavy eyelids open. "I told you." She teased one nail along his forearm, tracing a prominent vein and basking in his rapid pulse. "You're what I want. What I need."

He growled, a low and dangerous sound that would have sent her scrambling in the other direction were it anyone but him. "You trust me?"

Trust him? How could she not? This was Ludan. Her protector. Her gentle giant. "With everything." Hooking her fingers in the waistband of her panties, she lifted her bottom and slid them off, never once breaking eye contact. "I've never willingly bared myself to any man. Only you. That should tell you how much trust I have for you."

His gaze glided down her torso, a wild and possessive glint deepening the blue in his eyes. "Only me." He palmed her knees and pushed them up and wide, exposing her to his greedy perusal. Skating one palm along her inner thigh, the whites of his eyes glowed a soft but beautiful neon. Unnatural by human standards, but amazing.

"What makes your eyes do that?"

His avid stare snapped to hers, and the muscle at the back of his jaw twitched. His breaths grew heavier, chest rising and falling as though he'd bench-pressed a mountain. He slicked one finger through her folds. "Control. Mine's close to snapping."

Her hips bucked, eager for more, and a tiny whimper ripped past her lips. "You think that makes me afraid?"

A lewd and feral grin tipped the corners of his mouth, and he lowered his head toward her sex. "No. You're not afraid. You're fearless, at least in this." He pressed a teasing kiss high on the inside of her thigh, then raked his soft whiskers where his lips had been.

"Then let go."

His mouth whispered against her drenched and swollen labia, his hot breath dancing wickedly against her most sensitive flesh. "Oh, Brenna. I'm already gone."

He flicked her throbbing clit, and the contact ricocheted clear to her toes. Her eyes slid shut, any other sensation beyond the hot, velvet rasp of his tongue too much to process.

"Oh no." His hands slid under her ass, better angling her for his mouth. "You open your eyes. You watch me take you."

She couldn't. Already her sex quivered, too close to release. She wanted him with her when she fell, inside her when she wiped her past clean. "It's too much."

The warmth of his lips and tongue disappeared. "You want me?"

She tossed her head, willing his mouth back where it was. "Yes."

"You want my cock?"

Oh God. Flutters rippled deep inside, release so close it was all she could do to breathe.

"Answer me."

She opened her eyes, every muscle from her neck to her toes poised and straining for his mouth. "Yes."

Pure predator stared back at her, his intensity fragmenting what was left of her reason. "Then you watch.

Watch, and know I'll give you what you want as soon as you've come on my tongue."

Her core clenched a second before he swept his devious tongue through her folds, moaning his pleasure as he devoured. She'd wondered, even fantasized what such a wanton act would feel like, but she'd been nowhere close. No touch could compare to this. No contact as intoxicating.

He eased one finger inside her, pumping slowly as he played her clit with his lips and tongue. "Your pussy's trembling. Ready for release." He added a second finger, increasing his rhythm and pushing deeper. "I want that. Come for me, sweetheart. Give me what I want." Twisting his wrist, he rubbed his fingertips against a spot inside her.

Reality shattered, her strangled cry ripping free as the most beautiful climax took her. Nothing existed but emotion and Ludan's carnal kiss. Over and over, her walls clamped around his devious fingers, and shards of blue and red danced behind her eyelids.

"That's it." Slowly, he eased the pace, giving her time to circle back to earth, yet still rocking his fingers inside her, nurturing the simmering after burn. He kissed a leisurely path up her torso. "Look at me."

Her eyes. Somewhere between his naughty encouragement and his tongue's cunning efforts, she'd let them close. "Sorry."

"I'm not." He hovered above her, his voice strained and his eyes still glowing. "I love your eyes on me, but watching you come and hearing you shout my name was better."

He'd watched her. The muscles around his fingers fluttered, the mere thought of his eyes on her in those intimate moments sparking a fresh wave of desire.

He chuckled low and dirty. "You like me watching you."

She did. Enough so it felt a little indecent. She sat up, forcing him upright on his knees, and brushed her fingertips through the trail of hair above his waistline. "Does that bother you?"

The lazy smirk on his face evaporated, replaced with a scowl. "The only thing that would bother me is you denying what pleases you."

Oh, she liked that. The words and the protective edge that came with it. "Then you won't deny me seeing you?"

He swallowed, his Adam's apple bobbing so pronounced it looked painful. "I won't deny you anything." He tugged the opening to his jeans, popping the buttons free, then hesitated. He lowered his hands to his sides. "Take what you want."

Her confusion must have been evident, because he smoothed her hair away from her face and tucked it behind her ear. "You need to lead this. To know the choices are yours."

An odd sensation dipped and twirled in her belly, and her breath caught. She might have appreciated Ludan, even idolized him a little, but with his simple, profound words, he'd sunk lifelong anchors in her heart. Grazing her fingers along his barely opened fly, she pulled the edges wide. And nearly swallowed her tongue.

His cock stood tall and proud against his abdomen, no underwear beneath to block her gaze. Thick veins ran from the base to the ridge beneath its flared head.

She traced one and Ludan sucked in a harsh breath, his shaft jerking beneath her tentative touch. It wasn't the first time she'd seen or touched a man, but it had never been like this. At her own pace, and under her own control, for nothing but pleasure. Odd how his skin could be so soft and still so hard beneath.

"Wrap your hand around me." He couched it as gentle guidance, but there was urgency underneath. Desperation and strain.

She started to comply, noted her ugly, callus-laden palms, and stopped. She fisted her hand and sat back on her heels. "I don't think that's a good idea. Touching you should feel good, not rough."

A rumble rolled from his chest, and he held out one hand, palm up, putting his own thick calluses on display. "You think I don't like rough?" He fisted himself at the base, far more powerfully than she would have attempted. "I came thinking about you just like this not five days ago." He stroked up and down, over and over, not once breaking his stare. "I've felt your hands on my back. Felt your nails in my skin." He released his grip and let his hands fall to his sides. "Now I want them on my cock."

For long seconds, she sat there, too speechless to move, the image of Ludan working his shaft seared in her head. "For the record, I think I like watching, too."

He grinned and lifted his hand to resume.

"No." She caught him by the wrist and tugged his hand away. "I didn't mean now. Definitely later, but this time I want to." She wrapped her hand around him.

So much strength and power. Raw and unyielding, like the man.

Mirroring his actions, she marveled at his response. How his hips pressed into each pump of her fist and his heavy breaths. She had control. No one else.

A drop of pre cum pearled at the tip. He'd tasted her. Given her unbelievable release. She licked her lips and leaned in close.

He stayed her with a firm grip on her shoulder. "Not this time. I'd never last. Not with your sweet mouth."

Her shoulders slumped, and she opened her mouth to argue.

Not this time.

"We'll have more than once?" The second the question came out, she regretted it, hating the vulnerability behind it.

Ludan covered her hand and lifted it to his mouth, kissing the center of her palm. "As long as you want me, I'm yours. You have my vow."

The anchors in her heart etched deeper, and the desolate, fearful part of herself who'd lived in shadows took another step into Ludan's light.

He pulled away, stepping off the bed long enough to shuck his jeans, then crawled across the bed. He lay on his back beside her and fisted his length. Curling the fingers of his other hand around her wrist, he dragged his thumb across her pulse point.

Praise the Great One, she could look at him like this for hours. All muscle and masculine power, coiled tight despite his relaxed pose. "What are you doing?"

"I'm giving you control." He tugged her wrist and guided one leg over his hips so she straddled him. His cock lay thick and heavy just inches from her core.

Her insides fluttered in a mix of excitement and panic. Not once had Maxis ever taken her in such a fashion. "I don't know what to do."

"We'll figure it out." He pulled her closer, threading his fingers in her hair and slanting his lips across hers.

The head of his cock grazed her labia, and she sucked in a sharp breath.

"Easy." His fingers tightened in her hair, and his heavy exhalations mingled with hers. Back and forth, he teased his mouth against hers, his hands guiding her hips. "Slide yourself against me. Use me. Build yourself back up."

She gasped at the first glide, his shaft slicking easily through her swollen folds. His cockhead nudged her clit and she ground herself against it, chasing her rousing need. They were finally here. At the moment she'd fantasized about with the one man she trusted. No more waiting.

"Please." She opened her eyes, her hips never breaking rhythm. "Tell me what to do."

"Lift up," he rasped, strangled and broken. "Take me in your hand and guide me in."

Loath as she was to break contact, she rose higher on her knees and gripped him by the base. The angle was awkward. Not at all the sexy, sultry image she wanted to present.

"That's it." The tip of his cock slipped inside, and he clenched his jaw, a strangled grunt muffled behind it. "Your pussy's so damned wet. Tight."

Power fired hot in her veins. Sensual and primal. Cleansing and perfect. Slowly, she lowered herself around him, his girth plying her with a delicious stretch. Down, then up. Over and over, working his magnificent cock deeper and deeper and until he filled her completely.

"Your pace." Sweat dotted his forehead, and that wayward lock of hair that always fell across his face clung to one cheek.

No, not her pace. Theirs. She rode him. Experimenting and gauging each reaction. The way he held his breath. His hungry gaze as he watched his length tunnel in and out of her sex.

"Brenna."

Oh God, she ached. Needed release as bad as he did, but it hovered out of reach. "Help me." She gripped his shoulders, squeezing tight. "Please."

"Lean over." His big hand splayed behind one shoulder blade, and his tongue flicked out against one nipple. "Come for me, sweetheart. Let me feel you on my cock." He sucked the tip into his mouth and slid his hand between them, pressing her clit with his thumb.

Firework, heart-stopping release ricocheted through

every inch of her body. She clenched her knees tight to Ludan's hips and rode the storm, her core rippling around his shaft in hungry, avid clasps.

Ludan bucked, slamming his hips upward and releasing a ragged shout. Around them, streams of fire swirled with no visible source. A blanket of deep golden flames tinged with blue at the edge. Beautiful like the glorious release blasting through her, body and soul.

His arms coiled around her, his fingers buried in her hair as he bound her tight to his chest. Beneath her, his heart hammered ruthless and heavy, their torsos lined with sweat.

She pulled in a steadying breath, his earthy scent and the aftermath of their sex filling her lungs.

Rest and hold your mate.

Eryx couldn't be right. That could never be her reality, not as a human. But they had this moment. Explosive passion and a connection that transcended anything she'd ever imagined. Maybe, just maybe, it would be enough to keep him for a little while.

CHAPTER 23

*L*udan tugged his last boot on and reclined in the chair beside Brenna's bed. Nine o'clock in the morning and she was still out. He'd never seen her sleep so late or so deeply. Her hair lay tousled against the cream sheets, and her lips were barely parted. Perfect for fitting his mouth against and rousing her the same way he had throughout the night.

He stood and shoved the temptation deep. She deserved the rest, especially after the night she'd given him. Prying himself away from her warm, naked body had taken ridiculous discipline. If it hadn't been for the voices in the living room, he'd have said to histus with control and lazed the whole damned day beside her.

Feeding his hunger a tiny crumb, he brushed his lips across her temple. Her scent gripped him, the same vanilla sweetness, but now mixed with his own.

Mine.

The thought knocked him back a step. No, not his. In the long run, she'd find someone more suitable. Someone who could give her all the things he couldn't, like a fully functioning heart and emotions that weren't as gnarled as an ancient oak.

Using his mind, he silently opened the door and shut it just as quietly behind him. He'd be smart to keep her future in mind going forward. He hadn't lied last night. As long as she wanted him, he'd see to her physical needs. Hell, he'd see to her *every* need to the extent he was capable. But losing sight of her end game would be an emotional cluster fuck he couldn't live through.

In the living room, Eryx sat on the couch in jeans and a T-shirt with his bare feet up on the coffee table. One hand gripped the television remote and the other fisted a cup of coffee perched on the armrest. A very fresh cup of coffee if the steam coming off it was any indication.

"You just make that?"

"Lexi and Brenna's mom did." Eryx aimed the remote at the flat screen and punched a button. "They left about ten minutes ago."

"Shit, I didn't know she was coming." Although he should have. The only time they'd spent apart was for Abby to keep her meager administrative assistant job.

Eryx frowned at the television, punched the power button, and tossed the remote to the coffee table. "Don't worry about Brenna's mom. Lexi covered it."

"You didn't have to stay here." Though considering how things had worked out, he wasn't complaining.

"You've been covering my ass for over a hundred years. You really think I'd leave your back unprotected when your woman's at risk?"

"She's not my woman."

Eryx cocked an eyebrow. "Really? You shout the house down and do pyrotechnics for all the women you jump in the sack with?"

Ludan's head snapped back as if he'd been punched.

"Yeah, Lexi and I both scented the fireworks. Good thing you kept that shit contained. Not sure the other tenants would appreciate a fire drill."

Fuck.

Ludan strode to the kitchen and snagged a mug over the coffeemaker. He'd need the whole damned carafe before he could deal with Eryx's crap. Maybe he and Lexi staying wasn't such a benefit after all.

Behind him, Eryx's signature silver and winter energy pattern pinged against Ludan's senses. "She tell you she healed you?"

Ludan nodded.

"She tell you Galena couldn't? That her energy was the only one your mind would accept?"

In lieu of an answer, he shoved the coffeepot back on the burner, turned, leaned back into the counter, and glared.

"I'll take that as an obstinate yes." Eryx thunked his coffee to the countertop. "You're going to tell me you've found a woman who all but has a brand on her that says she's your mate and you're not going to honor it with a vow?"

"She's human. She can't take that kind of vow." His voice caught on the thought, and he swallowed to clear it. "Not that it's any of your business, but I gave her the best vow I could last night."

"She's a heck of a lot more than human," Eryx said. "I haven't seen any normal human heal a Myren. And I damned sure haven't seen a human with her kind of energy."

Ludan pushed off the countertop and set his coffee aside so fast the hot brew sloshed over one side. "How the fuck do you know what her energy looks like?"

Eryx grinned. A shit-eating oh-I've-got-your-ass-cornered grin. "I gave her a boost to mirror from. Your *mate* doesn't have a normal human essence. Histus, I don't think I've seen a Myren with energy like hers."

It was a platonic statement. Purely factual. But the fact Eryx had been inside Brenna that way, so innately intimate, made his fingers itch to choke the bastard. He paced his breathing and fought to keep from fisting his hands. "It's the impact of your healing. She couldn't mirror before. That's the only thing that's changed."

Eryx studied him, his shrewd, all too keen focus sucking in nuances few could escape. He rubbed his chin with the back of his hand and nodded. "Point taken. I'll see if Ian's up for sharing his. We'll compare notes."

And if Ian's wasn't the same? What did that mean? Could she take his vow?

Eryx chin lifted in Ludan's direction. "Speaking of healing, how's your head?"

"Nowhere near what I felt yesterday. A little quieter than normal, but the voices always are when Brenna's close by." He cocked his head and focused on the chatter. "Weird though. I don't hear the things I saw in Angus's memory. I can pull them up, but the sound doesn't echo like the others."

"Could be she wiped it before it embedded in long-term memory."

Maybe. Whatever she'd done, he was damned grateful. Living with his mother's screams was torture enough. Relieving Angus's abuse every day the rest of his life would be a whole new level of hell.

The front door opened, and Lexi's boisterous laughter spilled into the living room. A second later, she and Abby came into view, Lexi holding two big white boxes with green and red lettering on the top. "Hey, boys. Glad to see everyone's up and about." She scanned the room. "Well, everyone but Brenna. She okay?"

"She's fine." Ludan focused on Abby. "Sorry we weren't up when you got here. It was a rough night."

Eryx chuckled behind him. *"Man, you suck at this. You're*

talking to her mother." The snarky remark came with a slight echo behind it, and given the smirk on Lexi's face, it didn't take a giant leap to figure out whom he'd shared it with.

She covered it for him, though, heading to the counter and laying her boxes side by side. "Well, all rough nights are best healed with copious amounts of coffee and sugar. Brenna never got a chance to finish her Krispy Kremes, so we picked up more on the way home."

"I thought she was just sleeping in." Abby glanced at the hallway leading to the bedrooms behind her. "Is everything okay?"

"Everything's fine." Eryx sipped his coffee, then motioned toward Ludan with the mug. "We just had a little something to take care of with Ludan. Brenna's a bit protective where he's concerned." He tacked a little extra mental message on the end. *"And by protective, I mean pissed-off momma cub. Remind me to tell you how she nearly ripped me a new one later."*

Lexi plucked a doughnut from the box. "Trust me. After a good night's sleep and the little surprise you booked for her, she'll be a new woman."

"You think she'll like it?" Abby said. "It's not much. Just a little place I saw down the street when I was leaving the other day."

Lexi opened her mouth to answer, but Brenna's voice sounded from the hallway. "Ludan?"

Eryx and Abby spun toward her voice, and Ludan stepped out of the kitchen to bring her in his sights. Her hair was loose and still a little mussed, and she'd thrown on the simple yet ridiculously sexy cotton nightshirt she'd peeled off the night before.

Her gaze locked onto him, and her shoulders relaxed on a relieved exhale. A vibrant pink flush spread across her cheeks, and her fingers pushed and pulled nervously against the fabric barely covering her thighs. "Sorry. I thought you'd left."

Left. As in abandoned.

The three long strides to reach her were the most fundamentally necessary yet awkward of his life. Especially with Eryx, Lexi, and Abby weighting each step with their curious stares. He banded his arms around her and nestled her cheek against his chest. What his avid audience thought about his actions didn't matter. Only Brenna and her needs counted. He lowered his mouth to her ear, knowing all too well how his quietly murmured words would still register for Eryx. "Do you remember what I promised?"

Brenna pulled her head away enough to peek from beneath her lashes. "You're with me," she whispered.

"Until you decide otherwise." The clarification shredded his already shaken emotions, but it was important. Just because he was the first man she willingly chose didn't mean he'd be her last.

Movement sounded behind them followed by Abby's hushed voice. "Maybe I should reschedule."

Brenna stiffened beneath his arms, remembering their audience, and stepped out of his hold. "Reschedule what?"

Abby glanced at Lexi.

Lexi sipped her coffee, then motioned to Ludan and Brenna with her mug. "No way. It'll be a nice treat for the two of you. This is just morning after kissy-kissy." She winked at Brenna, then grinned at Abby. "I told you they'd end up together. The Lexi Mojo is never wrong."

"Oh." Abby rubbed her hand along the hollow at the base of her throat and quickly looked away from Ludan, centering on Brenna beside him. Given the bold flush that crept up her neck, he had a good idea which parent Brenna earned the blush from. "Well, I made us a spa appointment at a nail place down the street. Nothing fancy. Just a manicure and a pedi-cure." Her gaze flicked up to Ludan, then back to Brenna. "I can reschedule it for a better day though."

Brenna squeezed his bicep and a slow, delighted smile crept into place. Even with his limited profile view of her, he could see the thoughts churning behind her dark eyes.

The image of her in front of him, wrapping her tentative fingers around his shaft, blazed bold as the real deal in his head.

"I'd like that," she said. "Very much."

He barely bit back a moan and tried to will his cock into not responding. It didn't help. And something told him he'd end up liking the outcome of Abby's gift just as much as Brenna.

~

BRENNA STARED down at her smooth nails and smiled so big her cheeks hurt. Their length barely reached her fingertips, so she'd gone without colored polish, but they were even and glossy with a simple clear coat. Her palms beneath weren't completely free of the calluses she hated, but they were smoother, and the technician promised they'd go away completely in time.

She relaxed deeper into the massaging pedicure chair, closed her eyes, and wiggled her toes in the hot water. She'd tried to talk Lexi into joining them, but she'd insisted Brenna have time alone with her mom. Eryx hadn't helped the argu-ment, pointing out how Ramsay couldn't juggle the search for Serena alone.

Her mother's low voice sounded close beside her. "You like the surprise?"

"I love it." She rolled her head on the headrest and care-fully laid her hand over Abby's wrist so she didn't smudge the still-wet coral polish. "Thank you. I know in the bigger scheme having smooth hands and nails is silly, but I want to feel pretty."

Abby dipped her head toward Ludan sprawled in an uncomfortable-looking chair in the salon's cramped waiting area. "Because of him?"

Like it always did when she looked at him, her heart leapt a little stronger and tiny flutters whispered low in her belly. His arms were folded across his chest and his knees braced wide, ready for action at a moment's notice. Not once since he'd settled into his chair had he looked away from the television, but she'd bet her newfound freedom he knew every single thing happening in the bustling business. "Maybe a little before Ludan, but definitely now."

"So, Lexi was right? You really are...with him?"

Funny. Her mom seemed as nervous talking about intimacy as she was. Maybe it was a normal thing between mother and daughter. "Yeah." It came out daydreamy. As if her waking self hadn't really come to grips with last night actually happening or his beautiful promise.

A little girl in a yellow sundress with white polka dots toddled toward him. Given her unsteady gait and the limited amount of teeth lining her vibrant smile, she couldn't be more than a year and a half old. Clutched in her pudgy grip was a bright red plastic phone. She held it out to Ludan. "Hello."

Her mother stood sharply and started after her child, a mix of worry and fear on her face, but stopped short when Ludan took the phone and held it to his ear.

"Hello?" Even from twenty feet away his low voice vibrated through her, his simple, kind action for the child pushing tears to her eyes. He'd be a great father. Protective and indulgent.

Well, maybe indulgent with a daughter. For a son, he'd be

different. Kind but stern, teaching him how to be a protector in his own right.

"He scared me at first," Abby said, "but there's more to him than how he looks."

So much more. And Brenna imagined few people spent enough time with him to realize it.

"He's different around you," Abby said.

Brenna faced her mom. "Different how?"

Abby smiled, a little lopsided and distant, but a smile all the same. "The same way your father used to act around me. The rest of the world got a polite but closed-off mask, but for me, he was vulnerable." Her focus sharpened, and she cupped the side of Brenna's face. "He was that way with you, too. From the day you were born his eyes burned a little brighter. When he'd come home, you'd rush to meet him at the back door, and he'd sweep you up in a big hug. Nothing made him happier than hearing your giggles."

Memories rushed in fast and overwhelming. Her father's citrusy cologne and the suits he always wore to work. Swinging while he pushed her higher and higher. The way he'd read her stories before bed. "Ludan told me what happened."

Ducking her head, Abby brushed nonexistent lint from her jeans. "He blamed himself. I tried to tell him otherwise, but he couldn't shake it. Couldn't live with the guilt."

"It was my fault."

Abby's head snapped up. "No." She gripped Brenna's chin between her fingers and held it firm. "Never think that. Not for a minute. It's a parent's job to protect a child. Not the other way around." Her gaze slid to Ludan, then back to Brenna. "Someday you'll understand."

Oh, how she'd love that. Sharing a child with Ludan would be nothing short of perfect.

Her mother lifted Brenna's hand and studied her palms. "She did a good job."

Brenna nodded, already planning ways to experiment with Ludan and gaining his feedback on the improvements.

Smoothing her fingertip over one stubborn callus, Abby frowned. "I know you don't want to talk about how you know Ludan or the time you were away, but did he have anything to do with your disappearance?"

"He saved me." As soon as she spoke the words, she realized just how true the admission was. Lexi may have been the one to guide her from Maxis's house, but it was Ludan who'd tended her soul. "Lexi, Eryx, his brother Ramsay, and Ludan...they all saved me. But it was Ludan who brought me here and helped me find you."

In her periphery, Ludan shot to his feet. He prowled to the center of the salon, eyes locked on the television. The sound was down, so it barely registered over the constant whir of jetted water, but the closed captioning scrolled fast beneath the image on the screen.

A news anchor filled the screen. At the bottom the caption read, *Human Access to Eden Hinges on One Renegade*. A second later, a penciled image popped on the screen.

Her image.

It was roughly done and showed her with the braided pigtails Maxis had always forced her to wear, but it was her. Even the haunted glaze her eyes had held for the better part of her life was in place.

Ludan spun and stormed toward them. "Let's go." He urged Brenna from the chair and slid the sandals she'd worn closer to her feet. "Abby get your things."

Behind him, the TV shorted out and went dark. Throughout the salon, patrons reached for their phones and punched frantically on the bright screens.

Brenna fumbled with sliding her shoes on.

To her credit, Abby didn't argue, just scooped her shoes and purse up and hustled around to Ludan. "What's going on?"

"I'll tell you later." As soon as Brenna had slipped her last foot into place, he pulled both of them behind him, one of their wrists in each hand. "Stay close to me."

One of the women who worked at the salon came rushing forward. "It's her."

Ludan herded them both out the front door before she could close in on them and grabbed them both by each shoulder.

The woman hurried out the front door, looking in both directions, but never acknowledging their presence.

He'd masked them. Had completely blown his vow to keep his Myren existence secret in exchange for keeping her safe. "You shouldn't have done that," she whispered.

His arm settled on her shoulder, and he pulled her close beside him. His voice barely registered. "No one's touching you. Not on my watch." He glanced at Abby on his other side.

Her jaw hung slack, and her eyes were wide with shock.

"Abby." His command was low enough others around him wouldn't hear, but it was enough to shake her mother out of her stupor. "Keep one hand on me at all times. Don't let go. Understand?"

She swallowed, and her eyes cut to Brenna, but she nodded.

"Good." He guided her hand to his waist and squeezed her shoulder. "Just trust me a few more minutes." He started forward, carefully navigating the crowds so they never made contact with those walking the sidewalks.

Abby stumbled awkwardly behind Ludan, scanning the crowds along the downtown street. "I don't understand. Why don't they see us?"

"He's masking us." Protected beneath his arm, she couldn't reach her mother for comfort. Could only cast a sympathetic gaze across his broad chest. "We can see them, but they can't see us."

"He's one of the people from Eden," she muttered. "One of the people from Texas."

The last word had barely left her lips when they turned the corner into their apartment building, and Ludan urged her up the stairs in front of him. Whether her mother's tone had rubbed him the wrong way, or he was worried she'd do something to call attention to them, his tension jumped to a whole new level.

Brenna fisted her hand in his T-shirt at his waist. "She didn't mean anything by it. She doesn't know the whole story."

"I know she doesn't." He frowned and steered them both down the hall toward their apartment. "Just pisses me off Serena's the one doing PR for our race."

The apartment door swung open while they were still ten feet away.

Abby flinched and scrambled backward, plowing into Ludan's unyielding body.

"It's okay, Mom." Brenna urged her forward. "It's a gift. Nothing to be afraid of."

Gripping Brenna's hand, Abby plodded across the threshold. She might have been scared out of her wits, but as soon as the door shut behind them and Ludan dropped his contact, she faced him. "Tell me why my daughter's face is on national news and how she's caught up with a bunch of people who can do things that shouldn't be possible."

His scowl deepened, and the muscles at the back of his jaw took on a high-octane tick. "The man who took your daughter is dead, but his mate, Serena, is unfortunately still breathing. The two of them lead a cause that believes humans are lesser beings who should serve the Myren race. The best way to make that happen is to bring down the wall that separates our realms. From what I gathered, Serena's figured out your daughter is the key to making that happen and is pulling out all the stops to find her. Though I'll be damned if Serena gets anywhere near her." He paused long enough to huff a few haggard breaths. "That sums it up."

Abby opened her mouth, then closed it. Then did it again. She finally looked at Brenna and lifted both brows as if to admit she was so confused she didn't even know what to ask.

Brenna knew the feeling. She remembered all too well the confounding questions for the first year she'd been a captive, though she'd had zero demonstrations of goodness to counterbalance those inquiries. She laid a hand on her mother's shoulder. "For most of the time I was taken, all I knew were people who believed in the Rebellion. People like the man who took me, Maxis, and Serena. But what I've learned in the last few months is that most Myrens are good people. I told you Eryx, Lexi, and Ludan saved me. What I didn't tell you is Eryx is their malran. He's a good leader. One who's kept humans safe from people like Maxis for a long time."

Deep furrows marked her mother's brow. "Malran?"

"King," Brenna clarified.

"And the things you can do." Abby motioned toward the door. "Opening things without touching them and hiding us. How is that possible?"

"We're a different race." The edge in Ludan's voice was gone, replaced with a weariness that made Brenna's heart ache. "We're just like you, but with more abilities. And that bit in Texas you mentioned ended in Maxis's death, so I won't apologize for it. If it was up to me, he'd have suffered more."

The tension in Abby's shoulders eked out on a slow

exhale, and she jerked her head in a stiff nod. "I'm sorry. I've seen you with my daughter, and I know you care for her. You and your friends. I won't apologize for being frightened, but I shouldn't have jumped to conclusions."

The memory of her sketched image on the television and the odd caption beneath shook its way to the forefront of Brenna's thoughts. "Wait. You never said how my drawing ended up on TV."

The blue in Ludan's eyes sparked with barely contained fury. "Serena's newest play. She and a man they didn't name took a reporter, a reputable one no one would think of discrediting, to Eden. They demonstrated their powers and said those powers could belong to humans."

"Can they?" Abby said.

"No." As soon as Brenna answered, the truth of her own situation slammed anvil-heavy in her head. "Well, not without intervention. And even then, it's not the same."

"The truth doesn't matter to her." Ludan prowled to the window overlooking the street below them. "What does matter is you. By promising power to humans and telling them you're the renegade keeping them from crossing over, she's just turned every power-hungry human into a bounty hunter."

"But I'm not keeping anyone out." Not yet anyway. Though every time she'd considered what to do if faced with the decision, she'd immediately resolved to keep it in place. Forever.

"No, you're not. But no one else knows that. And thanks to Serena, a lot of people want into Eden now." Ludan let the curtains fall back into place and faced Brenna and her mother. "I fried the electronics with a pretty good pulse, but by now word's definitely gotten out you're in the area. You're not safe here. Not anymore. Everyone from nut jobs to the government will track you." His bitter frown sent shivers down her spine. "I want to take you back to Eden."

"I just found my mom. I don't want to leave her again."

"Then I'll take her, too."

"But it's against the rules." A knot as big as her fist formed in the base of her throat and burned as though coated with acid. "Eryx said the penalty for that is death."

"No fault will lie with you. Only me."

That was what she was afraid of. Just the idea of never seeing him again—let alone being the cause of his demise—was too much to even process.

He crept toward her. "You're overthinking this. You forget who the malran is. Don't think for one second Eryx won't throw down for either one of us. Now what's your decision?"

Her decision. Like everything else he'd done for her, he'd zeroed in on the one most critical aspect of the situation. It was her choice to make. Not one to be forced on her by anyone else. She glanced at her mom.

Ludan cupped Brenna's shoulder and pulled her close, lowering his voice. "Understand, there will be guards. Not to keep you under control, but to keep you safe. Life won't be like it has been here, not for a while. It won't even be like it was at the castle before we left."

"Would you let me stay if I said that's what I wanted?"

His lips tightened to the point they ran white, but he nodded.

Of course he would. The stubborn, proud, beautiful man would stay here until he couldn't function or died keeping her safe. No way would she put him at that kind of risk. Not when Eden and the support she'd find there was an option. "Then I'll go." She turned to her mom. "Will you come with me? I can't promise the outcome, but what the humans who visited said is true. It's beautiful." Far more beautiful than anything she'd found here.

A tremulous smile crept across her mother's face, and she framed Brenna's cheeks in both hands. "I've already lost you once. I won't lose you again."

CHAPTER 24

Serena trailed Uther from the misty gray portal out of New York City into the Underlands and nearly groaned beneath the sweltering heat. The soft pink velvet gown she'd worn to visit the reporter had been a tactical mistake for August in the muggy state, but for the Underlands it was torture. "Praise the Great One, I'll be glad when I can live in a region with a decent climate."

Uther stomped up the two steps to his raised, weathered porch and jerked his front door open with a thought well before he reached it.

She hurried behind him and shut the rickety closure against the unmerciful Myren sun. "What in histus is wrong with you? You've been nasty ever since we took the reporter back. You should be happy. Everything's going exactly like the Spiritu said it would."

"Is it?" He yanked open the small, rudimentary cooler near the back of his kitchen, and wisps of ice-cooled air swirled around the edges. He pulled out a large pitcher of ale and snagged a tall tumbler off the shelf.

"What's that supposed to mean?"

He poured the peachy brew nearly to the top, slammed the pitcher down on the counter, and gulped at least half the contents in one go. He lowered the glass and stared at the remainder. "You didn't tell me about the girl."

Actually, there were several details she'd left out when sharing the Spiritu's visit. "I didn't think the details mattered so long as we both got what we wanted." More importantly, what *she* wanted. As in the wall down and the powers that went with it.

"I realize a conscience is a novel concept for you," Uther said, "but I have one. I didn't join Maxis because of his precious Rebellion. I cozied up to him for one thing and one thing only. Information. Information leads to power, and power is everything. That doesn't mean I'm willing to slaughter an innocent human who's already been fucked over by Maxis. You said the bearer of the key would bring the wall down."

"Exactly. The bearer. Or more to the Spiritu's lingo, the judge, which is Brenna. And who said anything about slaughter?" Serena waved Uther off and strolled to the tiny living room. Normally she hated the cold that descended on the Underlands at sunset, but tonight she'd welcome it. She dropped none too elegantly into the worn armchair near the empty fireplace, her patience drained from their outing in Evad. "The girl is a means to an end. She'll wield the key and bring the wall down like we tell her to."

"And how am I supposed to be sure the power will go to me and not someone else? Someone like you?"

Five times he'd asked her that, poking and prodding for some slip in her story. She rested her head on the cushioned chair back, closed her eyes, and recited the same lie she had the night the Spiritu severed her links. "It's your family's destiny."

"You always say that as if you know the details behind it.

You certainly knew more about who's supposed to use the key. Makes me wonder if there's more you know."

Oh, she knew more. Much more. Scraps of information she had no intention of sharing with Uther. Like the fact that Brenna would actually choose who the recipient of the powers would be, as well as whether or not the wall stayed up.

Still, passing on a little history wouldn't hurt anything and might actually stop his repeated inquiries. She stared at him. "Your ancestor was one of six murdered by Hagan Xenese, a first-generation Myren no less powerful than the first malran, Kentar Shantos. Hagan was exiled to Evad and forced to live one millennium for each death. The Great One built a wall between the two realms. Hagan's powers were stripped to fuel it."

"Why?"

"Why what?"

Uther stalked toward her. "Why did he murder them?"

She sighed and went back to glaring at the ceiling. "Because the men raped and killed his human mate."

Silence filled the tiny room, only the approaching sunset's whipping wind sweeping around the worn down shack.

She rubbed one temple and tried to let go of the anxiety knotting her stomach. The next task she'd have to tackle came with extraordinary risk and little guarantee of success. Dealing with Uther's grumbling only scattered her focus. "Stop worrying, Uther. The power will go to you as the prophecy foretold. You'll take down Eryx, I'll be your advisor, and we'll all live happily ever after."

Well, one of them would live, at least, and she'd be the one in power. Whether or not Uther kept breathing depended on how well he fell in line. "If you want, you can gift our little pet with whatever she desires in return for our demands."

"What else?"

His voice cut like a whip, snapping across her already frayed nerves and jerking her to her feet. "The Great One take it. What's with all the questions?"

"I'm tired of being in the dark. Tired of theatrics in Evad that have no bearing on what we're out to do. I know you, Serena. You'd cut your own mother's throat if it meant getting something you want. I'm not stupid enough to think you're not holding more back. A detail that's bound to piss me off or get me killed. Considering I'm the only backup and muscle you have right now, I suggest you share, or you'll be on your own."

He wouldn't.

He scowled down at her. A hard, mercenary glint in his sage eyes that said he'd happily take her out of the equation if she pushed further.

Okay, maybe he *would* bail on her. Then again, if she didn't meet her obligations to the Spiritu, she'd be dead anyway.

She paced the length of the room and rubbed the back of her neck. Her heart thrummed a hummingbird pulse, and a bead of sweat trickled between her shoulder blades. She'd already fudged on some of the information Patrice had given her. A little more wouldn't hurt, assuming she could keep her complicated lies from getting tangled.

Pausing in front of the fireplace, she faced Uther and lifted her chin. "In order to get the information we needed, and in exchange for severing all my links, I had to barter something."

Uther straightened, his weight shifting as though ready to pounce.

"Nothing that has to do with you," she added quickly. "But one that will help us."

"And that is?"

Standing by the front door, she stared out the tall skinny

window beside it. The horizon blazed a scarlet red as the sun began its descent, heat radiating up from the sand in dizzying waves. "You remember how I explained there's a dark and a light contingent?"

"One for pure actions and one for passion."

"The dark and the light. They're supposed to stay in balance. Patrice's mate was part of a rogue faction who wanted the two sides out of balance. Wanted the dark passions to rule." She faced him. "The things I've been doing, bringing more people to Eden and interviewing with the reporter, it's all for that."

"And how is that supposed to help us?"

"Because if the dark passions rule, our race will more easily transition to natural order based on power and strength. But mostly, it gets us the final bit of information we need."

"So there's more?"

Not really. Patrice already had her over a barrel with a blood vow, so withholding information wasn't necessary. She'd actually felt the agreement bind her very soul when her blood mingled with Patrice's. Otherwise, she'd forgo fulfilling her debts and get on with bringing the wall down. Still, making Uther think there was more to the equation might help keep him in line. "Just how we initiate the actual rite. Patrice said it would be given to me when the time was right."

"Then what other parlor tricks are we committed for?"

"Something to make people panic. Something big that will get humans working against each other."

Uther huffed out a laugh and ambled to the couch. He sprawled against the faded cushions and propped one foot on the low table in front of him. "And how exactly are we supposed to do that with just the two of us?"

Serena edged closer. "A simple promise. A vow that the

first person to turn over Brenna will be the first to go to Eden and inherit Myren powers."

"Myren powers can't be given."

"I know that. You know that. But they don't."

Uther gaped at her. "You think humans will cut each other's throats for power?"

"Why wouldn't they? You already have more power than most average Myrens, yet you slit one of your peer's throats to gain more. Imagine what someone who has no powers would do to gain even a fraction of what we have."

Uther stared, the truth of what she'd just shared burning deep. "And how, exactly, are the two of us supposed to navigate all the leads generated on locating the girl?"

Serena gingerly sat beside him, a tiny bit of anticipation bubbling up from beneath the weight of the day's fatigue. "We won't have to follow those at all. Brenna will come of her own accord. Just as soon as we snare the right bait."

CHAPTER 25

*G*old and blood-red skies marked the portal's exit into Eden, silver energy streaks whizzing past the sunset skyline. Another hour and the sun would disappear below the horizon.

And Ludan would have Brenna safe.

Brenna's mother staggered beside him for the umpteenth time since they'd started the trip, and he tightened his arm around her waist. He'd tried to carry her, but she'd insisted on walking, keeping a death grip on her daughter's hand the whole way.

Brenna, on the other hand, had finally got the knack of the portal's bog-like surface. She smiled at Abby and pointed to the deepening colors ahead. "Not too much farther. See? There's the end."

A soft breeze swept through the tunnel, the scent of flowers from his father's garden, woodsmoke, and the bite of grass and algae from the nearby lake a welcome break from the portal's metallic edge. With every step, his powers surged with Eden's abundant energy.

They reached the edge, and Ludan guided Abby across

the tricky exit. Before he could turn to help Brenna, she was already out, her eyes wide and scanning the peaceful land-scape. Her gaze snagged on the gray stone cottage nestled at the base of a giant black mountain. "This isn't the castle."

"No, it's where my father lives." Ludan paused long enough to make sure Abby had her balance before he let her go. "That mountain range marks the farthest edge of Havilah."

"Your father?"

On cue, the front door of the cottage opened and Graylin strolled out of it, Orla beside him.

Ludan urged both women forward. "We hid Lexi here when we first brought her over. Dad thought it might be a good option for you, too. No one outside the Shantos family and their mates know where it is, so you won't have the guards. It also means we won't have to worry about Serena finding you."

Graylin met them at the sandstone path. Unlike his usual somber and patient expression, his eyes were bright and his skin a little flushed. He held out his hand to Brenna's mother. "Mrs. Haven. It's my pleasure to welcome you to my home."

Abby took the hand he offered, clearly anticipating a polite shake, but sucked in a delicate gasp when Graylin bowed over their joined hands in the most formal of greetings.

Formal.

As if meeting an intended mate's parents.

Ludan fought back a growl and scowled at his father. *"Don't blow this out of proportion."*

Graylin lifted his head and grinned at Abby, completely ignoring Ludan's telepathic message.

"Please, call me Abby. And we're very grateful to you for offering us your home. I hope we won't be too much of an imposition."

"No imposition at all." Graylin motioned to Orla. "This is Orla Weathers. She's part of the Shantos family and has agreed to stay and help us keep the cottage running smoothly while you're here."

Abby shook Orla's hand. "You're Eryx and Ramsay's mother?"

"Oh, I'd love to claim them, but no. I'm closer to nanny than mother. I've been with their family since shortly after Eryx and Ramsay were born." Orla winked at Ludan. "Spent just as much time around our gruff one here, too."

The wind snapped and whistled behind them.

Abby spun to gauge the source of the unexpected whirlwind. Above her, Eryx, Ramsay, Lexi, and Trinity were all aimed feet-first toward the grass right behind them.

"Oh!" Abby jerked back as they landed, one hand fluttering at the base of her throat.

Brenna giggled and wrapped an arm around her mother's shoulder, more delight coloring her face than he'd seen from her the whole time she'd been in Evad. "Isn't it marvelous? And it feels even better than it looks. Kind of like a really windy day, only you're part of the wind instead of something it fights against."

Abby's eyebrows hopped even higher. "You can fly?"

"Well, no." Brenna's gaze cut to Ludan, a shy blush stealing across her cheeks. "I've flown a few times with Ludan. It was scary at first, but once I relaxed it was lovely."

His shoulders pushed back, pride and something heady he couldn't quite identify surging thick through his veins. If he'd known how much she liked it, he'd have flown her the whole damned way to Florida.

Eryx and Ramsay ambled forward, Lexi and Trinity on either side. Unlike Ludan, the men wore standard-issue silver drasts and black leather pants. Trinity was her usual sunshine self with a yellow tunic and leggings, while Lexi rocked the malress image in a bold blue dress that clung to every curve.

Skipping formalities, Lexi wrapped Abby in a familiar hug. "I'd say I'm sorry for your trip down the rabbit hole, but the truth is I'm glad you're here. I doubt Brenna would have come back without you." She stepped back, keeping her arms clasped at Abby's shoulders. "I'm sorry we didn't tell you everything before. Sharing about our realm is a big no-no."

Swiping her hand along her stomach as though to try and settle it, Abby huffed out a shaky chuckle. "I believe I can see why."

Eryx grinned and offered his hand. "It's good to have you here, Abby." He motioned to Ramsay beside him. "This is my brother, Ramsay, and his mate, Trinity."

Abby nodded her head at both of them. "It's nice to meet you."

Orla stepped to Abby's side and motioned everyone toward the door. "Why don't we get Abby inside so she can have a minute to catch her breath? Or have the rest of you forgotten what your first portal trip was like?"

The whole crew kicked into gear, Abby naturally gravitating to Orla's side as if she'd known her for years instead of minutes. But then, Orla was good that way. Always treating strangers with the same radiating warmth that filled her kitchen.

Ludan crowded close to Brenna and wrapped his arm around her waist, resting his hand on the slope of her hip.

Graylin fell in step beside them, his gaze locked on the possessive touch and a pleased smirk curling his lips. *"Blowing things out of proportion, hmmm? I've watched you for a hundred and fifty-two years and not once have I seen you act possessive of a woman."*

His conscience kicked and demanded Ludan release her before anyone else got the same idea. The beast grunted and tightened his hold on her hip. Brenna might not need him tomorrow, or the day after that, but right now she did. He'd be damned if he didn't take advantage.

Once inside the cottage, Brenna craned her head from side to side, absorbing all the details she could while keeping up with the group. He'd never lived here himself, his father building the reclusive getaway after his mother's death, but it was just as warm and welcoming as the house he'd grown up in. Given the way she eyed the front living area with its gold and red decor and oversized couches and chairs, he figured it would be one of her first stops on a slower, self-navigated tour later. The only other room that outperformed it was the upstairs balcony with its view of the lake and mountain range.

The spice and herb scent of roasted aron drifted through the hallway, the heat of the kitchen's oven right behind it and weighted with cinnamon, caramel, and baked apples.

"Smells like Lexi's getting her lastas," Brenna muttered.

They rounded the corner just as Lexi sidled up to the cooling row of pastries and pinched the corner off the farthest one. She popped the bite between her lips, and her eyes slid shut. "I swear," she said around the mouthful. "These will never get old."

"They are addictive." Trinity rounded the far end of the long trestle table and took a seat beside Ramsay. The huge bay window stretched behind them, putting the spacious backyard on prime display. "Then again, everything Orla cooks is addictive. If it wasn't for the Myren part of my metabolism, I'd be as big as a house already."

Ramsay slung his arm around her shoulders, pulled her in close, and nuzzled her neck, not the least bit uncomfortable with his audience. "That's not genetics, sunshine. That's all the calorie burn we've been working on."

"Ramsay." Orla smacked her wooden spoon against the

stock pan and glared at him from the kitchen island. "Brenna's mother just got here. Let her get situated before you convince her all our men are playboys."

Ludan pulled a chair out for Brenna at one end of the table while Eryx and Lexi settled at the other.

Ramsay's eyes cut to Ludan where his hand rested on Brenna's shoulder. "Got a pretty good idea she's really only concerned with one of us."

All the poking, prodding, and wishful thinking converged at once, physical and verbal assaults queuing up for launch faster than he could process them.

"Enough." Eryx's low but lethal command sliced across the table. He held Ludan's stare until Ludan unclenched his hand from the back of Brenna's chair, then shifted his focus to Ramsay. He didn't speak, at least not where everyone else could hear, but the intensity behind his eyes said Ramsay was getting plenty between his ears. About five heartbeats later, he reclined in his chair and rested his arm on Lexi's chair back, his attention on Ludan. "Tell me what you heard on the news."

"High-level info at best." Finally comfortable with a line of conversation he could stomach, Ludan leaned against the wall behind Brenna's seat and crossed his arms. "Something about a big-name reporter, a new tour of Eden, and promising humans the same powers as Myrens. Brenna's picture came up with the renegade caption under it, so I fried the electronics and got everyone out."

Eryx nodded and glanced at Graylin next to Lexi and Abby. "Well, about ten minutes after Ludan contacted me, Ian and Jilly came back to Eden with the finer details. All this time we've assumed the person bringing people here was Serena. Now we know it is. She and a man who wasn't identified nabbed a reporter and a police sketch artist and took them to Eden. The reporter's name is Tilly Rhinehart, and she's covered some of the biggest stories in recent world history. Her reputation is spotless. So much so, there's not a single person who hears her story who won't give it credence."

"And the story Serena gave them was that Brenna is the person keeping the wall from coming down," Ramsay added.

Black burned the edges of Ludan's eyesight, and the muscles in his arms bunched with the need to squeeze Serena's neck until it snapped. "I want her dead. As long as she's alive, Brenna's not safe."

"We're looking," Eryx said, "but we've got almost nothing to go on."

Lexi laid her hand on Eryx's thigh. "Ian went back to dig through the reporter's story for details. Maybe see if there are any clues on where Serena might be staying."

"I've sent a crew to Orlando near the spa you guys went to," Ramsay said. "That news has to have traveled fast. If Serena's goal is to flush Brenna out, she'll show hoping to reel her in."

Ludan zeroed in on Trinity. "Anything else from the Spiritu?"

"Nothing. The Black King won't see me again."

"Well, someone has to be helping her." Lexi scanned the room and shared a sour scowl. "No way that dimwit translated the journal faster than us."

Her sassy bite cut the room's tension in half and painted a grin on Eryx's face. He squeezed her shoulder. "Easy, hellcat."

It was just a simple squeeze, nothing remarkable at all, but Ludan couldn't look away from Eryx's hand on Lexi. A tight, burning sensation noosed around his neck, barbed and jagged thorns stabbing so deep he couldn't breathe. Eryx had Lexi. Ramsay had Trinity. Histus, even his father had Orla now. Every damned one of them moved so easily with each other. Comfortable and familiar. He could never let himself get to that point with Brenna, not without coming out broken on the other end. Seeing her with someone else would slaughter him.

His gaze drifted to her arm, the yellow sundress she'd worn that morning for her day with Abby leaving the pale stretch of skin bare for everyone to see. Even if she wanted him long term, he'd never be able to mark her. To truly bond with her the way Myren mates did.

As if sensing his stare, she faced him. "What if we set up a trap?"

Everyone's attention lasered onto Brenna.

"Come again?" Eryx said.

She swiveled back to the rest of the table. "I'm what Serena wants. Why not use me to lure her out?"

Ludan pushed away from the wall and dropped his arms. "No."

"Why not?" Clearly knowing better than to try to sway him, she honed in on Eryx. "If rumors of me in Evad are enough to draw her notice, wouldn't rumors of me returning to Eden do the same?"

Ludan gripped the back of her chair and leaned in close. "No."

"Actually, that's a good idea."

Ludan snapped upright and glared at Ramsay. *"If you want to die tonight, you've found a pretty damned good ticket to get there."*

Trinity backhanded Ramsay in the chest. "Are you out of your mind?"

Ramsay held up his hands, eyes mostly on Ludan. "No wait, you're missing Brenna's point. She doesn't have to stay wherever it is we've set up. We just make a big deal of her being somewhere, make it look like she's going to be around awhile, but we mask her right out the back door."

"You really think Serena would fall for that?" Lexi crossed her legs and frowned. "I wouldn't."

"But Serena's greedy," Eryx said. "If she figured out the prophecy, then she knows what's at stake. Histus, she was ballsy enough to steal right out from under our noses."

They were idiots. Every damned one of them. "I don't like it."

Graylin, who'd been taking in the commentary with quiet observation, lifted a hand to halt the conversation. "Take no action yet. Wait and see if Ramsay's men are able to catch her in Florida. If not, reconsider. In the interim, you have time to plan and work through flaws." He ended the guidance with his eyes on Ludan. He might have staved off the idea for now, but the resignation and regret etched across his worried brow said he didn't think the respite would last long.

Which meant Ludan would have to amp up his game. "What about the Rebellion men who came forward?"

Eryx frowned. "Nothing of substance we didn't already know. The only common thread they offered was Maxis's strategos, Uther Rontal. Not one of them knows how to find him."

"No records of him at the capital? No relatives?"

"Not a thing." Eryx pinched the bridge of his nose and let out a tired sigh before he lifted his head. "I know you don't want to hear this, Ludan, but Serena's covered her tracks pretty damned well. I think you should consider Brenna's idea."

Like histus he'd go there. Not yet. Not unless they ran out of other options, and there was still one he hadn't played. He planted his hands on the back of Brenna's chair. "I want to scan them."

Brenna twisted so fast she'd have toppled her seat had he not been holding on. "No."

Ludan kept his eyes on Eryx. "I get more detail in my

scans than anyone. Even yours or Ramsay's. One of those men has to know something."

"No." Brenna shot to her feet, her dark eyes flashing with enough anger to fight a whole squadron solo.

His muscles slackened and his heartbeat leveled, the same eerie calm he'd felt when he'd broken his vow as Eryx's somo settling deep in his core. "You're willing to use yourself as bait. I'm willing to use my gifts. There's no difference."

"There's a huge difference. You didn't see the condition you were in, Ludan. You were barely breathing. Your mind was covered in gray ash, and you looked like you'd been flayed alive."

"I had been. Right along with Angus." He cupped the back of her neck. The room grew quiet and freakishly still, the weight of everyone's stares uncomfortable in such a private moment. Uncomfortable, but nowhere near the pain he'd experience if he got what he wanted. He kissed her forehead and pulled in her sweet, innocent scent. "I'd do it again if it gave me the answers I need to keep you safe."

Her lower lip trembled, and her eyes welled with tears.

Squeezing her shoulders, he lifted his head and zeroed in on Eryx. "Do you have the contacts I need or not?"

Eryx's gaze slid to Brenna, then back to Ludan, and nodded.

"Then set it up." Prying his hands free, he stepped away and stalked toward the kitchen's main exit before anyone could take another pass at changing his mind. "First thing tomorrow we start working through them."

CHAPTER 26

a door from somewhere beyond the kitchen slammed shut, and the crippling panic that had seized Brenna's lungs squeezed a little tighter. "He can't do this." She spun toward Eryx. "You can't let him."

Eryx sighed and scanned the other people at the table. "Give us a minute."

Slowly, everyone stood, only Lexi making eye contact as she squeezed Eryx's arm and smiled at Brenna.

Orla paused beside Abby. "Why don't you let me show you your room? Ludan's is belowground, but we have a pretty room made up for you near the sunroom upstairs."

Abby hesitated, seeking guidance from Brenna with just a look.

"I'll be okay, Mom. Let Orla show you around."

Ramsay trailed behind Trinity and slapped Eryx on the back as he passed. "We'll wait for Galena and Reese out front."

Graylin was the last to depart. He'd nearly crossed the arched opening that led to a cozy sitting room beyond, but he paused and offered her a sad smile. "You probably won't understand this, but as dangerous as what he's willing to do might seem, I'm grateful he has someone in his life he wants to fight for."

The weight of his remark slammed against her so hard she nearly staggered backward. By the time she'd caught her bearings, Graylin was gone.

Eryx motioned to the chair closest to him with a nod. "Sit."

Even with him sitting down and out of arm's reach, a shadow of her old self wanted to run. To double the distance between them. The new her, the one who'd found freedom and confidence through her gentle giant, lifted her chin and took her seat.

Through the huge picture window, silver swirls danced across a fast-deepening blue sky. Simmering coals from the still-warm oven crackled behind her. Otherwise, no sounds but her shaky breath registered.

Eryx studied her, reclined against his chair back in a relaxed pose. "I can't stop him."

"But you saw—"

Eryx held up a hand. "Even if I tried, he'd go around me." He frowned, then leaned into the table, crossing his arms in front of him. "I told you there are bigger things at play here. Things even Ludan doesn't comprehend yet."

"What's to comprehend? It's a suicide mission. You saw what happened."

"I did. But I also know that if anyone—human, Myren, or Spiritu—tried to get between me and protecting my mate, I'd annihilate them."

Rest and hold your mate.

Her breath caught, and if Eryx hadn't stayed rock solid in her field of vision, she'd have sworn the world spun wildly around her. "I'm not his mate. I'm a human."

"Lexi's half human. Trinity has the blood of all three races."

"But I'm *just* human."

"Are you?" One corner of Eryx's mouth curved into an ornery grin. "How many humans do you know who are capable of healing a Myren?"

Flutters winged behind her sternum, and she clenched her fist above her heart to try to still its rapid thump. "Don't."

"Don't what?"

"Don't give me that kind of hope." Even as she said it a bright, tingling sensation radiated through her chest, warming parts of her she'd long thought dead.

Eryx cocked his head, the grin replaced with profound solemnity. "Maybe hope is what you need. What you both need."

A future with Ludan. A bond beyond just the physical. So many years she'd tucked away the idea of a lasting relationship. Ignored the wish for fear no one would find her desirable. But Ludan wanted her. "He hasn't said anything. How can you even think he'd be interested in me?"

A low, self-satisfied chuckle rumbled from his chest. "I told you. He doesn't even see it himself yet. Or more to the point, won't let himself."

"Then how can you be so sure?"

"I can't. No one can." He narrowed his eyes and lowered his voice. "You could have curled up in a ball and refused to fight the whole time you were with Maxis, but you didn't. Why is that?"

"Because I wanted out. I wanted to survive long enough to find something better."

Eryx smiled, the glint behind his silver eyes that of a man who'd just proven his point. "You survived, Brenna. You survived, and now your something better is here. You'll just have to fight a little more to get it."

~

LUDAN TOSSED a stone into the lake and watched the stars' reflections wobble in the slowly growing ripples across the once smooth surface. A larken sang in the distance, too damned chipper and singsongy for his nasty mood. An hour now he'd sat on the cooling earth beside the lake and tried to calm the escalating voices in his head, but nothing worked. The only constant, the only image he could easily conjure, was Brenna's face, her tears as bright as the moon.

He pulled his knees up and rested his arms on top. Dropping his head against the tree trunk behind him, he scowled at the sky. At this point his only options were fighting with Eryx or drinking himself into a stupor.

You could go to Brenna.

He shoved the thought aside and rolled his neck from side to side. Being with Brenna was the last thing he needed. If he saw her, touched her, he'd cave. Her safety meant more than his comfort, and the only way to do that without letting her put herself at risk was finding Serena. That meant sucking it up long enough to do what needed doing. Getting his head firmly reacquainted to the noise between his ears well in advance probably wouldn't be a bad byproduct either.

Footsteps sounded near the winding sand path. A heavy, slower tread, not the least bit camouflaged. Definitely his dad because Ramsay and Eryx seldom went anywhere slowly unless there was stalking or an attack involved.

His father came into view. "You've been out here a while."

Ludan jerked his chin up in acknowledgment but otherwise kept his gaze on the lake.

"Orla got Brenna and Abby situated." He eased into the old rocker he kept beside the mammoth feelan tree. For years as he'd built the cottage and recovered from the loss of his mate, Graylin had gravitated to this quiet spot. He gazed up at the canopy of feathery leaves, the branches spanning almost as wide as the house. "She was a bit worried she'd overstepped by putting Brenna in your room, but I told her that's where you'd want her."

The muscles in his torso tightened, the thought of Brenna warm and pliant in his bed shoving him closer to giving in.

"Was she wrong?" Graylin asked.

"No." Ludan snatched another loose pebble and chunked it toward the lake. "She's where she needs to be."

Graylin rocked back an inch, and the teakwood rocker groaned. "The last thing I want to do is cross an unwelcome boundary, but I'm also your father. Part of being a father is teaching you what I can, and I suspect you're lacking in this particular area, so I'd like to offer some guidance."

Ludan picked up a twig and rolled it between his fingers. "Lacking in what area?"

"Relationships."

Boy, he wasn't wrong there. Ludan had thought he had a handle on things. Had accepted his place as short-term comfort, but just being away from her for a few hours had frayed his nerves.

"Perhaps if Brenna is in your room," Graylin said, "the place for you to be is beside her."

"I can't. If I do, I'll cave."

"To what?"

The twig snapped in half. "The scans."

Silence dropped hard enough to quiet even the wind and insects buzzing in the night.

"You're afraid you won't do them? Of what will happen if you do?"

Terrified was more accurate. Not that he'd ever admit it out loud. Histus, he could barely admit it to himself. "She needs me."

"There are other ways to help her, Ludan."

"Her acting as bait can't be one of them."

Graylin sighed. "No, I suppose that wouldn't be an option for me were I in your shoes either." He rocked back and forth, the motion lazy and soothing within their quiet space. "Why would you cave if you went to her?"

"Eryx told you about my gift? What it does and how she stops it?"

The rocking slowed and then stopped. "He did."

"Then imagine how hard walking away from that would be, knowing you're about to willingly add more to what's already there." Ludan hung his head. "I don't want to give myself that chance to balk. Not if I can make her safe."

"The same way you wished you'd made your mother safe."

Ludan froze. For a second, even his heart forgot to beat, then lurched forward at a limping sprint.

"I'm not naive, son. I knew you confirmed my brother's guilt through your gift and cast judgment, and I'm proud you avenged her. My only wish is that it could have been me who broke his neck instead of you."

Ludan forced himself to breathe, to wrap his conscious mind around the peaceful sounds around him and ignore the percolating screams in his head.

"I know you hold yourself responsible," Graylin said. "I've seen the guilt in every merciless chain of self-discipline you've bound yourself with. But if you blame yourself, then I'm guilty as well. I was serving our malran instead of protecting my mate. I could have made other choices. Eryx's father never would have begrudged me looking after Rista. If I'd put you both first, she'd be alive, and you wouldn't be tortured with her cries in your head. That's what you hear, am I right? Everything my brother inflicted, you relive?"

Ludan jerked a rough nod and fisted his hands at his sides. "I was with Eryx and Ramsay." The knot in his throat mushroomed to a razor-lined boulder. "You told me to be on time, but I didn't listen. I was late. You told me how important it was, and I failed you. I failed her."

"Son, you could never fail either of us. The only person you could ever fail is yourself. And my guess is, your mother would be far more disappointed in you not grasping love when it's offered. Seizing love and treasuring it is the greatest gift we'll ever be given. Predicting the future is impossible."

Praise the Great One, his mother had been beautiful. Dark, glossy hair and a willowy, elegant frame. He'd never met anyone with a smile as bright as hers. Everything about her was light and pure. As powerful as the first spring day after a cold and brutal winter. And she would have adored Brenna.

"I'm afraid I'll hurt her." The admission hopped out uncensored, but as soon as it caught air, a weight lifted.

"Hurt her how?"

Yeah, explaining wasn't nearly so easy of a task. One wrong word and his dad could either write him off as a loon or a pussy. He cleared his throat, searching for the right words. "There's a part of me that's different. Animal almost. Like it's got a mind of its own."

"And?" Not a judgment. Not a funny look to go with it. Just a calm, conversational request for information.

"It's stronger with her. Even more than when I fight."

"As it should be."

Ludan snapped his face toward his father.

"You're a warrior, Ludan. Every man has a primal instinct inside him, but for a fighter, a protector, that instinct is stronger. It's what feeds and gives us the strength to do what we do. It's not something to be feared, but something to guide you. To protect those you love."

Ludan slumped against the tree behind him, all the

assumptions and fears he'd juggled for years scattered and rearranged into a new truth he couldn't quite process.

"Do you love her, son?"

Ludan blinked over and over, his mind stumbling to catch up. How could he possibly answer that question? He knew he loved his family, that he loved Eryx and Ramsay as though they were his brothers, but Brenna? "I don't know. It's..." No words worked. "Without description."

Graylin's low chuckle slipped through the night's quiet. "I remember that feeling. But I found my definition, and you'll find yours." He stood and paced to the edge of the sand path. "You know, there is one other thing you could do."

"About Serena?"

"Not exactly." His gaze caught on a streak of energy high in the sky above the far end of the lake. "More for Brenna. As a precaution."

Ludan held his silence, waiting.

"She healed you."

"And?"

"If she can mirror our gifts well enough to heal you, she should be able to defend herself." He cocked his head. "Assuming someone took the time to teach her."

He could. Absolutely, he could. Emotions may not be his forte, but fighting sure as hell was.

For the first time since he'd stalked out of the house, he found his mental footing, all the avalanching worries he'd nursed about Brenna and the upcoming scan knocked sideways by simple yet very tangible action. "You think it would work?"

"I think anything is possible. It might take more time to teach her than an awakened Myren, but it would be time well spent if she finds herself in a difficult situation."

It was smart. Damned smart. The beast stomped and snorted from inside his cage, pissed he hadn't thought of it first. Ludan nodded, more to himself than his dad. "I'll work with her tomorrow." He met his father's gaze. "After."

Even cast in the moon's shadow, there was no missing his father's frown. "Then you still plan to wait until after to see her?"

"Could you have walked away from Mom?"

A sad smile tilted his lips. "No. I could never walk away from Rista."

"Then you understand why."

Graylin bobbed his head and turned for the house.

"Pops."

His father stopped and looked back.

"Ask Lexi to talk to her. Tell her I'll be back tomorrow. I don't want her to worry."

Graylin scratched the back of his head and sighed. "You've got a lot to learn about relationships, son. No matter what Lexi conveys, Brenna will worry." He started down the path. "But I'll ask Lexi to talk to her all the same."

CHAPTER 27

*M*orning sunlight slanted over the arena's east wall, its rays sparking off the torques and cuffs of at least a hundred warriors as they powered through their daily natxu. Most were new recruits, only a few years past their awakening and fresh to their vows. Ludan shut the entrance gate behind him and studied their dedicated yet unpracticed movements. He couldn't remember the last time he'd felt that eager. That lacking in cynicism.

Except the last two weeks. Those have been pretty nice.

The thought blasted so pronounced through his head, he flinched. Odd, because the voice wasn't his own. He blinked and tried to replay it, but unlike the memories he stored, it was gone, only a dreamlike whisper in its place.

He shook it off and strode along the stadium's far edge, angled for the tunnel entrance and the containment cells below. With every step, heads turned, curious gazes that should be focused on their drills.

Fuck if he could blame them. Hard not to ogle the only somo in history who'd filched on his vow. He threw the tunnel doors wide with a mental push and stomped down the carved stone halls. He should have picked someplace different to do his work, especially after how Angus's scan had turned out. If things went south a second time, he'd have a much bigger audience than the first go-round.

At the end of the hall, the thick blackwood door to the malran's private chamber stood ajar, shafts of morning light beaming through the solar tubes piped from the outside. For early morning, the place was eerily silent. A few more seasoned warriors patrolled the main hallway, but otherwise the energy patterns that registered were minimal.

He strode into Eryx's private space, opened his mouth to offer a greeting, and stopped.

No Eryx or Ramsay. Only Lexi and her somo, Jagger.

Jagger stood in the farthest corner of the room, his legs braced shoulder width apart and arms crossed. His gaze was rooted on some random spot across the room, an expression that most would take as distracted or distant.

Ludan knew better. He'd used that same pose for years. Not only did it give the person being guarded some semblance of privacy, but it made foolhardy attackers over-confident.

Lexi kicked back in Eryx's chair and propped one foot up on his desk. Gone was the refined gown of yesterday, replaced with combat boots, jeans, and a soft pink tank top that gave her a girly biker chick vibe. Considering the heat behind her glare, her attire was the only thing soft on the agenda.

Fine by him. After a night without Brenna and way too much adrenaline prepping for today, he'd lock horns with anyone. "Where's Eryx?"

"Running an errand for me." She lowered her foot, stood, and sauntered around her mate's desk.

"And Ramsay?"

"With Eryx." Her grin made him consider taking a step

back. "Don't worry. There won't be delays on your memory crusade. Jag and I have it covered." She glanced at her somo. "They ready?"

Jagger nodded.

"Okay then." Lexi motioned Ludan down the hallway. "Let's get busy scrambling your head, 'cause none of us got enough of it the first time."

With a huffed chuckle, Jagger uncoiled his arms and prowled down the hallway.

Ludan waited until Lexi followed and stalked behind her. "What the hell is your problem this morning?"

"Me? I don't have a problem."

Women. When you wanted them to talk, they wouldn't. When you didn't want them to, they wouldn't shut up. Except Brenna. Not once in the time he'd been close to her had she seesawed his brain like Lexi was now. He hoped like histus she was as levelheaded when it came to him being a no-show last night. Assuming he was still breathing on the other side.

"You talked to Brenna last night?" Better a mental thought to Lexi than one Jagger could overhear.

"Oh, I talked to her."

Ludan snatched Lexi by the forearm and yanked her to a stop.

Jagger spun, poised on the balls of his feet and ready to attack.

Waving him off, Ludan used every inch of his intimidating height and stepped in close so Lexi couldn't help but look up. "Talk."

"About what? The fact that Brenna's incredibly classy? Or the fact that you're a ginormous asshat? Seriously, Ludan, the only reason I haven't cut your nuts off this morning is you're an absolute neophyte at relationships."

"Fuck!" He whirled away and fisted his hair at the top of

his head. He gulped in giant lungfuls of air and still felt like he'd suffocate in seconds. Only when he was sure Jagger wouldn't go for a deadly tackle did he face her. His voice came out as haggard as he felt. "You wanna cut me a little slack and explain what the hell you're talking about?"

She studied him for way too long, mouth tight and eyes pinched. Finally, she sighed and motioned Jag toward the room at the end of the hall. "Give us a minute. We'll be right there."

Jagger's gaze slid to Ludan, not giving an inch.

Ludan cocked an eyebrow. "You're shittin' me, right? I've guarded her mate for over a hundred years. You think I'd let anyone hurt her?"

"Not worried about anyone else," Jagger growled, the golden aura that surrounded him 24-7 sparking brighter with his heightened energy. "I'm worried about you."

With an exasperated eye roll, Lexi shooed Jagger away. "He doesn't scare me. Go. Get the guys lined up so we can get this over with." She waited until Jagger was out of earshot before she turned.

Bracing, Ludan crossed his arms over his chest and lifted his chin.

"Jesus," she muttered. "You act like I'm about to come at you with a dagger."

At this point, he didn't know what to expect, but he damned sure knew to keep his guard up. "What's wrong with Brenna?"

"Nothing's wrong with Brenna. Well, except you left her alone and frightened in a place she didn't know."

"I asked you to tell her I'd be there after I'm done."

Lexi planted her hands on her hips, the ire she'd barely tucked away firing right back to full bright. "Right. After you put yourself at risk *again* on her behalf. That alone would screw with any woman's head. But you also left her alone the night after you'd just been intimate with her *for the first time*. That's a major fuckup, Ludan. Especially for a woman like Brenna who's just figuring out that maybe, just maybe, sex and intimacy aren't the worst damned things in the world."

"But I—"

"Don't." She held up a hand and hung her head. "I get it. We all get it. You want to make her safe, and you think digging around in a bunch of people's heads has a shot of working. You probably even have a good reason for doing it, but it was a seriously green move on your part."

He swallowed hard, for all the good it did him. The sand on the arena floor had more moisture than his mouth, and a whole bramble of thorn bushes had taken up root in his throat. "I didn't think about that."

She huffed out a tired laugh. "Yeah, I know. So did Orla, Trinity, and Galena. It took all four of us, plus a long, unplanned slumber party, to convince Brenna of it, but now she does, too. I know this whole twosome thing is new to you, but part of a relationship means thinking about things as a duo. Not you always being the hero."

"I wasn't trying to be a hero."

"No, but you're *her* hero. Sometimes that means you need to be beside her instead of out slaying her demons."

He was Brenna's hero? Really?

"Uh, yeah," Lexi answered without him actually putting voice to the thought.

He couldn't move. Hell, he could barely breathe with the shock ping-ponging through his head. "How do I fix it?"

Lexi's mouth quirked, and she waved him toward the room at the end of the hall. "You get these stupid scans over with, and avoid the chest-beating Neanderthal routine next time."

The next time. Which implied he wasn't totally screwed. Dumbfounded, he lumbered beside Lexi on autopilot. His dad had tried to tell him. To warn him. Maybe he'd have some idea how to make it up to Brenna.

The interrogation room sat empty save Jag and a wooden chair in the center. No color except the pale gray stone and soft yellow from the sun above. Cold and impersonal, exactly the same as the day he'd taken Angus's memories.

Jagger nodded toward the adjacent room. "We've got a whole roomful lined up. The top ranking according to what we got from those who turned themselves in."

Ludan stared at the empty chair. Tingles spider-walked down his arms, and a churning weight pooled in his belly. If this went wrong, Brenna would be alone. She'd never know how he felt about her.

Do you love her, son?

He still couldn't answer Graylin's question. The only thing he knew for certain was that he wasn't whole without her. Just one night alone had been torture. Apparently, she'd suffered the same.

Two warriors led a burly, barrel-chested man with scraggly black hair from the other room. He might have been a fighter for Maxis, but his brown boots, sturdy wool pants, and loose tan shirt marked him as a farmer now. He dropped to the chair and sneered at Ludan. "I thought the whole point of turning on the Rebellion meant a pardon and no further troubles."

Eryx's voice shot from behind Ludan. "The pardon was me feeling generous. Bad attitudes make me rethink the idea."

Thank the Great One, he was here. Lexi and Jagger were solid, but having his best friend at his back for this drill bolstered his courage. Still, he didn't turn. Didn't dare for fear he'd break and run like a little girl. He'd come this far. He may as well glean what he could and get back to Brenna.

If he was lucky, he'd have a semi-sane mind to grovel for forgiveness with.

He motioned the two guards behind the Rebellion man. "Hold him."

The man volleyed his gaze between the two guards and tried to stand. "Now wait—"

The guards shoved him back to his seat, and his breath *oomphed* out of him.

Ludan gritted his teeth and stepped forward. He could do this. For Brenna he could do anything.

"Ludan?" Brenna said from behind him, her voice quavering.

He glanced over his shoulder and nearly staggered back a step. He hadn't imagined it. She was here. Dark crescents marked the space beneath her eyes, but the rest of her brought the dreary room to life. Her near-black hair was loose and glossy, and her evergreen gown made her skin look like one of those delicate porcelain dolls.

Wait a minute. If Brenna was out of hiding, then anyone could find her. She wasn't safe. Even flanked by Eryx and Ramsay.

"Don't be mad at them." Brenna crept forward, uncertainty marking every step. "I asked them to bring me."

He faced Lexi, who'd taken up a front row view beside Jagger.

She shrugged and crossed her arms. "Okay, so my errand was also a tiny favor. Sue me."

Brenna sidled close and held out her hand, palm up. "You're right. Getting whatever information we can is smart, but you don't have to do it on your own anymore. Not if I can anchor you."

Her outstretched hand was steady, only a tiny tremor in her fingertips belying the courage it had to have taken to venture out like this. Or even to face his rejection.

As he enfolded her hand with his, the voices disappeared and his world righted. Like an anchor finding solid purchase, the emotional tug of war he'd battled all night settled and left a fluid, tranquil peace.

Lexi had been right in her guidance. He still wasn't sure if what he and Brenna had qualified as a relationship, but whatever it was he was tired of fighting it. She was here, ready to fight beside him, and it was her battle as much as it was his.

CHAPTER 28

This was it. The last debt Serena owed the Spiritu before she could set her plans in motion. One simple yet risky move in exchange for the sum of all Myren powers.

Assuming the Spiritu's plans worked.

Her mask in place, she scanned the Great Lawn of New York City's Central Park and blew out a slow, calming breath. The morning sun had only crested the tree line a few hours before, but the air was already thick and muggy. At the far end of the green, the stage crew prepped for the concert slated for later that evening, and the number of park goers milling on the highly manicured turf weren't significant enough to jeopardize her plans.

Twenty feet away, the news crew readied for their midday news segment. A pond was just a stone's throw away to their right. The Reservoir, they called it, or had before they'd tacked Jackie O's name to it. An idyllic place for what she was about to do and strategically perfect so long as Uther held up his part of the plan.

For the fourth time in less than thirty minutes, she second-guessed her decision not to re-forge a link with Uther. Confirming his location would have gone a long way to ease her mind, not to mention allowed for fluid communications, but she'd learned all too well the weakness links created. The price to break them was even higher.

No, she'd chosen the right path. If things went south, she'd simply mask herself, fly out of range, and port back to Eden. Clean and efficient.

The sun's position registered nearly eleven o'clock. Only a few more minutes to showtime.

Serena drifted closer to the news crew. She hovered a good foot off the ground, but her energy vibrated with such a heady mix of adrenaline and fear it reverberated off the soft soil and wavered over her skin in tiny pulses.

The female reporter paced to her spot before the cameras, head bent to the tablet in her hand. With her other hand, she smoothed her sleek blonde hair into place, the gesture absent, yet well-practiced.

"Two minutes." Her videographer hustled forward, one arm outstretched with the woman's microphone. "You're on after intros."

The reporter nodded and tucked her earpiece into place. "Be sure you get a good shot of the stage. Tonight's band is a crowd favorite."

Oh, they'd get a good shot. Not of the stage, but of something so much better.

The two support people stopped their chatter, and the man behind the camera centered himself in front of the reporter. "In five, four, three…" He motioned, *"two, one,"* with his fingers and pointed to the reporter.

The woman's false, bright smile clicked into place. "Good morning, Renee! And you're absolutely right, New York City is in for a treat tonight as we're expecting a sold-out crowd for our latest Summer Stage performance."

Floating closer so she levitated only a foot behind the reporter, Serena dropped her mask.

The videographer snapped taller, and the crew, who'd been focused on the small television in front of them, jerked their heads upright and gasped.

"What?" The reporter spun and stumbled back a step.

Oh, this was good. Perfect and oh so very public. Serena smiled. "Don't be afraid."

The woman noted the air between Serena's feet and the ground, and her eyes popped wide. She glanced back at her partner. "Are you getting this?"

"Yeah, yeah." He motioned her to go with it.

Of course he wanted her to go with it. It was television, sensationalism at its finest, and Serena had every intention of giving them their money's worth. "You know who I am?"

"You're the woman who's been taking people to Eden," the reporter said.

"I am." Through her peripheral vision, Serena noted one of the two support staff snapping pictures and videos with their phones. "I don't mean to frighten you, but I can't wait anymore. The time to bring down the wall that separates the Myren and human realms is growing short. There are those who would keep Eden from you, but I'm against that. Humans deserve their birthright."

Downshifting to a serious demeanor, the reporter inched closer. "You're still looking for the person you described to Tilly Rhinehart?"

"I am. Without her, humans will never find their true home. That's why I'm here today. I need help. To get it, I'm willing to make an offer." Serena zeroed in on the camera and focused her influencing gifts on those who watched.

"Those I've brought to Eden have shared how glorious our lands are. They've witnessed Myren powers. I'm willing to share those gifts. Whoever locates Brenna Haven and brings her forward will not only be the first to cross over into paradise, but will be granted all the powers of the Myren race."

The reporter's mouth opened and closed twice before she managed to speak. "You can do that? Powers are transferable? Flying, disappearing, and all the tricks with the elements?"

"They're more than tricks." Serena opened her palm face out to the side and sent a flame arching over the vacant space on her right. "They're quite formidable and very real. Not everyone can dispense these gifts, but I can. And I'm willing to do so in order to secure the birthplace of all humans. Your rightful land alongside your Myren brethren. This is what our Creator has always wanted. We cannot let one renegade and those who support her prevent it."

With one last influencing push, Serena focused on the camera. "Find Brenna and bring her forward. Spare no effort and trust no one. Only the Great One knows what lies ahead."

She shot high into the sky, slowing her ascent so the cameraman had ample time to track her flight.

Right on time, a gray mist swirled over the reservoir, its size twice that of what was actually necessary. Walkers and joggers along the lake's edge stopped and gawked at the sparkling creation. A few hustled closer to the perimeter and tried to follow, but they came up short when they realized they'd have to swim, or walk on water, to get there.

Perfect. Utterly fantastic as far as visuals went.

She felt more than saw Uther move into the portal, his energy pinging against her senses.

Serena hesitated at the entrance, turned enough to cast a

benevolent and beseeching look at those who gathered, then pushed her thoughts toward the camera. *Follow my guidance. Find her. Spare no one. Not friends or family.*

She spun with a dramatic flair and let the portal swirl shut behind her.

CHAPTER 29

renna tightened her grip on Ludan's hand, the faint tremor she'd first sensed an hour ago growing in its intensity. Three grueling hours he'd worked. Every second of it she'd stood beside him, never letting go as he plowed the memories of Maxis's highest ranks.

She glanced at Lexi behind them. She'd long ago given up pacing and now sat with one heel perched on the edge of a wooden chair. Her other leg jangled a nervous rhythm that matched the pinched worry in her eyes.

In the corner, Eryx exchanged low, terse words with a warrior she'd never seen before. He looked up, caught Brenna's stare, and scowled.

Motioning to Ludan with a slight nod, she whispered, "Something's not right."

Eryx dismissed the man beside him and prowled closer, assessing Ludan from head to toe in one fast sweep. "Stubborn shit, he's low on energy." He glanced at Lexi. "Get Ramsay and Reese in here."

Jolting into action, Lexi took off down the hallway, Jagger fast on her heels.

"I don't get it," Brenna said. "We're in Eden. How can he get low on energy?"

"Doesn't matter how much energy there is if your body's too maxed out to process it." Eryx splayed a hand between Ludan's shoulders.

Ludan inhaled sharply, and his shoulders snapped back.

Brenna pressed closer, checking Ludan's glazed and unfocused eyes. "What was that?"

"A boost. Ramsay, Reese, and I will feed him what he needs." Eryx offered her a small, assuring smile. "Trust me, he'll be fine. Unless he doesn't find what he's after. Then we're all in for a tirade."

Ludan released his grip on the man in front of him and stepped back. He shook his head as though to clear it and scanned the room until he locked eyes with the guard off to one side. "Any more?"

"That's the last of them," the guard said.

Ludan grunted and waved the Rebellion man away. He might not be making a big deal out of what Eryx was doing, but given the way his balance wavered, he clearly needed Eryx's energy.

"Anything?" Eryx grumbled.

"Nothing." Ludan's glower darkened, and the muscles along his neck and shoulders flexed. "They've all seen the guy Angus referred to. Worked with him and followed his commands once Maxis made him strategos, but not one shared a link. No one showed memories of him before their time in the Rebellion, or outside Rebellion activities. It's like the son of a bitch just popped out of nowhere."

The son of a bitch in question being Uther Rontal, the man they all suspected was the one helping Serena.

"Anyone else? Any details with Serena?

"Just her with Maxis. Nothing that caught my attention."

Ludan spun, knocking Eryx's hand free. "You've checked all of Maxis's haunts?"

Eryx crossed his arms, irritation and barely leashed impatience setting deep groves along his brow. "His manor, his Rebellion camp, the training ground…yeah, I think we've got it covered." One eyebrow kicked high. "Unless you got another locale we can check."

Ludan shook his head and paced the cell, rubbing the back of his neck. "No. Nothing outside of those."

"Then we've got it covered."

Ramsay strode through the doorway with Lexi, Jagger, and Reese close behind him. "We've got a problem."

Eryx huffed an ironic laugh, hung his head, and pinched the bridge of his nose. "Tell me something I don't know."

"No, a big problem," Ramsay said. "Serena upped her game. The warrior stationed with Ian in Tulsa just reached out and said Ian wants us there ASAP."

Ludan planted both hands on his hips. "Wants us there for what?"

"Details. He said shit's coming in too fast for him to stop what he's doing and come here. Said we'd do better to see it for ourselves anyway. To tell you the truth, the man I've got with him is a rock-solid warrior, and even he sounded a little off."

"Great." Eryx glanced at Ludan. "You coming or staying?"

"We're coming," Brenna said before Ludan could answer otherwise, and started forward.

Ludan clamped onto her wrist and stopped her mid-stride. "It's not safe."

She jerked her hand free. "Serena doesn't know where Ian lives."

"Actually, she does," Ramsay said. "That's where she and Maxis swiped him to begin with."

"Okay, fine," Brenna snapped. "She knows where Ian lives.

It's not like I'm planning on moving in." She locked stares with Ludan, all the anger, frustration, and fatigue she'd smothered the last few weeks bursting free. "I'm the one in danger. That means I get to have a say. Trust me, I don't want to end up with Serena any more than you do. I've been a prisoner and I'm not looking for a second helping, but I do want to know what kind of shit she's stirring up for me now."

The room fell silent.

Brenna exhaled what was left of her tantrum, and her shoulders sagged with relief. God, that had felt good. As in liberating, hear-me-roar good. Why the heck hadn't she done it sooner?

A snicker sounded on her left.

Lexi quickly covered her mouth, but the fact that no one else would meet Brenna's eyes and the way they fought back smiles said they weren't too far from doing the same.

"What?" Brenna said.

Lexi grinned, completely unrepentant. "That was beautiful. You just threw down with your man and used a pretty swear word to go with it."

"You're a bad influence." Eryx's words were scolding, but the tone was both playful and sweet. He grinned, wrapped an arm around Lexi, and focused on Ludan. "What's your play?"

"Do I really have one?

Eryx shook his head. "Not really. Once they get a stubborn streak, you're screwed."

Ludan studied Brenna, then sighed and held out his hand. "Then I guess we're going."

"Smart move." Eryx headed out the door with Lexi beside him. "Reese, I want you to stay here. Find Galena and keep her at the castle. Until I get a better angle on what Serena's up to, I don't want her out alone."

They hurried out of the training center and met Trinity at

an isolated stretch of land beyond the arena. The trip to Evad took less than ten minutes, but the loss of Eden's energy weighted Brenna with a bone-deep lethargy. She gripped Ludan's hand to keep from face-planting at the portal's tricky exit and stepped into Ian's backyard.

Oddly, the house wasn't all that much different than the one she'd grown up in. Even the August heat and humidity was the same, nearly stealing her breath. The yard was sparse but tidy, nothing more than slightly browning grass from the heat and lack of water, and an unadorned cement patio. "Aren't you worried about the neighbors?"

Eryx opened the sliding glass door and chin-lifted toward the eight-foot privacy fence. "We keep the portal and ourselves masked on the way in and out, but that goes a long way toward covering the risk."

"Are you kidding?" Lexi hooked her arm through Brenna's and guided her into the house. "The neighbors are probably so glad they don't have to look at Ian's craptastic landscaping anymore he could have an orgy back here and they wouldn't care."

Inside, the house held the same early-eighties feel as its exterior, though the carpet looked as new as the fence. The living room wasn't huge, but it was long with a built-in bookcase taking up the exterior wall. To the right was a small eating area with a kitchen at the far end.

"Dad, they're here!" Jillian's always chipper voice cut through Brenna's perusal. She snatched a remote off the coffee table and aimed it at a flat screen mounted high on the wall. "Sorry, he's running down something new on the computer. You're not going to believe what Serena's done this time." She switched to one of the recording devices, then punched a few more buttons.

A news crew splayed across the screen and seconds later Serena shimmered into view.

"No way." Lexi glanced up at Eryx, then to Jillian. "Are you kidding me?"

"Oh, it gets better." Jillian upped the volume.

Every eye stayed rooted to the screen. No one moved, too dumbfounded by Serena's ridiculous claims and grandstanding.

Ian ambled down the hallway just as Serena whirled and disappeared into the portal. "Can you believe that shit?"

Ramsay still hadn't peeled his eyes away from the television. "I can't believe she had the balls to do it."

"She's nuts," Lexi said.

"Yeah, well, it's working." Ian motioned toward the kitchen and wound his way through the bodies in his direct path. "I need more coffee. Anyone else want a cup?"

Eryx trailed him, but the frown on his face said it was for details and not a midafternoon caffeine fix. "What do you mean it's working?"

"I mean there's some crazy activity going on. It started right after she pulled her stunt with calls coming into all the major networks. They've got everything from people claiming they've found Brenna, to people stating Serena paid them a personal visit."

Ramsay settled in a chair behind the kitchen table. "That's a pain in the ass, but that's not crazy."

Ian rinsed his cup in the sink. "No, but it got the networks talking about it even more, which helped get Serena's message out." He poured a fresh cup, slid the carafe back in place, and faced the group. "Now, tell me this. If you were hunting for a woman who looked like Brenna, what target-rich environment would you pick for women in their early twenties?"

"Shit." Lexi wrapped her hand around Eryx's and squeezed, her usual vibrant skin tone blanching to a sickly white. "Colleges."

"Exactly." Ian leaned back against the counter. "At the one-hour mark, there were reports of breaking and entering in almost all the major universities and college cities. Dorms, apartments, homes—everything was fair game. And we're not just talking about people who know each other, we're talking about people busting into residences of complete strangers."

Trinity padded up behind Ramsay and clamped a hand on his shoulder. "How many people are we talking about?"

"A lot. Not everyone, mind you, but a lot." He pounded back a slug of his coffee. "You familiar with Black Friday?"

Trinity nodded.

"About like that, only with higher stakes. Police are reporting increased robberies and violence, and we're only four hours in. The more that happens, the worse it seems to get."

A booming masculine voice sounded from behind them. "That's because it is."

Ramsay shot to his feet, and everyone else spun toward the visitor.

The Black King stood at the kitchen entrance, his demeanor austere and cold. He dipped a minute nod toward Eryx and floated deeper into the small dining area. "Serena's in league with the rogues, and the goal they've sought to accomplish is at hand."

"You didn't think this was good information to share the first dozen times Trinity paid you a visit?" Ramsay shot back.

"The Spiritu are bound by the laws of the Great One. What you're seeing now—the riots, the chaos, the disregard for decency and kindness—is what happens when the balance is not kept."

Trinity's gaze slid to one side, her focus distant. "No action taken without a balancing sacrifice." She zeroed in on the Black King. "The rogues figured out we couldn't get an even trade on information if they offered up a sacrifice."

"I wouldn't call it a sacrifice," the Black King said. "Falon's mate, Patrice, had already been isolated as a result of his sentence. The ridicule she suffered made her position worse. For her, offering her life was more defiant retribution."

He faced Eryx. Even with Eryx having a good three or four inches on him in height, the king's presence seemed to fill every nook and cranny. "It will get worse. Without the steadying presence of the light, the atmosphere will shift, bringing with it storms and darkness the likes of which our realms have never experienced."

"It's already here." Ian pushed away from the counter and set his mug aside. "Just before you guys got here, meteorologists from Europe were reporting unexplained weather phenomena. Clouds and electrical storms that rolled in out of nowhere."

"Where's Serena?" Eryx demanded.

The Black King stared back at him. "If I could tell you that, I would have done so days ago."

Eryx prowled toward the Black King, not the least bit intimidated by his powerful aura. "Are you shitting me? She's single-handedly screwing all our races, and you're going to stand there and tell me you can't share?"

"I'm telling you there are destinies to be followed. Choices to be made by those deemed worthy by the Great One."

The room went still and quiet. Every gaze save the Black King's slid toward Brenna.

"No." Brenna staggered backward, her feet instinctively seeking space and fresh air.

Ludan stepped in close behind her and coiled his arm around her waist. His breath was warm at her ear, low, but solid. "You're not alone. Not in this. Not anymore."

The Black King's lips curved in a slight but pleased smile. "Indeed, she is not. And while it may seem otherwise, I assure you, all the information you need to triumph is yours. All that's left is to listen."

CHAPTER 30

The sun glowed bright through the solar tubes into Ludan's underground room, but Brenna still hadn't stirred. The old, unhealthy habits she'd learned with Maxis were breaking. Slight shifts others might miss, but Ludan hadn't. Not the fact that she'd taken to experimenting with her wardrobe, or how she'd gone head-to-head with him the day before. He'd bet she could count on one hand the number of times she'd stood up to a man in her life and still have fingers left over, but she hadn't so much as flinched with him.

He eased onto the bed beside her and smoothed a strand of her dark hair off her cheek. Her skin was so much paler than his, a soft, creamy color unlike the deeper tones of most Myrens. The hard years under Maxis's control might have built the calluses she detested on her hands, but every other inch of skin he'd sampled was soft and smooth.

Dipping close, he skimmed his lips across the path his fingers had taken. "Brenna."

Her eyelids fluttered open, her dark gaze unfocused and

relaxed from sleep. Vulnerable and honest. She grinned, let her eyes close again, and snuggled under the blanket.

She'd chosen him. Not someone smarter or kinder or better versed in how to navigate a relationship—but him.

He traced his thumb along her lower lip, and a choking knot clogged his throat. He swallowed to clear it. Now wasn't the time to get in touch with his soft side. He had a task. An important one he couldn't put off any longer. "Time to wake up, sweetheart. We need to get to work."

She blinked a few times, scanned the room, and pushed up on her elbows. "What time is it?"

The sheet slipped, and he nearly swallowed his tongue. The edge perched just above her nipples, leaving the upper swell of her breasts exposed. Hours he'd devoted to exploring her the night before, diverting her fears with far more enjoyable sensations, and yet the sultry image clocked him like it was brand new.

He fisted his hands. It was either that or yank the sheet out of his way and give in to the tactile exploration he craved. "A little after nine," he managed.

Following his stare, she pulled the sheet up to her collarbone. Her cheeks flushed a pretty pink, and her nipples hardened beneath the silk. "What work?"

An instant, almost volatile growl crawled up his throat, and he clenched his teeth to contain it. Lexi was right. He was horribly unprepared for a relationship. All Brenna had done was cover herself, but the simple act infuriated the beast. Made him want to tear the damned sheet to shreds. Hell, he wasn't just unprepared for a relationship, he was a freak.

Her hand stayed fisted in the sheet, holding it tight to her chest. It was all he could look at. All he could process.

"Training," he said.

"Training for what?"

His gaze snapped to hers. "To fight."

Rattled by the answer, her hand relaxed. "I don't know how to fight."

"You don't yet, but you will." He stood and paced to the wide dresser where she'd unpacked some of her things. Through the mirror above it, he watched her watching him. "The way things are going in Evad, we don't know how much time we have, so it's best we get started."

"Okay." Her thumb shuttled across her skin once. Then again. "I'll get dressed and meet you in the kitchen."

Oh no. That wasn't happening. Maybe it proved him the crass, knuckle-dragging jackass Lexi claimed he was, but he'd be damned if he let Brenna build walls between them. "You're hiding from me. Why?"

She opened her mouth as if to argue, then closed it.

It didn't matter. The fear swimming in her eyes said plenty. He stalked toward her, the darkness in him straining for release. "I've seen you. Touched you. Tasted you."

She snapped upright, and the defiant spark he'd glimpsed the day before fired bright. "It's different in the daylight."

"Different how?"

"Because it's normal." As soon as she said it, her eyes popped wide and she jerked her head to one side so he couldn't read her face.

Normal? That didn't make a damned lick of sense. "What's wrong with normal?"

No answer. No sass. Just hard, cold silence.

"I can stand here all day. You wanna see stubborn, I'll show you—"

"It gives me hope."

Man and beast both froze, for once in sync and utterly dumbfounded.

Slowly, Brenna lifted her head, her lips tight and eyes glassy with threatening tears. "Hope makes me want things that may not happen. I could take going home and being disappointed with what I found there, but I couldn't take experiencing normal with you and then losing it."

She thought...fuck, he couldn't even wrap his head around what she thought. That this was some nonchalant arrangement he could toss aside? That he'd willingly walk away?

The darkness swarmed, knocking aside what scraps of gentleness he had left. "Stand up."

Her breath caught, and her lips rounded on a startled O.

"Stand up and get dressed. I'm going to train you until both of us are exhausted and too tired for bullshit, and then I'm going to bring you back here and show you how there's not a thing about us that's normal."

"Didn't you hear—"

"If you want to argue, get up and do it. Get in my face. Histus, you can throw a punch if you want, but you'll do it the way you are now. The way a woman not ashamed of her body, or afraid of her man, would do it in the heat of the moment."

Emotions shifted across her face so fast he could barely keep up. Shock. Disbelief. A flicker of desire, then fiery anger. Like a whip, she tossed the sheet aside and flung her legs to the side of the bed. Her chin snapped high, and the Great One help him, she threw her shoulders back, making her breasts bounce and demand his attention. "Happy now?"

His dick stretched and hardened beneath his jeans so fast it was a wonder he didn't pass out from the blood rushing to it. He palmed himself and shifted to ease the grueling press of denim, for all the good it did him. "I'm pacified. *Happy* won't hit until I'm buried inside you and you're coming around my cock."

A tremor shook her, and one hand fluttered above her

abdomen. Her head tilted back as though she barely held back a moan, and her eyelids weighted with need.

He stalked closer.

Goose bumps lifted across her delicate skin, and her lips parted.

He couldn't touch her, not the way the beast demanded, or he'd never see to her training, but he could make a point. Something to hang on to, for the day ahead and the rest to come.

Starting at the base of her sternum, he dragged his knuckles down her belly. He palmed the space above her womb and splayed his fingers low, teasing the top of her mound. "It feels good, doesn't it?"

Her breaths deepened, and her nipples tightened to such pretty, tight points his mouth watered. Not a verbal answer, but likely more honest than he'd get with words. She couldn't hide, or run, from what burned between them any more than he could.

Drawing small circles against her tender flesh, he dipped his head and ghosted his lips across hers. "This is what hope feels like. I suggest you get used to it."

∾

BRENNA STRODE into the clearing behind Ludan, more frustrated and out of sorts than she'd been in her entire life. Her skin prickled beneath her pale blue tunic and leggings, and the ache between her legs wouldn't ease no matter what platonic thoughts she focused on.

Damn Ludan and his demands. In his promises and his wicked touch. Everything had been so much easier when she'd been the comfortable one. The one pushing, or more like shoving, things along.

She still didn't get it. Somewhere along the way their

dynamic had shifted. When or why, she couldn't pinpoint, but it was different.

"We'll work here." Ludan paused about fifty feet to one side of the lake behind his father's cottage. The red-rimmed sun was full bright, and along the water's edge, tall, skinny plants with periwinkle tops bobbed in the wind. He motioned her forward.

Ugh. He was still testy. Why on earth he was so irritated she still couldn't figure out. She was the one who'd had to reveal everything this morning, both physically and emotionally. And then he'd gone and done the one thing that scared her more than anything. Dared her to hope.

She stomped within slapping distance and mashed her lips together so tight she'd be lucky if they didn't bruise.

His mouth quirked on one side, and a devilish glint sparked in his icy-blue eyes. In that moment, he looked more animal than man. A panther who wanted to toy with its prey before it savored its meal.

Her core tightened and readied, the mere thought of his powerful body pressing into hers making her wet.

Oh yes. The tables had definitely turned. She cleared her throat and planted her hands on her hips with more bravado than she felt. "So? What are we doing?"

For the longest time, he stared at her, his expression so frustratingly neutral she had half a mind to pick another fight. He frowned and scanned the soft, silver-edged turf. His gaze locked on something at the lake's edge. In a smooth, well-practiced move, he held out his hand and a rock flew across the space, straight to his palm. He pinched it between his two fingers and held it up. "That's step one."

He gently lobbed the stone her direction, and she jerked forward to catch it. "Step one for what?"

"Telekinesis. The first thing you need to learn."

"I can't do that."

"Healing's more complicated. If you can heal, then this should be a cakewalk." He held out his hand again. "Send it to me."

"That was different. Galena guided me with her energy. Eryx did, too."

He flashed forward so fast his appearance blurred. Had it not been for his hand plastered at the small of her back, he'd have knocked her over. His other hand gripped the side of her neck, and his breath huffed in and out like he'd sprinted a mile. "Don't mention Eryx in that context. Not right now."

If it hadn't been for the torment pinching his face, she'd have balked or tried to argue. "I don't understand."

The hand at her back slid up until his fingers twisted in the hair above her nape. "His energy inside you. It's intimate." His breath fanned across her face. "He didn't mean it that way. I know that, but you have no idea how hard I'm fighting right now. I'm raw. Dangerous." He loosened his grip and cupped the side of her face. His hands shook with a ferocity that matched his gaze. "I've never done this before. Never been this close to a woman. The thought of Eryx inside you...I want to kill him."

A shiver snaked beneath her skin. He couldn't mean it. Not really. Eryx was his best friend. A brother, even if only by choice. The general sentiment and shift in his demeanor should have scared her to death. And yet, the admission pleased her. She nuzzled her cheek against his touch and kissed his palm. "Okay."

He dragged his thumb against her lips. His covetous gaze followed the simple act, then snapped back to hers before he stepped away. He held out his hand, palm up. "Send it to me."

The rock was smooth and white, its powdery surface leaving a chalky residue on her fingertips. She opened her hand and closed her eyes. The rock's weight was insubstantial, no more than one of the marbles she'd played with as a child. When she'd healed, she'd pushed her spirit forward. Maybe this was the same. A combination of will and thoughts.

"Feel my energy," he said. "Use it. Make it your own."

Even with the wind whipping around her, she felt his voice. His essence. A soft, downy blanket that wrapped around her. She pulled in a slow, calming breath, centered her thoughts on the stone's weight, and pushed.

The weight disappeared.

Brenna opened her eyes as the rock plummeted over her fingertips to the ground between them. "I did it. It moved."

The smile he gifted her with was unlike any she'd seen from him before. Bright and unguarded with absolute joy shining in his eyes. This was the man he had to have been years ago. Before life and the burden of his gift had tarnished his light. "Yeah, you did it."

The rock zoomed straight up in the air and landed back in her hand.

"Now, do it again." He stepped back another foot. "This time keep your eyes open and focus on sending it to me."

Keep her eyes open. Right. Because pulling off tricks her body hadn't been designed to perform was so easy with her eyes closed. She let out a slow exhale and braced her feet a little farther apart, eyes focused on the stone.

"Don't overthink it," Ludan muttered. "Use my energy like you did before, but carry it this time. Guide it to me."

Memories of the way her stream had curled and flowed through Ludan's body billowed to the forefront of her thoughts. The sun's warmth along her bare shoulders and arms gave way to the subtle tingle of Ludan's gifts. They were hers to use. All she had to do was channel them.

Visualizing the stream in her mind's eye, she wrapped the stone in a sleek, ivory ribbon and lifted. Smooth as the path she imagined, the rock drifted to Ludan and settled in his palm.

He pinged it right back to her and took three more steps back. "Again."

More confident, she reached for his powers again. The energy was hazy, more undefined and elusive than before, but still within reach. She drew from it, building a bigger well of strength before she set the pebble free. It launched just as powerfully as before but lost its steam midway and nearly missed her target. "Something's different."

Ludan gauged the ten feet between them. "It's the mirroring. You need my gifts to make it work. The farther away I am, the less you have to work from." He doubled the distance and sent the stone back to her. "One more time."

"It won't work."

"You won't know until you try. Knowledge in a fight beats power every time. Know your strengths *and* your weaknesses."

Ludan was right. This was war. Maybe not the knife-and-gun type, but a battle nonetheless. She fisted her hand around the rock. If she didn't push herself, she'd never know what she could do. Unfurling her fingers, she sought Ludan's power.

Fine, misty tendrils wavered just beyond her reach. There, but too insubstantial. "I can't latch on."

"Keep trying."

"I can't."

"Yes, you can."

"When I try, it slips past me."

"Then don't play nice," he snapped. "Take what you want."

The bossy jackass. If she could use her hands instead of his gifts, she'd hurl the rock at his head. She ground her jaws together so hard her temples ached. With a mental swipe, she yanked the soft-spun energy to her and thrust the stone forward.

It bypassed Ludan's outstretched hand and whacked him on the forehead.

Ludan gaped back at her and blinked over and over. A deep, slow chuckle shook his chest. The rumbling grew alongside his smile, bigger and bigger until he threw his head back and laughed to the sun-drenched sky.

He'd lost his mind. She'd hit him with a damned rock, and he was happy about it. "Why are you laughing?"

He sucked in a lungful of air and splayed one hand at his belly. "You hit me."

"It was an accident."

A fresh hoot doubled him at the waist. He planted his hands on his knees and let his laughter have full rein. "No it wasn't." He lifted his head, his smile stretching ear to ear. "You threw it at me."

Okay, maybe she had. Sort of. Though, she hadn't imagined her thoughts would manifest quite so literally. She studied her toes and fought the urge to fidget. God, she was an idiot. The guy tried to teach her something and she beaned him in the head. Classy.

Ludan's laughter trailed off, and his footsteps scrunched against the soft grass. His black boots came into her line of sight. Mirth still coated his voice, but it was soft, too, laced with care and concern. "Brenna."

Heat stung her cheeks. Too bad he hadn't taught her how to mask first. Invisibility would be a handy trick right about now.

He lifted her face to his with a finger under her chin, the touch so tender it resonated everywhere. "I'm not mad."

"You should be."

Pulling her closer, he cupped the side of her face and his

thumb swept across her check. "Why should I when I pushed you on purpose?"

Her churning guilt halted on a dime. "What?"

"Anger always pushes us past our fears. You got pissed and stomped right past your limits." His eyes sparked with a warrior's appreciation. "It was beautiful."

Her heart fluttered and her breath lodged in her throat. He'd used those same words with her before, but never with that look on his face. Enthralled. As if the world could vanish and he wouldn't care so long as she was with him. "You need to stop looking at me that way."

His mouth quirked. "Hope creeping in again?"

She bit her lip and focused on her fingertips resting against his chest. "Something like that."

He covered one of her hands with his, lifted it, and pressed a reverent kiss to her palm. "You'll get used to it."

She doubted it. No woman in her right mind would ever get used to this sensation. It was too powerful, too all-consuming to ever settle easy on the senses.

Before she could tell him as much, he squeezed her hand and stepped away. "Time to work on casting fire."

"Time to what?"

"You heard me." He dropped her hand but stayed close, turning her so she faced the lake. "Everything works the same way you moved the stone. Flying, the elements—you generate or move them all with your mind."

"How can you say this isn't different? Fire is, well, huge. I could burn everything down."

He cupped her shoulders and pulled her against his chest. "I won't let anything happen to you. Besides, you're aiming at water. The last I checked, fire's got nothing on it."

Great. Now he'd shifted into smarty-pants mode. Between the grouchy, bossy, and happy moods he'd already been through, it was starting to feel like she'd hooked up with the seven dwarves instead of a Myren badass. She frowned at the lake's center and sighed. "Okay, so what do I do?"

He laced his fingers with hers, the palm of his hand against the back of hers. "You imagine it, you set it free, and you direct it." He lifted their joined hands and aimed her palm toward the lake. "Simple as that."

Simple for him maybe. She hated fire. Had ever since she'd bungled her first round with an oven and burned her fingertips so they blistered. "Does it hurt?"

"It feels no different than when you moved the rock." He squeezed her shoulder with his free hand. "Now focus."

The wind sent ripples across the water's surface and whipped her hair against her cheeks. Water was safe. She couldn't do any damage, or at least not much.

A memory from her childhood slipped into her thoughts. A campfire her father had built on a camping trip. The wood snapped as tiny sparks drifted beside soft coils of smoke. That fire had been good. Relaxing. She narrowed her mind's eye on the flames. Rich, warm orange and gold with ribbons of red interwoven.

Along her arm, Ludan's gifts flowed in a powerful torrent. She wound the image along the stream and pushed.

A wide flame blasted in front of them.

Brenna flinched, nearly catching Ludan in the chin with the back of her head. She tried to wrench her hand from his, but he tightened his grip and pressed their joined hands across her stomach.

"Easy." He kissed her temple, giving her time to catch her breath. "You did just fine. You just need to give it form."

"But it was huge. And hot." The only time she'd seen anything like it was a flamethrower at the circus.

"Because you're using my gifts. Males carry stronger defensive gifts. Warriors even more so. If you're using mine, you'll wield what I wield." He lifted their hands again and aimed like before. "This time give it form. Make it reach the same way you moved the rock."

She sucked in a slow breath and tried to ignore her battering heart. Repeating the process she'd used before, she narrowed her gaze on the lake and thrust her energy forward.

A beautiful flaming arch reached from her palm to the lake, surpassing the center and nearly reaching the lake's farthest edge.

Ludan released her hand and cupped her shoulders. "Perfect. Now try it again."

And so it went. Fire. Add distance. Fire again.

Air came next. Then electricity. With each experiment, he started close, then gradually built distance.

A thin sheen of sweat coated the back of her neck, and her muscles ached. For the last thirty minutes, her stomach had rumbled as if she hadn't eaten in days. She lifted her hair off her nape and turned her back into the brisk, cooling wind. "Okay, I give up. I need food before I can do any more. And maybe a nap."

Ludan stayed silent. Odd considering how quick he'd been to banter back with her all morning, particularly when the words *can't* or *won't* slipped past her lips.

She released her hair and faced him.

He stared at the lake, hands resting on his hips and a distant, pensive expression etched on his face.

"Ludan?"

His gaze slid to hers. "I think we need to work on something else."

Her muscles squeaked in protest, and her stomach let out a mini-roar. "What else is there? I mean, I guess we could try water, but I have a feeling your dad likes the lake where it is."

His lips quirked as though he wanted to laugh but

couldn't quite muster the oomph over all the worry scampering around in his head.

"Oh, for Pete's sake." She stomped toward him and halted just an arm's reach away. "It can't be that bad."

"I want to teach you how to break out of a hold."

"A what?"

"If someone grabs you, I want you to be able to fight back."

She blinked. Then did it again. No matter what she tried, she couldn't connect whatever dots were putting him off balance. "And?"

"That means fighting."

She lifted her eyebrows, hoping it might move him along a little farther.

"Fighting like you would have with Maxis."

Her head snapped back as surely as if she'd been slapped. "Oh." Now that he'd put words around his concern, it made sense. Still, none of the panic she normally registered around other men bubbled up. "I'm not afraid. Not with you."

"You're sure?"

Tired, yes. Hungry as a teenage male, and looking forward to a long, hot bath, absolutely. But not afraid. "I'm sure." She sidled closer and cupped the side of his face. His beard tickled her palm, and his warm breath wafted across her face. "Though my body may demand payback by the time we're through. I already feel like I've done three days' labor."

His hands at her hips tightened in response, and his gaze dropped to her lips. "Whatever you want. However you want me."

A shudder trickled down her spine, and her sore muscles perked with interest. For that kind of promise, she could go at least another day. "Then come at me, bad man. I'm ready."

This time he gave in to his grin, the lopsided angle adding a vulnerability that made her lightheaded. He turned her around and wrapped her in a bear hug. "Remember, a Myren's powers are still available in a fight. You can use them to leverage yourself, or them, away the same as you did the rock."

"I hadn't thought of that."

"Neither will they. Especially with a human who shouldn't have powers. Use the advantage." Giving her a gentle squeeze, he widened his stance. "How would you get out?"

She wiggled within his hold, but he gave zero ground. With her arms pinned to her sides, she couldn't use any attacks. "You're too strong. I can't move."

"You can, you just need to get me off center. Keep your torso upright and squat. Make it sharp so my weight's thrown off balance."

She tried, and sure enough, her upper body slipped a little bit within his arms.

"Good, now take a big step to the side and twist. See how I'm opened up? Your hands are free enough you can push them like you did with the rock or fire something nasty at them. I prefer the latter." He pulled her back against him again. "Now, do it all at once."

Dropping her weight, she crossed one foot back and to the side, spun and pushed just enough to touch his chest.

He popped both eyebrows high as if to say, "That's all you got?"

"What, didn't I do it right?"

"The moves, yes. The shove was more of a tap. Hit me with it. Get me away from you."

"Are you out of your mind? I can't do something like that to you."

"You taken a good look at Eryx lately?"

"Yes."

"You get an idea of how much power he packs?"

"Well, yeah."

"I've taken all he can dole out and then some. I think I can handle you."

Ugh. Men. She huffed and gave him her back, ready for him to do the bear hug thing again. "Fine. I'll push harder. Let's just get on with it."

He struck, nearly knocking her forward, his grip sharper and more powerful than before. Aggravation sparked.

Drop. Cross.

Shove.

Ludan went airborne and shot back a good twenty feet, his shoulders hunched forward as though he'd been hammered by a battering ram.

"Ludan!"

Before she could chase after him, he was back in front of her, pride stamped on his face. "Just like that. Now, again."

Over and over they drilled, each attempt faster than the last with Ludan throwing different variations. Adrenaline flooded her bloodstream, and her mind clicked sharper than ever in her life. If this was what it felt like to battle, no wonder the men got that glazed, ferocious look in their eyes. It was exhilarating. Intoxicating.

Liberating.

Escaping his latest hold, she powered a huge punch toward his stomach.

His sharp grunt billowed out in front of him as he shot backward. Unlike all the other times before, though, he kept a good distance between them. "You ready for something a little more real-life?"

"What have we been doing?"

He grinned and did a gunslinger finger wiggle. "Warming up."

Oh boy. If she'd known that, she'd have saved a little energy for the real deal. As it was, moving for the next few days was probably out of the question. "All right, but after this I'm calling a break. You need to feed me and spoil me."

He dipped his head, a bull ready to charge. "Sweetheart, you get through the next few minutes, I'll make it so neither of us leaves the bed for days."

A flutter rippled through her belly, one strong enough to override her killer ninja mindset and leave her dumbstruck.

Ludan shimmered out of view.

Uh-oh. Definitely not good. The man was dangerous enough when she saw him coming. Not knowing what direction he was coming from was lethal.

Birds chirped and the wind whistled. The sun beat down on her shoulders, but goose bumps lifted across her neck and arms. She spun in a slow circle, scanning the landscape for some clue as to his whereabouts. The flowers spanning the lake's edge waved back, an innocent taunt of how real such a scenario could be.

Ludan's weight slammed into her back, knocking her breath out with an unattractive *oomph*.

She staggered forward and dug in her heels, pressing backward with everything she had to get upright. All at once, something tripped—instinct or divine intervention—sending strength through her tired muscles and guiding her feet through the simple routine needed to free herself. She escaped. He attacked. She dodged. He caught. Even as her lungs burned and demanded she call a cease, something far more primitive and raw spurred her further.

Faster than her eyes could register, he streaked toward her, wrapped her up, and spun them both, their bodies levitating through the air until she found herself pinned to the ground. His hands manacled her wrists, and his legs pinned hers.

Helpless.

She froze and her heart stuttered. She couldn't breathe.

Couldn't think. Whatever it was that had led her before was swept away on the cool breeze, leaving her bare and vulnerable beneath him.

And she liked it.

"Ludan." She wiggled her fingers, suddenly needing to touch him, to connect with his flesh and feel his pulse beneath her palm.

His gaze shot from her face to her fingers, and his eyes flashed wide. He shot upward, landing a good two feet away with hands fisted at his sides. "I'm sorry." He hung his head and shook it. "I went too far. I didn't...you seemed okay and I—"

"No!" In less than a blink, she stood in front of him. How she got there so fast she hadn't a clue, and from the surprise on Ludan's face, he didn't have one either. She'd merely thought to intercept him and had somehow made it happen.

She licked her lips and fought to steady her breath. To calm her heart. "You misunderstood. I wasn't afraid. I was..." What could she possibly say that made sense? That wouldn't make her sound crazy or twisted?

The only thing that would bother me is you denying what pleases you.

His claim from their first night together moved through her with surprising strength, bolstering her courage with the same intensity she'd felt while they fought.

She swallowed and stepped in close, nearly moaning when her breasts pressed against his chest. Meeting his rapt stare, she stroked her hands across his broad shoulders, prayed she wasn't making a wrong move, and rasped, "I liked it."

CHAPTER 31

*B*renna held her breath. Her heart punched an unsteady rhythm and her skin tingled as though electricity danced across the surface, but she didn't dare move. One wrong move and Ludan would bolt.

He stared down at her, hands fisted at his sides. His deep voice rolled across her senses, broken and oh so cautious. "You don't know what you're asking."

"Actually, I do." She smoothed her fingertip across his lower lip. Even scowling down at her the way he was now, his mouth was pure decadence. Lips full and commanding. "I want you. No holding back and no worries. Just you."

The corded muscles in his neck and shoulders strained and his face flushed. "You don't get it." He gripped her shoulders and squeezed, either to push her away or jerk her closer. "It's not safe. There's a part of me...it's different."

It. Not he. But then she knew that. Had sensed the untamed part of him from the first time she'd seen him. "I don't care."

"You should."

"I don't."

"Damn it." He yanked her flush against him, one hand palming the back of her head so she couldn't look away. His eyes were wild, the whites around the perfect blue glowing neon. "It wants to pin you down," he growled. "To mark you. To warn other males off."

"Then do it."

He stilled, his arms immovable steel coiled around her. His nostrils flared and his fingertips dug deep at her nape and back. Dangerous and unmistakably deadly.

But she was safe.

She wrapped her hands around his neck and urged him closer, her lips close enough to tempt but not enough for contact. "Let it out. I'm not afraid."

His breath came quicker. A savage on the edge. Within his hold, his powers surged and whirled against her in an erotic tempest. Just a fraction more and they'd both have what they needed. What they craved.

Emboldened, she slipped her hands beneath his T-shirt. The corded ridges of his abdomen tightened and goose bumps rose beneath her fingertips. Strength and vulnerability all in one. For her. She'd barely pushed the shirt to his pecs before he finished the job, tossing the soft blue cotton aside and dragging her back against him.

His heat seared through her, drawing her nipples to hard points beneath her tunic and rasping them against the soft fabric. She kissed the space above his heart, lips parted enough to sample his sweat-slick skin. His earth and spice scent surrounded her, pushed away what was left of reality and dragged her deeper into the intimate moment. "Don't coddle me." She lifted her gaze to his. "Let go."

"Brenna…"

Oh no. No more arguments. If she couldn't wrangle him across his self-restraint with words, she'd use something more effective. More potent and guaranteed to smash the padlock on his control. She slid her hand down his belly, relishing the flex of his abdominals beneath her palm, then cupped his rigid cock.

A low, animalistic growl rumbled from his chest and the furrow between his brows deepened, but he didn't stop her. Only watched her, the heat in his gaze ravenous and wild.

"You promised me." She yanked his button fly open and his cock unfurled, thick and proud, eager for her touch. Easing to her knees, she peeled the denim away and shimmied it down his hips, baring his perfect shaft and heavy sac for her perusal.

He lifted his hand, and for a moment, she thought he'd push her away. He caressed the side of her face, tremors making the touch unsteady.

Holding his stare, she leaned close and pressed a simple, lingering kiss near the base. His cock jerked in response, and a broken moan slipped past his lips.

She sucked in a sharp gasp, fascinated by his vulnerability. Willingly at her mercy and hanging on by a thread. She kissed the same spot and smiled against his velvet flesh. No more holding back. Not for either of them.

She licked a slow, deliberate path to the ridge beneath the flared head and traced it with the tip of her tongue. His deep forest scent permeated his skin, tinged with a potent musk that made her core clench. She wanted it, needed it on her own skin. A sensual brand to mark how far she'd come. How far they'd come together.

She paused, marveling at the pearly precum glistening at the tip. She'd done that. Her lips and her touch, readying him for pleasure with the same devotion he'd always shown her. Closing her mouth around his glans, she suckled deep and groaned as his bold, salty tang slid across her tongue.

Ludan hissed and rolled his hips, spearing his fingers into her hair and fisting his hand at the back of her head. Just as fast, he eased his grip and smoothed the same spot as though seeking forgiveness. His body quaked, barely restrained control on the brink of collapse.

Firmer, she fisted him at the root and took him deep, laving his length with the flat of her tongue, then hollowing her cheeks with each upward draw. Again. And again. Following the flex of his hips, her own need built, mindless to everything save her fierce warrior.

"Enough." He tried to pry her away.

She dug her nails into his hip and sank her lips as far as they would go. No way would she sacrifice this chance to set him free. For once she had the upper hand, and the odds of being there again anytime soon were slim. She cupped his balls and rolled them in her palm, the soft, smooth skin so unlike the rest of him. His sac was drawn tight, close to release.

"Brenna." Desperate, but angry too. His powers tingled against her skin, hot and furious. Dangerous and fearsome. A decadent pool for her starved desires. There had to be something, some way to lure him past the breaking point. More than once he'd driven her to near madness, teasing her with fingers, lips, tongue, and teeth.

That was it. He was a fighter, not some delicate weeping willow. If she wanted him to trust her with his aggression, she'd need to show her own. Fight fire with fire.

Sliding one hand around his flank, she cupped his ass, digging her nails in deep. His hips jerked, and she fisted the base of his shaft tighter.

Perfect. Just a little more. Something more surprising. More unexpected to draw him in.

She hollowed her cheeks and suckled, grazing her teeth across the taut head.

A roar exploded through the endless valley. Formidable and utterly majestic.

The ground disappeared and the world spun.

Brenna grappled for something to steady her and latched on to Ludan's powerful shoulders a millisecond before her back met soft Myren grass.

His mouth slanted over hers. Demanding. Punishing in his quest to draw sweet revenge. There wasn't a place she didn't feel him. His lips, bruising against hers. His fingers manacled around her wrists, and his powerful torso and legs pinning her to the soft ground. It was perfect. So far from the terror of her past it was as if Maxis never existed.

She writhed against him, the ache between her legs unbearable and frenzied for relief.

"Uh-uh." Keeping her pinned, Ludan jerked his hips away. His breath came fast and furious, and his muscles bunched in an exquisite display of dominance. "You don't think I know what you did? What tricks you played?"

He lowered his pelvis to hers and ground his raging cock square against her clit.

Her heart leapt and her wits scattered. Ludan wasn't just Ludan anymore. He was an animal. A predator ready to sate its hunger. The whites of his eyes no longer glowed. They burned. A supernova of neon white, blue, and gold.

He sat back on his heels, releasing her wrists while his knees straddled her thighs, pinning her in place. Every inch of him, save the jeans slung low and open below his hips, was on display. His broad shoulders. His narrow waist. The V at his hips, and his thick cock straining tall in front of her. He was like a god, and his mesmerizing gaze was locked onto her like she was breakfast, lunch, and dinner.

She tried to lift her hands and gasped, an unseen force holding her firmly in place.

His massive hands splayed across her rib cage and stroked upward until he palmed her breasts. His gaze was ravenous, almost fevered. Even through her tunic, his touch resonated with tiny sparks of barely leashed power. He scraped his thumbs across her spiked nipples, the soft fabric unbearably yet perfectly rough. "You wanted the beast. You've got him. Now I want what's mine."

The sound of ripping fabric registered a second before cool wind swept across her bared torso. He cupped her breasts, drawing them together and working their peaks with his wicked tongue and lips.

She undulated, needing more, but pinned in a way she couldn't make contact.

"Not yet." Back and forth, he licked and sucked, tormenting the aching peaks and building the escalating pulse inside her with relentless focus. "I want you to ache. To burn and beg." He latched hard onto one nipple and drew so deeply it speared straight to her core.

"Ludan!" She arched deeper into the commanding sensation, and her muscles trembled. "Please," she whispered, clenching her hands as the tantalizing ripples built stronger and deeper between her legs, release so close she could taste it. "Please don't make me wait."

A low, prurient growl rolled past his lips. "You'll wait." Slowly, he sat back on his heels. His hands spanned her hips, thumbs teasing the sensitive stretch above her hipbones as he surveyed her well-tended nipples. He licked his lower lip, and her core fluttered as though the velvet stroke had traveled between her legs. "You'll wait and thank me for it after."

Wind coiled around her tight breasts and teased the still-wet peaks.

She bowed upward, so captivated by the natural yet unexpected caress that she startled at Ludan's physical touch atop her mound.

"So pretty." He stroked downward, rasping the soft cotton against her sensitized labia then back up again. "I love the way you whimper. The way you strain for my touch."

Unpinning her legs from beneath his, he yanked her leggings off and splayed her knees up and wide, held open to his gaze with nothing more than his thoughts. He shucked his jeans, eyes locked on her throbbing center and the undeniable wetness lining her folds. "You're mine. All of you."

Slim streams of air coiled around each ankle and wound their way to the tops of her thighs. "Ludan!"

His unrepentant, almost devious chuckle surrounded her, and the wind-borne caress shifted. She couldn't see it, but oh could she feel it. More tangible and depraved than before. A cross between sparking energy and physical touch. He stroked his thick cock in languid pumps, a hunter planning his attack.

So erotic. So perfect she'd go to her grave remembering every detail.

"Change your mind? Want the tame side of me back?"

God, no. She might be pinned to the ground and buck naked in broad daylight, but she'd never felt more alive. Primed for the fight of her life. "What I want is you. Inside me. Deep." She lifted her hips, inviting him with the subtle flex as much as her splayed legs allowed. "However you want me."

He groaned and palmed the inside of her thighs. The pads of his thumbs teased the seam where her thighs met her core. "Anything?"

Tingles scampered down her torso. This was it. A crossroads between them. How she knew it she wasn't sure, but it resonated with a certainty she felt to her soul. As if some intrinsic, deep-seated aspect to her being had flared to life, ready and waiting. "Anything."

He slicked one finger through her sex and a low, gurgling growl clawed its way from his chest. He notched his fingertip inside her entrance and his eyes slid shut. "Drenched." Slow but firm, he pumped once. Twice. "For me." He added another, the intensity of each thrust growing stronger. "All mine."

The words washed over her, beautiful and perfect. "All yours."

With one hand anchored beside her head, he held himself over her, still building a release that threatened to swallow her whole with the other. His long, wavy hair hung loose around his face, strain etching the corners of his mystic eyes. "You want to know what I want? What I've fantasized about?"

At his neck, his pulse hammered to match her own, and a tempting sheen of sweat coated his tan skin. The heat generating from him and the wicked streams still swirling across her sensitized flesh jumped another notch. She ground her hips upward to meet his rhythm, bit her lip, and nodded.

"I want you on your hands and knees. Want to see your knees wide and that perfect ass of yours in the air. Want to cover your back and sink my teeth in that sweet spot you like me to kiss." He circled her clit with his thumb. "And when I feel your pussy quiver, I want to grip your hips, pound my cock inside you, and push you over the edge."

Sweet, unrelenting climax gripped her sex, cinching her muscles around his devious fingers. Colors to match Eden's landscapes danced behind her eyelids, and every muscle in her body contracted at once. Dimly, she registered a shout. Hers given the clawing ache in her throat, but she didn't care. Couldn't care with the powerful waves pulsing through her.

"That's mine." Ludan kept his tempo, bringing her off the edge but refusing to let her land. "I want it."

"Okay," she whispered, not at all clear on what it was he laid claim to. After that release, he could have whatever he wanted. Her mind. Her heart. Her life.

She sifted her fingers through his hair, only realizing they were free when the soft waves tickled her palms. Rolling her hips against his steady moving fingers, she pried open her eyes and gasped.

Possession. If a single look could convey an unequivocal meaning, that was Ludan's. Pure, animalistic ownership so potent every nerve ending buzzed on high alert.

He eased back and sat on his heels, slowly easing his fingers from her entrance and skimming his palms down the tops of her thighs to her knees. His touch was gentle, but a barely banked intensity burned beneath it. His powers crackled and popped with the force of a fast-approaching thunderstorm, snapping across her flesh in intoxicating zings. His gaze bore through hers and anchored in her very soul. "Offer yourself to me."

Tiny aftershocks fired in her sex. Spasms that shouldn't be possible after the release he'd just given her.

"You said anything." Slowly, he brushed mesmerizing circles with his thumbs on her knees. "Give me what I want. Offer yourself to me. Show me what's mine."

As in, on her knees. Vulnerable and exposed in the most hedonistic way possible. Her breath left her on a rush, and insistent need ramped from indolent to critical. Tucking her shaky legs under her, she rose to her knees, facing him. She skimmed her fingers through the soft scruff of his beard and cupped the side of his face, needing the connection, the strength that came from his presence. She could do this. With him, she could do anything. Be anything. Learn anything.

She trailed her hand downward, along the pulse at his neck and farther to his heart. She savored the powerful beat. Primitive but restrained. Asking instead of taking. As she dropped her hand, her own heart lurched. Her breath came shaky and short as she shifted, the world around her a little hazy from the rush of adrenaline jetting through her veins. The black mountain range stretched wide ahead of her, the huge expanse and the lavender-topped trees driving home just how exposed she was. Not just to Ludan, but to the universe.

Movement sounded behind her, and Ludan's heat registered at her back. Not touching, but close. His scent blended with the open world around her, earth and spice against crisp air and sweet grass. This was where she was meant to be. Physically and emotionally. Whatever sparked between them was nothing short of perfect. A divine gift worth any risk.

Even her heart.

Focusing on his presence, she drew on his strength and leaned forward.

A low, approving rumble sounded behind her, a masculine purr that vibrated against her skin. The cool grass tickled her palms, and gravity's pull against her heavy breasts made her arch her shoulders for more.

"Beautiful." His huge hand coasted from between her shoulder blades to the small of her back. "A faultless gift."

Faultless. All this time she'd thought herself damaged and dirty, but under his touch she felt clean. Whole for the first time in years.

He skimmed his callused hands over her ass and down the backs of her thighs, his thumbs skating along the inner seam.

Craving more of his touch, she widened her stance and lifted her hips.

He hissed in response, his fingers tightening against her legs and urging her further. "I wish you could see what I see." He ghosted the pad of one thumb down her center. "Your pretty pink pussy. Swollen and ready. Wet with your release." He increased the pressure, sliding his fingers on either side of her entrance. "You screamed my name when you came. Did you know that?"

Oh, she knew. And with the way he was touching her now, she'd do it again in record time.

His lips nuzzled the base of her spine, and he splayed his hands on each side of her ass. "I want to hear it again. Louder." His breath fluttered against her drenched sex. "Then I'll take you."

Contact. Hot and demanding, his lips and tongue devoured every inch of her, savoring every drop of her climax as though he'd die without it, demanding she provide more. Erotic was too tame of a word to describe it. Carnal and wanton, maybe.

He squeezed her ass and moaned against her flesh. His finger circled her clit, and his tongue speared inside her.

"Ludan!" She threw her head back and tried to catch her breath, all her senses focused on his wicked ministrations and the steady pressure he lavished on the throbbing nerves between her legs.

His mouth disappeared, but his powerful thighs brushed the backs of hers, and his raging staff pressed against her core. "Almost." He ground his hips against hers, teasing her with the delicious ridges that lined his velvet length. "But you can do better."

A slow, tingling sensation brushed her rib cage, lifting inch by inch until it cupped her breasts. She moaned and let her head loll back, pressing her ass into the cradle of his hips.

"That's it." He slicked his cockhead through her folds. "Give in to it. Let me take you there."

He wasn't taking her anywhere. Catapulting was more like it. Rocketing her into universes she'd never known existed.

"Let it out." He teased her entrance, barely notching himself inside. The sensation he'd created with his energy grew, centering on her nipples and sharpening even as the energy speared down her belly to her clit. "Give me my name."

The force tightened on each pleasure point and gave a none-too-gentle tug.

"Ludan!" She felt more than heard her shout, its lingering tone reverberating around her as his thick cock plunged inside her slick channel. Release slammed home, fisting her sex around his pistoning shaft and obliterating all thought in its path. Now was all that mattered. This moment. This man and what burned between them.

His heat blanketed her back, and he fisted her hair. His voice growled behind her ear. "No more hiding."

His hot breath sent shivers rippling down her spine. She whimpered and tried to nod.

He tightened his hold, and the tiny stabs of pain where he tugged her hair laid a fresh siege to her still-spasming sex. "Say it."

"No." She shook her head and angled her head farther, offering the last vulnerability she had. "No more."

He licked and sucked a path down her neck, his heavy pants streaming across her tender skin as his hips slapped against her ass. "This is real. This is us. This. Is. Hope." He rammed deep and sank his teeth where her neck and shoulder met.

Marked.

In her womb. In her skin. In her soul.

She trembled beneath him, her sex clenching around his jerking shaft. Gone was the preternatural sensation he'd created beneath her skin, replaced with reverent caresses from his hands. Cupping her breasts, smoothing across her abdomen, slicking between her legs where they were joined. Nothing mattered but his touch and their connection. Nothing but him.

Slowly, he eased back to his haunches, pulling her with

him. His lips roamed everywhere. Neck, shoulders, lips, every touch filled with devotion and care. A beast sated from his feast and languorous.

He curled one hand loosely around the front of her neck, a claiming gesture that once terrified her, but now brought peace. It felt right. Comfortable and soothing. "What you gave me, I won't let you regret it."

She rolled her head and kissed the tender skin beneath his jaw. His beard tickled her nose and his scent saturated her lungs. His energy coursed through her, as though it no longer understood the physical barriers between her body and his, very much the same way her heart seemed tied to his. "I hope not, because I am well and truly yours."

CHAPTER 32

Darkness engulfed Ludan's room, broken only by moon glow through the solar tubes overhead. He'd doused the bedside candles an hour ago, but their tallow scent still lingered. Brenna lay naked beside him, her legs tangled with his and her head pillowed against his chest. Since the first night they'd lain together, she'd slept deep, but tonight she was dead weight. Exhausted from hours of training and relentless, soul-wrenching sex.

He fingered the mark he'd given her. Crescents from the primitive bite had formed long before nightfall. He couldn't see it in the dark, but just knowing it was there calmed the beast. It wouldn't last more than a day, maybe two, but that was okay. Soon she'd have another mark. One that would only dim upon his death.

His mate.

If you had to save me or Brenna, who would you choose?

Praise the Great One, he'd been an idiot. Eryx had known all along. So had Lexi. And his father. And Ramsay. Histus, everyone had accepted it before him.

Did Brenna know, too? When he asked her, would it be a

surprise? Or had she already deduced what the Fates had tried to tell him?

He skimmed his hand along her hip, then over her ass. So soft and firm. If he dipped a little lower he'd find his seed still coating her thighs, the most gratifying mark of all. He didn't dare indulge. One slide through her folds, feeling his cum against her flesh, and he'd take her again. Already she'd given too much, tirelessly welcoming that dark, ugly part of himself inside her body and making him whole.

He should have tended to her after. Cleaned the remnants of his release and let her soak, but he couldn't do it. Just this once, he wanted a part of him left behind. A reminder and the promise of what would come.

The image of Brenna round with his child flashed in his thoughts. She'd be a brilliant mother. Patient and giving. As tireless and instinctive as his own mother.

They'd need a home. Something private and modest like his father's cottage. Not too modest, though. Brenna had wanted for enough in her life. She deserved to be spoiled. Not that she'd make that easy on him. Maybe he'd buy them a home in Evad, too. Someplace near the ocean with a stunning view.

His cheeks strained beneath an unexpected smile. Praise the Great One, he'd turned into a whipped little puppy. He was plotting out his future. He'd never once in his life considered he'd do such a thing, but here he was, staring into the dark and doing exactly that.

As quickly as it came, his smile slipped. Brenna wasn't safe. Not yet. Until she was, nothing else mattered.

"Are you ready now?"

He stilled at the feminine voice in his head. No link accompanied it, but the tone was familiar. Similar to his mother's, but softer. Airier than the rich, honeyed tone he'd grown up hearing.

His Spiritu.

He tensed beneath Brenna, instinctively shielding his soon-to-be mate as he cast his senses throughout the cottage. What was he supposed to be ready for? An attack? A clue?

"The Black King told you. All that's left is to listen. Are you ready now?"

Answers. How could they even ask if he was ready? He'd been ready for weeks, chasing every lead.

"But you didn't listen." Such a peaceful sound, yet laced with reprimand.

He opened his mouth to argue into the darkness, then hesitated. The voice was right. He'd acted, searching countless memories and rerunning them until his head throbbed. One scenario after another, always trying to think as he imagined Serena would. The one thing he hadn't done was listen.

The muscles at his neck and shoulders slackened. Maybe it was the darkness or the stillness that came when one day crossed to the next, but an otherworldly awareness sparked across his senses. As powerful as what he felt mid-battle, only grounded in something more profound. Divine.

A memory surfaced. The day he'd scanned Reginald after Serena's disappearance. On reflex, he zeroed in on the images and let them play across his thoughts.

Something had intervened. A presence halting the flow the same way a person or object might block his line of sight.

"Not what you saw. What you felt."

What he felt? What the hell did feelings have to do with answers?

"Perhaps you're not ready." The voice dissipated toward the end.

"Wait," he whispered into the shadows. He swallowed and tightened his hold on Brenna, drawing her sweet, cleansing scent deep to ground him.

That morning he'd been agitated. Pissed at Eryx for digging into Ludan's response to Brenna and hating the need to add more memories on top of all the others.

No, wait. That hadn't been everything. He'd been kicked off balance the second he'd stepped up to Reginald. Like someone had disconnected his will from his actions, especially when he'd touched on the memory of Reginald and Serena in their kitchen. Every second had registered, but his focus had been off and the words were muddied. What in histus was that? He'd been sucking down memories for over a hundred and thirty years. Never once had he felt such a sensation.

He reached for his father via link. *"You got a minute?"*

Shit. What was he thinking? It was almost two o'clock in the morning. Of course his dad wasn't up. Most sane men slept at night.

"It's late for you to be up," Graylin said, nearly jolting Ludan out of bed. *"Particularly for a man who carried a languid woman into the house just before sundown."*

So his dad had seen that. Not surprising. He'd gotten away with zilch growing up. Just because Ludan was an adult now didn't mean his dad wasn't still sharp. *"I was thinking."*

Graylin chuckled with far too much enjoyment. *"Thinking isn't how your mother and I spent our nights, but to each his own."*

"I need to talk to you about Serena's father," he said before Graylin could venture any farther down their awkward conversational path. *"Could he hide or blur his memories?"*

The link to his father buzzed. If Graylin had been asleep or dozing, he wasn't now, not with that kind of energy. *"Outside of delta sleep? No, not unless he could channel memories the way a solicitor does."* He paused and Ludan could almost picture his father's frown. *"Although, I've heard influencers can sway memory perception. Rather the way a human might throw a lie detector test off. Nothing conclusive, but enough to make the test questionable."*

"And influencers are prone to vendor-focused skills."

"They are," Graylin said. *"I take it this has something to do with Reginald or Serena?"*

He wasn't sure what to think. Not yet. But his instincts prickled the same way they did before an attack. *"I think Reginald dodged my scan. I checked his memories after Serena disappeared. There was a section with him and Serena talking."* He hesitated, reassessing what he'd felt. *"It may be nothing, but I can't afford to miss anything."* He combed his fingers through Brenna's silky hair. *"Not now."*

Weighted silence streamed between them before Graylin spoke. *"Have you found your definition then?"*

Ludan's arms tightened around her, a hoarder prepared to fight both seen and unseen threats. A fist-sized knot lodged in his throat. *"She's my mate."*

More silence, though emotion warm and saturated with pride echoed through it. *"Yes, son. She's yours."* His voice hitched before he added, *"Your mother would be pleased, as am I. You'll be a strong mate for her."*

He couldn't talk. Couldn't process the sentiment rioting in his head and heart.

Graylin spoke before Ludan could wrestle himself to steady emotional ground. *"You'll come to grips with it. When you do, you'll find contentment. Even peace."* He paused for only a moment. *"Goodnight, son."* And then he was gone.

Brenna's easy breath fluttered against his chest, the rise and fall of her chest hypnotic in the dark. He closed his eyes and gave in to the moment. To his father's reaction. To the promise of a future with her and all that brought with it.

He matched his inhalations to hers and focused on her scent. Sweet like Orla's kitchen. Bit by bit, his thoughts drifted. Random memories darted between consciousness and sleep. The first time he'd seen Brenna and how the voices dimmed when she drew close. How she'd anchored him while he scanned the Rebellion warriors' minds. The ugliness of Angus's youth, and snippets of Serena's time with the Rebellion.

"Did you see it?"

The Spiritu's voice jangled him to awareness, and his eyes snapped open. His heart slammed against his chest, and adrenaline spiked so high a ringing sounded in his ears. Only blackness and silence surrounded them. No energy registered save that of his father near the front of the cottage.

Maybe he'd dreamed the voice.

No, he hadn't been asleep. Merely drifting and recalling real memories. Serena's. She'd visited Maxis's strategos multiple times. Now that he knew the memory was there, it seemed clearer. Sharper than before. He'd grabbed it the one time she'd given them unprotected access to her memories, just after she'd been sentenced, but he'd glazed over it.

"Because she wanted you to."

So, Serena was an influencer like her daddy. No wonder she had so many men whipped. Though, he couldn't imagine the information would do much for Eryx's ego considering their history.

He backtracked, zeroing in on Serena's visits with Uther at a run-down shack. The land around it was barren. Desolate and empty.

The Underlands.

It was the perfect place to hide. Far below Serena's standards, but perfect for staying off Eryx's radar.

Gently lifting Brenna, he eased from underneath her and gave his anxious energy free rein, pacing the room while his thoughts zigzagged. If he could trail the memories close enough, he could track the place.

He yanked on his leather pants and drast, combating frustration and eagerness to follow his newest trail. All this time, everything he'd needed had been right there, waiting. He sat on the edge of the bed and pulled on his boots.

"Ludan?" Brenna lifted her head and blinked against the darkness. "Is something wrong?"

Far from wrong. This was the answer he'd been looking for. A chance to make things right. Shifting closer, he smoothed her hair away from her face and pressed his lips to hers. "Everything's fine." Or it would be. "Go back to sleep."

Her eyes fluttered closed, her dark lashes forming pretty crescents against her creamy skin. Everything he'd ever needed—ever wanted, but hadn't realized—was right here. He kissed her temple, fortifying his strength with her scent. He'd keep her safe. And then he'd make her his.

CHAPTER 33

*L*udan stalked through the cottage's darkened halls, following Graylin's link toward the study. Two in the morning was a hell of a time to take in a book, even for his night owl father. That meant either he hadn't been able to go back to sleep after Ludan woke him, or he was up to something.

Firelight spilled through the office door, the scent of leather and woodsmoke greeting Ludan before he crossed the entrance.

Graylin's head snapped up, eyes rounded in surprise. An ebony box no bigger than a foot long and half as wide sat on his lap. "Ludan." He shut the hinged lid and set it on the side table beside him. "Why aren't you with Brenna?"

Yeah, definitely up to something. No one snuck up on his father unless he was severely distracted. "Why aren't you asleep?"

A sheepish grin crept into place, and Graylin motioned to the box. "I'd forgotten about this until our talk. Your mother set some things aside after you were born. Things she planned to give your mate when the time was right." He stared at it, his eyes distant. "I never explored what was in it at the time. Turns out your mother was quite sentimental."

A gift for someone she hadn't even met yet. It was just like his mother, thoughtful and always planning for the best. He braced for the guilt, for the shame that always came with thoughts of his mother, but for once, the weight didn't crouch on his shoulders.

"She would have liked Brenna," Graylin said. "Very much."

And Brenna would have adored Rista. The Great One take it, they'd have been inseparable. Two graceful yet inherently strong women woven from the same cloth.

Graylin coughed and pushed from his leather armchair, headed for the gleaming bar along the far wall. Its carved mahogany woodwork featured Celtic details and winding ivy with lattice edges. Inside was every fine liquor a man could ever want. "Now you know why I'm up. Explain why you're dressed to fight instead of wrapped around your woman."

Ludan startled and shook his head. He had to be out of his mind, standing around ruminating on the past and future when the present was shooting by too fast. "I've got a lead. Something I missed in Serena's memories. I think she's in the Underlands."

"No one lives in the Underlands."

"Maxis's so-called strategos does. Near the border into Asshur."

"And you think to capture her alone? That's a hotheaded move, and you know it."

"Not capture. Confirm. I'm not stupid. If I bungle the intel, we risk Serena disappearing again. I'll follow the memories, mark the place if it's a plausible lead, then come back and strategize with Eryx."

Graylin set aside an unmarked crystal decanter, strasse given the auburn color and sharp berry scent. The frown he aimed over one shoulder said he wasn't entirely buying Ludan's plan.

"I'm not even sure I can find the place," Ludan said. "If I do, one person casing the perimeter's a hell of a lot safer if anyone's monitoring for activity." His shoulders pushed back a fraction, and he lifted his chin. "Plus, I've got incentive to keep breathing."

Graylin's mouth twitched. He sipped his drink to cover the smirk, but amusement shone in his eyes. "Indeed you do." He waved his hand toward the door and returned to his chair. "Your woman will be safe. If anything alerts me, I'll get her to the castle or the training grounds."

Ludan nodded and spun for the door.

"I expect regular communications." It was a command, one outranking warrior to another. "I know you want Brenna safe, but I won't lose my son in the process."

"You won't lose me." His lips curved, the movement far more awkward with his dad than it had been with Brenna. "I'm too stubborn to die."

Ten minutes later, Ludan was airborne and headed to the farthest edge of Asshur. The voices were back and as incessant as ever, but their edge was gone. Where the constant din had made him irritable and short before, now it was an annoyance. A bothersome gnat his psyche refused to engage.

Because of Brenna.

She was the difference. Not just the way she dampened his gift's impact, but the way she grounded him. Life wasn't just something to be endured from one day to the next anymore. It was something to experience and share. To look forward to.

He laughed into the dark night, not bothering to mask the clumsy, unfamiliar sound. It was a damned good thing Eryx and Ramsay couldn't see inside his head. They'd load him up with chocolates, maxi pads, and a lifetime supply of Midol.

Even more bizarre, he didn't care. They could razz him all they wanted, but he'd never be ashamed of Brenna or what he felt for her.

A silver stream of energy arced across the cloudy night sky, briefly illuminating the land below. Asshur was the dreariest of Eden's regions, seldom bearing sunshine and more prone to tumbleweeds than crops. No wonder Maxis had built his fortress in such a nasty space. Plenty of room to roam without anyone questioning his presence.

Another five minutes and the temperatures began to drop, marking his approach to the Underlands. Serena's memories hadn't shown her traveling more than a mile or two past the border, but the region spanned a good two hundred miles wide. Far more than he could cover in one night.

He slowed his flight and hovered high in the air. In one of Serena's memories, he'd noted a limestone outcrop he recognized from Asshur, not ten miles from where he was now.

Recalibrating his path, he backtracked to the location he'd recognized. It took everything he had not to pour all his energy into flying full speed, the seasoned, patient warrior in him pointing out that diligence and care were critical. The beast didn't give a shit. Only wanted the threats to his mate obliterated in short order. He'd give that side of himself free rein soon, but not at the risk of leaving Brenna alone and unprotected.

The scent of burning wood floated on the wind.

Ludan stilled and pulled his mask into place. This was it. His eyes had yet to focus on anything tangible in the inky darkness, but his body hummed with certainty. He lowered to the ground. The cracked clay surface was strewn with rocks and pebbles. The only thing blocking the empty stretch of land was a line of boulders.

One step forward. Then another. His heart thumped a

steady, almost deafening beat in his ears, and sweat coated his skin despite the chilled wind.

The clouds broke, and a flash of moonlight washed across the desolate landscape. Not three hundred yards ahead sat a simple hut built in sturdy, dark wood. The boulders he'd noted circled the perimeter, roughly a hundred yards in all directions. Darkened windows dotted a crude front porch, and smoke curled from the chimney. No light, though. If anyone was inside, they were asleep or hidden behind dark drapes.

Ludan inched toward the giant stones ahead. The moon flickered in between clouds, and light glinted off one of the boulders.

Odd. They'd been dark like the rest of the muddy surroundings when he'd landed. Not something he'd expect to reflect light. He skimmed the top of one.

Pain razored through his veins, ripping away his mask and consuming his powers.

A zeolite barrier.

He jerked his hand away and staggered back, loose clumps of dried dirt falling to show more of the crystal's sparkling surface. Before he could gather his balance, pebbles crunched behind him and warning tingles fired across his shoulders.

He spun.

Serena stood shrouded in the darkness, one long strand of her near-white hair slipping free of the hood she'd drawn over her head. "About time you got here."

He lurched toward her.

Solid iron bashed the back of his head and his legs buckled, leaving him sprawled against the cold, unforgiving clay. Pain speared from the base of his neck and ricocheted down his spine. Above him two figures stood, Serena and a man, backlit by the cloud-covered sky. Darkness crowded the edges of his mind, and reality slipped farther and farther from his grip.

He reached for his father's link with the last of his strength. *"Protect Brenna."* The connection wavered and the black took him.

~

A SHARP, heavy knock on the bedroom door jerked Brenna from sleep. Only a hint of light filtered through the solar tubes, leaving the room in a dusky glow. It couldn't even be six o'clock yet.

Blinking to clear her fuzzy vision, she lifted her head from the pillow and found herself alone in Ludan's rumpled bed. "Ludan?"

The door swung open, and Graylin strode into the room dressed for combat in full drast, leather pants, and boots. "Unfortunately not." Not pausing for any explanations, he jerked the top dresser drawer open, rooted around, and closed it. "Where are your things? We need to move."

"In the armoire." Her heart jerked into second gear, and she fisted the soft sheet in her palm. She'd never once seen Graylin dressed like the other warriors. She knew he'd been somo to Eryx's father years ago, but seeing him like this, clipped and ready for action, triggered all kinds of alarms. "What's going on?"

Graylin snatched the first outfit he laid hands on, tossed it to the bed, and turned his back to give her privacy. "I'll tell you on the way to the training center. Right now, I need you up and dressed. I'll have your things brought later."

She scrambled from the bed. The room's chill mingled with her surge of adrenaline and cast goose bumps out in all directions. "What about my mother?"

"Orla's helping her now. She's going with us."

Leggings in place, Brenna pulled her tunic over her head and wiggled it past her hips. "You can turn around."

Graylin turned, his gaze alert, but not once meeting hers. Something wasn't right. His eyes always held a hint of sadness, but there was more today. Worry or fear.

Ludan.

He'd been dressed for fighting when she'd woken in the middle of the night. But that made absolutely no sense, unless he'd gone and done something stupid. "Where's Ludan?"

Graylin grimaced and averted his face.

Nerve-numbing terror wrenched her heart. "Graylin, tell me what's wrong."

"I don't know." He snatched her hand and tugged her toward the stairs leading up to the main floor. "He went to check a lead last night. About thirty minutes ago, he reached out from the Underlands. I got his location via link, but the connection's gone fuzzy since. I can't track him. Eryx, Ramsay, and Reese have headed out with search squadrons."

She stopped dead in her tracks and jerked her hand from his grasp. "What?"

Graylin backtracked and moved in close, the same move Ludan used when he wanted to impress a point. "I need you to listen to me. I know you're afraid for my son. I am as well. But I made a promise to him to keep you safe. Until we know what's happened, I need you someplace defendable with ample guards. Once you're safe, I'll give you every detail I know. Until then, I need you strong and focused."

Strong and focused. That's what Ludan would want, too. What he'd expect. She swallowed and jerked a terse nod.

Answering with one of his own, he hurried her up the stairs and through the quiet cottage. She'd barely made it two steps past the front door when the enormity of Graylin's fears slammed home. At least a dozen warriors formed a protective barrier between her and the front yard, their eyes sharp and bodies poised for action.

Her steps slowed, the mere thought of being around so many men, particularly those she didn't know, jangling free fears she'd thought long gone. "I thought no one but Eryx's family knew where you lived."

"Until this morning, they didn't. I'm not transporting you without a guard."

"But—"

He gently squeezed her arm to cut her off. "You're my son's chosen. I would never favor something so selfish as privacy over your safety."

Her mother's voice sounded behind her, mixed with the hurried slap of Abby's and Orla's sandals against the soft stone walkway. "What's going on?" A flush tinted Abby's cheeks, but sleep and confusion still clouded her gaze.

"Ludan's missing." Brenna glanced at the men gathered close and smoothed her hand across her stomach to still her nerves. "These men are taking us to the training center."

Taking that as his cue, Graylin urged Brenna farther away from the house. His sharp command rang out against the still morning. "Tight formation. Make it quick. Phillip, you're with me."

Beside Brenna, Abby tensed, her gaze ping-ponging from warrior to warrior as they surrounded. "I don't understand. How can he be missing? I thought he was with you. And who are these men?"

"They're warriors." Brenna clutched her mother's hand in hers, feigning more confidence than she felt. "The men Ludan and Graylin fight with."

An older warrior with the white-gold torque and cuffs of an elite marched to the center. His loose chocolate hair and full beard gave him an edgy, pirate look, but the gray sprinkled at the temples and shrewd eyes spoke of experience.

Graylin pointed at Abby. "Phillip, you transport Mrs. Haven. I've got Brenna."

"Transport me how?"

Graylin frowned and scanned the skies. "Mrs. Haven—"

"Abby."

He nodded his head, his flagging patience showing in his tight yet still polite smile. "Abby. As you've learned, the primary means of transportation in Eden is flight. You do not possess that gift. Therefore, Phillip will have to carry you. Under normal circumstances, I'd approach the experience less abruptly. But the longer Brenna is in a vulnerable environment, the longer she's at risk."

Abby gaped at them both. "We're going to fly?"

"It'll be fine." Brenna squeezed her mother's hand. "You'll see. Once you relax, it's very pretty."

The color drained out of Abby's face, and her lower lip trembled. "O-okay."

Phillip inched closer, wrapping one arm around her mother's shoulder. He spoke so low Brenna could barely hear him, but his baritone voice resonated with confidence. "You'll be safe. I won't let anything happen to you." With that he dipped and scooped her up.

"Oh!" Abby circled his neck with her arms and hung on for dear life. The surprise and awkwardness would have been funny on any other occasion, but Brenna barely had a chance to ensure her mother had adjusted before Graylin swept her up in his own arms and shot to the skies.

The world around them was quiet, only the first soft rays of sun creeping across the vibrant landscape. The air was crisp and damp, still weighted by fog clinging to the mountain base in the distance. Absorbing the beauty felt wrong without Ludan.

Graylin's fingers tightened on her shoulder. "He'll be fine."

"Serena killed her own mate. What makes you think she'd hesitate to kill Ludan?"

For a second, the tension pinching his face eased enough for him to grin. "For your sake, I'll keep to myself that you dared put Ludan's defense skills on par with Maxis's."

That was likely true. As far as she knew, Maxis's only fighting skills centered on subduing those weaker than him. Ludan was a warrior, trained in warfare and capable of protecting the malran. That had to count for something.

Graylin sobered and looked Brenna square in the eyes. "My son is strong. Smart. He knew enough to send me a link and protect you. He'll be wise enough to bide his time and wait for the right move."

"But he's still alive?"

"I can't trace his link, but I can feel it." His eyes slid back to the horizon, scanning for any sign of trouble. "Besides, I don't think there's a force in nirana or histus that would keep him from coming back to you."

"You say that with an awful lot of certainty."

He held his silence, but countless thoughts and emotions shifted behind his blue eyes. His expression sharpened into one of resolution. A decision made. "Ludan's never once spoken of the future. Of wanting something more than exactly where he was in any given moment. This morning he did because of you. When I say he'll be back, I mean it. There's no way he won't fight his way back to you."

CHAPTER 34

A nauseating throb burned at the base of Ludan's skull, nudging him toward consciousness. Praise the Great One, he hurt. His head weighed a ton, and his tongue felt cemented to the roof of his mouth. What the fuck had he done? The last time he felt this bad he'd polished off a fifth of strasse solo.

He lifted his head and sharp stabs radiated out from his shoulders. Shit. He wasn't hung over, he was captive. Bound with his arms cranked behind his back and his legs roped to chair legs.

Adrenaline flooded his system, recounts of the moments before he'd lost consciousness carried on the wave. The throb in his head upgraded to a nuclear pulse. He forced his eyes open and bit back a groan. Candlelight was all that surrounded him, but it burned his retinas like a blowtorch. Wherever he was, it was dark. Rough rock walls reached at least twenty feet on either side of him with stone pillars evenly spaced to bolster the ceiling. A cave, from the looks of it, but not zeolite.

He reached for his links and came up short. They were gone. Dead the same way he'd feel in containment.

"Good to see Uther didn't do too much damage."

Ludan flinched at Serena's taunting voice and narrowed his eyes in the direction from which it had come. Only shadows registered. Not that he'd expect any less than full-scale drama from her.

She sauntered forward, her usual penchant for gowns replaced with a functional legging and tunic combination that looked way beneath her standards. She fingered Trinity's medallion around her neck. A sword twined with ivy that matched Lexi's mark and was believed to be the key in the prophecy.

"To tell you the truth," she said, "I was a little worried. Hard to hold your health and safety over your new lover's head if you're catatonic."

Bile surged and bubbled in his gut, and the ropes at his wrists razored into his flesh as he wrenched against them. The mention of Brenna wasn't unexpected. They'd all suspected Serena would figure out her role in the prophecy, but the fact that Serena knew what Brenna was to him was a game changer.

Serena grinned and cocked her head, obviously pleased at his response. "So it's true. When Patrice told me the two of you would end up together, I couldn't believe it. But here you are, ready and willing to protect the little human."

"I don't know what you're talking about." His voice sounded about as smooth as the crude walls around him.

With a wave of her hand, Serena slid a simple wooden chair from across the room to sit roughly five feet in front of him. Definitely not a zeolite cave if she was pulling parlor tricks. So how the hell was she containing his powers?

"No point in protesting and pretending indifference to your little woman," she said. "Patrice is a Spiritu, and if there's one thing I've learned, it's that they have the market on history." She perched on the edge of the chair and leaned in as though to share a secret. "And the future."

Fucking. Bitch. The first chance he got, he'd gut her and hang her with her own intestines. His eyes burned and his temples kicked from the strain of his clenched teeth.

"Ah, there he is. The meandering oaf who trots behind Eryx like a little lapdog. I knew your temper would come out to play sooner or later." She reclined in her chair and crossed one leg over the other as if she were discussing the weather instead of prodding a beast. "I would've thought you'd at least be smart enough to finagle details from me."

"Why? You're too vain to keep them to yourself."

She pursed her mouth and bounced her crossed foot, irritation sparking brighter than the candles around them. "I wouldn't call it vanity. I'd call it pride. Maxis came close to yanking the throne out from under Eryx, but I'll finish the job. The fact that I take pleasure in my accomplishments isn't something I'm ashamed of."

"Kind of getting ahead of yourself. Last time I checked, that throne was still toasty under Eryx's ass."

"It is now. It won't be for much longer. Not with the information I've got in my corner." Her foot kept bouncing, projecting her unease more than she realized. Surprisingly, she didn't dive into the details like he'd expected. A bonus considering his aching head, but not so good for intel.

"Did your soothsayer Spiritu tell you that, too?" he said.

"Oh, she told me lots of things." She waved her hand over her head, motioning to the space around them. "Take for instance this cozy little spot. You'd think an ancient ritual site for our race would merit stronger mention in the history books, but it's wasting away unattended."

"What ritual site?"

"You remember. The pile of rocks near the castle where

Ramsay so loved to practice his natxu? Turns out this was where the prophecy actually came into being. Where Kentar started his reign and held court." She scanned the length of the cave and sighed. "It's a little primitive for my taste, but handy considering that's where Brenna needs to be when she brings the wall down. You're just underneath the main altar."

Ludan opened and closed his fists, pumping as much blood to his tingling fingers as he could and straining for his gifts. But nothing came. Not so much as a flicker of power or the trace of a link.

"Frustrating, isn't it? Feeling like a worthless human?" Serena unfurled from her perch and strolled to the long table behind her. "That's another handy trick Patrice shared." She picked something up and winced at the contact.

A torque. One not unlike those given to warriors, but far more crude and embedded with shimmering zeolite.

"Maxis would have loved to know about these." She held the torque higher, letting Ludan look his fill. "It's what we used before containment. Not as effective for blocking links, but extremely helpful in restricting a prisoner's gifts once wrapped around his throat. Something about disconnecting the mind's connection with the body's inherent powers." She tossed it to the tabletop and shook her hand as though to get the blood moving again.

"What makes you think this Spiritu's not using you?"

Serena stilled, only her eyes shifting toward him from beneath her sultry lashes. A beautiful snake coiled and eager to strike. "Because she needed me for her cause. To help push the dark and light passions out of balance."

"The rogues."

Serena smiled, pure evil curling her pouty lips. "She said you knew of them. That the rogues had faltered in their plans one too many times." She strolled closer, hips swaying with confidence. "It was her mate who pushed that dagger in

328

Maxis's chest and screwed things up for the rogues. Patrice was smarter. She told me all I needed to know to make sure the balance not only shifts, but stays where it needs to be. The prophecy. Brenna. The wall and who the powers go to. I know it all. All I have to do is line up the pieces and make them fall."

She paused in front of him and pushed a stray lock of hair off his forehead. "She even told me about you. Pointed out how you were my only exposure, then showed me how to use it." She petted the top of his head and smirked. "I knew you were all brawn and no brains, but I thought you'd figure it out faster than you did."

Oh yeah, he'd kill her all right. Slowly. Then he'd offer her blood up in tribute. "Enjoy the moment, Serena. Futures change. No destiny is set in stone. Or did your Spiritu fail to mention that?"

"She mentioned it. Then she made sure I knew every variable needed to adjust accordingly." She dropped her hand and stepped away. "Don't worry though. I'll make Brenna's ending short and sweet. Just as soon as she gives me what I need."

She ambled toward the far end of the cave but glanced back over one shoulder. "I figured you'd enjoy thinking on that while I round up my reinforcements."

CHAPTER 35

*T*oo many stares, all of them aimed at Brenna. Lexi, Galena, Trinity, Orla, and her mother all watched her. Oh, they pretended to make small talk, but the chatter was distracted. As though they were waiting to jump into action at even the tiniest sign of distress from her.

She paced Eryx's private chambers, the only underground chamber complete with an escape route known only to a limited few. A fact that made Graylin only marginally satisfied as far as her safety went.

Her stand-in protector glared down at the huge rock tableau depicting Eden's regions. Carved to show the elevations in 3-D, it had to have taken years to complete and was spotlighted by a wide solar tube from aboveground. For the last fifteen minutes he hadn't moved, one arm crossed at his chest with his other elbow propped on top and his chin in his hand.

"I feel like we should do something." Galena abandoned her seat on the leather sofa and rubbed her hands. Considering how confident and graceful Eryx's sister always was, it was quite the telling gesture. "All this sitting around and looking at each other isn't helping Brenna."

"I'm fine." The mother of all lies, but if it meant less pity aimed her direction, it would be worth it. She crossed her arms and stopped beside Graylin. "Have they said anything? Found anything?"

Graylin's mouth tightened. As somo to Eryx's father and a warrior in his own right, he had all the links necessary to stay in constant contact with the search.

Before he could answer, Lexi sat forward in Eryx's desk chair and propped her elbows on the mammoth desk. "You know, I still don't get it. The Spiritu were quick to help us before, but now they're just lying low and being all cryptic."

"It's not that easy." Perched with one hip on the arm of the sofa, Trinity was a bold ray of sunshine in the otherwise somber room. Everything about her was bright, from her short, sassy blonde hair, to her turquoise painted toenails. "Their very existence is tied to fate and the balance of passions. They could share with us before because the rogues screwed up. This time, the rogues thought things through. Somehow, someone ponied up payment so the light wouldn't have leverage to help us."

Lexi scoffed and plopped back in her chair. "That's insane. It's gotten so bad in Evad that Ian won't let Jilly go with him anymore. Aggravated assaults have quadrupled in the US in the last twenty-four hours, and the atmosphere is behaving like something out of the first *Ghostbusters* movie. They're out of their minds not to help us."

Trinity frowned and smoothed her pretty leggings, the color a perfect match to her to Caribbean-hue painted toes. "They can't intervene with destiny, Lexi. I've never been dialed into the things they see and hear, but I know it almost killed my dad knowing what lay ahead for me and not being able to do anything about it."

"I wouldn't call giving up his life so you could have yours nothing," Lexi said.

"He made that choice, yes. But only after he gave me the chance to make my own." Trinity's gaze slid to Brenna. "If the Spiritu intervene beyond their role, then they undo what the Creator intended. This is your time. Ludan's time. Fate is the life we're given. Destiny is what we do with it."

"She's right." Abby sat in a comfortable, man-sized club chair angled against the corner, her feet tucked under her and her eyes locked on Graylin. Empathy and understanding lined her features, as though in watching him she relived the last fifteen years of her life. "It took me until Brenna's father died to figure that out. I stood there, staring down at his coffin, and tried to understand what I'd done to deserve so much hardship. I'd been a good mom. A good wife. Fulfilled my responsibilities. But my baby was taken and my husband took his own life."

She looked at Brenna. "Then one day I woke up. I decided I could follow my husband's path, or keep going and make a difference. I don't think I ever really took a full, easy breath until you found me, but I helped countless other families in the process. I held their hands. I listened. I helped search for other lost children when I couldn't find my own. It's nowhere near what you have to face, but you'll do what's right. You'll take what you're given and make it your own the way you have your whole life."

Brenna huffed and spun for a fresh lap across the room. Everything her mom shared was beautiful. Poignantly so. But right now she couldn't process it. She was too raw. Too exposed and angry at the universe for all it had thrust her direction. At the injustice of a man like Ludan, who'd only wanted to protect her, being subjected to a spoiled, socio-pathic woman.

A heavy boom resonated down the hallway, wood slamming against stone, followed by the rap of boot heels marching closer.

Graylin snapped from his thoughts and shifted, putting himself between Brenna and the door. Behind her, the women rose from their varied seats and gathered close.

The door opened and Eryx strode through, his glower frightening enough to scare the diabhal himself and the corded muscles at his neck bunched tight. Reese and Ramsay stood slightly behind him at either side, neither offering much better in their expressions.

Brenna rushed forward. "Did you find him?"

Eryx kept his gaze on Graylin, the mix of regret and fury behind his gray eyes jetting a fresh burst of panic through her veins. He looked to Brenna, and the muscles at the back of his jaw twitched. "We found Uther's home." He lifted one hand. Pinched between his fingers was a simple parchment, folded in half. "And this. Serena left it at Uther's place. She has Ludan, and she wants a trade in exchange for his life. The time, the location—it's all here."

"Then give it to her," Brenna said. "Whatever she wants."

Graylin's hand settled on her shoulder. Big, like Ludan's, and just as steady. "What she wants we can't give her, Brenna."

She faced him, the resignation in his voice sparking a wildfire she couldn't contain. "Why not? Nothing's as important as saving him. He's your son. How can you not give her what she wants?"

Pure torture smoldered behind his blue eyes, their surface glossy, bordering on tears. "Because what she wants is you."

Her breath left her on a rush, her middle hollowing out as though she'd been punched in the gut. Of course that's what Serena wanted. She was the judge, and Serena wanted power.

The one task she'd wanted to avoid, the fate she'd tried to dodge, was the one thing that could save Ludan. If the mere thought of being alone with someone like Serena didn't terrify her, she'd have laughed at the irony.

Fate is the life we're given. Destiny is what we do with it.

Stillness seized her. The world around her grew hazy, and the voices of those gathered around her turned to muffled, distant chatter.

You survived, Brenna. You survived, and now your something better is here. You'll just have to fight a little more to get it.

Eryx was right. What threat could Serena possibly pose that Brenna hadn't already endured and overcome? If the roles were reversed, Ludan wouldn't hesitate. Histus, he'd already be halfway there and unleashing an unholy wrath on those who'd dared to hurt her. He wanted her to hope? She'd give him hope and then some. She'd fight. "If she wants me, she can have me."

The voices ceased, and all heads turned to her.

Lifting her chin, she squared her shoulders and looked Eryx dead in the eye. "I don't care what we have to do or how we have to do it, but I'm not leaving Ludan there."

Eryx glanced at Graylin, then Lexi before settling back on Brenna. "Aside from the fact that Ludan would gut me for even considering Serena's trade, this is way more than just one person for another. This is the wall we're talking about and all the powers that go with it. It's one thing for you to make the choice on our future based on what you deem best. It's something else for you to be forced into a choice."

"She can't force me into a choice any more than you can stop me from going. Both are my decisions. My fate."

"You're telling me that if she threatens to kill Ludan if you don't make the call she wants, you're willing to watch him die? I don't buy it."

Brenna shook her head, a dizzying determination mush-rooming up that made her feel three feet taller. "No, I'm saying I'm ready to go head-to-head with her. If she wants a battle, we'll give her one." She held out her hand, drew from Graylin's power beside her, and yanked the letter from between Eryx's fingers with the slightest thought.

It sailed toward her and settled in her outstretched palm.

Eryx gaped, and more than one shocked inhalation sounded behind her.

Lexi moved in close. "When the hell did you learn how to do that?"

"Ludan taught me. And how to use fire and electricity, too." She refocused on Eryx. "I might be human, but I'm not an ordinary one. If Serena wants a fight, then I'll bring her one."

∾

YEARS LUDAN HAD TRAINED, every moment preparing him for torture or death. Yet here he was alone. Powerless with nothing to do but pray Serena didn't get her hooks in Brenna. It was brutal. The worst torment the Great One could give him.

Surely Brenna would be smart and keep her distance.

As soon as he thought it, the proud, stubborn lift of her chin when she'd stood up to him yesterday morning flashed bold and beautiful in his head. Right behind it came the obstinate heat in her dark gaze as she'd sucked his cock between her lips hours later.

Shit.

She wouldn't hide. Weeks ago she might have been content to do so, but not anymore. She'd grown. Slain both their demons and done it with a steady, unwavering confidence found only in the most seasoned rulers.

Oh yeah. She'd fight, but she'd do it honorably.

Serena wouldn't.

Straining his arms, he wrenched against the rough hemp

335

binding his wrists, pouring his strength into the act even as his shoulders demanded he stop. Wetness trickled across the back of his fists. Blood or sweat. Probably the former given how slow it seeped against his skin.

Fucking zeolite. Though, at least with just the torque around his neck it didn't drain the rest of his energy.

Darkness pooled at either end of the cave. The only furniture distinguishable was the table across the room and a few wooden chairs around it. Too bad the chair his feet were bound to was metal. Otherwise, he'd have smashed it.

He closed his eyes and reached for his link to Eryx. To Ramsay or his father. Anyone who'd stand a chance in histus of keeping Brenna away.

Nothing happened.

The slow grate of stone on stone echoed from the far end of the cavern, and the candles wavered on a draft. Serena couldn't have been gone more than a few hours. An awfully short trip for rounding up reinforcements.

Heavy boot heels rapped against the stone floor, growing closer with each second. A man strode from the darkness, the same build as the person he'd seen before he'd blacked out.

So this was Uther Rontal. One way or another, he'd return the whack he'd served the back of Ludan's head, but he'd make damned sure the son of a bitch didn't wake up.

Uther paused just inside the pool of light. Short dark hair, shrewd eyes, and a perma-scowl. He dressed like a farmer in sturdy wool pants and a loose dark shirt, neither of which were high quality. An empty burlap sack dangled from his fingers. "I can't decide if I'm glad you proved the Spiritu right or pissed you made it so easy."

Ludan's gut clenched on reflex, the barb striking home as strong as any fist. "Shouldn't you be off with your boss pulling together reinforcements? Or has she already relegated you to grunt duty?"

Uther frowned, a blip of confusion quickly smoothed away with indifference. "She's not my boss. No one is."

"Strategos implies second in command. Not first. Last I heard, that's the only title you've ever had."

"I couldn't give a shit about the Rebellion. They were a means to an end. Serena's no different."

Interesting. Usually Serena had men whipped and put in their place in no time. Understandable now that he knew her gifts ran to influencing, but Uther seemed indifferent. No, not just indifferent. Disgusted.

With one last dismissive once-over, Uther strode to the opposite end of the cave, moving a few candles through the air with his mind as he went.

Crude shelves lined the farthest wall, and a small pile of tattered animal furs filled one corner.

Uther pulled items from the shelves and stashed them in the bag.

Weird how he'd responded to the bit on reinforcements. Like he didn't understand what Ludan meant. But that couldn't be right. If they were in this shit together, he'd know what Serena was up to.

Unless Serena was using him like she used everyone else.

"You sure you can trust her?" Ludan said.

Uther paused, then resumed his packing. It was a small tell. Hardly anything to hang his hopes on, but it beat the shit out of sitting here dress-rehearsing worst-case scenarios.

"She killed her own mate," Ludan said. "That's gotta give you at least a little doubt."

Uther glared at Ludan over one shoulder. In his hand was Trinity's journal. Given the size and shape of the now weighted bag, he'd bet his life the translations were in there, too. "The Spiritu took her free will. She's too weak to kill anyone on her own."

"Physically weak, maybe. But smart enough to find someone like you to do the heavy lifting. If you think for a second that she wouldn't do the same to you, you're wrong."

Uther went back to his task.

Damn it. There had to be more he could use. "You know she's an influencer. That she pushes people to do her bidding with her gifts."

A low chuckle filled the room. "Oh, she's tried it. I'm immune." He cinched the bag, sent the candles floating back to their perch, and headed back toward Ludan. "I'm immune from a lot of things."

He should have been focused, digging for something else to needle Uther on, but Ludan couldn't look away from the bag. Why the fuck did he need the journals? If Serena had all the answers, then Uther should, too.

"You don't trust her." Ludan zeroed in on Uther's face. The flinch was there. Barely, but still there. "You believe the Spiritu are the ones giving her the paint-by-number instructions, but you're not so sure she's passed it all on to you."

Uther held stock-still. Almost. Except for his fingers around the neck of the bag.

Oh yeah. Definitely a raw nerve there. One he could exploit if he dared to try. Of course, it could screw Brenna if he spilled something neither Uther nor Serena knew, but if he tipped the scales of distrust on Serena, it might be worth it.

"Tell you what." Ludan sat up as tall as his binds would allow. "How about I share what we know of the prophecy. You compare my story to Serena's, and we'll see just how forthcoming the little snake's been this time."

CHAPTER 36

*D*arkness, quiet, and the Great One only knew how many hours had passed. Without his gifts, Ludan couldn't gauge the sun's location, but his hands and feet were numb. He wasn't sure he could even straighten his back at this point if he needed to.

For the umpteenth time, his thoughts drifted back to his conversation with Uther. He still couldn't get a bead on how his gamble went. He'd spilled his guts like some chatty Cathy drunk on cheap wine, and not once had Uther so much as flinched. No narrowed eyes. No furrowed brows. Nothing. The son of a bitch had to be the best damned poker player in history.

Ludan rolled his head and stretched his neck. The zeolite torque pressed heavy on his collarbone, the links jingling with the subtle movement. From what little he'd glimpsed of the one Serena had lifted off the table, they were crudely made. Nowhere near as fine as his warrior marks, but unfortunately efficient.

The same scrape of stone on stone he'd heard before sounded at the far end of the cavern. Uther strode into view only moments later, his steps slowing as his gaze swept the room.

"Your partner in crime's not here." Ludan pumped his fists, willing the blood to move. "I told you she's not trustworthy. Be smart and—"

"Shut it." Uther paced the length of the cave. He paused at the table, one hand resting on the back of a chair as though he meant to pull it from underneath.

The soft pat of light, rushing feet sounded from the entrance.

Serena hurried from the darkness, her near-white hair mussed and her cheeks a mottled red. If the shadows weren't jacking with his eyesight, there was even a hint of sweat near her temple. She smiled at Uther. "It's time."

Uther stomped toward her, herding her to the farthest corner of the room. His face was pinched and inches from hers.

Ludan strained to make out the conversation, but only managed a few broken words amidst Uther's grumbles. Whatever the conversation was about, Uther wasn't as happy as she was.

A bonus for Ludan. He'd work that angle until the Great One gave him something else to use. One way or another, he was getting out of here. And, if the Fates played along, he'd take that bitch out along the way.

Serena stroked Uther's arm, her face soft and comforting.

Uther's frown smoothed, and he stepped away.

So much for Uther being immune. Serena might not be able to influence him with her gifts, but she obviously had something else to keep him in line.

Uther stalked toward Ludan.

Serena trailed more slowly, a snide, pleased-with-herself grin stretching ear to ear.

Behind Ludan, metal *zringed* against metal, and the cold, sharp tip of Uther's dagger pressed against his carotid.

"Ready to see your lover?" Serena crooned.

Ludan eased his head back, trying to gain distance from the blade. "Whatever your Spiritu told you about Brenna and me is way off base."

"Please." She tsked and folded her hands in front of her. "I saw the way you responded to her name. It's cute, really. The fearsome somo enchanted by a lowly human."

"Even if Brenna comes for me, do you really think you can hold Eryx at bay with only me as a hostage?"

Her smile deepened, pure evil and confidence glowing in her otherwise pretty blue eyes. "No. I don't." She sauntered closer and trailed her fingertips along his jaw, her head tilted, considering. "But I'm ready if he tries anything." She stepped back, lifted her gaze to Uther, and nodded. "Bring him."

Never easing the dagger away from Ludan's neck, Uther unwound the ropes binding his legs with his mind, then yanked him upright.

Ludan's knees buckled, but Uther's powers jerked him upright and held him steady.

Fuck. He couldn't feel anything. It was like his legs didn't even exist.

"Oh, this is priceless." Serena stood back and waited. "If I'd have known I'd get a sideshow to go with this, I'd have done this years ago."

"Enough." Uther shoved Ludan forward. "I want this done."

Ludan staggered behind Serena, relying more on Uther's unseen hold than he cared to admit, but grateful for its presence. Part of him wanted to analyze it. To gauge whether or not Uther had nursed a few of Ludan's warnings. Most of him just struggled to put one foot in front of the other.

As he stepped from the cave, the late-afternoon sun

slanted across his face, blinding him for three painful steps. He blinked, grinding his jaw through the stabbing pain at his temples and the growing pinpricks in his feet and legs.

The red sun inched toward the horizon, no more than an hour away from sunset. In the east, silver swirls of Eden's surplus energy dipped and streamed at a more frenzied pace than normal. Black clouds marked the western sky, the most sinister Eden sunset he'd ever seen.

Goose bumps lifted across his skin, and a weird foreboding pitched his stomach. Despite the aches and cramps in his muscles, his mind lasered to a fine point, poised for any break in Uther's focus.

The standing stones waited straight ahead, the flat rock in the center sparking with gold flecks in the sunlight. The space was roughly fifty feet wide and twenty deep and formed a natural dais. Countless times he'd seen it, joining Ramsay for natxu or just escaping for quiet, but never had he felt this awareness. This bone-deep dread.

A square structure covered in a black tarp sat at one corner of the dais. No, not just one. Four of them, one at each corner. Serena had to have added them, though why still remained to be seen. Wind whipped at the heavy fabric and odd sounds issued from underneath, something he couldn't quite identify.

At least he could feel his feet again. One bad move on Uther's part and he'd make his move, hopefully before Brenna came into play.

In front of him, Serena glanced over one shoulder and smirked. "Good to know your lover's punctual at least." She stepped aside so he could see.

Brenna's small, delicate form drifted forward in the distance. Her chin was lifted, proud and sure, and her stride was slow but purposeful. Damn, but she'd grown. So much different than the fearful waif who'd tried to slip through the castle unnoticed. Under other circumstances he'd have pushed his shoulders back with pride, but right now all he wanted was to command she turn around and go the other direction.

And where the fuck was Eryx? Ramsay? His father?

Brenna halted at the base of the raised ledge.

Uther's fist tightened on the dagger held to his neck. "We've got company."

Eryx and Ramsay shimmered into view on either side of Brenna. Graylin and Reese were positioned directly behind her, as were Lexi, Trinity, and Galena. Around the standing stones were at least two hundred Myren warriors, all poised and ready for action.

Serena and Uther were screwed. Even if they tried to run, they'd be caught in seconds.

For the first time since he'd woken in the cave, Ludan sucked in a decent breath. Though he'd like it a fuck of a lot better if Brenna was behind the line of warriors instead of in front.

Eryx took two steps forward. "Stand down, Serena. You can't win this."

Serena's chuckle echoed off the monoliths. "You're so predictable, Eryx. Do you really think I'd be so foolish as to think you'd let me just waltz in and take what I want?"

She waved her hand, lifting the tarps from the squares at either corner of the dais with a dramatic mental flourish.

Humans huddled inside the tight space, bound together and gagged so they could hardly move. There had to be at least thirty to each pen, crammed so close they couldn't have moved even without the binds.

Whimpering. That was the sound he'd heard. The reinforcements.

Uther growled beside him. "Where did they come from?"

Serena jerked her head in a terse, nearly imperceptible

shake to silence him. She faced her audience and opened one hand. A small remote rested against her palm. "I really should give humans more credit. What they lack in powers they make up for with technology. One little button and I can end their paltry lives." Her head cocked to one side, taunting. "You might be willing to sacrifice your somo, but I can't imagine you'd be so tolerant at the loss of innocent lives."

She'd nailed that one. His own life or warriors he'd sacrifice in a heartbeat if it meant the safety of his race, but innocents? Never.

Eryx stayed rooted in place, no response whatsoever. If anything he looked bored. "You're right. I wouldn't."

Brenna inched forward.

Ludan jolted toward her, but Uther jerked him back, the tip of the dagger digging into his flesh. Blood trickled down his neck, and Uther's fingers dug into Ludan's strained shoulders.

Closer and closer Brenna drifted, her moves slow and calculated, her mouth tight and her eyes on the device in Serena's hand.

Concentrating on the device.

No surprise from Eryx.

Shit. They'd anticipated Serena would make a dirty play and came with their own game plan. Brenna was the key. That had to be it. Serena wouldn't know what Brenna was capable of. How she could draw from the powers around her. She'd try for the device. Or the key. But one misstep and she'd have the lives of innocent humans on her hands.

He couldn't let that happen. Not if he could help. She needed leverage. Anything. Something.

"The powers won't be yours," he murmured to Uther. "No matter what Serena told you, the powers will go where Brenna directs them. Do you really think she'll give them to someone like Serena? Someone willing to put innocent lives at risk?"

Brenna was only fifteen feet away, close enough that she could draw from Serena's powers.

Ludan's heart lurched. He needed more time. "Damn it, man, think. Serena won't let the humans go. She can't. She's set herself up to be some benevolent God. If she lets them live, they'll get the truth out and ruin it for her. Whatever you're in this for, Serena is in it for something else. You'll never control her."

Brenna took another step closer.

Uther's dagger hand shook.

Serena's hand shot out, angled for Brenna.

"No!" Uther released his clasp long enough to push Brenna away with a mental shove and knocked the remote from Serena's palm.

Ludan spun, ripping free and racing to cover Brenna.

Shouts rang out, warriors jetting toward the dais and bracing and dodging electrical strikes emanating from behind him.

He toppled Brenna to the ground, covering her body with his own. "The torque! Get it off!"

Fire and lightning strikes blazed behind them. Too much for only Serena and Uther to generate.

With a sharp tug and an ugly grunt, Brenna yanked the torque free and toppled back to the grass.

Ludan's powers surged to life. He twisted, snapping the ropes that bound his wrists with a blast of fire and crouching in front of Brenna.

Rogue Spiritu filled the dais. At least twenty in number and generating three times the manpower of the warriors they engaged. They surrounded Serena, her eyes wide and her skin deathly pale. Uther lay crumpled at her feet.

Brenna scrambled out from behind Ludan. "The key!"

One rogue wrestled Serena, his hand twisted in the thick chain.

"No!" Brenna's hand shot out, and her mirroring powers ripped through Ludan.

The chain around Serena's neck snapped, and the key shot to Brenna's outstretched hand.

Light exploded, a deafening shockwave with an unforgiving pulse that billowed out in all directions and slammed him to the ground.

The world fell away and darkness consumed him. Whether it was a dream or some other world he couldn't tell, but it wasn't reality. Whatever it was, he needed out. To get to Brenna and keep her safe. He tried to move but found no purchase. No physical substance connected to his spirit.

"You don't need to struggle. I'll help you." A misty gray light broke through the blackness, and a woman shimmered into view. Not just any woman. His Spiritu, her voice the same as the one who'd led his thoughts. And she was a warrior. Her armor glinted off an unseen light source, and her black hair whipped in a nonexistent breeze. "Focus on me and I will show you to the light."

What. The. Fuck. He didn't want light. He wanted Brenna. "Who are you? Where am I? Where's Brenna?"

She smiled, as unrepentant and proud as any victorious fighter. "You've already accepted who I am, but my name is Morigan. You hit your head with the blast and now drift between reality and imagination. As to your mate, she touches the Great One."

The Great One. As in the prophecy. His spirit thrashed, clawing in all directions for escape.

"Be at ease, warrior." Morigan's glow intensified, full-moon soft but dazzling in its power. Calm descended on him, and his heart slowed to a steady beat. "In the Great One's arms, she will know no harm. It's in the days to come she will need you. Are you prepared now to accept her? To give her the future she deserves?"

"I would give her my vow. My life, if she would have it."

Morigan dipped her head, acknowledging his words with the reverence he'd offered them. "Then go to her. Find your mate."

A loud whirring noise rushed past his head, and the space around him blurred in a stream of every color. A second later, he stared up at the cloudless Myren sky.

No clouds.

No shouts.

No fighting.

Only silence.

He rolled to his knees, lungs burning and limbs shaking with the sting of adrenaline. The rogues and Serena lay motionless on the dais. Eryx's warriors fared slightly better, some staggering upright from the blast, others shaking their heads as though stunned. The rest stared mesmerized at the massive opaque column of light in front of him. It reached from the ground into the heavens, thrumming with a powerful force. Spiritu surrounded it. Not the rogues, but a sea of beings dressed in both black and white, all poised as though ready to defend to the death.

And Brenna was locked inside the light.

~

QUIET. An infinite absence of sound, and yet a presence thrummed through Brenna, filling her head with a steady hum. A pinkish-white stretched as far as she could see, tiny glimmers like fairy dust the only thing that gave the space dimension.

"Hello?"

The void swallowed her voice as soon as she spoke, and an odd, soul-reaching peace settled deep inside her.

"I'm here, child. I always have been."

Tingles danced along her skin, recognition sparking at the rich, velvet voice. She'd heard that voice countless times. In the dark the night after she'd been captured. As she'd trembled and hugged her knees against her torso the first night Maxis defiled her. In the moment when her feet had slipped from the bluff before she'd fallen into Ludan's arms.

She tilted her head back and stared into the white. "Are you who I think you are?'

"Why do you ask what you already know?"

The Creator. The Great One.

Her muscles quaked, and sweat dampened the skin at her nape and between her shoulder blades. Should she bow? Kneel? For all the warning she'd had, she'd never once imagined actually being here, or how she should act.

"My greatest joy is when you simply are who I made you to be," he said.

A comforting touch whispered across her face, soft-spun cotton carried on a sweetly scented breeze. She had no need to fear. No cause to fight or worry. In this moment, she could never be safer. More protected or cherished.

The expression etched on Ludan's face in the second she'd broken free of his shelter and reached for the key flashed in her mind's eye. "Ludan. Is he okay?"

"Your mate is well and safe. Frantic that he cannot reach you, but the White Queen will not let him suffer. The two of you have had enough in one lifetime for any soul."

Hope shook her voice, and the muscles in her torso clenched, braced for disappointment. "My mate?"

"The soul intended for you alone. You know this already, though you've hesitated to accept it."

"But Ludan—"

"Has no such misgivings. His realizations are new, but they are fierce and without question."

Warmth blossomed in her chest, and her cheeks ached from the size of her smile. "He wants me," she whispered into the void.

"Of course he does, child. How could he not love someone so brave and genuine as you?"

For long moments, she stood rooted in place, clutching her newfound knowledge. When her breath evened out, she lifted her chin and gazed up at the endless space above her.

"When can I see him?"

"When you've completed what you were born to do." The air around her thickened, and she could have sworn the presence leaned in as though to hear her secrets. "You are the judge. The one chosen to guide the futures of the races I've created. You've watched them. Suffered at their hands, and lived the lives of both. What choice will you make?"

From the day she'd witnessed Ramsay's visions and seen her ancestor dead and broken at her mate's feet, she'd vowed to keep the wall in place. She straightened taller and opened her mouth, the choice poised on the tip of her tongue.

And froze.

Yes, a Myren had taken her. Raped her. But a Myren had also saved her. And another had healed her. One by one, they'd gathered round her, offering their strength and friendship.

The memory of the ellan the day she'd shared her memories flittered through her thoughts. The woman had been a stranger, but she'd wept at what she'd witnessed. Had offered up her most sincere regrets and motioned for Maxis's sentence.

And Ludan. Her sweet, gentle giant. He'd given up his life for her. Gone against his most sacred vow to bring her happiness, then offered his heart as only a warrior could. Bravely. Unhindered.

"Most people are good," she said into the nothingness. "Some on the fringes go too far, but most want to grow. To learn and get along."

"Those are the faithful. The ones unafraid of work and exercising courage," the Creator said.

Courage.

The simple word rattled through her, recalibrating things she'd thought cemented in place and setting free her deepest, darkest fears. "Take it down."

She flinched the second the words came out, panic firing hot in her belly, but an equal, almost defiant surety standing battle-strong in her heart. "They can do this. Both races can do this. They're ready."

The all-encompassing love and peace of the Creator swirled around her, spring-breeze warm and light. "Your judgment and belief in my children brings me much joy. What gift can I give you in return for the faith you've shown them today?"

A gift? He'd already given her the world in confirming Ludan's place in her life. Peace between the races aside, nothing short of a life with him could make her future better.

Actually, there was one other thing. Something well deserved. "There's nothing I need. But if you could ease Ludan's pain, let him be free of the voices he carries from all the memories he's taken, it would be a beautiful blessing."

The Creator's presence pulsed and shimmered, and the hairs along the back of her neck and arms danced as though in the midst of an electrical storm. "You are offered a gift, yet you request on behalf of another."

Silence stretched for seconds that felt like eons.

"I hope that the races you champion come to appreciate your giving soul." Colors swirled, slow at first and pale in color. Blues, reds, and yellows, all mingling and deepening with each moment. "Your judgment and your request have been rendered. The weight of your mate's gift no longer exists. The wall will come down and the powers within it bestowed upon you."

Brenna snapped to attention. "Me? But I thought...Serena said you'd ask me who to give them to."

"Information provided to her by those who held no conscience. I love all of my creations, but some cannot move beyond their greed. Serena opted to believe the lies she was told. The powers are yours, a gift granted for the brave path you have chosen."

Fire and sharp sparks licked her fingertips and toes. The sensation deepened and traversed her limbs, creeping slowly toward her heart. Powerful. Altering something not entirely flesh as it moved.

"Be at peace. Live in joy with your mate. Be fearless in the days ahead, and lead your race with the same wisdom you've shown today."

Bit by bit, the white around her faded. Above her, the rainbow skies stretched clear and free of the black clouds she'd witnessed before the battle. Row after row of Spiritu surrounded her, all eyes locked on her and smiles wide and bright as a noonday sun.

Power pulsed in her palms. Her neck arched as energy surged up through her belly and to her crown. Pain and pleasure rolled into one, encompassing all she was and who she'd yet to become. This was her awakening, the wall's powers surging through her in one bold rush. She couldn't fight it. Already her body was shutting down, bracing for the change.

"Brenna!" Ludan's voice shot across the clearing.

With the last of her strength, she twisted toward his voice. The world spun and her knees buckled, but strong arms caught her before gravity could take over.

Just like the day he'd caught her at the bluff, he cradled her tight against his chest and brushed his lips against her temple. His breath came short and fast against her skin, thick with relief. "It's over. You're safe."

It wasn't over. Not really. If anything, life had just begun. She smiled at the thought and let the weight pressing her eyelids take over, not the least concerned at the future's hurdles. Beneath her hand his heart beat strong and steady.

He was right. She was truly safe. With her heart. With her life, and her future. With him, she always would be.

*B*renna peeked between the white wood blinds covering her bedroom window. Outside her private villa, near white sand and mesmerizing turquoise waters stretched as far as she could see and only a few Divi trees dotted the landscape. According to the real estate agent Ludan had hired, Aruba's Eagle Beach was the best in the Caribbean. Considering how isolated and protected the beachside haven was, Brenna had been afraid to ask what *the best* would cost.

Not that Ludan had given her time to ask. He'd agreed to the purchase before they'd even finished the tour. Now here she was, less than an hour from sunset, enjoying a horizon coated in everything from rich mangos and red on one end, to violet and cobalt blue on the other. Beautiful and not unlike to the sunset she'd watched with her parents all those years ago.

Except that now, Eden shimmered high in the eastern sky.

With no barrier between the two realms, it shone as a translucent arc. The yet to rise moon reflected off it, highlighting a ring of soft pink clouds and swirling silver energy streams.

Eden was real. Everyone accepted it as truth now. Granted, the only way humans could get there for the time being was with the help of a Myren via portal, but it was only a matter of time before humans found a way to bridge the realms on their own. Especially since Eryx had vowed to help make that happen, a promise that had earned him all kinds of backlash from his ellan.

Both sides would have to adjust, the same way she had. In the last six months, her life had gone from one of suffering and obscurity, to lavish and painfully public, but she'd done her part to ease her race's worries. Shared not only her story, but her faith that both races were destined to live and thrive together.

The bedroom door whooshed opened, letting in the cheerful chatter of the women who'd gathered to help her prepare for her special day. So many years she'd been almost entirely alone, devoid of female companionship save Maxis's aged slave who'd trained her. Now she had her mother back and four strong women who'd proven they'd stand beside her come hell or high water.

The latch snicked shut, and soft footsteps sounded against the soft gray tile floors.

Brenna glanced over her shoulder, loath to leave her view behind for long.

As always, Lexi was the epitome of casual elegance. Her flirty sundress was a rich, raspberry sorbet and accented her tan skin to perfection, but it was her striking blue-gray eyes that really caught everyone's attention. "You nervous?"

Shaking her head, Brenna resumed her beachside watch. "Nervous was facing Serena." Her cheeks strained on a wide smile as Ludan, Eryx, Ramsay, Reese, and Graylin ambled into view, guiding a somewhat nervous and starstruck minister toward the simple white trellis only twenty feet from the shoreline. The soft white tulle Orla and Jillian had wound around the slats and posts wavered on the ocean breeze.

"Really? That's the nerve-racking experience you'd pick? I'd have thought your one-on-one with the Big Guy would have ranked higher." She paused right behind Brenna, checking out the men over her shoulder with a pleased sigh. "We are seriously lucky girls."

Lucky indeed. As she had on an almost daily basis since her mating night two months ago, she skimmed her fingertips over Ludan's mark on her forearm. She didn't need to look at it anymore. The unusual yet bold ivory mark was burned forever in her memory. A panther, perched at the edge of a thick tree branch beneath a full moon. One paw rested easy atop the branch and the other dangled downward. A deceptively relaxed pose, but his eyes bespoke an alertness that stole her breath. Watchful. Always waiting to pounce and protect.

Just like her mate.

From his place near the trellis, Ludan threw back his head and laughed so loudly it reached her through the thick glass wall.

The space behind Brenna's sternum tightened as though her heart had simply run out of room with all the happiness pumping through it.

"Never thought I'd see him do that in a million years," Lexi muttered. "It looks good on him."

Boy did it. Between their mating and the lack of voices ransacking his head, a whole different side of Ludan had shown itself. The part of himself he referred to as the beast was still there, ready to attack at a moment's notice, particularly if someone got too close or ruffled his mate. For the most part, though, the intense side of him seemed content to bask in the aftermath of their victories.

He sobered and twisted, aiming his penetrating gaze in the direction of their bedroom.

Lexi and Brenna both jerked back, and Brenna yanked the cord on the blinds so they snapped shut.

Two short raps sounded on the door, and Galena poked her head in. "You two ready?"

How she could have flutters over a simple wedding was beyond her, especially after all the mystery and intensity of their mating night, but her stomach did the butterfly thing anyway. She smoothed her hand down her simple white sheath dress and blew out a calming breath. The strapless cut displayed Ludan's mark beautifully and worked well with the intricate braid Orla had helped her with. If there was one thing Ludan got antsy about in short order these days, it was her going out in public without her hair bound, one of the most honored traditions of a mated man or woman. "Yeah. I'm ready."

With a quick, reassuring smile, Galena ducked back into the other room and hurried to the beach alongside Trinity and Orla.

Lexi handed Brenna a waterfall bouquet made of delicate white orchids, only a few with tender pink streaks lining the inner petals. "You know, the whole double ceremony thing is pure genius. Two ceremonies means two honeymoons."

Heat blasted across Brenna's cheeks, and she ducked her head to hide it. She might have grown a lot more comfortable with her sexuality with Ludan in the last many months, but it was still hard for her to be as open about it with Lexi and the rest of the women. "That wasn't the reason."

The real reason was just between her and Ludan, and they'd keep it that way for a little while longer. Besides, a human-style marriage set a good tone for the many people with a keen eye on her every move. A demonstration of how open Myrens were to human ways as well as their own.

"Mmm hmmm." Lexi's too-shrewd eyes sharpened, and she pursed her mouth, considering. Just as fast, she shrugged it off and let whatever ideas were traipsing around in her head go. Waggling her eyebrows, she slid open the glass door that led to the patio and the beach beyond. "It's still genius." Then she was gone, strutting out to her place of honor as only Lexi could.

The warm Caribbean air gusted through the open doorway, tinged with salt and cool against her heated skin. Today was her wedding day. She'd dreamed of it as a little girl, but had let those dreams fade in her time with Maxis. Now it was here. Beautiful, set in an exotic paradise, and very, very real.

Her mother clasped Brenna's hand and squeezed encouragingly. "Your father would be so happy today. I wish..." She clamped her lips tight, and tears welled in her eyes. "He'd be proud. Proud of the man you've chosen and everything you've done."

Sorrow clogged Brenna's throat and left an awkward weight in her stomach. "I miss him, but I'm glad I have you."

Releasing her hand, Abby wrapped Brenna up in a fierce hug, the two of them swaying slightly in the quiet moment. She kissed Brenna on the forehead and guided her forward. "Let's go get you married."

Voices sounded from the beach, Eryx and Ramsay's rich baritone mingling with Lexi's sassy banter. Jillian giggled, and Ian's sharp laugh followed right behind it. Everyone was happy. Finally. They still had a ton of obstacles to figure out, mainly those centered around political and military concerns, but Eryx had proven himself extremely savvy and more than a little persuasive when needed. Without the prophecy hanging over everyone's head, negotiations had been a cakewalk in comparison. Even the threat of the Black rogues was no longer an issue, an assurance delivered by the Black King himself.

Brenna stepped from the villa's shelter with her mother by her side, and the chatter stopped. The setting sun warmed her shoulders, and the powder-soft sand tickled her bare feet. Even the wind whipped a little more strongly in greeting, but the only thing her senses processed was the man waiting for her in the center of those gathered.

Her mate.

Barefoot and dressed in the loose silver silk pants and tank reserved for the most formal council events, Ludan stood tall and proud with Eryx at his side. As it always was now, he'd knotted his wavy dark hair high at the back of his head, but loose strands had escaped and whipped around his ice-blue eyes. His warrior torque and cuffs were back in place, the unique design marking him as somo to the malran. While the ivory mark he'd given her was more subtle against her pale skin, her family emblem reflected boldly against his deep tan flesh.

An owl. She still couldn't believe her mark was one so beautifully detailed or majestic as the wise creature the Creator had given her. His wings stretched tall, nearly reaching Ludan's shoulders, and clutched in his talons was the prophetic sword twined in ivy. But it was his eyes that moved her more than any other feature. So sage and confident.

Before she knew it, her mother kissed her cheek and placed her hand in Ludan's. His warmth settled her angsty nerves and enveloped her in a soul deep peace. Relaxing into the moment, she let the minister's words wash over her, giving her answers when asked and keeping her gaze locked tight to Ludan's. She was so riveted, so deeply connected to the unspoken love shining in his eyes, she almost missed the minister saying, "You may kiss your bride."

Ludan's gaze dropped to her mouth, and that salacious, pleased-with-himself smile she'd grown to love stretched wide. *"Now I've bound you every way a man can."* He dipped his head and teased her lips with his. *"My mate."* Another glide. *"My wife."* He settled his mouth firmly against hers and brushed a mental caress across her abdomen. *"The mother of my child."*

Shivers danced along her spine, the rich possessiveness of his words mingling with the thrill she experienced every time she thought of the life they'd created.

He pulled her flush against him and plied her lips with his until they parted. His tongue swept inside, branding her with the velvety caress, uncaring of the crowd or the cheers sounding around them.

Brenna surrendered. To his touch. To the safety of his embrace and the glorious hope burning bright in her soul. The past was behind them, the barbs that had once trapped them worn dull and the sting of old wounds now unbreakable scars that strengthened their bond. The future was theirs, full of promise, happiness, and the sweetest liberating love.

BOOKS BY RHENNA MORGAN

The Eden Series

Unexpected Eden

Healing Eden

Waking Eden

Eden's Deliverance

Men of Haven Series

Rough & Tumble

Wild & Sweet

Claim & Protect

Tempted & Taken

Stand & Deliver

Down & Dirty

Ancient Ink

Guardian's Bond

Healer's Need

NOLA Knights

His To Defend

Hers To Tame

Mine To Have

Standalone

What Janie Wants

Now Available From Carina Press and Rhenna Morgan

Sometimes the safest place is in the arms of a dangerous man.

ROUGH & TUMBLE
Book one in the Men of Haven series

***Live hard, f*ck harder, and follow only their own rules. Those
are the cornerstones the six men of the Haven Brotherhood live
and bleed by, refusing to conform to society's expectations,
taking what they want, and always watching each other's
backs.***

A self-made man with his fingers in a variety of successful
businesses, Jace Kennedy lives for the challenge and he
always gets what he wants. From the start, he sees Vivienne
Moore's hidden wild side and knows she's his perfect match,
if only he can break it free. He will have her. One way or
another.

Vivienne's determined to ditch the rough lifestyle she grew
up in, even if that means hiding her true self behind a bland,
socialite veneer. Dragging her party-hound sister out of a
club was *not* how she wanted to ring in the New Year, but
Viv knows the drill. Get in, get her sister, and get back to the
safe, stable life she's built for herself as fast as humanly
possible. But Viv's plans are derailed when she finds herself
crashing into the club's clearly badass and dangerously sexy
owner.

Jace is everything Vivienne swore she never wanted, but the
more time she spends with him, the more she starts to see
that he loves just as fiercely as he fights. He can walk

society's walk and talk society's talk, but when he wants something, he finds a way to get it. He's proud of who he is and where he came from, and he'll be damned if he lets Vivienne go before showing her the safest place of all is in the arms of a dangerous man.

Turn the page for an excerpt of this gritty and oh so sexy contemporary romance!

CHAPTER 1 - ROUGH & TUMBLE

Nothing like a New Year's Eve drunk-sister-search-and-rescue to top off a chaos-laden twelve-hour workday. Vivienne dialed Shinedown's newest release from full blast to almost nothing and whipped her Honda hybrid into a pay-by-the-hour lot in the heart of Dallas's Deep Ellum. Five freaking weekends in a row Callie had pulled this crap, with way too many random SOS calls before her current streak.

At least this place was in a decent part of town. Across the street, men and women milled outside a new bar styled like an old-fashioned pub called The Den, with patrons dressed in everything from T-shirts and faded jeans, to leather riding gear and motorcycle boots. Not one of them looked like they were calling the party quits anytime soon.

Viv tucked her purse beneath the seat, stashed her key fob in her pocket, and strode into the humid January night. Her knockoff Jimmy Choos clicked against the aged blacktop, and cool fog misted her cheeks.

Off to one side, an appreciative whistle sounded between low, masculine voices.

She kept her head down, hustled through the dark double

doors and into a cramped, black-walled foyer. A crazy-big bouncer with mocha skin and dreads leaned against the door-jamb between her and the main bar, his attention centered on a stunning brunette in a soft pink wifebeater, jeans, and stilettos.

The doors behind her clanged shut.

Pushing to full height, the bouncer warily scanned Viv head to toe. Hard to blame the guy. Outside of health inspectors and liquor licensing agents, they probably didn't get many suits in here, and she'd bet none of them showed in silk shirts.

"ID," he said.

"I'm not here to stay. I just need to find someone."

He smirked and crossed his arms. "Can't break the rules, momma. No ID, no party."

"I don't want a party, I want to pick up my sister and then I'm out. She said she'd be up front. About my height, light brown, curly hair and three sheets to the wind?"

"You must mean Callie," the brunette said. "She was up here about an hour ago mumbling something about *sissy*, so I'm guessing you're her." She leaned into Scary Bouncer Dude's formidable chest, grinned up at him, and stroked his biceps with an almost absentminded reverence. "May as well let her in. If you don't, Trev will spend closing time hearing his waitresses bitch about cleaning up puke."

Too bad Viv didn't have someone to bitch to about getting puke detail. Callie sure as heck never listened.

Bouncer dude stared Viv down and slid his mammoth hand far enough south he palmed the brunette's ass. He jerked his head toward the room beyond the opening. "Make it quick. You might be old enough, but the cops have been in three times tonight chomping to bust our balls on any write-up they can find."

Finally, something in her night that didn't require extra

time and trouble. Though if she'd been smart, she'd have grabbed her ID before she came in.

"Smart move, chief." The woman tagged him with a fast but none-too-innocent kiss, winked, and motioned for Viv to follow. "Come on. I'll show you where she is."

An even better break. The last search and rescue had taken over thirty minutes in a techno dance bar. She'd finally found Callie passed out under a set of stairs not far from the main speakers, but the ringing in Viv's ears had lasted for days. At least this time she'd have a tour guide and an extra pair of hands.

The place was as eclectic on the inside as it was out. Rock and movie collectibles hung on exposed brick walls and made the place look like it'd been around for years even though it reeked of new. Every table was packed. Waitresses navigated overflowing trays between the bustling crowd, and Five Finger Death Punch vibrated loud enough to make conversation a challenge.

The brunette smiled and semi-yelled over one shoulder, never breaking her hip-slinging stride. "Nice turnout for an opening week, yeah?"

Well, that explained the new smell. "I don't do crowds." At least not this kind. Signing her dad's Do Not Resuscitate after a barroom brawl had pretty much cured her of smoky, dark and wild. "It looks like a great place though."

The woman paused where the bar opened to a whole different area and scanned Viv's outfit. "From the looks of things, you could use a crowd to loosen up." She shrugged and motioned toward the rear of the room. "Corner booth. Last I saw your girl she was propped up between two airheads almost as hammered as she was. And don't mind Ivan. The cops are only hounding the owner, not the customers. My name's Lily if you need anything." And then she was gone, sauntering off to a pack of women whooping it up at the opposite end of the club.

So much for an extra set of hands. At least this part of the bar was less crowded, scattered sitting areas with every kind of mismatched chair and sofa you could think of making it a whole lot easier to case the place.

She wove her way across the stained black concrete floors toward the randomly decorated booths along the back. Overhead, high-end mini sparkle lights cast the room in a muted, sexy glow. Great for ambience, but horrid for picking drunk sisters out of a crowd. Still, Viv loved the look. She'd try the same thing in her own place if it wouldn't ruin the tasteful uptown vibe in her new townhouse. Funky might be fun, but it wouldn't help with resale.

Laughter and a choking cloud of smoke mushroomed out from the corner booth.

The instant Viv reached the table, the chatter died. Three guys, two girls and the stench of Acapulco Red—but no sister. "You guys see Callie?"

A lanky man with messy curly blond hair eyed her beneath thirty-pound eyelids and grinned, not even bothering to hide the still smoldering joint. "'Sup."

The redhead cozied next to him smacked him on the shoulder and glowered. "She's after Callie, Mac. Not stopping in for a late-night chat." She reached across the table and handed Viv an unpaid bar tab. "She headed to the bathroom about ten minutes ago, but be sure you take this with you. She stuck me with the bill last night."

Seventy-eight bucks. A light night for New Year's Eve, which was a damn good thing considering Viv's bank balance. She tucked the tab in her pocket. "Which way to the bathroom?"

The girl pointed toward a dark corridor. "Down that hall and on your left."

Viv strode that direction, not bothering with any follow-up niceties. Odds were good they wouldn't remember her in the morning, let alone five minutes from now.

Inside the hallway, the steady drone of music and laughter plunged to background noise. Two scowling women pranced past her headed back into the bar. One glanced over her shoulder and shook her head at Viv. "May as well head to the one up front. Someone's in that one and isn't coming out anytime soon from the sound of things."

Well, shit. This was going to be fun. She wiggled the knob. "Callie?"

God, she hoped it was her sister in there. Knowing her luck, she was interrupting a New Year's booty call. Although, if that were the case, they were doing it wrong because it was way too quiet. She tried the knob again and knocked on the door. "Callie, it's Viv. Open up."

Still no answer.

Oh, to hell with it. She banged on the door and gave it the good old pissed-off-sister yell. "Callie, for the love of God, open the damned door! I want to go home."

A not so promising groan sounded from inside a second before the door marked Office at her right swung wide. A tall Adonis in jeans and a club T-shirt emblazoned with The Den's edgy logo blocked the doorway, his sky blue eyes alert in a way that shouldn't be possible past 1:00 a.m.

Two men filled the space behind him, one shirtless with arms braced on the top of a desk, and another leaning close, studying the shirtless guy's shoulder. No wait, he wasn't studying it, he was stitching it, which explained the seriously bloody shirt on the floor.

"Got more bathrooms up front. No need to break down the damned door." Adonis Man ambled toward her, zigzagging his attention between her and the bathroom. "There a problem?"

Dear God in heaven, now that the Adonis had moved out of the way, the shirtless guy was on full, mouthwatering display, and he was every book boyfriend and indecent fantasy rolled up into one. A wrestler's body, not too big and not too lean, but one hundred percent solid. A huge tattoo covered his back, a gnarled and aged tree with a compass worked into the gothic design. And his ass. Oh hell, that ass was worth every torturous hour in front of her tonight. The only thing better than seeing it in seriously faded Levi's would be seeing it naked.

"Hey," Adonis said. "You gonna ogle my brother all night, or tell me why you're banging down one of my doors?"

They were brothers? No way. Adonis was all...well, Adonis. The other guy was tall, dark and dirty.

Fantasy Man peered over his injured shoulder. Shrewd, almost angry eyes lasered on her, just as dark as his near-black hair. A chunk of the inky locks had escaped his pony-tail and fell over his forehead. His closely cropped beard gave him a sinister and deadly edge that probably kept most people at a distance, but his lips could lull half the women in Texas through hell if it meant they'd get a taste.

Viv shook her head and coughed while her mind clam-bered its way up from Smuttville. "Um..." Her heart thrummed to the point she thought her head would float off her shoulders, and her tongue was so dry it wouldn't work right. "I think my sister's passed out in there. I just want to get her home."

Adonis knocked on the door and gave the knob a much firmer twist than Viv had. "Zeke, toss me the keys off the desk."

Before either of the men could move, the lock on the door popped and the door creaked open a few inches. "Vivie?" Callie's mascara-streaked face flashed a second before the door slipped shut again.

Months of training kicked in and Viv lurched forward, easing open the door and slipping inside. "I've got it now. Give me a minute to get her cleaned up and gather her stuff."

Adonis blocked the door with his foot. The black, fancy cowboy boots probably cost more than a month's mortgage payment, which seemed a shame considering it didn't look like she'd be able to pay her next one. "You sure you don't need help?"

"Nope." She snatched a few towels out of the dispenser and wetted them, keeping one eye on Callie where she semi-dozed against the wall. "We've done this before. I just need a few minutes and a clear path."

"All right. My name's Trevor if you need me. You know where we are if you change your mind." He eased his foot away, grinned and shook his head.

"Oh!" Viv caught the door before it could close all the way and pulled the bar tab out of her pocket. "My sister ran up a tab. Could you hold this at the bar for me and let me pay it after I get her out to the car? I need to grab my purse first."

He backtracked, eyeballed Callie behind her, and crumpled the receipt. "I'd say you've already covered tonight." He turned for the office. "We'll call it even."

Fantasy Man was still locked in place and glaring over one shoulder, the power behind his gaze as potent as the crackle and hum after a nearby lightning strike.

She ducked back into the bathroom and locked the door, her heart jackrabbiting right back up where it had been the first time he'd looked at her. She seriously needed to get a grip on her taste in men. Suits and education were a much safer choice. Manners and meaningful conversation. Not bloody T-shirts, smoky bars and panty-melting grins.

Snatching Callie's purse off the counter, she let out a serrated breath, shook out the wadded wet towel, and started wiping the black streaks off her sister's cheek. A man like him wouldn't be interested in her anyway. At least, not the new and improved her. And the odds of them running into each other again in a city like Dallas were slim to none, so she may as well wrangle up her naughty thoughts and keep them in perspective.

On the bright side, she didn't have to worry about the tab. Plus, she had a fresh new imaginary star for her next late-night rendezvous with BOB.

~

Damn if this hadn't been the most problematic New Year's Eve in history. It wasn't Jace's first knife wound, but getting it while pulling apart two high-powered, hotheaded drug dealers promised future complications he didn't need. Add to that, two more customers arrested at his own club, Cross-roads, in less than three days, and nonstop visits from the cops at The Den, and his New Year wasn't exactly top-notch.

Thank God his brother Zeke wasn't working trauma tonight or he'd have had to have Trev stitch him up. That motherfucker would've hacked the shit out of his tat.

"You 'bout done?" Jace said.

Zeke layered one last strip of tape in place and tossed the roll to the desk. "I am now."

"Took you long enough." Jace straightened up, tucked the toothpick he'd had pinched between his fingers into his mouth and rolled his shoulder. It was tight and throbbing like a son of a bitch, but not bad enough to keep him from day-to-day shit—assuming he didn't have any more drug dealer run-ins.

"I don't know. Our straitlaced partygoer didn't seem to mind me taking my time." Zeke packed his supplies into one of the locked cabinets, the same triage kit they kept at every residence or business they owned. It might have been overkill, but it sure as hell beat emergency rooms and sketchy conversations with police. "Thought for a minute there the sweet little thing was going to combust."

"Sweet little thing my ass." Trevor dropped into his desk chair, propped his booted feet on the corner of his desk, and fisted the remote control for the security vids mounted on the wall. "I'd bet my new G6 that woman's got a titanium backbone and a mind that would whip both your asses into knots."

Jace snatched a fresh white club T-shirt from Trev's grand opening inventory and yanked it over his head, the wound in his shoulder screaming the whole time. "Based on what? Her courtroom getup or her uptight hairdo?"

"Like I judge by what people wear. You know me better than that." Trev punched a few buttons, paused long enough to eyeball the new bartender he'd just hired ringing in an order on the register, then dropped the remote on the desk. "You ask me, you're the one judging. Which is kind of the pot calling the kettle black."

The setback hit its mark, the Haven tags he wore weighting his neck a little heavier, a reminder of their brotherhood and the code they lived by.

It's not where a man comes from, or what he wears, that matters. It's what he does with his life that counts.

Twenty-seven years he and Axel had lived by that mantra, dragging themselves out of the trailer park and into a brotherhood nothing but death would breach.

"He's right," Zeke said. "You're letting Paul's campaign crawl up your ass and it's knockin' you off course."

Damn, but he hated it when his own mantras got tossed back at him. More so when he deserved it. He let out an exhausted huff and dropped down on the leather couch facing the string of monitors. "Play it again."

Trevor shook his head but navigated the menu on the center screen anyway.

"Not sure why you're doing this to yourself, man." Zeke pulled three Modelos out of the stainless minifridge under the wet bar and popped the tops faster than any bartender. God knew he'd gotten enough experience working as one through med school. "Paul's a politician with a grudge, nothing else. Watching this again is just self-inflicted pain. Focus on the real problem."

Jace took the beer Zeke offered as the ten o'clock news story flashed on the screen. The third-string reporter's too-bright smile and pageant hairdo screamed of a woman with zero experience but eager for a shot at a seat behind the anchor desk.

"Dallas's popular club, Crossroads, is in the news again this New Year's Eve as two additional patrons were arrested on charges of drug possession with intent to distribute. Undercover police are withholding names at this time, but allege both are part of a ring lead by Hugo Moreno, a dealer notorious in many Northeast Texas counties for peddling some of the most dangerous products on the street."

"She's not wrong on that score." Zeke plopped on the other end of the couch and motioned to the screen with his bottle. "The number of ODs coming in at Baylor and Methodist the last six months have been through the roof. The guys from DPD swear most are tied to some designer shit coming out of Moreno's labs."

Trevor leaned in and planted his elbows on the desk, eyes to Jace. "You think Otter's going to hold out long enough to waylay Moreno?"

If Jace knew the answer to that one, he'd be a lot less jumpy and minus one slash to his shoulder. Pushing one pharmaceutical genius out of his club by strong-arming him with another was a risky move at best, but it sure as shit beat ousting Moreno on his own. "Otter's a good man with a calm head on his shoulders and a strong team. If he says he'll only let weed in the place and keep Hugo at bay, I'm gonna give him all the backing he needs. DPD's sure as hell not going to help. Not the ones in Paul's pockets, anyway."

"Paul doesn't have any pockets," Trev said. "Only his daddy does."

Right on cue, the camera cut to an interview with Paul Renner as reporters intercepted him leaving another political fundraiser.

"Councilman Renner, you've been very vocal in your run for U.S. Representative in supporting the Dallas Police Department's efforts to crack down on drug crime, and have called out establishments such as Crossroads in midtown Dallas. Have you heard about the additional drug arrests there tonight, and do you have any comments?"

Renner frowned at the ground, a picture-perfect image of disappointment and concern. Like that dickhead hadn't been trying to screw people since his first foray from the cradle.

"I continue to grow more concerned with establishments like those run by Jace Kennedy and his counterparts," Renner said. "It seems they continually skirt justice and keep their seedy establishments open for business. It's innocent citizens who end up paying the price, courted by heinous individuals peddling dangerous substances and amoral behavior. My primary goal, if elected to the House of Representatives, will be to promote legislation that makes it difficult for men like Mr. Kennedy and Mr. Moreno to escape justice."

The toothpick between Jace's teeth snapped in half. He tossed it to the coffee table in front of him and pulled another one of many stashed in the pocket of his jacket.

"It's official, now." Trevor raised his beer in salute and tipped his head. "You're an amoral son of a bitch leading innocent citizens to ruin."

Motion registered in one of the smaller security screens, the bathroom door outside Trevor's office swinging open enough to let Little Miss and her seriously drunken sister ping-pong down the hallway. The two were about the same height, but you couldn't have dressed two women more differently. Next to Little Miss, her sister was best suited for a biker bar, all tits, ass and wobbling heels. Not that she was bad to look at. She just lacked the natural, earthy grace of the sober one.

Damn it, he needed to pace. Or get laid. Just looking at the ass on Little Miss in tailored pants made him want to rut like a madman. Never mind the puzzle she presented. Trev wasn't wrong—she had a shitload of backbone blazing through those doe-shaped eyes. The combination didn't jive with her image. Nothing like a paradox to get his head spinning.

"Guess we found one way to get his head off Renner." Zeke knocked back another gulp of his beer.

"What?" He back and forthed a glare between his brothers.

Trevor chuckled low and shifted the videos so Little Miss's trek to the front of the bar sat center stage. "Zeke said the only thing you've done amoral was that freak show you put on with Kat and Darcy at last month's barbecue."

"Fuck you, Trev."

"Fuck her, you mean," Trev said. "No shame there, brother. You didn't even see her up close. If you did, you sure as shit wouldn't be sitting here rerunning sound bites of asshole Renner."

"Hell, no," Jace said. "A woman that uptight is the last thing I need. Or did you miss her casing not just Zeke patching up my shoulder, but the bloody shirt on the floor, too? You'll be lucky if the cops don't show from an anonymous tip called in."

Little Miss and her sister stumbled into the front section of the bar, the sister's arm curled around Little Miss's neck in a way he'd bet would still hurt tomorrow morning.

Nope. Sweet hips, fiery eyes and a good dose of mystery or not, she was the last thing he needed right now.

Two men blocked Little Miss's path.

The women stopped, and the drunk sister swayed enough it was a wonder she didn't topple onto the table beside her.

One of the men palmed the back of Little Miss's neck, and she jerked away.

Jace surged to his feet, grabbing his leather jacket off the table. "I'm headed to Haven. You hear more from Axel at Crossroads or get any more grief from the cops, let me know."

Both men let out hardy guffaws and waved him off.

"Twenty bucks says our buttoned-up guest gets some help on the way out the door," Trev said.

Zeke chimed in behind him. "Yeah, let us know if Sweet Cheeks tastes as good as she looks."

Bastards. The sad thing was, Trev was about to score a twenty from Zeke, because Jace might not be willing to curl up with Little Miss, but he wasn't watching men paw her either.

Don't miss
ROUGH & TUMBLE by Rhenna Morgan
Available February, 2017 wherever
Carina Press ebooks are sold.
www.CarinaPress.com

Copyright ©2017 by Rhenna Morgan

MEET THE AUTHOR

Rhenna Morgan is a happily-ever-after addict—hot men, smart women, and scorching chemistry required. A triple-A personality with a thing for lists, Rhenna's a mom to two beautiful daughters who constantly keep her dancing, laughing and simply happy to be alive.

When she's not neck deep in writing, she's probably driving with the windows down and the music up loud, plotting her next hero and heroine's adventure. (Though trolling online for man-candy inspiration on Pinterest comes in a close second.)

She'd love to share her antics and bizarre since of humor with you and get to know you a little better in the process. You can sign up for her newsletter and gain access to exclusive snippets, upcoming releases, fun giveaways, and social media outlets at www.rhennamorgan.com.

GLOSSARY

Aron - Mainstay livestock in Eden used for food and clothing. The hide is tanned to provide a soft, supple leather and is the predominant source of protective outerwear in the colder regions. The animal's fur is a cross between that found on a buffalo and a beaver in the human realm. The thickness and warmth of buffalo, but shiny and soft as beaver.

Asshur - A region in Eden. Sun isn't unheard of, but Asshur tends to be cloudier and rainier than other regions. The population has dropped off in the last few centuries with inhabitants moving to more hospitable areas.

Awakening - A Myren ceremony where people between the ages of eighteen and twenty-one are brought into their powers. The father (or paternal representative) is typically the trigger for the process, where the mother (or maternal influence) acts as an anchor for the awakened individual.

Baineann - The female within a bonded union.

Briash - The Myren equivalent of oatmeal. Its color is deep brown and the flavor has a hint of chocolate and cinnamon.

Brasia - A region in Eden. The terrain is mountainous. Heavy snow and difficult conditions prevail in the higher elevations.

Briyo - Brother-in-law.

Cootya - A type of cafe that sells common Myren beverages and snacks. Myren fruits and vegetables are the most common menu items, but some pastries can be found. Most feature an open air area where customers can relax, while kitchen and serving areas remain indoor.

Cush - The capital region of Eden, densely populated with elaborate buildings.

Diabhal - Devil.

Drast - Field-issue protective garment worn by warriors to protect their most vital organs in battle. Made of fine, metal threads, the garments fit their bodies closely. Day-to-day drasts are sleeveless, but the more formal version covers 3/4 of their arms. The necks are boat shaped to allow for greater comfort when fighting. Metal threads block most fire and electrical attacks.

Drishen - A fruit found in Eden. Looks like a grape and tastes like lemonade.

Eden - Another dimension, unknown to humans, within the fabric surrounding Earth.

Ellan - Elected officials who govern the Myren race alongside the Malran or Malress. Like most governing bodies, there are a mix of honest servants who seek prosperity and growth for the Myrens and corrupt lifers who stand on antiquated ideas and ceremonies.

Evad - The realm in which humans reside.

Fireann - The male within a bonded union.

Havilah - A more affluent and less populated region in Eden. Rain occurs, but mostly in the evenings with pleasant days full of sun and comfortable temperatures.

Histus - The human equivalent of hell.

Kilo - A fish that swims in many lakes in Eden, but is most prevalent in Brasia. A popular mainstay of protein in the Myren race, most often prepared by smoking in apple wood and basting with an apple and cinnamon glaze.

Larken - A long-winged bird known for its sing-song chirp. Primarily cobalt blue, while their wingtips are lavender.

Lastas - A favorite Myren breakfast pastry.

Leabrash - Library

Lomos Rebellion - A faction of Myrens that has long pursued the enslavement of humans and sought to overthrow the tenets of the Great One.

Lyrita Tree - An exotic tree exclusive to the Havilah region. Trunks are dark brown. Leaves are long, slender, and sage-green. The blooms are exceptionally large and run from pearl to pale pink in color. Average height for a mature lyrita is thirty to forty feet.

Malran - The male leader of the Myren people and the equivalent of a king in the human realm. Leadership has descended down through the Shantos family line since the birth of the Myren race, with the mantle of Malran (or Malress) falling to the first born.

Malress - The female leader of the Myren people and the equivalent of a queen in the human realm.

Myrens - A gifted race in existence for over six thousand years that lives in another dimension called Eden. They are deeply in tune with the Earth and the elements that surround her. Their powerful minds and connection to the elements allow them to communicate silently with those they are linked to, levitate, and command certain elements. Women typically have more healing or nurturing gifts, where men trend toward protective and aggressive abilities.

Natxu - A regular and expected practice of physical discipline for all Myren warriors. The moves and postures are grueling yet meditative, resulting in peak physical performance and enhanced ties to the elements.

Nirana - The human equivalent of heaven.

Oanan - Daughter-in-law.

Quaran - The Myren equivalent of a General within the warrior ranks.

Runa - Region in Eden, predominantly used for farming. The black soil is rich and sparkles with minerals. It's surrounded by a crescent-shaped formation of mountains that appear blue from ground level.

Shalla - Sister-in-law.

Somo - Sworn personal guard to the Malran or Malress.

Strasse - A highly intoxicating Myren beverage made from berries found only in Eden.

Strategos - Leader of the Myren warriors.

Torna - An annoying Myren rodent. Larger than an armadillo, but similar in color to an eel. While not typically aggressive, their teeth function similar to a shark. Torna almost always come out fighting.

Underlands - Not considered a region by most, but

more of an uninhabited wasteland. Lack of rain makes agriculture nearly impossible.

Vicus - A vegetable known for its extremely tart flavor, popular among the older generation.

Zurun - A thick flaky pastry with a thin layer of icing in the middle, twisted in the shape of a bow.

CPSIA information can be obtained
at www.ICGtesting.com
Printed in the USA
LVHW030930100720
660313LV00001B/43

9 781945 361036